WHAT THE PRESS SAYS ABOUT JAKE NEEDHAM

"*The Big Mango* is a full-blown work. There's no room for improvement. It's as good as it gets." — *THE BANGKOK POST*

"*Tea Money* is a racy financial thriller set in Asia. Needham certainly knows where a few bodies are buried." — *ASIA INC.*

"At last, a grown-up modern novel about Bangkok. Jake Needham has a huge talent." — *THE NATION* (Bangkok)

"Fans of . . . Leonard Elmore and Carl Hiaasen will find lots to like in *Tea Money:* wise-cracking crooks, tough broads, nefarious government agents, an ordinary Joe who finds himself out of his depth, plot twists and scenery with character." — *ASIAN REVIEW OF BOOKS*

"Jake Needham seems to have discovered a secret formula. Why do some people have all the luck?" — *THE BANGKOK POST*

"The most delightful improbabilities are artfully woven together to form the plot of *The Big Mango*. This witty, inventive, and most of all thrilling thriller is ... [a] heady, bloody, luxurious, sordid fictional romp." — *THE NATION* (Bangkok)

"It moves at a crackling pace. The scenes are always changing, people are always going somewhere and doing something ... surreal contrasts illuminate this City of Angels." —*THAILAND TATLER*

"*The Big Mango* was universally acclaimed. As for *Tea Money*, you will not want to put it down and will resent every phone call or visitor who interrupts you." —*THE PATTAYA MAIL*

"The dialogue crackles and the action gallops ... a pleasant change from the usual Bangkok novel about feckless expats, sleazy bargirls, and venal cab drivers." — *THE PHUKET GAZETTE*

"Intrigue, colorful characters, and a power-packed thriller you will remember for a long time." — *LOOK EAST MAGAZINE*

LAUNDRY MAN

With best regards,

Also by Jake Needham:

KILLING PLATO (coming Autumn 2002)

TEA MONEY

THE BIG MANGO

LAUNDRY MAN

a novel by

Jake Needham

Chameleon Press

A Chameleon Press book

LAUNDRY MAN
ISBN 962-86319-2-6

Published by Chameleon Press
www. chameleonpress.com
23rd Floor, 245-251 Hennessy Road, Hong Kong

Typeset in Adobe Garamond by Alan Sargent

Cover design by PPC Ltd, www.powerpointcreative.com
Cover photograph by Virapoj Asavajarn
Author photograph by Sanskrit Jadsadapatipat

Printed and bound in Hong Kong by Elite Printing Co. Ltd

A substantially different version of this novel was published in Thailand for limited distribution in Thailand, Myanmar and Indochina, under the title *Tea Money.*

For Ruby Needham

Ninety-one years old,
she's survived damned near everything.

"You're an expatriate. You've lost touch with the soil. You get precious. You drink yourself to death. You become obsessed by sex. You spend all your time talking. You are an expatriate, see? You hang around cafés."

"It sounds like a swell life," I said. "When do I work?"

"You don't work. One group claims women support you. Another group claims you're impotent."

Ernest Hemingway
The Sun Also Rises

ONE

I'VE ALWAYS THOUGHT THAT driving a convertible is an awfully fine way to enjoy the soft-toned stillness of Sunday twilight in Bangkok.

Normally the city's foreign residents went to considerable lengths to avoid breathing the air, at least until after it had been thoroughly dried, adequately chilled, and comprehensively decontaminated. Not only was the stuff hot and soggy, frequently it smelled spoiled and a little sour, like it had been inhaled and exhaled by way too many people already. Generally the whole experience was pretty much like having a wet dog sit on your face.

But this was January, the middle of winter in Thailand, and the southern-most edge of a large dome of Siberian air had slipped down from China and momentarily broken Bangkok's muggy heat. The air had turned pleasingly cool, even sweet, and it was richly thickened with the syrupy fragrances of frangipani, jasmine, and gardenias.

The Thais hated that, of course. At the first sign of sliding temperatures they hauled out parkas fit for winter in Alaska and swapped their flip-flops for fur-lined mukluks. The city's foreign residents usually reacted to the onset of winter in a somewhat more measured fashion. At most, they rolled down their sleeves.

With the top on my Volvo open to the afternoon breeze, I eased through the gates of my apartment building and nosed into the light Sunday traffic. At Ploenchit Road I crossed under the concrete pillars of the BTS, the city's elevated train system, and headed south. Skirting Lumpini Park, I turned west on Sathorn Road toward the Chao Praya River, the defining feature of the flat, marshy plain over which the city of Bangkok lay scattered.

I could smell the rancid, vinegary aroma of rain in the distance and the sky in front of me looked like a bruise, dark brown at the center fading to a greenish tinge at the edges. Deeply saturated with gathering moisture, the sunset glowed with an eerie iridescence. Thunderstorms at dusk were a local staple much of the year, although it was unusual for one to blow up in winter. Still, I had no doubt at all that a big one was coming tonight.

After crossing the Taksin Bridge high over the Chao Praya, I took the first turn to the left, exactly as the message on my answering machine had told me to.

The concrete ramp made a wide downhill arc and turned me back toward the river. After a few hundred yards I found myself at a busy intersection below the bridge's western ramp. Continuing to follow the instructions with care, I turned left and looked for a way to get underneath the bridge itself, to where the woman had said I would find a parking lot.

I had not driven very far before I noticed a narrow street that seemed promising. It was a tiny *soi* that disappeared between an apartment building and a small park, and I pulled to a stop and examined it in the dim glow of a streetlight. High concrete walls blocked my view on both sides and I couldn't make out much, but nothing about it looked out of the ordinary and I could see no other road nearby that appeared to lead in the right direction. I took one more quick glance around and turned in.

It was only a short distance to where the little *soi* ended at the bank of the river and became a wide asphalt pad separated from the dirty water by strands of barbed wire strung between rusty metal posts. I could see a scattering of small, red plastic stools along the wire and on the left behind another barbed-wire fence was what looked like a children's playground. A yellow and blue swing set, a wooden sand box, and three green teeter-totters sat in the gloom beneath some broad-leafed rubber trees, all as quiet and empty as the stools along the river bank.

I looked at my watch. The woman had said for me to be there at eight. It was twenty minutes past. That made me as close to on time as anyone in Bangkok ever was for anything.

I hadn't recognized her voice nor did I get the impression she had expected me to. She sounded youngish — nice, with a cultured accent that seemed slightly English perhaps, but with a touch of something else I couldn't quite place. She told me that she was calling for a man named Barry Gale. He had to see me urgently, the woman said, and very discreetly. After giving directions, she had asked me to erase the answering machine tape and to tell no one about her call.

I flicked my lights to high beam and looked around. A narrow track just ahead appeared to continue under the bridge, easing between the riverbank and the western anchor, then disappearing into the darkness beyond the range of my headlights. There didn't seem to be much else for me to see where I was, so I took my foot off the brake and let the Volvo roll slowly forward. As I passed underneath the bridge I could hear the rattle of traffic high above my head, but except for that it was almost unnaturally quiet.

After a blind bend to the left that paralleled the river, the track quickly petered out into another parking lot that was as deserted as the first. A line of slender, three-story buildings walled one side of the small pad and the bank of the river marked the other. They looked like godowns, the small warehouses that had serviced shipping on the river for centuries, but these were dark and appeared derelict. A high wall conspicuous in a fresh coat of fluorescent green paint ran from the last godown to the riverbank, closing off the far end of the area. There might have been room for someone on foot to slip between the wall and the river, but certainly not enough for a vehicle. The only way into the lot, or out of it again, was by the narrow road on which I had just come.

The godowns were grimy and run-down, their exteriors cracked and ancient-looking. There were paving stones, rusted barrels, pieces of discarded machinery, and oddly enough, a head-high mound of brown metal folding chairs piled around the lot's perimeter. Thick stands of weeds poked up through wide splits in the surface of the asphalt. The whole place had a dilapidated yet still almost dreamlike air to it, like an empty stage set lighted and waiting for the actors to appear.

I nosed the Volvo toward the waist-high wall that separated the parking lot from the river and rolled forward until my bumper nudged it. Then I shut off the engine and set the brake.

Okay, I was here. Now what?

I couldn't imagine what reason the woman had for leaving such a message on my machine or even what was supposed to mean, but I knew absolutely what it could *not* mean. It could *not* mean that a man named Barry Gale was going to meet me there in that parking lot that night in Bangkok, at least not if it was the only Barry Gale *I* had ever known.

That Barry Gale and I had once been partners together in a large and well-connected Washington law firm. The firm was huge and had over two hundred partners — it was one of those legal factories that only American-style commercial zeal seemed to have spawned — so in spite of our common title, I had run across him only occasionally. Truth be told, I could remember very little at all about Barry Gale.

Except, really, for one thing.

Barry Gale had been both the outside legal counsel and a member of the board of directors of the Texas State Bank in Dallas when it was engulfed in scandal, a hugely psychedelic mess involving a bunch of Russian mobsters from New Jersey who had been using the bank to clean and press their income from a variety of rackets up and down the East Coast. The character at the center of the imbroglio was an Armenian named Jimini Zubokof, who was better known as Jimmy Kicks because he had once, so the legend went, personally taken his gleaming Ferragamos to an FBI informant and kicked the poor bastard to death.

Somehow it happened that Jimmy became inexplicably possessed by the idea of shifting his money-laundering operations from Texas to Asia — *anywhere* in Asia, really — and he demanded his underlings get it done immediately no matter what it cost. Of course all Jimmy Kicks actually knew about Asia was how to order Chinese take-away and he wasn't even very good at that, so in the ensuing upheaval at Texas State Bank offshore accounts and foreign currencies were whizzing all over the place and quite a lot of money disappeared. Tens of millions of dollars, or so the press reports claimed, were lost by the bank through dealing forward contracts in the foreign exchange market, although whose contracts they actually were or how the losses had been incurred was never made entirely clear.

Just as the whole saga was starting to sink out of sight, weighed down by technical obscurity, the disappearance of one of the bank's directors, and what the Dallas cops called the suicide of another, freaked out the conspiracy buffs and the stories about the Russian mob connection with Texas State Bank cranked up all over again.

As far as I knew, no trace had ever been found of the director who vanished, but the so-called suicide had been dramatic enough to grab all the attention anyway. There was a guesthouse in North Dallas that the bank leased for the use of out-of-town directors. That was where Barry Gale had been found, at the bottom of the swimming pool, pinned to it by a manhole cover tied around his neck with barbed wire.

I took a cigar, some matches and a cutter out of my briefcase and snapped it shut. Then I got out of the car and walked to the low wall separating the parking lot from the river. Settling myself on the pitted concrete surface as comfortably as I could, I snipped the end of the Montecristo and lit up. The sweet smoke filled my mouth and the intense aroma mingled with the rich perfume of the Bangkok night. I lifted one knee to support my forearm and took a long, slow pull.

To buy the official story that Barry had committed suicide, I figured you had to be the sort of person who could find a potato at the supermarket shaped like the Virgin Mary and then anoint himself the prophet of the second coming. Still, I supposed I should allow for at least the remote possibility that Barry Gale's death really *had* been a suicide. It had occurred in Dallas after all, the spiritual capital of one of America's more peculiar regions. Either way, I guessed it didn't really matter much as far as I was concerned whether Barry jumped or was pushed into that swimming pool. The question at the moment was why someone was using his name a couple of years later to get me to meet them in a parking lot underneath a bridge in Bangkok.

I drew on my Montecristo again and exhaled a slow stream of smoke into the darkness. I could hear the river sloshing against the base of the retaining wall and occasionally a large vehicle crossing the Taksin Bridge would rattle its substructure with a rumbling like distant kettledrums. The only other sound was some faint music in the distance, and I listened quietly for a long while as the mournful voice of a young girl sang Thai love songs full of sorrow and loss. Her voice had a quavering, reed-thin quality, and the sound of it drifted over the black water like wisps of river fog.

This was the same river along which nineteenth-century European traders had cautiously approached the alien splendor of the Thai capital, the same dreamy, fabled waterway that had once enthralled Joseph Conrad and Somerset Maugham. It had been called the River of Kings then, and sometimes it still was when the local tourism authority was feeling expansive, but now instead of kings it carried mostly mangled soda cans, chunks of soggy cardboard, pieces of lumber, bags of garbage, and blue-green oil slicks.

The air smelled of ozone and rancid water. Lightning leaped soundlessly between clouds off in the distance, and the breeze cranked up a notch.

A small boat roared by heading downriver. It was a longtail, one of the narrow, canoe-like vessels powered by salvaged automobile engines that were the usual form of transportation on the rivers and canals of Thailand. The little boat skimmed the tidal currents like a stone, glancing lightly off the chop and misting the air with dark fans of spray. I wondered briefly if it was going to swing toward me, but then the longtail slalomed around a broad-beamed rice barge plodding silently along in the middle of the channel and disappeared from view underneath the bridge.

As I pulled on the cigar I studied the bank opposite my post on the wall. Where I waited everything was covered in gray-green dimness, but over there Bangkok sparkled with an astonishing radiance. Most of the city's towers were brightly lit, etched into the night sky by lights so blindingly white that they seemed to drain the color from everything around them. The rank of luxury hotels standing watch along the riverfront glistened with jolly red, gold and blue lights, shards of which snaked over the surface of the water and reached out toward me. In spite of itself, I thought, Bangkok could sometimes be such a beautiful city.

To the north the river curled westward and eventually slid out of sight. In the distance I could just pick out the floodlights on the soaring, golden spires and preposterous-looking green and red tile roofs of the Grand Palace. Once the heart of a dazzling, secret world ruled over by a god-king, this eccentric collection of whimsical structures had lately fallen on less glamorous times. The King had long since decamped for more modern quarters and the Grand Palace was now neither grand nor a palace. These days it amounted to little more than a faintly shabby attraction for the hordes of tourists that swept over Thailand year around.

There was a sudden flash of lightning, and moments later, a single, crunching boom of thunder that seemed to drive the air out of the night. I dropped the cigar and ground it out with my foot, then walked quickly back to the Volvo. Starting it, I raised the top.

Just at I snapped shut the two latches above the windshield, the storm hit like a fist.

TWO

I TURNED ON THE WIPERS FIRST, and then the headlights. The driving rain was already so intense that the car's lights looked like they were nothing more than a couple of feeble flashlights, two cones of pale white disappearing into the darkness without touching anything. The wipers struggled to clear the deluge from the windshield, but with little success.

The sudden storm had put an end to speculation. The message had obviously been a prank and I needed to make my way back to the main road before the parking lot and the little *soi* were flooded. Go home, maybe open some red wine.

I sighed and punched off the parking brake. Before I could put the car in gear, however, my cell phone rang. I opened the briefcase again, dug around, and fished it out. The number on the screen was unfamiliar, and I thought fleetingly of just shutting the phone off and ignoring it, but habits are hard to break, even when you wish you could, and so I answered it.

"Jack Shepherd."

"Hello, Mr. Shepherd."

It was the same voice that had left the message on my answering machine.

"Who is this?"

The woman ignored my question, which didn't particularly surprise me.

"I'm sorry we left you sitting in that parking lot," she said instead.

Her voice sounded genuinely concerned, like a school nurse who had just given a small child a shot she wasn't absolutely certain was really necessary.

"I realize my message must have sounded awfully strange," she continued when I said nothing. "We just had to find out what you'd do."

"What makes you think I did anything?"

The woman laughed. It was a surprisingly warm laugh, and the sudden and unexpected way she did it completely disarmed me for a moment.

"We were watching, but please don't take that as a threat. I'm sorry we had to do it. We just didn't feel we could take any chances."

I didn't feel threatened, but I *did* feel thoroughly pissed off and I wondered if she cared as much about that. What the hell was this woman up to? First she lured me into driving halfway across town by leaving a bizarre message on my answering machine, and then, instead of meeting me, she had apparently just sat off in the darkness somewhere and watched me wait for her.

"Look, lady, Barry Gale's dead. I know it and I'm sure you know it. So unless you're Madam Zena the Medium with a message from the other side, you can cut the crap. What do you want?"

I heard a scraping noise and then the woman's voice became muffled. I gathered she must have covered the phone with her hand and was talking to someone else. Then the scraping noise came again.

"I'm in deep shit here, Jack," a male voice said.

The man who had apparently taken the phone from the woman cleared his throat.

"I know it's not like we were war buddies or anything, but I need your help. I really do. I figure I got no more than a week before somebody cuts off my nuts and feeds them to the ducks."

The man spoke slowly and deliberately. He didn't sound much like someone playing a practical joke.

"You don't recognize my voice," the man went on when I didn't reply immediately. "Well, it's been a long time. That doesn't surprise me, Jack."

"Look, I know you're not Barry Gale. He's been dead for at least a couple of years."

The man seemed to consider my remark briefly.

"What makes you think he's dead?"

"Barry's synchronized swimming routine with the manhole cover was pretty flashy. It got a fair amount of attention."

"Oh, yeah. The body in the pool."

The man drew his words out with a drawl that made me think momentarily of Dallas.

"I'll bet an awful lot of people saw it when they pulled it out," he said.

"Probably."

"Of course, it had been in the water almost a week before anybody found it, so they couldn't get fingerprints. Also I hear the face was too badly smashed up to recognize. Must have caught the manhole cover when he hit the water. Anyway, nobody thought it was worth bothering with DNA so they just did the ID from dental records."

"And didn't the dental records match Barry's?"

"Well . . . they would, wouldn't they?"

I wasn't quite sure what to say to that, but I wasn't feeling particularly subtle right then so I settled for the obvious.

"Are you telling me that the body they pulled out of the swimming pool wasn't Barry Gale's?"

"Not likely, Jack. Not likely at all. Especially not seeing as how we're talking to each other right now."

I tried it another way.

"Look, I'm a reasonably approachable guy," I said. "Why don't you and your girlfriend just tell me what you want and drop all this Barry Gale stuff?"

There was a brief silence and then the man started talking again. He spoke softly, and in what I thought was a tired-sounding voice.

"Your name is Jonathan William Shepherd, but your father started calling you Jack when you were a kid to keep your mother from calling you Johnny and it stuck. You're admitted to the bar in the District of Columbia and in New York, too, aren't you?"

I wasn't sure if the man expected me to say anything, so I didn't. He must not have cared because after a moment he went on again.

"When you lived in Washington your address was 1701 Great Falls Road in Potomac, a big white house with a lot of columns and two statues of little naked colored boys at the end of the driveway. Your wife, the lovely Laura, had taken up with that proctologist somewhere out in Virginia, Dr. Butthole, you called him. How am I doing?"

"Very impressive," I said.

"I'm an impressive guy. You want more?"

"Sure. Knock yourself out."

"Everybody at Stassen & Hardy called you the Old Asia Hand, and you hated that, didn't you?"

Whoever the man was, he was certainly right about that. I had never been one for nicknames in general, but that one had particularly annoyed me. It fairly reeked of black and white movies, Robert Mitchum when he was thirty-five and more or less sober, glamorous men in rumpled linen suits lounging in exotic bars with wooden ceiling fans creaking slowly overhead, and dark-eyed, accommodating women lurking in the shadows, smiling inscrutably. The Old Asia Hand business conjured up a sense of dilapidated romance that I truly despised. Being an international lawyer was serious stuff, judgment and diligence, not a bunch of half-baked, dreamy fantasies. Anyway, that was the way I had looked at it back then.

"But you *were* the Old Asia Hand, Jack. You really were. Somehow you could get incredible stuff done out here when the rest of us were just sitting around Washington with our thumbs up our butts. Maybe it was because all the flaky shit that drove the rest of us mad really turned your crank. You loved every bit of it, didn't you?"

The man had me there, too. Love it I did from my very first trip back in the mid-eighties. Asia was the home field of hustle, the headquarters of hype. You could grab a seat at almost any bar in a dozen countries and watch corporate cowboys flimflamming conmen, arms dealers rubbing elbows with intelligence agents, and criminals on the lam cutting deals with diplomats on the take. It was a murky, outrageous world, and the guy had nailed me cold. I absolutely couldn't resist the place.

"Is that it?" I asked. "You recite a few bits of my bio and some things you've heard about me, and now I'm supposed to believe you're Barry Gale risen from the dead?"

"Hell, Jack. I could go on all night. How about this? In Washington your office was about as far away from the reception area as it was possible for you to get and still be in the same building with the rest of us. You had a big glass table that you used for a desk. Goddamn, Jack, I'm sure you were the only lawyer in the world with a glass desk. It was like you were trying to look purer than the rest of us hiding behind our big hunks of mahogany. Was that it, Jack? Was that what the glass desk was all about? And, oh yeah, you had that big yellow couch with the deep cushions where you took naps in the afternoon."

"Look, I don't know who you are, but. . . ."

"One time you fucked that part-time receptionist, the little Vietnamese girl who was going to law school somewhere and worked as the relief girl on weekends. Remember? You did it right on that yellow couch one Saturday afternoon and then you told me about it after you'd sucked up a couple of extra martinis one night at the bar in the Mayflower Hotel. You said you hadn't told anyone else. *Had* you told anyone else, Jack?"

I hadn't. All at once the beating of the rain on the Volvo seemed abnormally loud. I listened as the car's fabric top began to rumble from the weight of the deluge.

"Say something, Jack. Are you listening to me? Or has living on cheap pussy and shitty beer completely wiped you out? Pay attention, man. What I'm saying here is. . . ."

"I heard you."

After that the man shut up and didn't say anything else for a while. Maybe he'd picked up the edge in my voice and thought he'd better give me a chance to think. When eventually he did start talking again, it was in the same low, tired voice.

"How'd a guy like you end up living in a place like Bangkok, Jack?"

His question surprised me, but even if it hadn't I wouldn't really have known how to answer it.

When people first began to hear that I was leaving Washington for Bangkok a few of them jumped to the conclusion I was trying to make a point of some kind, abandoning the land of my birth for reasons that were probably political and no doubt wacky. Others who'd heard what I was doing — and I noticed this group seemed to be composed mainly of women — attributed my change of address to middle-aged male *angst* fueled by overly moist fantasies of slim, submissive Thai women serving me brightly-colored tropical drinks with little umbrellas in them.

Most people who heard, of course, fell into neither of those categories. Most people just assumed that I had lost my damned mind, not that unusual an occurrence in Washington.

Part of the problem was that the whole idea was just so *strange* to most Americans, particularly since very few of them had ever seriously entertained the thought, however fleetingly, of packing up one day and going off to another country to live. After all everyone wanted to come to America, didn't they? Half the population of the earth was fighting to live in Orange County and work in a 7-Eleven, wasn't it? Why in God's name would an American even *think* of going anywhere else?

This man, like many before him who had asked me the same question, eventually got tired of waiting for an answer and tried a different approach.

"You're a teacher now, I hear. In some business school."

"That's right. At Chulalongkorn University."

"No more lawyering? No more of that big-time stuff we used to do?"

"I don't practice law anymore if that's what you mean."

"Miss it?"

"Not particularly. I still do a little consulting sometimes."

"Consulting, huh? Is that right?" The man barked an abrupt laugh. "You want to consult with me, Jack?"

"I don't think so."

"Still a fucking hard-on, aren't you?"

"I just don't particularly like being the butt of some clown's crappy little joke."

"Oh, this is no joke, Jack. I wish to Christ it was, but it isn't."

Then there was another long silence and again I waited the man out, listening to him breathing over the phone.

"Do you know that place called Took Lae Dee?"

The man's voice sounded an entirely new note, that of a salesman who sensed he had a sale and wanted to get it closed before the mark had a chance to think it over.

"Sure you do, Jack. It's that counter up in the front of the all-night Foodland behind that rib joint on Sukhumvit. Meet me there tomorrow night, would you? About midnight."

"Midnight?"

"You got a problem with that?"

"Yeah, I got a problem with that. What makes you think I'd even consider showing up in some damned supermarket at midnight because this wacko pretending to be a dead guy calls me up and tells me to?"

"Oh, you'll be there, Jack. Unless you've changed an awful lot these last couple of years, you'll be there."

"I don't know how you found out all those things about me, but if you think that just because of that. . . ."

The man started laughing.

"I know you're coming, Jack, so don't give me that crap. You're coming all right. This is just the kind of shit you love."

The storm was moving away. Thunder rumbled distantly and I listened to it without saying anything.

"I know you, Jack. You'd never pass up a chance to hear a story like the one I've got to tell. Especially not now, not after I've gone and gotten myself dead."

And with that, the man hung up.

I guess I should have been seriously annoyed that someone had rousted me into chasing halfway across city that Sunday night on a fool's errand, particularly since he had left me sitting in an empty parking lot in the middle of a thunderstorm. Oddly enough, I wasn't especially. This was Bangkok after all. If I didn't have genuine affection for strangeness, I'd probably still be living in Washington.

The rain had become little more than a warm drizzle — storms here never lasted very long no matter how nasty they might seem to be at first — so I put the Volvo in gear and started home. Crossing back over the river, I followed Sathorn Road east, driving slowly and enjoying the city. The sudden deluge had scrubbed it clean and emptied the streets. It wasn't a bad time to be out and around.

My apartment was in a mid-rise tower called Chidlom Place, a fairly new and attractive building, but one with a silhouette that, some said, bore an unfortunate resemblance to male genitalia in full flight. The apartment itself was bright and spacious, and regardless of the building's shape, it was one of the city's better places to live. Actually I probably could never have afforded an apartment there except that the previous owner of this one had been a Burmese amphetamine producer who had apparently gotten himself involved in a fairly serious business dispute. One night someone settled it by putting a full clip in him while he was sitting on the toilet reading a copy of *Penthouse.* That had brought the price right down into my range.

I came to the end of Sathorn and turned north on Wireless Road, heading toward the American Embassy.

Only a generation or two ago Bangkok had been a gracious place crisscrossed by canals rather than streets, an uncluttered scattering of mostly wooden buildings set in thick groves of mango trees that cast cool shadows as they swayed in the tropical breezes. Only the gilded spires of the Buddhist temples reached up any more than two or three stories, and life took its rhythm from the moods of the muddy Chao Praya.

Now it was a lot different. Almost all of the city's small shops, family homes, and neighborhood restaurants had long since been swept away by a flood tide of soaring condominium towers and massive shopping malls. The things had sprouted everywhere, toadstools in a rainforest, lavishly fertilized by a potent combination of hot money and obliging bankers. Jagged mountain ranges of gleaming marble, anodized aluminum, burnished chrome, and bronzed glass now lined what not long ago had been narrow, tree-shaded lanes, turning them into deep valleys grid-locked bumper-to-bumper with traffic. Concrete, steel, and the Mercedes-Benz had nearly buried Bangkok in less than a generation.

Yet, some said, when the breeze was right you could hear the old city whispering still. The shadowy deals, the tangled mysteries, the murky alliances, and the dark, treacherous scheming that had always been Bangkok's very soul were there in the wind even now. That was true, of course. I'd heard the murmuring myself, and it always came to me like a remembrance of an old and reliable friend.

Bangkok always made me think of that old joke about a kid who wants a pony so badly that he drives his father nuts, so the old man eventually fills up a room with horse manure just to show the little bastard what owning a pony is all about. Instead of being discouraged when he sees the room, however, the kid starts rooting around in the crap, flinging it cheerfully in all directions.

"What in the world are you doing, son?" the father asks.

"Well, Pop, I'll tell you," the kid says. "With all this horseshit, there's got to be a pony in here somewhere."

Bangkok was like that.

So much horseshit, but there were sure a whole bunch of ponies in there, too.

THREE

WHEN I GOT HOME, I found some chicken in the refrigerator and some leftover rice in the cooker. I heated them both in the microwave while I opened a Heineken, and then I doused the chicken and rice in hot Sriracha sauce and took everything into the living room and watched a replay of yesterday's Redskins game on ESPN while I ate. That's not exactly the way I used to eat back in DC when I watched the Skins play, of course, but I've always been an adaptable kind of guy.

Anita got home around ten, and as soon as she closed the door behind her she took a couple of little quick hopping bounds across the room and dived over the back of the couch. Then she rolled into my lap and hung one arm around my neck.

"I missed you, darling."

I tilted my head down and kissed her lightly on the lips. "I missed you, too."

"Am I interrupting your game?"

"Not really. I wasn't paying much attention." I groped for the remote control and pressed the mute button. "How was the dinner?"

"It wasn't a dinner. It was just another gallery opening. A new place at the Emporium."

"I've never really understood what you get out of going to those things."

"And I've never really understood what you get out of jogging around the park at dawn, my darling."

Anita and I had been together for a little more than a year. She was a true child of the world, having been born in Paris of an Italian mother and an English father and then moved to Hong Kong by her parents when she was ten. She went to high school in New York and eventually graduated from UCLA with a degree in film.

Now she was a painter of considerable note, although I had to admit somewhat sheepishly that I'd never heard of her when we first met at a Sotheby's auction in Bangkok. Actually I suppose that I had never heard of many painters, except for a few who died in the fifteenth or sixteenth century and all of them had beards, but it wasn't long before I discovered that Anita had a huge reputation in Europe as a young artist to be watched. I too thought she should be watched, although I was pretty sure what I was watching and what the European art critics were watching were completely different things. At least I hoped they were.

Anita had simply packed up her whole studio and moved from London to Bangkok a few months after our meeting at Sotheby's and it wasn't very long after that she became white-hot in European art circles. She always said that it was the sensuality of Thailand that had given her work the push it needed to make that happen, but I naturally held to the theory there might have been another factor at work as well.

Anita was much in demand among the art set in Europe these days and she traveled there frequently to do publicity for galleries that sold her work. Of course she was also much in demand by me in Bangkok, and it pleased me beyond reason that she made such an effort to strike a balance between those two tugs on her life.

"So what did you do tonight?" Anita asked me as we watched maroon-and-gold uniformed giants silently smashing into some blue-and-white ones.

I hesitated before I answered, not entirely sure what to say about my drive down to the river and the call from the man who claimed to be Barry Gale. It was just a beat, but Anita jumped all over it.

"Ah *ha!* Out chasing bargirls, I'd bet."

"Look here now, I'm not taking any crap from a painter. Particularly not one who's spent the evening standing around some drafty gallery, sipping Campari from a plastic glass and listening to strange men feign fascination with the paintings in a transparent effort to get into her pants."

"Which bar is your favorite these days, my darling? Is it King's Castle? That used to be the place to go in Patpong, wasn't it? Or are you local boys avoiding the tourists these days and going to Soi Cowboy again? What's hot there? Is it still Long Gun? Do they still do those lesbian shows like they used to?"

"I think you know way too much about a lot of things, and this is obviously one of them."

Anita grinned and brushed her lips quickly over mine, then she swung her feet to the floor and pushed herself off the couch. There was nothing special about the whole movement but, just the same, the grace in the way she did it took my breath away.

"Don't go away, big boy. Got to pee. Then I want to hear the whole story about the little honey who latched onto you tonight before I go over and scratch her eyes out."

I would have married Anita in a moment, but she never mentioned it and there was something that made me hesitate to ask. To do that would risk changing everything that made life so good right then, particularly if she said no, and that was a chance I was not prepared to take.

After Anita came back we leaned against each other on the couch and made small talk for a while, but eventually of course I got around to telling her about the message that had taken me down to the parking lot by the river and the man on my cell phone who had claimed to be Barry Gale.

"That's shocking, Jack," she said when I'd finished.

The word took me aback me a little. It sounded quaint and outdated somehow, out of place in a world that now had little room and less time for people who were shocked by anything. Yet it was a word that Anita wore well. I liked it on her.

"Do you think it really *was* him?" she asked.

"Well. . . ."

The answer was pretty obvious, but I'd been trying not to admit it to myself yet.

"Then whose body was that in the swimming pool?" Anita leaned toward me and tilted her head.

"Got me."

"What does this man want with you now?"

"He didn't say."

"Well, Mr. Laconic, I want to thank you for clearing everything up so nicely for me."

"Hey." I opened my hands in the universal gesture of coming clean. "You know what I know. It's just not much."

Abruptly Anita pushed herself away from me and stood up. She walked to the window and stood there looking out at the city, her arms folded around herself as if the air had suddenly turned unexpectedly cool.

"You went out there tonight to meet this man." She spoke without turning around. "Down to the river."

"I just told you I did."

"Why did you do that?"

"To find out what the message meant."

"And you went alone?"

"Yes."

"All by yourself?"

"That's what 'alone' means."

"I'm not stupid, Jack . . . but sometimes I think *you* are."

I would have though that diplomacy would come naturally to someone who was half Italian, half British, and born in France; but in Anita's case at least, it didn't.

"Going down there alone was really stupid, Jack. You could have been killed."

"Oh, Anita, don't be ridiculous."

She turned quickly.

"Ridiculous? Didn't you just tell me that the embassy had been warning Americans to keep a low profile and to be especially alert?"

"The embassy does that all the time, Anita."

"Do they? They warn Americans in Thailand to be careful all the time?"

"They warn Americans *everywhere* to be careful all the time. Look, the embassy's just covering its ass. Nobody really pays any attention to these things."

"Well, maybe you *should."*

"Now don't go getting. . . ."

"You Americans are all alike, aren't you, Jack. All a bunch of tiny John Waynes at heart. Well here's a news flash for you. *Life is not a movie.* You've got to have the sense to know when to be afraid."

"Look, come over here and sit down." I patted the cushion next to me with my open palm. "Let's start over."

Anita stayed where she was just long enough to make it unmistakable that she was sitting because she chose to, not because I had asked her to. Then she walked over and perched on the couch.

"I didn't see any danger in going out there tonight or I wouldn't have gone, Anita."

"You didn't see any danger in going to an empty parking lot in a deserted part of town that you don't know very well and waiting for some nut who left a strange message on our answering machine? You *really* didn't see any danger in doing that in the middle of the night?"

"It wasn't the middle of the night. It was eight o'clock."

"You *know* what I mean. Don't try that lawyer crap on me, hot shot."

"Look, Anita, when was the last time you heard of a foreigner being assaulted by anyone in Bangkok?"

"The week before last."

"What are you talking about?"

"That French photographer. It was in all the papers."

Come to think of it, Anita was right. A couple of weeks before a motorcyclist had shot to death a middle-aged Frenchman as he'd been walking back to his apartment after an evening spent drinking at the Crown Royal in Patpong. The foreign community had fretted about that for a few days, but the whole incident quickly slid off their radar when the *Bangkok Post* reported that the shooter had been hired by the Frenchman's Thai wife and her nineteen-year-old Thai boyfriend.

"I figured I was safe since you were busy tonight."

"Ha, ha, ha, ha."

"Look, Anita, I wouldn't have gone if I'd thought it was dangerous. And besides, I was very careful."

Anita folded her arms again and drew her mouth into a tight line.

"If it wasn't dangerous, why were you so careful?"

She had me there. Never argue with an Italian woman who was born in France, I reminded myself for not the first time.

"I'm very tired," Anita suddenly announced in a voice that left no room for speculation as to whether I was going to be forgiven my sins anytime soon. "I'm going to take a shower and go to bed. Good night, Jack."

And with that she stood up and left the room, and everything was suddenly very quiet.

FOUR

AFTER ANITA WENT TO BED I sat without moving for a while, then I got a Montecristo out of the humidor behind the couch and walked out on the balcony. I cut and lit the cigar, then stood there smoking, looking out over the city for a long time.

Mostly Bangkok felt like home now, but occasionally looking at it in the silence and the darkness like this left me with an oddly untethered feeling, as if the lifeline that secured my existence to the real world had unaccountably come untied, and now here I was, hanging in space, drifting in the unknown, maybe even in the unknowable.

How had that happened? The question came less frequently now, but still, from time to time, it came.

As all the really important turning points in life seem to, the whole business had started out in an utterly unremarkable way when I bumped into a man during a business trip to Singapore, a man who I had known for a long time and liked quite a lot.

For a couple of decades Stanley Ratikun had been the managing partner of one of Bangkok's oldest international law firms, then he retired and became director of the Sasin Institute of Business Administration at Chulalongkorn University. Chula was Thailand's premier university, and Sasin its premier graduate school of business, so the directorship was a post of considerable prestige.

Stanley didn't need the prestige. Although he had been born in New York, his grandmother was obscurely related to the Thai royal family and he still had his Thai passport. That was one of the two reasons that his law firm had represented just about every significant international corporation that did any business at all in Thailand after the mid-sixties. The other was that Stanley and the other members of his firm were all first-rate lawyers.

It was on the second day of the trip that I unexpectedly ran into Stanley in the lobby of the Grand Hyatt. When he suggested we have dinner together, I proposed that we go to Dan Ryan's for burgers and a couple of beers, but he was a far more refined fellow than I was and he insisted instead on taking me to the Raffles Grill.

The veal chop I ordered was wonderful, but the bottle of Brunello di Montalcino that Stanley chose to go with it was even better. As we ate, our conversation rambled here and there, touching on the things that lawyers as members of a common lodge talk about when there aren't any civilians around. He asked me about my practice, and I voiced the usual complaints about its monotony and soullessness. I asked Stanley how he was enjoying the academic life, and he told me how much fun he was having.

"You mean to tell me that you don't miss all that great stuff you used to do?" I asked.

"Like what?"

"Well . . . how about winding up the Merchant Group? That must have been a real adventure."

Stanley sort of grunted, but he didn't actually say anything.

We had first met when Stanley's firm had been lead counsel for a company called the Merchant Group that had gone suddenly and spectacularly belly up and left a good number of Stassen & Hardy's banking clients holding embarrassingly empty bags. The company had technically been a Luxembourg corporation with its operating headquarters in Bangkok, but in reality it was as Australian as a red kangaroo. Lyndon Merchant ran the whole organization out of Perth, and he referred to it as a private international merchant bank, whatever that crafty assembly of buzzwords was actually supposed to mean.

What the company really did was equally difficult to divine. It did deals of course, as the players liked to say back in the eighties when the expression was still socially acceptable if not exactly laudable. It bought companies all over the world, mostly with money borrowed from gullible and greedy bankers whose primary interest was in pumping up their quarterly results with fat fees; then it either flipped the companies quickly for a fast profit, generally to some sucker lined up in advance, or it cut them up, pulled the valuable assets out, and dumped what was left.

When Stassen & Hardy sent me out to Bangkok to fish around in the wreckage of the Merchant Group, it wasn't long before I was up to my butt in a morass of untraceable fund transfers and funny-money loans involving shell companies headquartered in places like the Cook Islands, Vanuatu, and Tonga. While the gamy odor that arose from the whole sordid mess was unmistakable, I never got the real story quite straight; and in spite of trying like hell, I couldn't develop any solid connections between the Merchant Group's operations and the usual suspects in international scams of that sort — the intelligence agencies, drug traffickers, and arms brokers who were generally skulking somewhere in the shadows.

Stanley, as I recalled, seemed to find the whole muddle more amusing than anything. Nevertheless, working that case with him turned out to be the finest graduate course in Asian commercial skullduggery that I could have hoped for.

Stanley called for our second bottle of Brunello, and when the waiter went off to get it, he casually mentioned that there was a vacancy on the faculty at Sasin for someone to teach international business and corporate planning. Then he asked if I was interested.

I laughed. "You're not serious."

"Absolutely."

"Me? Move to Bangkok?"

"Uh-huh."

"Give up my partnership? Just like that? And become a law professor?"

"A business school professor."

"Oh." I nodded, managing to keep my expression suitably grave. "That's different."

"Yes, it is. You said as much yourself a few moments ago, as I recall."

Lawyers have a tendency to bitch and moan to each other about the monotony of their profession, and naturally I did my share. Still, I hated the constant bellyaching most lawyers did about how crappy and boring their lives were, and it embarrassed me a little to have been caught out by Stanley yammering on like that myself.

The waiter appeared and presented the new bottle of Brunello for Stanley's approval. He nodded without looking up from his *veal Milanese* and the fellow went into the ritual of uncorking it.

I used the silence to try and decide what I was going to say to Stanley's offer. I gathered that he was quite serious, and I didn't want to be so rude as to be entirely dismissive. Nevertheless, the whole idea was obviously ridiculous. There was no way anyone could seriously consider giving up a partnership in one of Washington's most influential law firms to become a business school professor at an obscure university in Thailand, of all places.

"I'll tell you something," Stanley went on after the waiter had finished pouring the wine and disappeared. "Guys like you hit forty and every one of you start doing the same chant. 'I'll get out,' you say. 'I'll get out just as soon as I have enough money.' I'm sick of hearing it. Not one of you is ever going to do it."

"Look, Stanley, I appreciate you thinking about me, but you couldn't seriously believe I'd. . . ."

"I'd be sadly disappointed to find out you're just like all the rest of them, Jack. I've heard you talk about quitting, and you just told me you're bored to death with the garbage you have to wade through every day. Then I offer you the perfect out and you laugh at me."

"Now that's not fair, Stanley."

"So what's your plan, Jack? Keep on fighting the good fight? Go on scratching and scheming so people you have no respect for can make a little more money until you're too old to come into the office anymore? Then what? Open a bookstore in Portland?"

I contemplated my glass and waited, sensing that Stanley was just warming up.

"Do you want me to tell you what the real secret is to surviving all the horseshit people like you live with, Jack?"

"Okay, Stanley. I'll bite. What's the real secret?"

"You have to know just one thing for sure, my friend. Just one thing."

The moment suddenly seemed quite portentous, although looking back, even now I don't understand why.

"You have to know that anytime you want to — *anytime* — you can walk away." Stanley sloshed the rest of the Brunello in his glass back and forth a couple of times and then downed it all in one long hit. "That's all you have to remember. You're not stuck with the life you've got. If you're not happy with it, you can get yourself another one. Know that's true — that you've got the balls to *make* it true — and they can never get to you."

"Nobody's always happy with his life, Stanley," I said. "Running away isn't the answer."

"It depends on what the question is, Jack. It really depends on what the question is."

I had to admit I could see the point Stanley was making, but still. . . .

"And there's another thing, Jack. You never know how many chances you're going to get to put things right. You remember what happened to Lyndon Merchant."

When the Merchant Group had collapsed, the welter of charges and counter-charges that brought it down were unsurprising. They had included the customary allegations of fronting for CIA shell companies, funding arms smuggling operations, supporting international commerce in drugs, and laundering money for a whole bag full of exotic specimens. Lyndon Merchant disappeared from Perth when the balloon went up and he wasn't seen or heard from again for three months. Then a bunch of Thai kids were driving around looking for a place to party near Hua Hin, a moldy beach resort about a hundred and twenty miles south of Bangkok, and they solved the mystery. Or maybe they stumbled on a bigger one, depending on which way you wanted to look at it.

Down a dirt track that led to a deserted beach, they discovered a dark blue, late-model Mercedes parked with its doors locked. Lyndon Merchant was lying across the front seat. His body was in an advanced state of decomposition, and the gray grit that was smeared over the inside of the windshield ultimately turned out to be a good part of his brain matter.

The Thai police soon announced that Merchant had shot himself in the mouth with both barrels of the Remington twelve gauge that was found lying across his body. It apparently didn't concern the local cops all that much that Lyndon's arms would have had to have been nearly four feet long to squeeze the triggers himself after the gun's long barrels were wedged in his mouth. This was Thailand after all. If a foreigner was dead, and you couldn't call it natural causes, then it must have been suicide.

"Lyndon probably figured he had all the time in the world to sort things out, too, don't you think, Jack? But that's not the way the cards came down for him. Maybe they won't be the way they come down for you either."

"Are you saying somebody is going to shoot me, Stanley?"

"Don't know." Stanley chewed reflectively on a piece of veal and consulted a spot on the tablecloth that was right above his plate. "I guess it depends on what you're mixed up in these days."

"I'm all grown up now, Stanley. I've gone straight."

"Then I guess you don't have to worry about anybody putting the hammer down on you like they did on poor old Lyndon."

"I don't."

"Actually it may not matter, Jack. From what I hear you saying, you're already doing a damned fine job of killing yourself."

The silence stretched on for a while after that, Stanley continuing to nibble at his veal without looking at me. I knew if I didn't say anything we'd probably sit there like that all night.

"You're making too much out of a little harmless bitching, Stanley. I'm a senior partner in one of the best law firms in the United States. I do a good job for them and they pay me more money than I really know what to do with. That's the way employment works, at least it does if you're lucky. Nobody asks you to swear an oath that you love every minute of it."

"You still married?"

"No."

For one horrible moment I thought Stanley was about to ask me why, and I knew that I didn't have a clue what I'd tell him if he did. But he didn't.

"You don't have any kids, do you?"

"No."

"Got a girlfriend?"

"At my age, Stanley, that expression sounds a bit threadbare. Sometimes you're with women you sleep with. Sometimes you're with women you fall in love with."

"Which."

"Which what?"

"Which is it for you now?"

I cleared my throat, unnecessarily. "Neither really. I'm between engagements."

"So what's keeping you in Washington? No important work. No wife. No kids. No girlfriend. You must really love that city."

"Well, not that much, but. . . ."

"Then change your life, Jack. The power's yours. You can do whatever you want to do."

Stanley bent toward me, snapping the words out in a crisp cadence and tapping his finger on the tablecloth in rhythm with each syllable.

"Change. Your. Life. While. You. Still. Can."

I looked away and shook my head.

"Christ, Stanley, listen to yourself. You sound like some cheesy motivational speaker haranguing a used car dealer's convention."

"Tell me one thing I've said that's not true."

I desperately wanted just to shut up and sit there until Stanley ran down and abandoned his pitch, but somehow I couldn't. The words kept coming out of my mouth as if an unseen magnet was tugging at them.

"You don't just pick up and move halfway around the world because everything's not great. You find a way to make it better," I said.

Stanley backhanded the thought away as if it had been a gnat hovering over what was left of his veal.

"I'm *offering* you a way to make it better. That's what this conversation is all about."

"I understand that, Stanley, but. . . ."

"I'm a happy man, Jack. I've found my spot."

"But you've retired. You've left the firm and started doing something you really love."

Stanley blinked at that, his eyes opening and closing slowly with the calm deliberation of a frog. Then he smiled and returned his full attention to his food.

While no doubt the retelling of the story now makes it seem commonplace, perhaps even a little silly, I can only describe what came over me right about then as an epiphany of sorts. There were no trumpets, no chorus of angels singing hosannas, but as far as I was concerned the whole damned heavenly host might as well have started boogying away right then as one. It was as if I had suddenly been gifted with an inexplicable, entirely unexpected, and almost magical vision, a vision that I can say, without exaggeration, changed everything that was to come afterwards for the rest of my life.

I *could* do anything I wanted, couldn't I? It really *was* just that simple.

I wasn't lashed to the mast of Stassen & Hardy. I didn't have a family counting on me to provide a future for them. I was responsible for no one except myself. No one's life depended on my decisions except mine.

Stanley was absolutely right. How could I *not* have seen that before? I *could* do anything I wanted. I could climb mountains. I could sail oceans. I could become a rock star. Well . . . maybe not that.

But, God help me, I *could* go to Bangkok and become a professor of international business at Chulalongkorn University. Actually, now that I thought about it, that has a kind of a ring to it. *Professor Shepherd.* Yeah, that had a sound. You could dance to it.

As I recall it now, when I eventually spoke again my voice sounded embarrassingly small.

"If the time comes when I really *should* move on, Stanley — and I'm not saying it has, you understand — how will I know it? How can I know I'm doing the right thing?"

Stanley glanced up without moving his head, and I remembered clearly the look on his face. He looked like he had a small animal trapped in his mouth and wanted to make certain it didn't escape. He had me, and he knew he had me.

I cleared the table and carried my dirty dishes into the kitchen. As I rinsed them off and put them away in the dishwasher, I thought back again over what Anita had said.

Had it really been foolish for me to go down to the river alone? Could I actually have been in danger?

To be a foreigner in Thailand was, in many ways, to live a charmed life. Thais were so famously courteous that most of the time they wouldn't bother a foreigner no matter what he was doing, and the rest of the time your status as a native of realms beyond the sea that the average Thai could only imagine afforded you a considerable degree of deference whether you deserved it or not.

It was a dream for most of us. You could, by turns, convince yourself that you were invisible, or command almost unlimited privileges. Of course, you were anything *but* invisible, and the privileges rarely had much real substance, but the feeling was still awfully seductive.

It had never occurred to me that going anywhere in Bangkok at any hour, not even down to the river on a Sunday night, might put me in harm's way. Yet still, it niggled at me that maybe Anita had a point. Maybe I should have been more careful.

If I was going to meet whoever this was on Monday night, Barry Gale or not, maybe I should approach the whole idea a little less casually. Do some homework. Get prepared. Think everything out in advance. Not just stumble into the Foodland at midnight like some simpleton and hope for the best.

Or maybe I should just forget about the whole thing. Pretend that none of this had ever happened and get on with my life.

I *could* do that.

Yeah, right.

FIVE

CHULALONGKORN UNIVERSITY is right in the middle of Bangkok, and the Sasin School of Business is in the northwest corner of Chula's main campus. Sasin is housed in two medium-rise buildings that make up in mediocre design what they lack in construction quality. My office was on the sixth floor of the larger building, around on the south side where I had a fine view of the golf course at the Royal Bangkok Sports Club and the towers of the Silom Road financial district just beyond it.

I had gotten in early on Monday morning. It had rained in the night, but the new day was glorious, a sky so blue that it reminded me of Hawaii and a promising breeze out of the south that carried the smell of salt all the way up from the Gulf of Thailand. My secretary hadn't appeared yet, so I walked down to the little kitchen at the end of the hall to make some coffee.

Bun always made coffee as soon as she got in, but to tell the truth, I preferred to do it myself. Most Thais who drank coffee at all stirred a couple of spoons of Nescafé into some tepid water and figured that was that. As for me, I couldn't get the stuff down.

My second day in the office, I had walked up to the Isetan Department Store and bought an overpriced drip coffeemaker. Bun gamely wrestled the thing to the death every morning, but usually the machine won. She would have taken great offense at the suggestion that I didn't trust her, so I had to let her do it. Most generously,

I even drank the terrible stuff that she managed to coax out of the machine. At least, I reminded myself, it wasn't Nescafé.

As I was waiting for the Mr. Coffee to finish dribbling, I walked back to the office and gathered up the weekend's harvest of incoming faxes from the machine behind Bun's desk. I flipped quickly through the first few sheets and saw that the schedule for a board meeting I had to attend the following week in Hong Kong had been shortened from two days to one. That was good news. When you lived in Bangkok, one day in Hong Kong was generally a lot better than two.

I was on several boards of directors around Asia. There was Southeast Asian Investments in Hong Kong, a bank in Australia, an Indonesian manufacturing group, the Thai distributor for Volvo, a Singapore media group, and a Hong Kong aircraft leasing company that was domiciled in the British Virgin Islands although as far as I knew no one connected with the company was entirely certain where the British Virgin Islands actually *were*.

Directorships were an undemanding way to pick up a little extra money, I had discovered, as well as a nice excuse to get out of the office every now and then and do some traveling at someone else's expense. In return, all I had to do was show up for meetings, look wise, and stay more-or-less awake.

Occasionally some company's management would politely ask for my views on a pending matter, but then, regardless of what I said, usually they went right ahead and did whatever it was they had intended to do in the first place. Once in a while, however, when the legal issues were particularly technical and convoluted, I noticed that some of the advice I gave was actually followed, at least after a fashion.

In Washington I had generally functioned as the hired gun for one of the parties to some international dispute, slugging it out remorselessly with all comers on behalf of whoever was paying the freight. When I wasn't doing that, I was usually puffing up my chest like General Patton for the sake of my clients, keeping them continually reassured that they were as safe as little children in the hands of a big-time, hard-balling bastard like me.

Now, newly swathed in the impartial cloak of academia, I had begun to think of myself as less like a mercenary and more like a canny old surgeon who was brought in only when a patient required a particularly delicate procedure. Best of all, when I was called to consult on a case, I didn't have to lean over the operating table, shake hands with the fellow lying there, and ask, "So, how's the family?" All I had to do was show up, cut the sucker, and go home. The rest of the deal was somebody else's problem.

I walked back to the kitchen carrying the faxes, picked out what looked like a clean mug from a cabinet above the sink, and poured myself some coffee. When I got into my office, I dumped the faxes on my desk, took a sip of coffee, then fished the *Asian Wall Street Journal* out of my briefcase and settled back to read.

Mondays were undemanding days for me since I taught only one class. It was an eleven o'clock lecture course entitled "Legal Aspects of the Regulation of Multinational Corporate Acquisition Finance Transactions in the Countries of the Pacific Rim," or "Wheel, Deal and Steal" as the kids called it. The course was a second-year elective that I gathered had never been very popular before I took it over, but now the enrollment was well above a hundred and the meetings had been moved to one of the large lecture halls to accommodate the crowd. I had no illusions that the mob of students was there because of some reputation I might have for imparting unimaginable wisdom. The real reason, I knew full well, was something a bit less noble.

The word around campus was that my lectures were entertaining, and I suppose they were. Moreover, if you turned up with reasonable regularity, at the end of the semester full course credit was yours without a great deal of fuss. I was a charter subscriber to Woody Allen's Postulate — at least eighty percent of life is about just showing up.

There was another reason the course drew so well, I also knew; one I had decidedly mixed feelings about. The curriculum was supposed to focus on case studies of the financing structures of major corporate acquisitions in Asia over the past couple of decades, but I always made an effort to sprinkle my lectures with a few war stories to lighten up what otherwise would have been a dreary discourse on tax treaties, banking practices, and securities regulations. Almost all of my stories naturally concerned money — frequently very large amounts of it — and I had quickly discovered that money was an even better topic than sex for keeping my students absolutely riveted.

The lectures generally featured anecdotes drawn from my own recollections of the bad old days of the eighties, of gunslingers who had bought companies with big gestures instead of money and somehow gotten away with it for a while. My stories were obviously popular with the students, and that was what bothered me. I often got the uncomfortable feeling that they were less interested in absorbing whatever moral object lessons I was trying to impart than they were in figuring out how they could pull off the same kind of scams for themselves.

Today however I was entirely free of the need to fret over what my students might make of my tales of greed and daring-do because I didn't have to tell any. I was about to engage in the oldest ruse known to academia — the guest lecturer ploy.

When I had guest lecturers in my class, usually I roped in local guys, but now and again I was able to lure somebody visiting from overseas, mostly to remind my students that there actually *was* a real world out there. Regardless of who I got however, the whole thing was a perfect parlay. The lecturers liked it because they got to preen their ego in front of a rapt young audience; the students liked it because it was clearly a day off and they didn't have to remember what they were hearing for the final exam; and I absolutely loved it because all I had to do was introduce the guy and then sit back, my face arranged in an expression of appropriate attentiveness while I thought about whatever I damn well pleased.

The designated hitter for this day was an old Bangkok hand named Dollar Dunne, an American-born lawyer who had been Stanley Ratikun's partner before Stanley retired to become the director of Sasin. As unlikely as it seemed when we were first introduced, I had subsequently discovered that Dollar actually *was* his real name, one hung on him by a mother with either a strange sense of humor, or given his ensuing success dealing his way around the back alleys of Asia, one who was startlingly prescient.

After supplying the kind of effusive and deferential introduction my guests always said was unnecessary but would have been mortally wounded not to receive, I settled into a seat up at the back of the hall and watched as Dollar leaned against the podium and launched into what were no doubt wildly embellished tales of his adventures as a legal mercenary stalking the commercial jungles of Asia.

He had to be at least in his mid-fifties, I knew, but his wiry build and the way he wore his thick, silver hair in what was almost, but not quite, a Marine Corps buzz cut made him look much younger. His skin was perfectly tanned, and despite his age, his features still had a boyish, open quality to them. Instead of the predictable uniform of dark expensive suit and a white shirt, Dollar was wearing rumpled khakis and a green golf shirt that looked faded from many hours in the sun. His choice of wardrobe said a lot about him. He was a bit of this and a bit of that, and he was probably happiest when he was doing exactly the opposite of whatever was expected of him. Those eccentricities, although a little studied for my taste, gave him a sort of raffish quality that a lot of people apparently found irresistible.

Dollar had just downshifted into a story about the Merchant Group, winging his way to the considerable amusement of the class through some of the wilder conspiracy theories about Lyndon

Merchant's death, when he suddenly looked up at the back of the hall and cut me a wink that was impossible to miss. A few of the kids twisted around in their seats to check out my reaction and I reflexively returned a half-smile, but it left me a little unsettled.

The wink seemed to imply that Dollar and I shared some secret concerning Lyndon Merchant, one that he couldn't impart to the class, but I couldn't imagine what he thought it might be. Had I missed something I should have picked up concerning Merchant's death back when Stanley and I had been jousting over the remains of his empire? If I had, it was plainly something that Dollar assumed I had eventually figured out on my own.

I was still thinking about that when the class started to applaud and I realized that Dollar had finished. The kids gathered their stuff, slid out of the narrow rows of theater-style seating that were tiered up off a single center aisle, and began to make their way down to the main floor and out of the hall. By the time I got to the bottom of the steps, the hall was almost empty and Dollar was sitting on the desk at the front of the room, waiting for me.

"What was that all about?" I asked before he could say anything. "Was the wink supposed to mean something to me?"

"You're getting kind of Canadian in your old age, Jack. Anybody ever tell you that?" Dollar eyed me for a moment with a detached smile, folding his arms across his chest. "You've heard the song. 'A kiss is just a kiss; a smile is just a smile; a wink is just a wink.' Like that."

Dollar wasn't normally one for empty gestures. Regardless, he now apparently wanted to let this one slide, whatever it was supposed to have meant at the time he made it. Still it still bothered me for some reason, but I didn't press the point.

"Anyway, forget that." Dollar stood up abruptly. "I've got something I need to talk to you about."

"Maybe we should move this outside, Dollar."

The man's voice came from behind me, and when I turned, I saw John Hanratty slouched down in a seat in the front row right at the main entrance to the lecture hall.

Everyone I knew called John by his nickname, Just John and the source of that name had become the stuff of local legend.

Whenever someone who knew only John's first name asked for his last, so the story went, John would invariably reply, "It's just John." Popular rumor had it that Just John was retired from the CIA. That of course interpreted his gesture concerning his name as a penchant for secrecy rather than just an indication of friendliness. Anyway, I thought the story far too colorful to be true, but I really didn't know Just John all that well, so I had never asked him about it.

He wasn't a lawyer, not as far as I knew anyway, although he worked for Dollar's law firm in some capacity. I had never been absolutely certain what Just John actually did for Dollar's firm, but I gathered he functioned as a sort of greeter for out-of-town clients when they came to Bangkok — something most of them were happy enough to do whenever they could come up with an excuse that their wives would buy. Clients were always flying in for what were euphemistically called conferences, only to spend most of their time on a stool next to John at one of the city's justly-famed go-go bars.

"I didn't know you were coming this morning, John."

"Shit." He grinned as he pushed himself out of his seat. "Neither did I until a couple of hours ago."

Just John was a big man, and all of his features seemed slightly over-scale — big hands, wide forehead, barrel chest, prominent nose. He must have been in his sixties, but he was tanned and fit looking despite a beer gut that rode his middle like a kangaroo's pouch. His gray hair was long enough at the back to curl down inside the collar of the neat, button-down white shirt he wore tucked into sharply creased, dark gray trousers.

"Come on, Jack." Dollar placed a hand against my back and nudged me gently toward the door. "Let's take a walk."

We turned north across the campus when we left the building. Just John said nothing at all, but Dollar and I made small talk as the three of us strolled unhurriedly in the general direction of Mah Boonkrong, a massive, lumpy pile of masonry that looked like a bomb shelter built inexplicably on the surface rather than underground. In actual fact it was an eight-story, windowless shopping center with a doubtful reputation. A lot of Chula students hung out there between classes, eyeing each other over the vendors' stalls heaped with knock-off clothing, cloned cell phones, and pirated CDs.

Finally I got bored waiting for someone to tell me what this conversation was really about.

"What's on your mind, Dollar?"

"As I recall, Jack, we referred Howard the Roach to you last year. That's right, isn't it?"

I nodded. Howard Kojinski liked to pose as a big-time financier, but he was really one of those guys who seldom made it past the fringe of anything that mattered. He had earned his colorful moniker, so I understood, because of the way he operated on those rare occasions when he accidentally stumbled into something that actually involved real money. "Why is it that cockroaches are so unpleasant?" the question went. "It's not because of what they eat," came the answer, "it's what they fall into and mess up."

"You organized a shell company for him in Hong Kong, didn't you?" Dollar kept walking, his hands folded behind him. "Then you used it to set up an LA property deal he had doing with a some Chinese hustlers."

"That's right."

"I've asked John to work up some stuff on what Howard's been doing lately. What have you heard from the little asshole?"

"Nothing."

Then I thought about Dollar's question and realized how odd it was.

"Why would you think I'd heard anything from Howard?"

"Well, Jack." Dollar gave me a tentative look. "You know more about manipulating corporate structures than anyone I've ever heard of. You're the man when it comes to all that shit. If Howard had a problem with some of his funny-money stuff, I thought he might have called you."

"And does he have a problem?"

"Sure he does, Jack. Howard always has a problem."

Howard claimed to have business interests around the world, but all I knew for certain was that he had done a few minor real estate deals here and there and that he owned a California company named In The Pink Inc. The company had been a nearly defunct distributor of pornographic videos when Howard bought it, but even after he unloaded the porno inventory on some Iranian students, Howard still loved the name of the company so much that he never changed it.

The only other thing of any value that In The Pink Inc. owned was a small tract of land in Hollywood that was just east of the old Warner Brothers studio lot. A broken-down karaoke club occupied the site, one improbably enough named Bangkok Nights although it had probably seen better days, and Howard wanted to redevelop the property with a small strip mall. That was just what LA really needed, of course, and he had somehow convinced three young Hong Kong Chinese disco entrepreneurs to put up the money. That had been the reason for setting up the development company in Hong Kong, or so I had been told. Regardless, before I even managed to get the titles to the land straightened out and the property transferred into the new company, Howard's backers lost interest in the deal and he told me to forget the whole thing.

"Oh man, Dollar. Please don't tell me that the Bangkok Nights deal is alive again."

Dollar didn't answer right away. I got the feeling that he might still be trying to read between the lines of my reaction to Howard's name coming up; but read what?

"No, it's not about all that shit," Dollar finally said, but that was all he did say.

We had reached the edge of the campus, and I thought that Dollar might be steering us toward one of the student cafés in Mah Boonkrong, but he turned abruptly east and headed for Phayathai Road, a busy north-south thoroughfare that bisected the campus. I still couldn't see where this was going, but I trailed along anyway, waiting Dollar out. Just John had dropped a few paces behind us, apparently losing interest in the conversation. I could easily see how that might be.

"I need to understand exactly how much you know about this mess Howard's got himself in, Jack."

"I just told you, Dollar. I don't know anything about Howard or any mess he's in. I haven't heard from him since last year."

I couldn't imagine why Dollar was suddenly so interested in Howard. I certainly wasn't.

Then it occurred to me what all this might be about, and I stopped walking so abruptly that Just John stumbled into me from behind.

"Are you suggesting that I'm trying to hijack one of your clients, Dollar?"

Dollar's firm called me in to consult with their clients on specialized corporate matters fairly frequently, I even had a small office of my own in his building, and I thought Dollar knew me pretty well by now. I didn't want any clients, and even if I did, I'd certainly be able to get them without stealing them from him. If that was what Dollar was implying, I didn't like it one bit.

"No, Jack. Nothing like that."

"Then maybe you'd better explain to me exactly what you *do* mean."

Dollar shifted his eyes off mine. He appeared to consider the possibility, but then seemed to find the whole idea unappealing.

"Why don't we just forget all this for now, Jack?" he eventually said. "If you haven't talked to Howard recently, you haven't. Just let me know if he calls. Will you do that for me?"

"What's going on here, guys?" I looked back and forth between Dollar and Just John. "Why don't you just lay it out for me?"

Dollar sighed heavily, but it was Just John who answered.

"Howard's gone and done something stupid, Jack. We need to straighten it out." John lifted his arms from his sides, palms up. "That's all. We just want to be sure nobody gets hurt when we do."

That seemed to me to be an odd thing to say.

"Is there something you're not telling me here, guys?"

Dollar looked exasperated.

"Jack, there's a *ton* of shit we're not telling you. Do you think we're completely stupid?"

I started to say something, but Dollar pointed a finger at me, cutting me off.

"Keep your nose clean. We'll be in touch."

Then he wheeled and walked away. Just John tossed me a little salute, half-smiled, and followed without another word.

Within a few strides they were moving crisply in lockstep, Just John slightly ahead and to Dollar's right, and they looked to me like they were making directly for Phayathai Road. I imagined that Dollar's driver was hovering somewhere there, idling in Dollar's big Mercedes, ignoring the traffic backing up and waiting patiently for the boss to appear.

SIX

ON THE WAY BACK TO MY OFFICE I stopped to get something to eat at one of the sidewalk food stalls that clustered between the campus and the National Stadium. At a green metal cart shaded by a torn umbrella an ancient woman was whacking a cleaver against a chopping block, cutting raw chicken into long strips and threading them onto wooden skewers. A tiny man who looked even older than the woman took the sticks as she made them, squatted down, and carefully lined them up across the grill of a charcoal brazier that sat on the sidewalk behind the cart.

When the woman noticed me, she looked up and broke into one of those all-purpose Thai smiles — shy, even deferential, but with a touch of disquiet around the edges. I held up two fingers, and she reached out with her free hand and patted the old man's arm, murmuring something as she did. He selected a pair of sticks from his grill as carefully as if he were sorting diamonds and I handed him a green, twenty-baht note.

"Nee aroi maak," I said to him after my first bite. "That's really good."

The man looked startled, and the woman turned her head and covered her mouth with one hand in a gesture of surprise and amusement.

"Poot Thai dai mai krap?" the old man asked in a shy voice.

"Poot dai nid noi." I speak a little.

Actually I thought my Thai was pretty good, particularly for someone with a tin ear for the subtle tones that were required to speak it properly. Nevertheless I erred on the side of modesty whenever the subject came up.

The man and the woman glanced quickly at each other, smiled, then returned to their work as if I had just disappeared in a puff of smoke. That hardly surprised me. Foreigners in general made many Thais uneasy, which was probably why they either ignored us most of the time or hid their disquiet in elaborate courtesy.

On the whole, Thais had nothing against foreigners. They simply had no idea how to fit us into their rigid, almost feudal, social order. Foreigners were, well, different. All those complex rules that Thais learned from birth, formulas for plotting their position in the universe relative to everyone else, made no provision at all for foreigners.

That was why Thais used their language against us like a long stick, wielding it to keep foreigners at a distance just as one might wave a stick to ward off a big, hairy dog. When a foreigner spoke Thai to a local, he took their stick away. Then Thais always did what they did when they didn't know what to do. They smiled, looked away, and did nothing.

I took the satay and went over to one of the miniature metal tables that stood in a row against the low wall at the edge of the campus. Using my foot to nudge out a plastic stool, I settled myself and chewed thoughtfully at the richly charcoaled chicken.

Was I being naïve to meet this guy alone tonight just because he'd pitched me a tale that had tickled my sense of the bizarre? Besides, I told myself, it almost certainly would be Barry Gale in the flesh who would turn up, and surely Barry meant me no harm.

Even if it turned out not to be Barry Gale, what mischief could occur in a supermarket that would be crowded with other people? I couldn't think of anyone I'd offended enough to want to do me any damage, at least not recently, and it seemed unlikely that someone would mount such an elaborate ruse even if I had. Anybody who wanted to get to me would certainly have no difficulty doing it without all this.

No, meeting somebody I probably knew in a crowded, public place like a supermarket didn't seem to be too alarming a risk, even at midnight. On the other hand, I knew I still ought to make an effort to find out whatever there was to know about Barry Gale's death before I turned up.

Fortunately Bangkok was a pretty good place to be when you needed some information in a hurry. It was a dream of a place for people who were in the information business whether they were working for governments or involved in some private enterprise or, as was not infrequently the case, doing both at the same time. The city was the doorway to Southeast Asia, and the Thais didn't much care what anyone did there as long as it didn't involve them. That made Bangkok an irresistible base of operations for almost anyone who was up to anything.

Everyone was there. There were the Americans, the Chinese, the Russians, the British, the French, the North and South Koreans, the Vietnamese, the Indians, the Pakistanis, the Japanese, the Burmese, the Libyans, the Israelis, the Iraqis, the Iranians, and a bunch of other countries that few even suspected *had* intelligence services. These gangs of cowboys were jumbled up with the local old hands — an expatriate community full of shady characters, or those who wanted to be; spooks, retired and semi-retired; ex-military hard cases; and a menagerie of men and women on the run from things that ranged from financial problems to murder charges to demons most people couldn't even begin to imagine.

Government intelligence officers, private security services, renegade operators, law enforcement agencies, freelance journalists, and international crime mobs ran amok and nobody really cared. So they all took comprehensive advantage of the opportunity. They bugged offices and restaurants; broke into hotel rooms and apartments; harassed the opposition; watched for new targets who were drinking more than their fair share or cavorting with too many bargirls; and ran surveillance on every visitor who might be doing anything remotely interesting or, when times were slow, on each other.

In narrow back streets, mysterious buildings lurked behind high walls, suggestive of even darker and more mysterious activities within. Fortress-like embassy compounds bristled with radio towers and satellite dishes, and guards armed with automatic weapons turned dead eyes on anyone who ventured too close. Tanned, crew-cut Americans in short-sleeved shirts sat in darkened corners of grimy bars watching the girls, sucking down cold beers, and talking in low voices to swarthy, Middle Eastern men who watched the door as they listened. Bangkok was a wide-open frontier town. You could get drunk on the intrigue.

My reputation as a reliable guide to the murky underbelly of international finance had led me over the years into meeting quite a number of people who operated on the fringes of Bangkok's intelligence community as well as a few who were probably closer to the center of it, although I wasn't exactly sure how close. Several had even become my friends, and I flipped through my mental Rolodex looking for the right name to call to dig out the real story of Barry Gale and the Texas State Bank. One person came to mind immediately, and the more I thought about it, the more I was sure it was the right call.

I finished off the second stick of chicken satay, tossed both wooden skewers into a sidewalk bin, and glanced at my watch. I had nothing scheduled until some student appointments at three, so there ought to be plenty of time.

I walked back to Sasin's main building and went straight to the garage. A few minutes later I was back out on Phayathai Road, headed north. The traffic was unusually light and I got to Arlene's a lot faster than I thought I would. She lived in one of Bangkok's older neighborhoods, out near Chitrlada Palace where the king maintained his official residence for most of the year. It was a part of town where you seldom saw foreigners, and that suited Arlene Rice just fine.

After Arlene retired from more than thirty years of working for the U.S. government, some of it in Washington and the rest in various postings around Asia, she took her whole pension in a cash settlement and headed straight for Bangkok. She'd already found a house there she wanted to buy and it took her less than a week to complete the full process.

The place had been vacant for a long while and was in poor repair. It needed almost everything, but it was a huge, two-story mansion of classic proportions entirely surrounded by a high wall. Although real estate was pretty cheap in Thailand, at least if you measured the prices by international standards, the old house still took almost every penny of Arlene's savings to buy. In spite of that, she still somehow proceeded to transform it into an astonishing sanctuary.

The house was at the end of a tiny *soi* that branched off Wisut Kasat Road at an Esso station. If you didn't know exactly where you were going, it didn't look like a street at all, but just part of the station's driveway. Behind the Esso station the *soi* made a sharp bend to the right and ran along a row of nondescript shophouses for about a hundred yards until it dead-ended at a green metal gate set into a high ginger-colored wall. Thick stands of rangy bamboo tumbled over the wall from inside and gave the whole area a slightly overgrown appearance, but the bamboo had a very specific purpose. Concealed within it was a sophisticated security system that encircled the entire property. It was an exceptionally thorough piece of technology and it effectively ensured the total privacy of the occupants.

I met Arlene shortly after she had retired to Bangkok. She had made it her business to look me up and introduce herself, and at first

I had wondered why, but after I got to know her better I understood very well. Arlene was in the business of collecting information, and therefore she also collected people who *had* information. For a year or so I heard from her only occasionally, mostly when she needed me to explain some arcane twist of international finance, but gradually the calls and our visits increased in frequency and a friendship developed.

Arlene had never spoken to me about her background except in general terms, however I had no difficulty reading between the lines. Although it would have been an obvious guess, I doubted Arlene had ever been CIA. My own theory was that she had been with the NSA, the National Security Agency, or No Such Agency as old Washington hands called it.

NSA was so secretive that it made the CIA look like the *New York Times.* What's more, they did the stuff that few people even knew was going on — the computer break-ins, the telephone and email intercepts, the satellite surveillance, and the other black-art wizardry that almost anybody out of the know would have been inclined to dismiss as paranoid fiction rather than real life. That was exactly the kind of stuff Arlene seemed to know all about.

Her computers occupied all of a two-story cottage across a swimming pool from the main house, and they were fat with data. There was little Arlene could not get access to. She could nail down details about intelligence networks and the activities of individual agents that conventional corporate investigative agencies had never heard of. The end of the Cold War had scattered a welter of unemployed, free-booting intelligence operators across the globe. A lot of them had tried to do the same thing Arlene had, but there were few others who could claim the sophistication of the operation she had created in Bangkok. It was nothing less than a private intelligence agency, one with capabilities equal to any competitor and to not a few governments.

I pulled the Volvo to a stop just behind the Esso station and took out my cell phone. Arlene had asked me always to follow a strict security procedure whenever I came to her house. It all seemed a bit melodramatic to me. A straightforward telephone call to ask if I could come around ought to have done the trick, I thought. After all, I was just a simple professor of international finance, not Carlos the Jackal.

Dialing the number she had given me, I waited for the tone that indicated a computer response. When I heard it, I punched in the number of my cell phone, followed immediately by 002. The additional numbers were the time in hours and minutes before I intended to arrive. If the computer disconnected me it was a wave-off; but if it gave three beeps, it meant Arlene could see me at the time I had entered.

The three beeps came almost immediately and I disconnected the call and tossed the phone onto the passenger seat. I never could figure out how the computer worked out so quickly whether Arlene was willing to see me then or not, but I guessed I really didn't *need* to know.

At the end of the *soi* I stopped in front of Arlene's gate and lowered the driver's window. Before I could push the button on the intercom box, the gate split into two panels and began to swing inward. I gave a little wave in the direction where I knew the security camera was concealed and the intercom speaker click-clacked in acknowledgment.

Parking on the gravel of the circular driveway, I got out and made my way up the short brick walk between rows of tropical plants so carefully tended and perfectly formed that they might have been stamped out of plastic injection molds. Arlene opened the door and stepped onto the house's wide front porch. She was a smallish woman, a few years past sixty, trim with a pleasant but forgettable face, and she wore her silver hair in a tightly fitted, masculine crop. As always when she was at home, she was dressed in a white silk blouse and an ankle-length sarong, today's selection being in the brightest shade of saffron I had ever seen.

"It's been months, mister." She pecked me on the cheek and held my arm in a kind of embrace as we entered the living room of the house. "Where the hell have you been?"

"Out chasing women. What else does one do in Bangkok?"

Arlene laughed and gestured me toward a couch in the elegantly proportioned living area. She sat on the one opposite and folded a leg up under her. A maid appeared almost immediately and placed sweating glasses of cold water in front of each of us, positioning them carefully on tiny squares of coarse, white cotton.

Arlene smiled at me and waited until the maid had glided silently out of the room before she said anything else.

"Nata is out in the cottage running some stuff. She ought to be in any minute."

Nata had been Arlene's companion for almost fifteen years, and not surprisingly, she was one of the primary reasons why Arlene had chosen Bangkok for her retirement. The daughter of a Thai general who had ended up on the wrong side of some long-forgotten military coup, Nata was a stunningly beautiful woman who must have been in her late forties. She was very slight with wispy, wide-set eyes, and she seldom wore make-up. Her skin was smooth and milky-looking, so white that you could go snow-blind just looking at it.

Sometimes I thought I was the only foreigner I knew who hadn't ended up in Thailand mostly because of the women.

"So tell me, doll, what's on your mind? I get the feeling you didn't come all the way out here looking for a free lunch."

"I guess I did in a manner of speaking. I need something."

"Don't we all."

"I've got to meet somebody tonight, and I don't want to sound completely stupid when I do."

"Uh-huh."

Now Arlene's face was professionally empty, waiting.

"I just need a little background. Nothing heavy duty."

"Tell me the story. Let me decide that."

I told Arlene about the telephone call and about my summons to Foodland that night, as well as what I remembered about Barry Gale's so-called suicide and the stories linking the Texas State Bank with money laundering by Russian mobsters.

"What I need to see is the press coverage around the time Barry Gale is supposed to have died, particularly the *Wall Street Journal* and the local Dallas papers," I finished up. "Can you manage that?"

"Exactly what are you looking for?"

"I'm not sure. Anything that would prepare me for the conversation tonight, I guess."

"Piece of cake. But I don't see how any of the public press stuff is going to help you figure out whether this really *is* your guy, if that's what you're trying to do."

"Well. . . ."

"Yeah, I know." Arlene laughed. "You'd also like to see if I could come up with anything that might not have made the papers."

"Something like that."

"For you, doll, anything."

Arlene stood up and held out her hand.

"Let's take a walk over to the cottage."

SEVEN

THE BUILDING THAT ARLENE CALLED a cottage was actually the size of a whole house. Two stories tall, had it not been for an ordinary-looking door on the first level and two small windows on the second, it would have resembled nothing quite so much as a solid cube of concrete.

The first floor was a single, brightly lit room with at least a dozen computer workstations positioned around its outer walls. Three matronly-looking Thai women, all apparently well into their fifties if not older, moved silently from station to station checking the screens and occasionally tapping a few characters on one of the keyboards. In the center of the room, on a low platform, there was a far more elaborate workstation equipped with two huge thin-panel displays, both supported by sleek, black pedestals and set at right angles to each other.

Nata perched at the center of the platform in an orthopedic chair and rested her folded forearms on the table in front of a keyboard. She was looking from one display to the other, twisting her brows in concentration. A thin microphone on a chrome boom curved in front of her mouth and I had the impression she had been murmuring into it when we came in, but when she saw us she pushed herself back from the table and flicked the boom up over her head like a surfer chick flipping up sunglasses.

"Hey, Jack boy! Long time."

"Well . . . I was in the neighborhood, so. . . ."

"Yeah, yeah. What do you need?"

Arlene stepped in and in a few clipped phrases related the high points of the story I had just told her to Nata. She took it in and then winked at me.

"Too easy, Jack. At least try to bring me some kind of a challenge next time, would you?"

Nata turned back to her keyboard and boxes began appearing on one of the big screens in front of her. I watched her type "Texas State Bank" into a space in one of them and after ten or fifteen seconds a list rolled up on the other screen. She typed "Barry Gale" into another box and waited until a second list replaced the first. Then she typed something that appeared on the screen as nothing but a row of asterisks, hit the Enter key twice, and waited.

After a few seconds an index of news stories appeared back on the first screen, each entry providing a headline, a newspaper's name, a date, and the first few words from the story. Nata started working her way methodically through every item, calling up the full text of each account. By the time she'd been at it for ten or fifteen minutes, we had pretty much everything that had been reported in the press concerning the death of Barry Gale.

Barry had been at the bank's North Dallas guesthouse for several weeks while preparing the Texas State directors for their formal meetings with the federal banking examiners. The examiners were awfully curious as to exactly how millions of dollars of the bank's deposits managed to wander away without anyone noticing, and they were themselves preparing to ask the directors a lot of tough questions.

It was a Thursday afternoon when Barry told everyone he was exhausted and was going to knock off and go to Acapulco for a few days, so no one really wondered very much where he was until he failed to turn up for a conference with some Treasury Department people the following Wednesday. The next day, exactly a week after Barry had last been seen, a maintenance man found the body in a lap pool behind the guesthouse off Preston Road.

"Your ghost was right on the money," Nata pointed out. "No useable fingerprints and the corpse's face was too badly smashed up to get an ID except with dental records."

"Was there an autopsy?" Arlene asked.

She and Nata were talking to each other now. I had been designated a silent observer.

"If there was, there's nothing about it here."

"That manhole cover looks like a pretty big loose end," Arlene mused. "What do those suckers weigh? They'd have to go at least fifty, maybe a hundred pounds, wouldn't they?"

Nata nodded absentmindedly, still studying one of the screens.

"Staggering around with a cast-iron manhole cover and then using barbed wire to tie it around your neck and leaping into a swimming pool is a pretty flashy way to commit suicide, if you ask me," Arlene said. "At least it is if you're doing the committing entirely on your own."

"It sounds like the Russians all right," Nata nodded. "Those guys love stuff like that."

Arlene bent forward, reading a *Dallas Morning News* story over Nata's shoulder. It concerned the unexplained disappearance of another director of the Texas State Bank about the same time Barry took his swim, a guy named Harold Wilkins. The details were pretty sketchy since the story of Barry Gale's drowning was so much sexier, but there was enough to work out the gist of what had happened. Arlene pointed to the monitor.

"Wilkins had been buying phony currency futures for a year or more before he disappeared. He was running all the positions himself, using the name of Westmoreland Oil and Gas, which was apparently a real oil trader in Dallas."

"How could he do that?" Nata asked. "Wouldn't somebody have started asking questions?"

"Not necessarily," I offered.

Arlene and Nata both looked at me as if they had just remembered that I was there.

"If Westmoreland had been reasonably active in the foreign exchange markets hedging their exposure on future deliveries like most oil traders do, it would have been normal enough. And I'm sure Wilkins would have been smart enough to set up dummy accounts to run his trades through. If he had, Westmoreland itself would never have noticed anything and there would have been nobody else to blow the whistle."

Arlene and Nata took that in, glancing at each other, then all three of us went back to reading silently through the rest of the story. I gathered I had been readmitted to the inner circle.

As we read, the rest fell into place. Wilkins had been using accounts he'd set up in Westmoreland's name to conduct his trading operations all right. He was buying and selling futures contracts in a half-dozen different currencies for what on the surface appeared to be routine hedging of exposure on crude oil deliveries that provided for payments in Japanese yen and Singapore dollars. When the market turned on Wilkins, however, his losses began to pyramid quickly.

He kept ahead of them for a while — mostly by running hard, shuffling papers fast, and doubling up his losses — but when the magnitude of the debacle became so large that he couldn't hide it any longer, the entire mess collapsed in a heap. That was when Wilkins disappeared without a trace. He left his house to drive to the bank one morning and stepped right off into the twilight zone.

Two weeks later, Barry Gale — or someone — was found at the bottom of the swimming pool. The suicide was quickly attributed to the close working relationship between Gale and Wilkins. There was even some speculation that Barry Gale could have been the real mastermind behind the whole currency-futures scam and that he might have been using the less-experienced Wilkins as a front man; but with one man dead and the other missing, following up the speculation would have been difficult. In the end, no one seemed to have bothered.

Arlene got to the end of the story first and started to say something, but Nata waved her into silence until she too had finished reading.

"Maybe this Gale guy really *is* still around," she said when she had.

"Then who was the stiff in the pool?" Arlene asked.

No one bothered to answer her. If Barry Gale was still alive, that obviously made Wilkins the prime candidate for the Esther Williams role. Moreover it strongly suggested that Barry might have had something to do with arranging the casting.

"You think this guy might be indexed somewhere in EDGAR?" Arlene asked Nata.

"What's. . . ." I started to ask.

"Never mind," Arlene interrupted, and I obediently fell silent.

Nata typed briefly and then slid her hand over a trackball sitting next to the keyboard. As she rolled the cursor around one of the screens and clicked here and there, both she and Arlene leaned in closer. After a moment I saw them exchange a look and then Arlene leaned over Nata's shoulder and typed a few keystrokes. After that they both watched the other screen in silence.

"That's pretty amazing," Nata finally said, more to herself than to Arlene or me.

She clicked the left mouse button on the trackball twice, looked at the screen for a long time in silence, and finally rotated her chair until she was facing me.

"I don't know what to tell you, Jack."

Up until then we had been doing just fine, but suddenly I didn't much like the way things were shaping up.

"I found the name Barry Gale in a keyword search of EDGAR's primary data index," Nata explained. "But when I went to the locations referenced in the search, there was nothing there. All the references came up as invalid entries."

"Does something like that happen a lot?"

Arlene shook her head. "Never."

"What are you saying?" I asked, looking from one to the other.

"There are a couple of possibilities, I guess." Nata took over again. "Three, really. Mistakes in data paths can occur. Maybe this is just the result of a simple input error."

"But you don't think so."

I was sure, at least, of that. Her face made it plain.

"What else?" I asked her.

"The references may have been there once, then deleted for some reason and the index entries were overlooked."

"I didn't think database entries were usually deleted, just updated."

"Right. Usually not."

"So then what's the third reason?" I asked.

Nata hesitated, glancing at Arlene, who nodded once.

"The entries may be encrypted with a unique key that we don't have," she said. "That's never happened before either, but theoretically I suppose it's possible."

"And what would that mean?"

"There's generally a turf battle of some kind going on in Washington, Jack. It might just be that one agency has something going and it's taking particular care to make sure that another agency can't find out about it. It could be that sort of thing."

"*Could* be?"

"Look, Jack, we're good, but we're not perfect. Some of the really big hitters can bury stuff so deep we can't get to it. To tell you the absolute truth, it hasn't happened before, but it *is* possible."

"Really big hitters? What are you telling me? What kind of database is this anyway?"

Nata felt silent, then glanced toward Arlene again. Arlene sighed and folded her arms.

"Don't put me in a bad spot here, doll. Let's just say that it is a comprehensive summary of . . ." Arlene paused, weighing her words with obvious care, ". . . of nonpublic U.S. intelligence data concerning foreign organized crime activity. If there was any real connection between your man, the Texas State Bank, and the Russian mob, it would be in here."

"In other words, you've hacked the FBI."

I had always thought the expression about someone's eyes twinkling was pure poetic exaggeration, but right at that moment Arlene's really did.

"If we had, you wouldn't want us to tell you, would you?"

"So what *can* you tell me that won't get me twenty to life?"

Arlene and Nata looked at each other.

"My gut says you're about to step into it here, Jack," Arlene finally said. "I'd back off and let it go if I were you."

That wasn't exactly what I had been expecting to hear from her.

"Don't you think that's sensationalizing this thing a little, Arlene? How can it hurt just to meet a guy at Foodland and talk to him?"

"He may tell you something you'd be better off not hearing," she said.

"What the hell is *that* supposed to mean?" I asked, looking from one to the other.

"Do you want some help?" Nata asked me, dancing away from a direct answer.

"Help? Doing what?"

"If you're really going to meet this guy, it might be a good idea to have somebody throw a loose net over you. That way you'd pick up on any surveillance that might be on you or any other funny business that might be going on."

"I don't think I like the sound of this very much."

"You asked for our advice and I'm just giving it to you."

"Look, if there's really something nasty going on here, the last thing I want is to get you two involved."

"Oh, not us," Arlene jumped back in. "You know my policy about avoiding operations. But we could find somebody to cover you without much trouble."

"How about Mango Manny?" Nata asked, looking at Arlene.

"That's a good thought," she answered. "You know him, Jack?"

"I don't think so. I imagine I'd remember meeting somebody named Mango Manny."

"His real name is Emmanuel Marcus. He's a Brit. Used to be a top hitter in London, but he made a couple of silly mistakes and had to relocate on short notice."

"Mistakes?"

"Oh, you know. Hit the wrong people a couple of times. That sort of thing."

Arlene made it sound like the fellow had done nothing worse than misdirect a few Federal Express packages.

"He's been in Bangkok . . . oh, eight or ten years now, I think. He owns Q Bar, that place on Soi 11 where the hipper-than-thou crowd hangs out. You've been there, haven't you?"

"Nope. Too expensive for me. I'm more a Cheap Charlie's kind of guy."

"Manny's very well connected. Plays golf with all the right generals and government ministers. But the important thing is that he's got a really first-class organization."

"You mean at his bar?"

"No, not that. Manny brought the marijuana business here into the twenty-first century. Really made it fly, so to speak."

"He's a *drug dealer?*"

"Nope, nope." Arlene looked down and kicked her toe at the carpet. "He's more of a . . . management consultant. Besides, he won't touch anything but grass. The man's not a criminal, Jack."

"Oh, he's not?"

"No. He's okay. Really."

"Then just let me be sure I understand what you're saying here, Arlene. Just because you can't find a couple of references to Barry Gale in your magic machine, you're seriously proposing that I get some screw-up cockney hitman turned management consultant to the marijuana trade to work security for me when I go to the Foodland tonight to meet a dead guy. Have I pretty much got it?"

"Manny's not a cockney. He went to Cambridge."

I stared wordlessly at Arlene.

"Oh, well. That changes everything."

"He's really a pretty good guy," Nata put in. "I think he just watched too many Bob Hoskins movies when he was young and never got over it."

There was a little silence then and Arlene and Nata both watched me expressionlessly. In the quiet I thought I could feel something stirring around me. I didn't know what it was, but it felt large and unpleasant. I looked at Arlene — hoping, I suppose, to see nothing — but from her eyes, I could tell that she felt it, too.

"What do you think I should do, Arlene?" I finally asked.

Arlene placed one hand gently on my back. She had the sort of look on her face I imagined a mother might give a son who was going off to war, a look that said there wasn't a thing she could do but wish him well and hope for the best.

"Be careful, Jack. Be very, very careful."

EIGHT

TOOK LAE DEE TRANSLATES FROM THAI as "cheap and good." At least it does if you pronounce it right, using a falling tone for *took*. If you use a rising tone instead, *took* becomes "sorrowful."

Since few foreigners struggling with Thai could manage the tones particularly well, the usual thing was for *took* to come out occasionally one way and occasionally the other — making the place either "cheap and good" or "sorrowful and good," depending. That was not entirely an abuse of the Thai language. Took Lae Dee was a primary hangout for the Bangkok nightshift, and it seemed to me that the alternating pronunciations framed the place perfectly.

During daylight hours Sukhumvit Road was one of Bangkok's principal arteries, four lanes jammed with vehicles and the BTS running on massive concrete pillars down the center. It slashed like a fault line across the part of the city where almost every foreigner in town lived. For miles it was lined with luxurious shopping malls, expensive restaurants, and multi-starred hotels, and it was generally thronged with well-heeled tourists, foreign residents, and those adventurous Thais who didn't mind so much mixing with either.

In the hours after dark, however, a different breed took over the street. Even at its most benign, Bangkok was part Miami and part Beirut, and there was nothing benign about midnight on the fault line. In the late, late hours, Sukhumvit Road became *Blade Runner* country.

Few Americans seemed to know much of anything about any place that was not America, but still it surprised me that I didn't know even one person back in Washington who would have had anything at all to say about Bangkok, other than on one of two topics.

Food was one of these topics, of course. Everyone I knew claimed to love Thai food. Sending out for Chinese was cheap. Sending out for Thai seemed somehow a lot hipper. Of course, most Westerners had no real idea what they were actually eating in either case, but Thai food was both cheap *and* hip, so how could you beat that?

The other topic, of course, was sex. Bangkok was inexorably intertwined in most people's minds with stories they'd heard somewhere, although few would admit to remembering exactly where, of an unabashedly dissolute life and the easy availability of free sex. Well, perhaps not exactly *free,* but certainly pretty inexpensive sex, at least by world standards. Thai sex was a little like Thai food, cheap but with a kind of exotic style to it. Couldn't beat that combination in *any* context, could you?

With all that going for it, you'd think then that the idea of living in Bangkok would be a pretty enticing idea to a lot of people, wouldn't you? You might think that, but you'd be wrong.

A couple of times I tried joking that, well, a man could sure make a lot worse choice than taking up residence in a city that was internationally famed for food and sex, but when I saw the solemn expressions that crack engendered in most Americans, I swiftly eliminated it from my repertoire. Maybe the suggestion that food and sex were actually significant parts of life made Americans uncomfortable. Maybe I ought to have more friends from France.

Anyway, the reaction I typically got when people found out I lived in Bangkok was something I had gotten used to. Oh, the place was exotic and interesting, they murmured, but yet . . . somehow it was still a city where a lot of people went who weren't particularly *nice.*

Oddly, on the whole, that perception had more substance to it than I really would have liked.

I had always thought there had to be some kind of international network devoted to coaxing social rejects and dropout cases worldwide into coming to Bangkok, because come they did. By the thousands. They walked away from third-shift jobs in places like Los Angeles, London, Sydney, Berlin, and Toronto, packed what they had, bought a cheap airline ticket, and made their way to the Land of Smiles. Some were looking for a cheap tropical paradise; others thought they'd found Sodom and Gomorrah; but almost every one of them was hoping in some way to make a fresh start on a life that up until then probably had little to recommend it. Many of these refugees from reality probably couldn't have located the city on a map before they'd decided it was the place for them, maybe they still couldn't, but now Bangkok had become their last, maybe their only hope.

In the empty hours it was this army of the dispossessed that took control of Sukhumvit Road. *Tuk-tuks,* little three-wheeled motorcycle taxis, flew up and down the street most of the night ferrying carousers between the two clumps of go-go bars that anchored the neighborhood: Nana Plaza on the west and Soi Cowboy about a mile to the east.

They were all there: the lonely, the frightened, the guilty, the depressed, and the psychotic. Soaked with sweat, they rushed back and forth from one bar to another, reeking of that peculiarly sour, metallic odor habitually given off by the emotionally overmatched and underachieving. It was this floodtide of the lost and abandoned that made the hours after midnight Took Lae Dee's busiest.

The Foodland was across the street from the Amari Boulevard Hotel, about a hundred feet off Sukhumvit and up a narrow *soi* nearly barricaded by *tuk-tuk* boys and motorcycle taxis looking for a fare.

Took Lae Dee was really nothing more than a little counter stuck up at the front of the supermarket that served hot food twenty-four hours a day.

I had gotten there early to have a look around before I went in, although I wasn't really sure what I was looking for or whether I would recognize it if I saw it. Finding myself a spot on one of the pedestrian overpasses that arched across Sukhumvit, I leaned on the railing for a while and watched the entrance to the little *soi.*

I didn't see anything particularly interesting and after a while people were beginning to glance strangely at me, so it occurred to me that cruising a few blocks in each direction might be a lot less conspicuous than just standing there. It had been a while since I'd last done the midnight shuffle on Sukhumvit, and I wondered briefly if I might have been a bit hasty in passing up Arlene's offer to ask Mango Manny to cover my butt; but it was way too late to change my mind about that, so I shoved my hands into my pockets and backtracked along the overpass to the sidewalk opposite the Foodland.

Walking east I passed under the Nana BTS station. The station rested on a concrete platform the size of a football field that was at least forty feet over my head and its green-roofed staircases flopped down to the sidewalks like the collapsed wings of a huge and weary prehistoric bird. On the bottom step of the stairs closest to me a middle-aged Thai wearing Groucho glasses was sitting with his knees pulled up, thumping at a ukulele. I wasn't even going to try and guess what that was all about.

I passed a tailor shop still open even at that hour. A turbaned man dressed entirely in white was leaning in the doorway talking on a mobile phone and he automatically thrust a business card at me as I passed. I declined the card with a shake of my head, but he hardly seemed to notice.

A little further along a midget wearing a blue vest with a large white number 29 printed on it sat outside a bar on a tiny stool and yawned. Just past him a teenaged girl sprawled on a straw mat chewing on an ear of corn. She watched me and smiled as I walked past her. Everywhere you looked in Bangkok you saw somebody eating something and everywhere everybody smiled.

A red and blue taxi trolling for passengers slowed at the curb and the driver beeped the horn to get my attention. I waved him away and stopped in front of a currency exchange booth that was closed for the night, pretending to study the past day's rates posted on a wrinkled sheet of paper taped to the inside of the glass.

What in God's name did I think I was looking for? All I could see was what every tourist on Sukhumvit saw and all I could smell was exhaust fumes and sweat. To hell with it, I decided. This was ridiculous. And with that, I turned around and walked straight back to the Foodland.

About two dozen high-backed wooden stools with gray seat cushions faced the narrow, L-shaped counter just in front of the checkout stands. I slid onto an empty stool and looked around. A small vase of flowers sat on the counter next to a stainless-steel water pitcher and a bottle of chili sauce. The flowers were plastic, but somehow they still looked a little bedraggled.

Behind the counter a Chinese-looking woman in a white cap scraped fried rice from a wok onto a plate. A plastic ID badge with a tiny picture was clipped to her apron and made her look more like someone employed in a defense plant than a counter girl at an all-night diner. Another cook was showing off, flipping a wok full of noodles into the air and then slapping the wok smartly with a long-handled ladle before catching them again. When he saw me watching him, he flashed me a big grin and bowed slightly from the waist.

There was a group of men in their twenties a few stools to my left, four sitting and a fifth roaming back and forth behind the others.

Their clothes were scruffy and they looked like the kind of guys who had a lot of time on their hands. They hammered loudly at each other in thick, British working-class accents and I leaned away and gave them room.

On the other leg of the counter three Arabs in white robes sat drinking tea and whispering quietly among themselves. Beyond them, two sweating, middle-aged men spoke German to each other and halting English to their young Thai companions. The older of the two men was with a girl who was round and dark with a pleasant face and a nice smile, probably not long out of some upcountry rice field. The other had a stunner draped all over him.

She was tall and slim with skin like poured honey and a cascade of glistening black hair hanging around her shoulders. Stylishly dressed in a short, red leather skirt, white blouse, black spike heels, and a matching belt with a heavy silver buckle, she was a real showstopper. The guy looked like he was about to have a stroke from all the attention he was getting from such a gorgeous creature.

I suspected he might very well, not right then perhaps, but almost certainly a little later when he got down to business and discovered his dazzling companion was actually a *katoey,* a man. The guy was about to learn the most fundamental rule for hitting the streets after midnight in Bangkok. Nothing was ever quite what it seemed to be.

"Help you, sir?"

The girl who had walked up behind me was young, not more than eighteen probably, with big eyes and a slightly dumpy air about her. I wondered what she saw when she looked at the Germans and their companions for the night.

"Café dum." Black coffee.

The girl bobbed her head and scribbled briefly on a thick pad before walking away. A few moments later a different girl, one of those who was scurrying around behind the counter, put a white ceramic mug down in front of me. I watched her pour the coffee, nodding in acknowledgement of her slight smile. I was jumpy enough already and didn't need the caffeine, but I lifted the mug anyway and reflexively began to sip at the thick, bitter coffee. With my free hand I pushed myself around on the stool and warily began to check out what I could see of the interior of the Foodland. I spotted the man almost immediately.

He was half obscured by a tall stack of Diet Coke cans, looking me over without trying to hide it. I saw him glance at a woman standing next to him and place his hand on her arm. Then she followed his eyes and examined me, too.

The man was a Westerner about my age. Either he was completely bald or he had shaved his head so cleanly that his scalp gleamed in the light. Oddly, however, he had a thin rim of neatly trimmed gray beard that ran all the way from ear to ear, and it made his oval face look almost upside-down. He was wearing khaki shorts, an expensive-looking golf shirt hanging over his belt, and dark loafers without socks. At a glance he was largely interchangeable with the lean, tanned, middle-aged Western guys you could find around any of the five-star hotels in town favored by visiting business executives — well-off, confident, poised, cocky almost.

The woman was another story. I doubted she was interchangeable with anybody.

She was probably in her twenties and looked Chinese, except that she was at least six feet tall. Slim, graceful, and feminine in spite of her height, she was dressed in loose, dark slacks and a man's white shirt. Her dark eyes looked tranquil, yet something gave her a quality of vigilance. She made me think of a cat lazing in the shade of a summer's day, ready to spring into motion at the first sign of a pigeon. Since it looked almost as if the woman was standing guard over the man, and I was already willing to bet this was the guy who'd called me, I wondered briefly if that meant *I* was going to turn out to be the pigeon here.

The man gave a little tug on the woman's arm and they started walking toward me. When they were still fifteen or twenty feet away, she moved slightly to one side and leaned back against the chrome railing separating the store's grocery section from Took Lae Dee. Her posture remained relaxed and she cupped her hands around the top rail and stretched out her legs, crossing one ankle over the other. I couldn't help but notice that they were very nice ankles indeed.

The man slid onto the stool next to me and rested his forearms on the counter.

"I didn't think you'd recognize me," he announced without preamble.

But he was wrong. I had no earthly idea how it could be — it made no sense at all — but there was absolutely no doubt in my mind. It was Barry Gale.

I took a shallow sip of my coffee and studied him over the rim of the cup. He was far leaner than he had been back in Washington, and his facial features appeared to have been scrambled up somehow, although I realized it might have been the absence of hair and the addition of the beard that gave me that impression.

"You've changed a lot," I finally said.

"That was the idea, Jack. That was the whole idea."

Barry's eyes went away from mine, sought out the woman leaning against the chrome railing, and then came back to me.

"I guess when we started redecorating I should have specified that I wanted to look more like Keanu Reeves and less like Jerry Ford, but I didn't give it enough thought. We were in a hurry."

"Who's 'we'?"

Barry ignored my question and looked off toward where a thick-legged blond woman who looked Russian was pushing through one of the checkout stands with a white plastic carrier bag, holding the hand of a tiny Thai girl who didn't appear to be more than sixteen. Suddenly he dug down into his baggy shorts and produced what looked like a card of some kind, thrusting it out and wiggling it at me.

"They fixed me up with a whole new life, Jack. Look here."

I first thought the card was an American driver's license, but when I took it from him I saw that it was actually a Hong Kong Identity Card. It certainly looked authentic enough, although I was certainly no expert on such things, and had what was probably supposed to be Barry's picture laminated onto it. As with most ID cards, however, the photograph had a vaguely generic look to it and I wouldn't have sworn an oath that it was the same man who was sitting in front of me right now. The name on the card was Arthur Daley.

"Stupid fucking name they picked for me though. Can't imagine where they got it."

Barry seemed to think about it a moment as he contemplated something else that was off in the direction of the checkout counters.

"Normally I wouldn't give a rat's ass, but I ask you, could I ever be somebody who's called Arthur Daley, Jack? Could I?" He took the ID card back and shook his head. "Shit, man, no way."

Barry had always told everyone that he had grown up as the only Jewish kid in Lufkin, Texas, and I had often thought that a childhood spent among the East Texas peckerwoods must have taught a little Jewish boy a lot about survival. He had been thought of around the firm as a bit of an oddball, not because he was a Jewish kid from East Texas, but because he would never let any of us forget it for a moment.

He had a huge framed poster behind his desk from a concert back in the seventies by some country and western band with the unlikely name of Kinky Friedman and the Texas Jewboys. Most of us thought Barry had the poster printed himself just to stick his thumbs in our eyes, but he swore it had been a real band.

"For Christ's sake, Barry, what the hell is going on here?"

"I'm not sure I really know, Jack."

He spoke quickly, furtively, his eyes rolling around the room.

"I'm living in a dark place and I don't know exactly how to get out of it. God help me, but I think you might be the only guy who can do anything about it."

He turned his head and looked at me as if he could hardly believe things had come to that.

"I really do think you might be, Jack."

Barry stopped talking, and since I didn't know what to say, I said nothing. Instead I looked away and ran my index finger around the rim of my coffee cup.

"Let's walk a little, Jack. Sitting in one place for too long makes me real nervous these days."

All of a sudden everybody wanted to take walks with me.

Barry stuffed a red hundred-baht note into the wooden cup that held the check for my coffee and stood up, taking my elbow and tugging me up with him. I did nothing to resist and we covered the short distance outside to the *soi* in silence. Threading our way through the jam of empty *tuk-tuks* and parked motorcycles, we turned right and walked out to Sukhumvit Road.

When we got there Barry stopped and glanced cautiously in both directions. A food vendor a few steps up the sidewalk was folding up his tables and chairs for the night, but other than that there didn't seem to me to be all that much to see. The usual late-night groups of foreigners were still trolling the sidewalks for action, but since it was well after midnight they were quickly thinning out to the hard core. Even the traffic on Sukhumvit was starting to move at something like a normal speed rather than crawling along bumper-to-bumper as it did for most of the day.

As far as I could tell, there was nothing going on that should to make Barry particularly nervous. Sukhumvit Road may have been a little freaky after midnight, but that was about it.

When the food vendor had folded up his last table, Barry shoved both hands into the pockets of his shorts and turned east, walking slowly with his head down. I followed, waiting for him to say whatever he wanted to say, but Barry just stared intently at the rough concrete of the sidewalk as if he might be trying to divine some message that had been left for him there.

I shot a quick glance over my shoulder and saw that the tall woman was following us at a discreet distance. However much Barry might have drifted off into his private reverie, she was more than making up for it with her concentration on both of us. I caught her eyes full on when I turned back, but she didn't look away — didn't even blink — and after a moment I did both.

Barry cleared his throat tentatively as if he didn't know exactly what to say, but then abruptly he started talking anyway.

"Okay," he said. "Here's the whole thing."

NINE

"YOU KNOW ALL THAT STUFF about Texas State Bank, don't you, Jack?"

Barry looked at me and twisted his eyebrows into question marks.

"Yeah. I looked it up."

"Good man, Jacko. Still doing your homework, aren't you? Always prepared. Real Boy Scout. I'll bet you wear two rubbers just in case one breaks, don't you?"

I looked away without saying anything and Barry kept talking in a low voice while we walked east along Sukhumvit.

"Harold Wilkins had been fronting for Russian mobsters for years. Mostly it was nickel-and-dime money laundering, but eventually he started thinking bigger and cut a deal with Jimmy Kicks. Jimmy had a soft spot for banks like Texas State that were in crappy, middle-sized shitholes like Dallas. He thought he was safer staying away from big money centers like New York and London because he didn't like dealing with sophisticated people. He always figured that sophisticated people were the most dangerous, and yokels were the greediest. Me, I'm not so sure. It just might be exactly the other way around."

"Uh-huh," I said.

It wasn't much, but I didn't know what else to say.

"Anyway, what he had Wilkins doing was pretty straightforward. Jimmy's mules delivered bags of cash to him, mostly from the big Russian drug operations in the Northeast. Then Wilkins would see that all the money was booked to legitimate bank depositors, companies whose names he'd used to set up dummy accounts without them knowing anything about it. He always picked companies that had big cash operations for his patsies, of course. Pawn shops were his favorite, but he liked restaurants and motels, too."

"A lot of people like motels."

Barry ignored me and went on talking.

"After the deposits were booked and a decent interval had passed, Wilkins would start transferring the funds into other accounts, shuffling them around until it was impossible to trace where the money had actually come from. Eventually he would funnel everything out of Texas State and into Jimmy's foreign bank accounts in a series of small transactions so they wouldn't attract any attention."

Two backpackers, a boy and a girl in their twenties who looked Scandinavian to me passed us on the sidewalk trudging doggedly in the opposite direction. They were bent forward under the weight of two massive yellow and black nylon packs, and the boy had his head buried in a guidebook, looking like someone who thought he might have made a wrong turn a way back. Barry fell silent until they were both out of earshot, then he went on again.

"I guess it was inevitable an idiot like Harold would eventually get sticky fingers. He decided he was slicker than goose shit in a greased tube and Jimmy Kicks was just some Russkie asshole, so Harold started wheeling and dealing with the money while it was lying around in the accounts he'd set up. He figured he could use the float to make a few bucks playing the forex markets before he shifted it out to Jimmy's offshore accounts."

"How'd Jimmy catch him?" I asked.

"He didn't. There was an audit while the stupid prick was off chasing pussy in New Orleans with the rest of the rubes."

"The auditors were onto him?"

"No, it was strictly some routine stuff. They just started pulling foreign exchange contracts at random, spot-checking the bank's exposure when it occurred to somebody that the number of open positions the bank was running seemed pretty high for a bank of that size. It was just a matter of time before they also noticed that almost all of the open positions were Wilkins'. That was when the whole fucking thing came unraveled."

"But didn't they just close out the positions when they found them? How could the losses have been so big?"

"I told you Wilkins was an idiot. I don't think he got the market right even once. Every time a contract went bad he'd cover it by doubling his next position. By the time the auditors got on to him, he was so far underwater he was shitting seaweed."

"How much did he lose?"

Barry hesitated, and I glanced over at him just in time to see a sly look slide across his face.

"The official number was just over sixty million dollars, so they say. Something like that."

"I still don't see how it could have been so much."

"It wasn't. Not really."

I looked at Barry and shook my head. "You lost me."

"Wilkins really did piss away a million or so fucking around with forex futures — that much of the story was true — but that was dogshit to Jimmy. It only mattered because it gave him an idea. He started wondering what would have happened if Wilkins had been thinking bigger? And that was when it came to him."

"What came to him?"

"That if he could find a way to hang some really big losses around Wilkins' neck instead of just the lousy million or so he had actually pissed away, then when the bank paid off those contracts the money would flow straight into a black hole. Wilkins would take the fall for the whole pile of shit and Jimmy could waltz away with all the money he'd scammed without the slightest chance anybody would ever work out what really happened. I got to hand it to the guy, Jack. The whole concept was golden."

I had no difficulty in seeing where this was going, and Barry didn't waste any time proving me right.

"There was one problem, of course. Jimmy had to have an inside man at the bank to pull that kind of thing off. I'd been put in charge of investigating Wilkins by the rest of the board and had full authority over all the bank's foreign exchange operations."

Barry turned his head and gave me a rueful look.

"I guess I was the obvious choice."

"What was your end?" I asked, not all that certain that I really wanted to know.

"Jimmy told me he'd put twenty percent of whatever I could scam for him into a Hong Kong bank and give me a fresh start anywhere I wanted."

Barry kicked at a pebble with his toe. It rattled off a garbage can that was turned upside down on the sidewalk and bounced into the gutter.

"That's the real American dream, isn't it, Jack? To disappear into some tropical paradise, rich and reborn?"

"I don't think. . . ."

"Americans have been reinventing themselves since the fucking pilgrims hit the beach," Barry interrupted. "It's one thing we're really good at. Today we just do it a little faster than we used to, that's all."

Barry stared into space as if he saw meaning in the air.

"Of course, if you're going to go to all the trouble to start over again, you sure want to avoid the big mistakes you made the first time around — like being poor. Everybody wants to come back rich, and I was sure as hell going to do that. I mean big *fucking* rich. Shit, I knew I could get forty or fifty million out of Texas State without even breaking a sweat. That would mean eight or ten million for me, at least."

Barry suddenly brightened and barked a quick laugh.

"You ought to understand starting over better than anybody, Jack. It's what you did, isn't it?"

Arguing with Barry's implication that we had both done more-or-less the same thing didn't seem worth the trouble, so I didn't.

"How did you pull it off?" I asked him instead.

"It was an easy sting. I phonied up a bunch of new contracts for bigger sums than Wilkins had ever dreamed of and then I slipped them into the system with his trades so they'd look right. Then I audited the trading accounts myself and simply discovered them. How the hell was I going to get caught? Nobody really knew what had been going on but Wilkins, and who the fuck was going to believe *him* when he said most of the contracts I found weren't his? Hell, the contracts I stuck in didn't even have to be good phonies since everybody was more than ready to believe that a boob like Wilkins would have made a mess out of his own swindle."

The look on Barry's face was not quite a smile, more just a crinkling around the eyes.

"Eventually I gave my solemn opinion to Texas State that legally they had to make good on every one of the contracts I'd found, and they did. When the smoke cleared, I'd creamed off just under fifty million for Jimmy. That meant I'd cleared almost ten million for myself."

We were passing in front of the Ambassador Hotel. As soon as he spotted us, a pudgy, neatly-dressed local man put on a big smile and broke out of the pack of touts that habitually lay in wait there to ambush passing male tourists. He approached us in an odd, crab-like gait, scuttling almost sideways.

"Massage, boss? Many sexy girl. Take look?"

The tout poked a tattered brochure toward Barry and started to open it for him to see, but then he abruptly froze. The man jerked the brochure back, turned away, and darted back to the safety of the other touts without another word. As we walked on by, I could feel the men following us with their eyes and I wondered what the tout might have seen in Barry's face when he had gotten up close.

"I don't know what to say, Barry."

"Then don't say anything, Jack. Just shut the fuck up and let me finish here."

Barry's voice trailed off for a moment and then he sighed heavily and went on.

"Anyway, that was when Jimmy got an even bigger idea. He was sick of getting screwed by banks, he told me. He had the fifty million I'd just scammed for him and so he figured this was his big chance. He wanted his own bank. He told me that if I'd put my ten million into the deal with him, he'd give me a free hand and a thirty percent shareholding."

"Shareholding in what?"

"Our bank."

I stared at Barry and stumbled on a piece of the splintered sidewalk that had jutted up unexpectedly in front of me.

"What are you telling me here, Barry? The Russian mob not only asked you to buy a bank for them, but to put some money into the deal yourself and become their partner? And you *did* it?"

"I didn't become partners with the whole fucking mob, Jack, just Jimmy Kicks. Don't go all hysterical on me here."

"You can't be serious."

"Serious as a heart attack, Jack. A chance to own thirty percent of an international bank and run it any way I wanted? I'd have been completely nuts to say no."

"How could you even *think* of fronting for a mob bank, Barry?"

"Now don't get so high and mighty on me, Jack. We both came out of the same fucking pile of crap. You took your way out, and I took mine. What the hell's the difference?"

"That's the second time you've tried the say that we both took the same road, and this time I'm not going to let it slide. There's nothing remotely similar about the choices you and I made, Barry. Not a damned thing."

"Then tell me the difference."

"The difference is that I didn't fake a suicide and go into business with a bunch of Russian mobsters."

"No, Jack. That's not it."

Barry offered me the faintest of smiles.

"The difference is that they didn't ask you to."

TEN

I WAS LISTENING TO WHAT BARRY HAD TO SAY because I really did love a good story. After he was done, I intended to do nothing more taxing than wish him a nice life and go home and go to bed, so it wasn't particularly difficulty for me to ignore the bait. An argument with Barry over ethical principals just wasn't on my agenda for the evening.

We were crossing the driveway next to Robinson's Department Store before I spoke again.

"You almost sound proud of what you've done, Barry."

"Yeah. A little, I suppose."

"I guess I just can't understand that."

"Well, you know the old saying, Jack. Every man loves the smell of his own farts."

In spite of myself, I burst out laughing.

"Did you just make that up?"

"Old Icelandic proverb."

I laughed some more and followed Barry as he angled off to the left and climbed half a dozen steps toward a McDonald's that was closed for the night. When he reached the last step he turned around and sat down, looping his arms around his knees.

"Was that Wilkins in the swimming pool?" I asked as I sat down next to him.

"Who the hell do you think it was, Jack? The fucking Tooth Fairy?"

Barry sounded genuinely annoyed.

"Look, Wilkins was a dead man anyway. You don't steal from somebody like Jimmy Kicks and then tell your grandchildren funny stories about it."

"So you let them kill Wilkins to cover for you, and you took off."

"Jack, I didn't fucking *let* Jimmy Kicks do anything. Harold was going to get whacked. That's all there was to it. Jimmy offered to use Harold's body to fake a suicide for me and give me a clean start if I'd do the bank deal for him. It was just that simple."

Barry looked off into the darkness and I wondered what he was seeing.

"Maybe if I'd had some more time to think about it. . . ."

He left the thought unfinished, but my professional curiosity had been whetted and I changed the subject, letting him off the hook.

"How could you buy control of a bank for the Russian mob without anyone finding out?"

"It was no big deal. I set up a string of shell companies to hold the stock, corporate cut-outs that kept anyone from tracing its real ownership. I used a private investment fund registered in the British Virgin Islands, a venture capital group in Luxembourg, a Panamanian shipping line, two Hong Kong insurance brokers. A whole bunch of others. Companies that owned companies that were in partnerships that owned other companies. Like that. Hell, Jack, you know how it's done. You're better at it than anyone I ever knew."

"What bank did you buy?"

"The Asian Bank of Commerce."

I stared at him.

"In Manila?"

"You got it."

The ABC was a very minor Philippine bank that would have been utterly unknown had it not been making headlines over the past few months with sensational allegations of corruption on a grand scale.

The cast of characters rumored to be involved was colorful if a touch familiar — the usual contingent of corrupt government officials, fabulously wealthy sheiks, shady arms dealers, out-of-control intelligence agencies, and Asian criminal gangs. In fact, about the only international villains who hadn't been getting press in connection with the ABC were Russian mobsters.

"When the peso went down the toilet a few years ago, the ABC was fucked. They tried to sell some convertible bonds to raise capital, but the market just laughed. My shell companies scooped up most of the bonds for a couple of cents on the dollar, then we waited for the shit to get even deeper and converted them all into common stock."

"And that gave you control of the Asian Bank of Commerce."

"Yep. Only nobody knew it because it looked like a whole bunch of different companies each had a small piece."

Barry lifted his arms from his sides and let them fall back.

"As they say, it seemed like a good idea at the time."

I had to admit that Barry had gotten it exactly right. He had struck on what was one of the best places in the world to find exactly the right combination of credibility, stupidity, and greed he needed to make his deal bulletproof.

Manila was anything but a financial center. On the other hand, it had just enough cachet as a real place to make the whole thing work. Best of all what passed for the banking authorities in the Philippines were mostly local politicians, none of whom would have particularly cared what Barry and his friends were actually doing with the ABC as long as they weren't too conspicuous about it and they didn't do it in the Philippines.

The gist of the story that Barry had told me was beguilingly simple, but the implications were breathtaking. On the surface, he had just bought a broken-down bank that was operating in a reasonably respectable place and used a string of untraceable shell companies to control it. As a practical matter, however, Barry had done nothing less than hijack an entire country as a front for a gang of Russian mobsters.

"It sounds to me like you delivered pretty well for your new pals, Barry. So why are we having this conversation? I can't believe you've discovered a sudden need to confess your sins."

"Well. . . ." Barry rolled some words around in his mouth for a few moments, but didn't seem to like the taste of any of them. "The bank's wiped out, Jack. Somebody scammed us bad."

He said it exactly like the death sentence he must have known it was.

"In the last three months we've lost more deposit money than we can cover from capital. I swear to God I don't know who took it, but eventually Jimmy's going to decide it was me."

I could feel a chill coming off Barry. He glanced past me toward the street, and I turned, following his eyes. The tall woman was standing on the sidewalk about fifty feet away. She was looking into some shop windows and seemed to be paying no attention to us at all.

"This is going a little fast for me, Barry."

"Yeah, it went a little fast for me, too, Jack. But listen up now. Once you know what I'm going to tell you, there'll be no turning back."

"It's not a question of turning back, Barry. I'm not going anywhere in the first place."

"Maybe, maybe not. But you'll know what I know, and that will make you a threat to them."

"To who? I'm not going to be a threat to anyone, because in just about a minute I'm going to turn around and walk off."

"No, you're not."

"I'm not?"

"Not a chance, Jack. I know you. You wouldn't miss the rest of this for the world."

I motioned vaguely for him to continue. What could it hurt to listen?

"Whoever it was, they got to us through our overseas depository accounts and drained most of our foreign currency holdings. About a hundred and eighty million dollars disappeared a couple of months ago. Poof! Just like that. Somebody cleaned us out and then burned us to cover their tracks. That's when all that shit started turning up in the papers."

"A hundred and eighty million dollars?"

"Give or take."

Barry nodded slowly at me. He did it carefully, like a man with a really bad headache.

"As a practical matter, Jack, it's like this. The Asian Bank of Commerce had been robbed. Somebody else's crooks fucked my crooks."

I would have laughed, but I didn't have the heart.

Barry stood up and stretched, then started walking slowly again, his head down. I followed him in silence to a pedestrian bridge that crossed Sukhumvit to the Sheraton Hotel. The woman maintained her position about fifty feet away, and now it was pretty obvious why she was there.

"So what does Jimmy have to say about all this?" I asked anyway.

"Are you fucking *kidding* me, Jack? You remember Harold Wilkins? He only lost *one* million dollars, and you know what happened to him."

"In other words, you haven't told Jimmy?"

"No fucking way, man. No way he'd believe I wasn't scamming him. Why do you think I'm hiding out in Bangkok?"

I glanced back at the woman again.

"So what are you going to do, Barry?"

"The way I figure it, I have to find the money, get it back, and prove to Jimmy that I had nothing to do with it disappearing in the first place."

Barry seemed reluctant to go on, but eventually he did.

"You know more about international banking and money laundering than anyone I know, Jack. I need your help to find the money."

I was too stupefied to say anything for a moment.

"Me? You want *me* to find your money?"

The nod of Barry's head was barely visible.

"Son of a bitch," I said, having no idea what else to say.

"Money's hard to hide. It always leaves footprints. A guy who knows how can follow them anywhere. You're the best there is, Jack, so you're my guy. I need you to find the footprints and tell me where they lead."

I was still too dumbfounded to say anything else right away, so I just watched as Barry looked for the woman trailing us and held her eyes briefly. Then he lifted his left index finger and twirled it in a tight circle. She immediately walked toward us, passed by without a word, and started up the concrete steps that led onto the pedestrian overpass.

"Come on, Jack. You can do this. Give me a hand here. I'm twisting in the wind."

I wanted to put a quick end to any hope Barry might actually have that I was going to help him, and I wanted to do it firmly without leaving the slightest chance he might think the door was open even a crack. While I was searching for just the right words to do that I vamped a little.

"Look, Barry, even if I was willing to help you out, and even if I found the money somehow, what good would it do? Somebody else would still have it, and you'd still be screwed."

"Yeah, but you haven't heard the rest of my plan yet."

The woman was about halfway up the steps, walking lightly on the balls of her feet like someone poised for a fast take off. There was no one within earshot, but still Barry leaned slightly toward me.

"After you find the money, I want you to steal it back," he whispered.

And with that he turned away and trotted up the steps, the woman advancing a dozen feet in front of him.

I watched them until they had crossed over Sukhumvit Road and approached the Sheraton. They avoided the main entrance and headed instead for a smaller door that was off to one side. They pushed through it, and I watched them until they were gone, but neither one looked back.

Driving home later I took Sukhumvit back west toward my apartment. Even late at night, Bangkok traffic could suddenly bog down without warning, so I wasn't particularly surprised when just past the Airport Expressway I found myself surrounded by a swarm of motorcycles and stuck behind an articulated bus momentarily rendered inarticulate. As I sat there waiting for the traffic to start moving again, I turned over in my mind all the things Barry had told me.

I had always operated on the assumption that I had a fairly sophisticated understanding of the Asian financial scene. Finding out that a regional bank, even a modest one, had been taken over by Russian mobsters came as a considerable surprise to me, to say the least.

Regardless of Barry's confidence that he had perpetrated his coup in complete secrecy, I doubted that. I was absolutely certain in fact that there had to be quite a few other people around who knew all about it. It was a common enough conceit among foreigners doing business in Asia, particularly Westerners, that they had some kind of advantage over the locals and were invariably a step or two ahead of them. That was a presumptuousness that many people I knew had ultimately come to regret.

Government officials, particularly those in Third World countries like the Philippines and Thailand, might seem sleepy to foreigners, but in my experience most bureaucrats around the region had a shrewd eye for opportunity. They were usually far from stupid, even if they played the part of bumbling provincials, and their nose for valuable gossip inevitably turned out to be formidable.

I didn't believe for a moment that every one of them had missed Barry's little ploy. Of course, as long as the arrangement wasn't general knowledge and the payoffs kept arriving regularly — tea money was the polite euphemism used in Asia for the practice of such official bribery — no one would make a fuss.

Still stuck behind the bus, I flipped the catches above the windshield and hit the switch that opened the Volvo's roof. A light breeze was blowing and the night air was laced with the smell of salt from the Gulf of Thailand, an odor that always seemed to me to be laden with enticing prophesies of imminent romance.

The jam started breaking up just as the roof finished retracting, which was happy timing although I didn't remember anyone ever honking at me when I got stuck with the car's roof half up or half down in Bangkok. It boggled the mind to think what might happen if I was stopped in the middle of the street back in Washington calmly lowering my convertible top. Forget honking. Someone would probably get out of another car and knock the damned thing off with a tire iron.

There were a lot of screwy things about Barry's story, I reflected when I was moving again. It was unlikely — probably impossible — for vast amounts of money to have disappeared from ABC accounts all over the world at exactly the same time without the active collusion of somebody inside the bank. But Barry didn't appear to have thought of that. Or if he had, he had chosen not to mention it to me.

When I walked into my apartment, I noticed the blinking from my answering machine before I flipped the lights on. There were three messages waiting for me the LED said, and I pushed at the replay button.

The first message was a hang-up, and so was the second. That meant almost certainly that both calls had been from Thais. Thais never left messages on answering machines and seemed genially puzzled at the entire concept. Generally they just listened to your recorded greeting, shook their heads, and hung up, writing off the whole idea of an answering machine as just another unfathomable mystery of the West.

When the third message began to play, however, I leaned toward the machine and strained to get every word. Anita was taking an evening flight to Sydney and must have called me from the airport before she boarded. The background noise corrupted her voice with a tinny echo; nevertheless the sound of it warmed the dark and empty apartment from her first words.

"Jack? Are you there? Pick up if you are. Jack?" Anita's voice buzzed slightly in the machine's tiny loudspeaker.

Sometimes when I was home alone I didn't bother to answer the telephone. Anita couldn't stand listening to a phone ringing without answering it — she was too curious to find out who it might be — but I had no problem at all. I held to the theory that anybody I really needed to talk to would eventually catch up with me somehow, and therefore it was completely unnecessary for me to do anything to speed the process along.

"Okay . . . I guess you're not there. I tried your mobile, but you're not answering it either. Out cruising the bars again, I guess. I hope you found something good tonight."

I hadn't told her that I was meeting Barry Gale, of course. After she had abruptly terminated our conversation the night before we had in fact said very little to each, and I certainly hadn't been foolish enough to risk reigniting everything.

"I just wanted to call before I left. I'm sorry . . . ah, that I missed you. Oh, by the way, I'll be back Thursday morning instead of Wednesday night. Some television station is doing a thing on this new gallery that's opening and I've agreed to an interview on Wednesday so they can make a big piece out of it. You know me. Anything to sell a few more pictures."

Did I know her? I hoped so, but there were times I felt a tiny foreboding that I might not.

"Anyway, don't worry. I'll still be around to make you look legitimate at whatever this grand occasion of yours is on Friday night. Wouldn't want you to have to take one of your bargirls along to chat up the politicians, although come to think of it, they might prefer it. Uppity Western women don't go down so well in Thailand, do they? Night night, my darling. I miss you."

I was too wired to go right to sleep as well as a little lonely from listening to Anita's voice on the answering machine, so I just sat on the edge of the bed naked for a long time, listening to the sounds of the city and replaying the conversation with Barry over and over.

After a while I fell back against my pillows and pulled the duvet up over me. I rolled and tossed for a long time, feeling helpless to put Barry's story far enough out of my mind to unwind and slip away. Eventually I drifted off into a shallow, fitful kind of sleep, but even then I dreamed of Barry Gale.

He was chasing me down a street somewhere. I couldn't tell where we were exactly, except that it was obviously a large city. From the faces of the people watching us as we ran, I eventually worked out that we must be somewhere in Asia.

Barry kept waving his arms and shouting something at me, but I couldn't slow down to find out what he was trying to tell me because right behind him and closing fast were at least a dozen guys in blue suits and dark fedoras, and every one of them carried a handgun that looked big enough to take out Pittsburgh.

They were going to get Barry. I could see that clearly. And there was absolutely nothing I could do about it. I wasn't even sure that I *wanted* to do anything about it.

We ran on like that for a while, our little parade winding deeper and deeper into a maze of exotic streets lined by curious faces that watched us with a maddening neutrality, then the men caught up with Barry and I looked away, not wanting to watch what was going to happen to him. Instead I just kept running like hell.

Eventually, of course, my curiosity got the better of me and I shot a quick glance back over my shoulder to see what was happening. Barry had disappeared completely, but the well-dressed posse was still coming hard.

And it was then that I realized that they weren't after Barry at all.

They were after me.

ELEVEN

I OVERSLEPT THE NEXT MORNING and woke with the conviction that I needed a run to clear my head more than I needed a pot of coffee. I pulled on my shorts and a clean T-shirt, laced up my Nikes, and trotted off toward Lumpini Park. Forty-five minutes later I was back home. In the interval, I had come to my senses.

I showered and dressed quickly, got the Volvo out of the garage, and made straight for Starbucks. With any luck, I thought, I could soak up enough caffeine and sugar in a half hour to set me up nicely for my ten o'clock class. The course was a real yawner, even for me — a lecture series on the application of American securities regulations to capital raisings in the United States by foreign companies — and I assumed my students really hated it. Without a caffeine high and a sugar buzz, I didn't see a hope in hell of getting through it today.

There were some people I knew who vilified Starbucks as an American corporate giant heartlessly homogenizing the unique cultures of the world in the headlong pursuit of profits. Strangely, I had noticed that the people who generally put the most energy into their vilifying were other Americans, mostly the kind you met abroad who were trying way too hard to be perceived as high-minded citizens of the world rather than just Yanks on the loose.

Thais didn't seem to care much one way or another about such things, particularly as long as the coffee, pizza, Coca-Cola, burgers, and other sustenance of middle-class America kept on flowing, but I still wondered if perhaps it wasn't my moral responsibility as an American expatriate to contemplate the issue of colonialism through fast food just as soon as I found the time. Maybe the upright types who worried about it had a subtle understanding of something I had missed. Until I could get around to that sort of serious pondering, however, it was good enough for me that Starbucks' coffee was strong and rich, and the bran muffins were usually pretty tasty.

It was a nice morning again, certainly by local standards. The night winds had come and gone, and they had left behind a dazzling blue sky without the usual layer of brown crud to spoil it. I whipped up Ploenchit Road and pulled into the McDonald's parking area just behind the Grand Hyatt. Smiling at the brown-uniformed security guard who came over to check me out, I transferred a red one-hundred-baht note smoothly into his lightly sweating palm.

"Korp khun maak krap." Thank you very much, I told him. Then I went on my way ignoring the prominently posted signs that said PARKING FOR MCDONALD'S CUSTOMERS ONLY.

That was something I had to admit honestly I loved about Thailand. The joyous, unrestrained air of corruption that permeated everything made life pretty simple once you had learned to go with it.

I selected a plump cranberry and bran muffin, got a tall low-fat latte, and carried them both to a window table along Ploenchit Road. Someone had abandoned a copy of the morning's *Bangkok Post* there and I flipped it to the front page so I could skim the headlines while I ate. Reading an English-language newspaper in Thailand was always an adventure. Probably reading a Thai-language newspaper was an adventure, too, but I couldn't read Thai nor could any other foreigner I knew, so I wasn't absolutely sure.

The Thai language had forty-four characters, and to the foreign eye they all looked more or less the same. To make matters worse, sentences, even whole paragraphs were usually written in one line without a break. If you asked a Thai what rules you should use to figure out where one word stopped and another began, he told you that it was just something you knew. I always thought that was a pretty good illustration of how everything else in Thailand worked, too — there weren't any rules exactly, you were just supposed to know.

Reading the *Bangkok Post* almost always put me in a pretty good mood. When I first moved to Bangkok, I had discovered that the *Post* wasn't exactly like a real newspaper at all. The standard fare of most American newspapers — graphic crime stories and breathless accounts of various groups demanding special treatment, preferably at the expense of other groups — was largely if not entirely absent from its pages. Instead, the *Post* seemed to make do mostly with photographs of watch shop openings and incoherent stories about Thai politics, although I was never certain whether it was the stories or the politics that were the more incoherent.

When I got through reading the *Post,* which seldom took more than ten minutes, I was usually pretty certain that nothing much had happened anywhere in the world that was of any great significance at all. I already suspected that, of course, but having it confirmed officially was still deeply gratifying.

My head was buried in the sports section trying to pick the previous day's NBA scores out of some microscopic type when I heard a familiar, rumbling voice at my elbow.

"Sawadee krap, Ajarn." Good morning, Professor.

That deep, resonant sound made me think of James Earl Jones every time I heard it, as did a number of other things about Jello.

His real name was Chatawan Pianskool, and beside the obvious fact that it was largely unpronounceable, I had never been absolutely certain why everyone called him Jello instead. I always surmised that the name had something to do with his physique since he had a prominent potbelly, unusual for a Thai. The first time I had met Jello

I noticed that his nylon shirt was stretched awkwardly in a hopeless effort to button over it. Jello was one of those guys a lot of people took lightly when they first met him. After all, the popular image of the jolly fat man has little to do with intelligence or subtlety, but that didn't seem to bother him. On the contrary, it was something he frequently turned to his advantage.

Jello was a Thai police captain and he had been assigned to the Economic Crime Investigation Division as long as I'd known him. Whatever Jello didn't know about what was happening in Bangkok just wasn't worth knowing, at least when it came to finance and commerce.

"You waiting for someone, Jack?"

"Nope," I answered, folding the *Post* and tossing it onto the empty table next to me. "Sit down, partner."

Just then a half-dozen giggling college girls tumbled in through the door and we both glanced over at the commotion. All of the girls were dressed in the customary Thai university uniform of tight white shirts and straight black skirts, worn either very short or very long, with wide brown belts looped loosely around waists that looked so tiny they had to be optical illusions. Bare legged and smooth skinned, the girls were decked out in an assortment of high-heeled, sling-back shoes and were uniformly so slim that they looked like a clump of reeds waving in the wind.

Jello and I both paused respectfully to take in the passing procession. Even at that age, there was a gliding grace about most Thai women that left men slack-jawed. Of course in a lot of countries two middle-aged men watching college girls in a coffee shop automatically spelled trouble, but in Thailand things were different. Feminine beauty was the country's hallmark and its pride, not the humdrum landscape of its countryside. To admire it when you saw it was as natural and acceptable a pastime as it would have been to enjoy an ocean view in Hawaii.

"So." Jello pulled out a chair and laid two chocolate croissants on a napkin alongside a large coffee. "What's new?"

He wouldn't believe me if I actually told him, I mused to myself, but of course I had absolutely no intention of doing anything of the sort. Having Barry Gale hanging around me was bad enough. Telling ECID about it was out of the question.

"Not much," was all I said. "Not much."

"Seen Dollar recently?"

"Not for a few days. Why?"

"Heard something strange about him this morning."

It struck me that Jello was choosing his words with particular care and my antenna automatically extended and made a couple of quick rotations.

"I talked to Just John about an hour ago," Jello said. "John told me Dollar got beaten up last night."

"Beaten up? Oh, come on. He must have been pulling your leg."

Jello picked up his cup and blew on the coffee before he tasted it. He didn't say anything and I noticed he wasn't smiling.

"I don't think so, *Ajarn.* He said that Dollar and some client got jumped by two guys when they came out of the office last night."

"Dollar's office? Dollar was mugged coming out of the United Center?"

"Yeah. In front of that Délifrance on the ground floor. Even knocked over one of those tables with the umbrellas when they were all rolling around."

I still couldn't believe it.

"Was he hurt?" I asked anyway.

"Apparently not. They didn't even bother to report it."

"What time was this supposed to have happened?"

"About ten." Jello's mouth was half full and he dribbled a few crumbs of croissant onto the table.

"That's impossible, man. No way."

Jello looked unimpressed by my skepticism, but that did nothing to change my point of view.

Residents didn't get mugged in Bangkok, only tourists, and even then mostly Taiwanese tourists for some reason. That approach had apparently become something of a firm rule among muggers since Taiwanese tourists seldom had much interest in returning at their own expense to testify against them, even if the mugger was unlucky enough to get caught — which he almost never was.

"Who was the client?"

"What client?"

"The one Dollar was with when he was mugged."

"Oh." Jello started in on the second croissant and sipped at his coffee again before he answered. "Just John didn't say."

It was hard to believe that Dollar could have been mugged coming out of the United Center on Silom Road at ten o'clock at night. That was one of the highest profile spots in Bangkok, and at that time of night the sidewalk should have been crowded with punters going back and forth to Patpong, which was just down the street.

"Why don't you call Dollar and check on him?" Jello suggested.

I knew Jello was probably less concerned about Dollar's welfare than he was with getting the gossip straight. I looked at my watch. Coming up fast on ten. I had a class and had to get going.

"It all sounds like a lot of nothing," I said. "Maybe later."

Although I still doubted that such a stupid story might actually turn out to be true, I figured it wouldn't hurt to call Dollar anyway. The last few days had been turning gothic on me and I supposed anything was at least theoretically possible.

Jello and I said our goodbyes and I headed back to the Volvo. If the traffic didn't get me, I'd be just about on time for my class.

As I pushed out the door I took a quick glance back over my shoulder. Jello was silently twisting his coffee cup with one hand and polishing off the second of his chocolate croissants with the other.

He licked the last crumbs off his thumb and forefinger and stared straight ahead into the street, apparently watching nothing more important than the traffic flowing past on Ploenchit Road.

He looked to me exactly like a man who didn't have a thought in his head. Somehow I really doubted that was true.

TWELVE

MY TEN O'CLOCK CLASS went surprisingly well. The sugar and caffeine did an impressive job. I hadn't been back in my office for more than a few minutes when my telephone rang, and since Bun had taken an early lunch, I answered it myself.

"Hello."

"Could you come to the office tomorrow afternoon to talk over a couple of things, Jack?"

Dollar had not only omitted the usual pleasantries, he also skipped his usual bantering small talk.

"About five or so would be good for me, Jack."

If Dollar could be brusque, I supposed I could, too, so I just ignored his question.

"I was going to call you later. I heard you got knocked around last night."

There was a short silence.

"Where did you hear that?" Dollar eventually asked.

"Jello told me. The way I hear it, Just John told him."

"Jello? The ECID guy?"

"Yeah."

Dollar let that hang there for a moment, then I heard an exasperated grunt.

"Figures."

I waited a moment for him to offer some explanation, but he didn't.

"So is it true?" I finally asked him.

"Well. . . ." Dollar hesitated. "It was no big deal."

"No big deal."

"No."

"What happened?"

"It's not much of a story."

I waited him out. Eventually he filled the silence.

"We were coming out of the office and two kids jumped us while I was calling my driver. The little shits were probably just a couple of pill-heads trying to grab our briefcases. It happens."

"Not really. Not in front of the United Center at that time of night."

"Sure it does."

I ignored that.

"You hurt?"

"A little, I guess. Bruises, and I'm sore as hell, but I'll live."

I thought I could almost hear Dollar thinking before he went on.

"Look, just keep this under your hat, would you?"

"If it's such a big secret, why did you tell Just John about it?"

Dollar paused for a long time, and I sensed he was trying to decide how much he had to say to make me let it go.

"It's his job to look after firm security," he finally said, then fell silent again.

That was the first I had heard of that. I always thought Just John was just a glad-hander and a boozer. Dollar telling me that he did security work for the firm opened up several questions — most conspicuously, exactly what was John supposed to be securing Dollar's law firm *from.* But before I could ask, Dollar started talking again.

"Anyway, a couple of tourist police came along right after we ran the fuckers off. They'd have told somebody, and then somebody else would have told somebody, and eventually John would have found out even if I hadn't told him myself. That would have pissed him off real good. This town is too goddamned small for me sometimes."

It crossed my mind that it was odd Dollar would care one way or the other if Just John was pissed off. Who worked for whom? But another question elbowed past that thought and went right up to the front of the line.

"Who's 'we'?" I asked instead.

"What?"

"You said 'we' were coming out of the office and 'we' ran them off."

Dollar hesitated, and because of something in the way he did, it suddenly occurred to me what he was going to say.

"Howard the Roach," he muttered just as I was thinking exactly that. "Look, Jack, I could have told you something else instead of admitting right off that it was Howard, but you'd probably. . . ."

"Was he hurt?" I interrupted.

"Not really," Dollar replied after a second's hesitation. It seemed to surprise him that I hadn't asked him anything else and the relief in his voice was evident.

"I'm glad to hear that," I said, thinking back over the conversation we'd had about Howard while we were doing laps around Chula yesterday.

Dollar didn't volunteer anything else after that and as we sat there in silence I sorted through the possible implications of what he was telling me, and far more likely, not telling me.

"Look, Jack, can you come around tomorrow like I asked?" he eventually resumed. "It's important."

"I'm going to Hong Kong tomorrow. I'll be back Thursday night as far as I know."

"Hong Kong?" I could swear Dollar sounded startled. "Why Hong Kong?"

"Board meeting. Southeast Asian Investments."

"Oh, yeah."

There was a tinge of relief in his voice. I was certain of it.

"Then how about Saturday morning?"

Whatever Dollar had on his mind must really have been important. As far as I knew, no lawyer in Bangkok had *ever* gone to the office on a Saturday before.

"I could manage that if you want."

"I know you'll probably be tired from the trip and all, and I hate to ask, but. . . ."

"It's okay," I interrupted, taking Dollar off the hook. "I'm only going to Hong Kong, not Honduras. It's not a problem."

"Okay, yeah. Good."

Dollar took a breath and rushed on.

"Look, Jack, there was one more thing I was calling about."

"Uh-huh."

No surprise there. I'd already worked out from his voice that there had to be something else.

"You haven't heard from Howard since last night, have you?"

"Oh Christ, you're not going to start all that again?"

Dollar's obsession over whether Howard was talking to me was taking on comic proportions.

"If you don't believe that I haven't heard from Howard, why don't you just ask him yourself?"

Dollar cleared his throat.

"I don't know where he is."

"I don't understand. Didn't you just say he was with you last night?"

"Yeah, but I can't find him this morning."

"Where's he staying?"

"He's been at the Regent for almost a week, but I called there and they said he checked out."

"Well, I can promise you he's not sleeping with me."

I let the silence that fell stretch on a bit.

"What is it you're not telling me here, Dollar?"

I could hear him take a deep breath.

"If Howard hasn't called you, Jack, why did he have your cell phone number written across the top of his notes?"

"I don't understand."

"What's not to understand?" Dollar sounded annoyed. "Yesterday afternoon in the office I was looking at some notes Howard had made about this deal he's working on. Your cell phone number was written on the top of the first page."

That stopped me. Directory information in Bangkok was a bad joke and as far as I knew it was pretty tough to get anybody's cell phone number, at least legitimately, unless they gave it to you. I had never given Howard my number. I was absolutely certain of that.

"I don't know how he got the number, Dollar. Look, I haven't heard from him. Other than that I just don't know what to tell you."

"You sure?"

"Goddamn it, Dollar, I'm tired of all this crap!"

Dollar sighed.

"Yeah. Me, too. Sorry, Jack. Rough night."

Then the obvious finally occurred to me.

"Are you asking me all this because you think those guys were after Howard? Is that why he took off?"

"Who knows? Who the fuck knows why that silly little shit does anything."

"Well, it seems to me that a guy gets. . . ."

"So you'll be at the office on Saturday?" Dollar interrupted.

His voice rose to make a question out of it, but of course it wasn't since I'd already told him I'd be there.

"Eleven, didn't I say?"

"You didn't say."

"Well, I'm saying now. Eleven. Okay?"

It was clear that Dollar wanted to put an end to our conversation about Howard the Roach before it got any more specific, and I had had more than enough of Howard for the moment myself, so I let him. After he hung up, I walked down the hall to get some coffee, came back to my office, and sat looking out the window for a long time.

I had always liked Dollar a lot in spite of his reputation for skating close to the edge. I even wondered sometimes if I might not like him better *because* of his reputation. I had always looked at it this way. If you were going to ride the range, you had to be either a cowboy or an Indian. And any four-year-old could make the right choice there, couldn't he?

For several decades Dollar had worked the territory around the Pacific Rim, a place that was a mystery as dark as the creation for most Westerners, and as far as I knew he had always done it with confidence, style, and not a little grace in spite of the high wire I suspected he might have been walking from time to time. He never seemed to get rattled, and I admired his capacity for taking on the most unsettling information at the worst possible time without blinking. And yet now something had him pretty well shaken up. That had been impossible to miss, even on the telephone.

Out the window I watched a helicopter as it clattered across Bangkok's clear winter sky and settled onto the pad on top of the Police Hospital a quarter mile away. Probably picking up some general for a golf date, I thought to myself, so why was I sitting in my office fretting about Dollar Dunne and Howard the Roach while Bangkok's only decent weather of the year was being left to the generals to play golf in?

Within five minutes I had locked away my files, shut down my computer, and was out the door. Bun was still at lunch, so I left a note asking her to cancel my other classes for the day and to reschedule the student conferences that had been set up for the afternoon. I enjoyed writing that note a lot. It reminded me vividly of why the academic life had become so appealing to me.

Taking the elevator down to the parking garage, I mused over what I ought to do with such a nice afternoon. One of the disadvantages of not playing golf was that the answer wasn't automatic. On the other hand, that was also one of the advantages of not playing golf.

Maybe I'd just drop the top on the Volvo, slip some ZZ Top into the CD, and cruise on down to Pattaya. That sounded good. Actually, it sounded *really* good.

Pattaya was an unremarkable beach resort on the Gulf of Thailand, a couple of hours drive southeast of Bangkok. Most of the time it had very little to recommend it, but right at the moment I could think of at least two things that spoke very well for it. There was an ocean in the neighborhood, and it was not Bangkok.

While the elevator was grinding down to the garage, the problem of how I was going to get rid of Barry Gale popped back into my head, pushing right past my curiosity about Dollar and the reasons for his sudden obsession over Howard the Roach. I knew I would be hearing from Barry again soon — that much appeared inevitable from the way our last conversation had ended — and I didn't have the slightest idea what I was going to tell him. I just wanted him to go away and leave me alone, but it was obvious that simply telling him to buzz off was not going to work. I was still stirring the problem around in my mind when the elevator lurched to a stop and the doors slid open.

I saw the man immediately. The way he was bending over into my Volvo, I could hardly have missed him. Still, he was such an unexpected sight that it took me a moment to react.

I had left the top of the Volvo down as I usually did when it was parked in the faculty garage and the man was taking full advantage of that. His back was to me and he was leaning over the driver's door, reaching into the car with both hands. I couldn't see what he was doing, but it seemed unlikely he was leaving me a winning lottery ticket.

The man was a Westerner, and when I thought about it later, it seemed to me that his appearance must have been average in every respect because absolutely nothing came back to me to distinguish him from most other Westerners in Thailand, other than perhaps the fact that he was wearing a suit and tie. It was a dark blue business suit, and it would have been unexceptional anywhere else, but it made him very conspicuous in Bangkok where the usual style was for men to leave their jackets at home because of the heat.

When I stepped out of the elevator and started toward the Volvo, the man must have heard my footsteps on the concrete. He immediately straightened up, and without turning, began to walk quickly away.

"Hey! Excuse me!"

The man didn't answer. Instead he quickened his pace and angled off toward a stairwell that was on the opposite side of the building.

"Hey!" I shouted as I broke into a trot.

The sound of my feet echoed loudly in the garage and the man bolted.

The door to the stairwell had been propped open with a concrete block, and in a dozen quick strides he reached it and shoved the block away with his foot. The man disappeared through the door and it clanged shut behind him. I knew from the click it made that it would be locked even before I got to it.

It was of course, and I could only stand and listen as the man's footsteps clicked down metal steps to street level. Then I heard another door open somewhere below, and after a moment, close.

When I got back to my car I looked it over cautiously but saw nothing unusual. Then I went back and examined it more methodically. I felt foolish letting the idea of a bomb even cross my mind, but the thought was there and I couldn't make it go away by pretending it wasn't.

Seeing nothing obvious in the car's open interior, I swung back first the driver's door and then the passenger door. I felt carefully under the front seats, then folded them forward and checked just as carefully in the back seat and on the floor. Finally I bent down and looked underneath the car like I'd seen people do in the movies. As far as I could tell everything seemed normal enough there, too, so I pushed myself to my feet again, reached in, and popped the Volvo's hood release.

I stood with my hands on my hips and stared into the engine compartment wondering exactly what I thought I was looking for. Finally I put my hand on a couple of cables and hoses and jiggled them and gave a tentative shake to a black, circular thing on top of the motor that I was reasonably sure was the air filter. I was certainly no mechanic and probably hadn't had the hood open more than twice since I had bought the Volvo, but everything looked very much as it seemed it should. At the very least I was pretty certain that there wasn't a bundle of dynamite hanging off anything. When I started to feel foolish enough, I closed the hood quietly and leaned on it until the catch clicked shut.

Just because some pretty strange things had been happening to me recently it didn't mean that I had to turn some ordinary-looking guy poking around my Volvo into a car bomber. Probably it was just somebody who liked convertibles, I told myself, and no doubt I scared the crap out of him when I bellowed like a madman as soon as the elevator door opened. Why had I jumped immediately to the conclusion that the guy was up to no good without even giving him the chance to explain himself?

Jesus, I thought to myself, if I'd thought before that I needed to get out of town for a while, I was absolutely certain of it now.

I made it to Pattaya in ninety-five minutes, successfully throttling my mind back into a fugue state nearly the whole way. Taking the first exit off the freeway, I made my way into town and turned left into Beach Road.

When I rounded the long bend in front of the Dusit Resort, I finally caught sight of the near-perfect half circle of Pattaya Bay, its tiny outer islands scattered and hazy along a tan horizon. The sea was flat and gray-brown.

There was a slight breeze coming off the ocean, and although it was warm instead of cool, it was still sea air. I filled my lungs with great gulps of salty air and tilted my head back, letting the tepid wind wash over me. A junk was coming in trailing a dingy. It floated right up to the beach and a crowd of people jumped overboard and began swimming at its stern, washing themselves in the tide.

I passed an old man riding a bicycle who must have been at least seventy. He was tanned and lean, wearing baggy shorts and a white T-shirt, and under one arm he carried a small, black and white dog. The dented red tank bike he peddled appeared to be close to collapse, and holding onto the dog was obviously a struggle for him, but still the old man pumped steadily. His eyes were locked straight ahead, unswerving in their concentration. He and his dog seemed to be on a mission and I wondered momentarily what it might be.

It was while I was watching the old man that it suddenly came to me exactly what I would tell Barry Gale when I heard from him again.

Barry, I could already hear myself saying, *I'm just not the same guy you knew in Washington anymore.*

I've managed to stumble into a life I like a lot better, one that no longer includes living with other people's troubles. And the truth now, you see, is that I just want to get on with it.

Try thinking of it this way, Barry. My deposit-your-bullshit-here window has been permanently closed for business, even to guys who've recently been dead.

Goodbye, partner.

And chok dee. *Good luck to you.*

THIRTEEN

I HAD GONE INTO THE OFFICE late Wednesday morning to collect the stuff I needed for the board meeting in Hong Kong, and since Anita was away and I had nothing better to do I hung around doing a bit of this and a bit of that rather than go back home again. The Cathay Pacific flight didn't leave until four and I was in no hurry, so when Jello pushed the door open and stuck his head in, I had my feet on the desk and was reading the *Asian Wall Street Journal.*

"Hey, Jack," he said. "Where's your secretary?"

"Lunch, I guess." I lowered the paper. "Bun's always at lunch."

"What a good idea." Jello smiled and patted his stomach. "How about us getting something, too? My treat."

"Nah," I said, shaking my head. "I'm not really hungry."

"Yeah, you are."

I folded the *Journal* and laid it on the desk while I thought that one over.

"I'm sorry?"

"I said I think you're hungry." Jello jabbed his thumb over his shoulder toward my door. "Let's go."

"Then you didn't just drop around to say hello? I'm deeply hurt."

"We need to talk, Jack."

"I see," I said, but of course I didn't. "So . . . you want to tell me what this is all about?"

"Not really, but I will."

Jello looked uncharacteristically somber, so I shut up and stopped arguing with him. I swung my feet off the desk and followed him out into the corridor, locking my door behind me. There would be plenty of time to come back for my things later before I went to the airport.

"Did you talk to Dollar yet?" Jello asked as we walked toward the elevator.

I glanced at him, but he was looking straight ahead down the corridor.

"Yeah," I said. "Yesterday."

"And?"

"And nothing. He said it was just a couple of kids grabbing briefcases."

Jello grunted slightly, but he didn't say anything else.

We rode down to the lobby in silence and then walked outside to where Jello had left a brown Toyota parked in Sasin's circular driveway. He started the car and drove off toward Mah Boonkrong Center. I let the silence go on until we passed the Princess Hotel and turned left into Phayathai Road.

"Where are we going?"

"Anna's."

Anna's Café was only a short distance away on Soi Saladaeng, just beyond the shadows of the office towers bunched together at the south end of Silom Road. Soi Saladaeng was a quiet street that cut directly across one of Bangkok's most venerable residential neighborhoods.

It was a lovely little *soi* really, lined with high concrete walls shielding the aging, slightly shabby villas of some of the city's old-time rich who so far had spurned the money to be made by turning their property into condos and office buildings. A peaceful canopy of gum trees overhung the street, and it sprinkled the *soi* from end to end with a cooling, dappled light.

Recently Soi Saladaeng had become the unlikely home to a procession of new and trendy Bangkok restaurants that were wildly popular with young Thai stockbrokers and other locals who wanted to be seen as cosmopolitan without actually having to mix with anyone but other Thais. I figured we were no more than a year or two away from the last of the old walls being flattened and all the gum trees being plowed under so that the little bastards could have even more places to buy Budweiser.

In spite of all that, I liked Anna's a lot, partly because the food was good and the surroundings pleasant, but even more because I thought of it as a kind of monument to the extraordinary adaptability and endurance of Thais.

When the Bank of Thailand gave up trying to support the baht in the mid-nineties, the country's financial collapse had wrecked almost everybody. Financiers fled the country, corporate executives turned to selling sandwiches, and one particularly luckless investor put a gun to his head in front of the stock exchange and pulled the trigger. He missed. That struck a lot of foreigners as the perfect metaphor for how Thailand had gotten into such a mess in the first place.

Property developers were particularly hard hit. Dependent on loans from local banks to keep all their plates spinning, when the banks stopped lending in a knee-jerk reaction to the financial crisis and starting calling in the loans they had already made, most of the plates came crashing down. Even now, years after the economy had begun to move again, Bangkok was still littered with the rotting carcasses of huge structures that had been abandoned by ruined developers who couldn't afford to finish them. Some parts of the city looked like a movie set being readied for another remake of *Planet of the Apes.*

The developer who had owned the site where Anna's now stood had been luckier than most, having gotten no further than building a sales office touting an improbable high-rise condominium when the crash came and the bank loans disappeared. What to do? An American property developer would no doubt have called his lawyers and sued everybody he could think of. The Thai developer, in happy contrast, had taken the ruined condo's sales office and turned it into a stylish, profitable restaurant. It had always seemed to me that there was a useful lesson in there somewhere.

We turned between Anna's gateposts and followed the driveway around to the parking area in back of the restaurant, where Jello took the first open spot he found. He got out, slammed the door, and started toward the front entrance without looking back. I followed him wordlessly.

Anna's was a one-story, white-pillared building of vaguely colonial design with a wide, red-tiled veranda running all the way across the front. Most people preferred to sit indoors since the large dining area was airy and spacious, but the weather was still unusually cool and the veranda looked inviting. I wasn't particularly surprised when Jello walked to the end furthest away from the front door and settled himself at a round teak table shaded by a white canvas umbrella. I pulled out a chair and joined him, folding my arms and leaning forward attentively against the table in hopes that my posture might encourage him to resume the conversation.

Jello sat slouched down, his body relaxed, but his dark eyes flicked around with the alertness of a pool shark cruising a game.

"I like to sit out here when I've got some serious thinking to do," he said, not looking at me.

"And is that why we're here now? To do some serious thinking?"

"Not really."

Jello pointed to the two menus that a boy with an uncertain smile and fluttering hands had just put on the table.

"We're here to have lunch. Okay if I order for us both?"

He scanned one of the menus, and without waiting for an answer, ordered several Thai dishes and two bottles of Heineken. That marked the end of the pleasantries. When the waiter was out of earshot, Jello got straight to the point.

"What do you know about a man named Howard Kojinski?" he asked in his cop's voice, the one that gave away nothing, but implied everything.

After being mentioned as far as I could recall exactly never, Howard the Roach had suddenly started popping up like crab grass after a wet winter.

"Couldn't you have asked me that on the telephone?"

Jello shrugged slightly.

"You never know about telephones. Shouldn't say anything on a telephone you're not ready to read in the newspapers tomorrow morning."

Jello's reluctance to use the telephone for what seemed to me to be an innocent enough inquiry would have verged on the comic if I hadn't already been a little uneasy over Dollar's recent obsession with Howard. I was developing a strong suspicion that nothing involving Howard the Roach was likely to turn out to be innocent, or for that matter, comic.

"For instance," Jello went on, "what do you know about his background?"

The answer of course was little or nothing. Howard was Dollar's client, not mine. I had always worked on the premise that I was advising whatever firm hired me, not any specific client of theirs. The clients were their problem, not mine.

"Not a lot," I said truthfully. "He told me once that he was from Poland."

I thought about it some more.

"Isn't he an accountant?"

"What kind of work have you and Dollar been doing for Howard recently, Jack?"

"Whoa," I said, and raised my right hand, palm out. "What does that mean?"

"It's a simple question. Seems clear enough to me."

"Then I'll give you a simple answer. I won't tell you. I'm not going to talk about anything that Dollar's firm is doing for its clients, and you ought to know better than to ask me to, Jello."

The young waiter returned and set sweating bottles of Heineken on cardboard coasters in front of each of us. Jello waived the proffered glass away, wrapped a big hand around the green bottle, and downed half of it in one hit. When the boy reached to put a glass in front of me, I shook my head as well, and he snatched it back and scurried away.

"Don't give me the lawyer crap, Jack. Just tell me the truth."

First Anita and now Jello. I wasn't all that fond of being a lawyer, but every damned time somebody said that kind of thing, it still rubbed me the wrong way.

"Look," I said, giving my indignation free reign to strut its stuff, "why don't you just ask Dollar? Don't try to put me on the spot."

Jello nodded, still looking off toward the trees. A chubby blond woman was getting out of a taxi on the other side of the road. She had leathery skin and was wearing a red dress that was much too tight and far too short. Lugging two large Fendi shopping bags she struggled up Anna's driveway toward the front door, the bags slapping awkwardly against her heavy thighs.

"I'm going to tell you something that I shouldn't, Jack. I'm going to tell you because I think you're entitled to know exactly what's going on here, but you're not going to be happy to hear it."

Jello sounded like a librarian who was about to describe the best way to burn books.

"Are you okay with that?"

I exhaled in exasperation.

"Look, Jello, you're buying lunch. You can tell me anything you want to, but I'm not going to talk to you about Dollar's clients and nothing you can say is going to change that."

The waiter reappeared, settled his tray on the empty table next to ours, and stilled his hands long enough to serve the food. Jello inspected each plate as it was placed on the table — *somtam,* a papaya salad with chilies; stir-fried morning glory in oyster sauce; prawn curry; lemon grass chicken; and spicy noodles. Apparently everything met with his approval, because he began spooning bits of each dish onto his plate of rice even before the waiter had collected the tray and withdrawn.

Jello ate for a while, saying nothing while I served myself, and then as I started to eat, he cleared his throat lightly.

"Howard Kojinski isn't an accountant from Poland."

"Really?"

I hoped my tone of voice reflected my general lack of interest in the subject.

"He was born in New Jersey, did ten years in the U.S. army, mostly in Germany, and then became an airline reservations agent. A few years later he somehow wound up working as a mid-level coke mule for the Colombians. He got busted making a run to Honolulu and did a few months in prison in Hawaii."

"Gee," I said. "That's fascinating."

Jello ignored me and went on.

"He must have used his time there making friends and learning new skills because he went to Hong Kong right after that and set himself up running a small-time money laundry. He turned out to be pretty good at it, and now he moves cash all over Asia for a lot of people you don't want to know about. Recently we think he's become the primary money launderer for a group of major Burmese heroin producers."

I burst out laughing, but I gathered that wasn't exactly the reaction Jello had been expecting.

"You think that's funny?" he snapped.

"Christ, I think it's *hysterical.*"

I shook my head and finished off the Heineken.

"Look, Jello, unless you're just generally full of crap, you've got the wrong man. Howard the Roach couldn't launder money if you gave him a new Whirlpool and a steam iron. If the Burmese are using *him* to handle their cash, I can promise you it's a giant step toward wiping out the drug business in Asia."

"The Burmese used to run their money mostly through Hong Kong, Jack, but a couple of years ago they started spreading it around, mostly to banks in Thailand and the Philippines. Howard's their man. There's no doubt about it."

I was still shaking my head. How anyone who knew Howard could think he was equipped to handle anything more complex than taking a whiz without soaking his shoes was utterly beyond me.

"Howard doesn't just move their money around," Jello continued. "He invests it for them. Suddenly Howard Kojinski has started turning up in all kinds of strange places."

"Such as?"

"I can't tell you that, Jack."

I snorted, and Jello looked annoyed.

"Have you told Dollar any of this?" I asked.

Jello sighed deeply and his expression softened.

"Yeah, sort of."

"What does that mean?"

Jello chugged the rest of his Heineken in one gulp and stuffed a heaping spoonful of *somtam* right behind it.

"I told him and he said it was bullshit, but he refused to tell me anything about Howard's business. He said it would be a breach of ethics."

"Yeah, well, there's your answer."

"But it's not bullshit, Jack. That's the point. It's all absolutely true."

Jello tapped the empty Heineken bottle against the table with a crisp little rat-a-tat-tat.

"That's when I started wondering if Dollar might be involved, too."

"Involved in what?"

Jello just sat there impassively, looking at me with dead cop eyes.

"You're not saying that you think Dollar Dunne and Howard the Roach are working together to launder money for a bunch of Burmese heroin producers, are you?" I finally asked.

Jello looked at me with what might or might not have been a slight smile. Then he nodded.

What in the hell was happening here? First Barry Gale in cahoots with the Russian mob and now Dollar Dunne supposedly moving money for Burmese drug lords. Whatever happened to the good old days when the worst thing you could accuse a lawyer of was ambulance chasing?

"How long have you known Dollar?" I asked Jello.

"Nine or ten years. A little longer maybe."

"And you're sitting here now, seriously telling me that all of a sudden you've decided he's the kind of a guy who launders drug money?"

"I think he may be, Jack. God help me, but I think he may be."

Jello spun the empty Heineken bottle in his big hand.

"Are you willing to help me find out for sure?" he asked.

I should have seen it coming, I thought to myself. I should have seen it coming, but I hadn't.

"All I want you to do is poke around a little, Jack. Nothing heavy duty. Just keep your eyes and ears open, really, then let me know what you see and hear."

"You can't be serious, Jello. Dollar's been your friend for a long time. He's my friend, too."

"Friendship's got nothing to do with this."

"Well, it does for me. I'm not spying on Dollar Dunne for you or anyone else."

I pushed back from the table and stood up while Jello watched expressionlessly.

"This is the end of this conversation, Jello."

"I can see that."

"I'm going to get a taxi back to my office and you're going to let me do that without arguing about it. Then I'm going to forget we were ever here today, along with everything you've said, and you're going to let me do that, too. Do we understand each other?"

Jello just looked at me without answering, and after a moment I turned my back on him, stepped off Anna's veranda onto the grass, and started walking toward Silom Road where I would be able to find a taxi.

Jello didn't try to stop me, and I didn't look back.

FOURTEEN

THE GLAMOUR OF INTERNATIONAL TRAVEL is frequently much exaggerated, chiefly, I've always suspected, by people who don't do much of it.

Still, since I flew mostly on business and somebody else was paying for it, I did have the decided benefit of first class tickets and I had to honestly admit that I enjoyed that part of it. I could lean that big luxurious seat all the way back, raise the footrest, and pull out some tacky novel I'd been meaning to read without the slightest twinge of guilt to mar the fun. No telephone would be ringing with a peremptory demand for attention; no fax was going to arrive with a narrative of problems demanding immediate solutions; and no one was about to burst into my office with tales of impending catastrophe. Once I was settled into that comfortable seat, I could be absolutely certain that — short of the airplane falling out of the sky — nothing unhappy was going to loom up on my personal horizon any time soon.

Other than one thing, of course. The guy in the next seat might want to talk.

Most people who flew a lot felt the same way I did. Normally it would have taken nothing less than an attack by a North Korean MiG to get anyone in first class to raise his head, let alone speak actual words. Not only did people in first class not talk to each other, they seldom even made eye contact and probably couldn't pick each other out of a line-up after a flight was over.

Although Thai International had far more flights out of Bangkok and more convenient departure times than any other airline, I was on the Cathay Pacific four o'clock to Hong Kong. I usually flew Cathay or Singapore Airlines instead of Thai because of something an official in the Ministry of Foreign Affairs had once said to me at a cocktail party. He was a man who had to fly on Thai a lot, and making small talk, I had asked him how he thought it compared to other airlines. "Whenever you fly Thai International," he had observed with a glum expression, "always remember that your pilots got their jobs exactly the way everyone else in Thailand got *their* jobs."

My seatmate on the Cathay Pacific flight introduced himself even before I had buckled my belt. In spite of my best efforts not to, I learned in short order that the man was a microchip importer from San Francisco and that he was going to Hong Kong to meet with a financial consultant after attending a trade show of some kind in Bangkok.

This consultant, the man explained to me, was going to reorganize his entire company using offshore banks so that he could completely avoid paying any taxes. The scheme had something to do with utilizing offshore deposits to guarantee loans made to him through California banks, but I was paying as little attention as possible and that was all I got. The guy was reading a book to prepare for his meeting and he held it up for me to see. I glanced over politely and had to bite my tongue to keep from laughing out loud. The book was called, *Offshore Money Havens: How to Live Tax Free for the Rest of Your Life.*

When the guy asked me what kind of work I did, I thought fast. We were going to be sitting together for the next three hours and telling the truth seemed to be an absolute guarantee that every one of them would be hell on earth for me. I briefly considered saying I was an Internal Revenue Service agent on vacation, but that would have been too cruel. Instead I told him I was a life insurance executive from Minneapolis. That was the dullest thing I could come up with on short notice and it must have been a good choice. The man hardly said another word for the rest of the trip.

Why was it that so many people thought that offshore banking amounted to some sort of occult wizardry? I had a sudden vision of huge airplanes stuffed with microchip importers from San Francisco whizzing endlessly around the globe in search of a fabled and mystical land called Offshore, a place that was forever beyond the reach of greedy governments, combative creditors, and vengeful ex-wives.

I myself had always pictured Offshore as a land ruled by Peter Sellers, but now that he was dead, I imagined that Rowan Atkinson must have taken over the throne. I wondered what people spent their days doing in Offshore? What did they eat? What did they wear? Did they have sex? Well, I could guess the answer to that one. Not with all that money around. Money was generally so much more interesting than sex for most people.

Exactly on schedule we landed at Chek Lap Kok, the new Hong Kong airport that had been built at enormous expense on a man-made island far to the southwest of the city to replace ancient Kai Tak which had been conveniently located right on the harbor. Instead of a few minutes, it now generally took an hour or more to get into the financial district, another example of progress that seemed to me, on the whole, not particularly progressive. Southeast Asia Investments had sent a driver to the airport to pick me up, and the fellow made the long haul into town in what must have been record time, getting me to the venerable Mandarin Oriental Hotel on Connaught Road in Central a little before nine.

It was too late to do anything really, but too early to go to bed, and Hong Kong television was too awful a thought to contemplate.

I stuck my head in the Captain's Bar off the lobby, but it seemed to be filled almost exclusively with middle-aged Englishmen entertaining their daughters and that was a depressing scene. I had skipped the meal on the plane, and it occurred to me that I could probably manage to eat something, so I decided to set out on a walk and see where I ended up.

I liked walking in Hong Kong. In winter the climate was balmy and the humidity was low, and in every season the intensity of the place was overwhelming. Bangkok was a tropical city and no matter how busy it might be there was a sort of languor in the air that you could never really shake off. Hong Kong, on the other hand, was all action and energy. It was like being inside a pinball machine.

When I left the Mandarin, I turned right, walking east toward the Wanchai district, or as it was more colorfully called by the American troops who took their R&R there during the Vietnam War, the Wanch.

The Wanch had a history, but then like a lot of history, most of it was made up. From the day William Holden first came to Hong Kong, moved into a hotel filled with good-hearted whores, and fell in love with Suzie Wong, Wanchai became the real Hong Kong in the eyes of most of the world.

Not wanting to disappoint anyone, particularly if there were a few dollars to be made out of it, Hong Kong people promptly created the Wanch so the world could have the kind of Hong Kong it was looking for — booze, music, women, and hot-sheet hotels. What did it matter that Hong Kong was really about banks, sweat shops, hustling, scheming, and getting stinking rich? Hollywood had invented the Exotic East and Hong Kong could give the punters what they were looking for.

Nightlife in the Wanch never attained the status of Bangkok's of course, not even at the height of the Vietnam War when thousands of fresh-faced kids from places like Nebraska and Ohio flooded its streets, all of them looking for a Suzie Wong of their very own. Most of the bargirls in the Wanch were more like bar grandmothers and put on their make-up with a garden trowel, but maybe that wasn't so important when you were nineteen years old, it was three in the morning, and the ninth bottle of San Miguel had just gone down so smoothly, and best of all, stayed down.

I circled around the golden glass-clad bulk of the Admiralty Centre, its bronze-mirrored surface twisting and shimmering with the city's garish nighttime lightshow. Heading up Queensway, I fought my way through the crowds still flowing out of the financial district even at this hour. Almost entirely Chinese, the throng pulsed and surged as if driven by some otherworldly energy source. Walking in Hong Kong had always seemed to me like playing a giant game of bumper cars. There was nothing personal in it and the concept of courtesy or discourtesy wasn't really involved. Most Chinese just didn't care much about protecting the space around them, at least not quite in the same way that was part of every Westerner's cultural baggage.

About a half-mile down Lockhart Road, I spotted the dirty brick façade of the Old China Hand pub on the opposite side of the street. The Hand was something of a local monument and had been a Hong Kong expat hangout longer than anyone I knew could remember. I could hardly imagine the deals and schemes that had been whispered of within its dingy interior.

I cut diagonally across the road and ducked inside the dark wooden door that was stained black from decades of exposure to Hong Kong's rancid air. The room was as gloomy as I remembered it, and like most expat bars in Hong Kong, it was chilled down to the temperature of a meat locker. From a loudspeaker somewhere up near the greasy ceiling Tony Bennett crooned about leaving his heart in San Francisco and for a moment I remembered the microchip importer and wondered if he was tucked up in bed somewhere nearby dreaming of Offshore Land.

I slid into a chair at an empty table and in a few moments a dumpy Filipina girl of indeterminate age shuffled over. She was dressed in jeans and a man's shirt and thrust out a menu that looked dirty and dog-eared. She didn't smile.

"A pint of San Miguel," I said, not bothering with the menu. "And fish and chips if you've got any left."

The girl pulled the menu back and walked away without a word. I gathered they must still have some fish and chips. Or maybe not.

The transition from Bangkok to Hong Kong was always a bit of a shock no matter how many times I went through it. Board meetings for Southeast Asian Investments brought me up every three or four months and that was just about enough for me. Any more often than that and I probably would have ended up slugging some local when I'd had enough of the surliness that was the daily currency of Hong Kong life, and that really wouldn't have been a good thing. Anyway, welcome back to Honkers, I reminded myself. *Jai yen yen.* Keep cool.

Most of my students seemed to imagine that becoming a director of a company, particularly a company located in some major financial center like Hong Kong, was a big deal. It wasn't. Directors from outside the ranks of management were pretty much useless appendages on any board no matter where the company did business. Generally just a bunch of semi-retired old geezers with nothing better to do than attend meetings a few times a year, outside directors were seldom expected to do anything other than keep their mouths shut and vote the way management told them to.

On the other hand, I didn't particularly mind. The occasional paid trips here and there made for a good counterbalance to life in Bangkok. If nothing else, they reminded me what I was missing, and how happy I was to be missing it.

Actually the only significant drawback to being on SAI's board was that four of the eight other directors were former English solicitors who were now partners in Hong Kong law firms. I had always hated dealing with English solicitors — their inevitable and hugely supercilious disdain for American lawyers was a real pain in the ass — but there was at least one thing that was a lot worse: dealing with Hong Kong solicitors who *used* to be English solicitors.

There was an acronym commonly applied to the small army of British lawyers and bankers in Hong Kong — FILTH. It stood for "Failed In London, Try Hong Kong." More often than not it fit the useless little prigs just fine.

I glanced around while I waited for my food and saw that the China Hand wasn't very busy. A group of loud, over-aged English schoolboys huddled around the L-shaped bar in the back, chain-smoking cigarettes and slamming back pints of beer like they'd just heard a shortage was coming and were laying in a supply. Every now and then a howl would go up from the group and I noticed they were watching rugby on a silent television hanging over the bar.

At the scarred wooden tables around the edges of the room, a dozen or so flabby, middle-aged Western men — most of whom seemed to be accompanied by Filipina women with noticeably empty faces — sat separately, and for the most part silently, staring into mugs of beer. The Hand had always been a Hong Kong refuge for the American diaspora that had sloshed around Asia ever since the Vietnam War ended. There was at least one place like it in every Asian city, usually a bar, where the displaced and bewildered gathered together, huddled in the certainty of the past and frightened by the upheavals of the present, feeling safe there at least, among each other.

Nothing about the Hand had really changed since I'd first come into the place more than twenty years ago. The men around me could have been the same men I'd seen back then sitting at the same tables with the same women.

The unsmiling girl returned with a lukewarm mug of San Miguel, a plate of greasy fish and chips, and a sticky bottle of vinegar. I doused the fish liberally with the vinegar, sliced off a piece with my fork, and chewed reflectively as I glanced around the Hand again.

Come to think of it, maybe they *were* the same men.

FIFTEEN

THE BOARD MEETING STARTED promptly at nine the next morning and was routine as usual. We were shown a detailed presentation about a Mekong River hydroelectric project that of course no one understood and then we listened to a droning recitation on the future of the shrimp industry in Cambodia that was so dull I think one director may have passed away during it without anyone noticing.

We all dutifully voted to approve both projects, and management rewarded me for my support with a small retainer to organize the shrimp farm's financial structure. For some reason that was unclear, at least to me, I was asked to use a shell company that SAI had already formed in Hong Kong to package the venture. It didn't matter, I supposed, but that probably meant several sour days dealing with the local solicitors that I could well have done without.

The entire excursion to Hong Kong would have been utterly and completely unremarkable, had it not been for one thing.

The meeting ended just after twelve and a light lunch was served in the boardroom. I was making small talk with some of the other directors and looking out across the panorama of Hong Kong Harbor when a slim, red-bound volume in a bookshelf caught my eye. Normally *A Register of Hong Kong Banking Institutions* probably wouldn't have raised much interest, but with the saga of Barry Gale in the back of my mind I pulled the book off the shelf and flipped to the index. About a third of the way down the first page I saw the Asian Bank of Commerce.

I turned to the page number listed in the index and found very little there since the ABC had only a restricted banking license in Hong Kong. That meant essentially that it had a little capital, but not much, and that it was legally entitled to take only very large deposits and make certain kinds of corporate loans in Hong Kong. No vaulted lobby, no cute tellers, no toasters with every new account.

The *Register* did at least have an address. The Hong Kong office of the ABC was on Duddell Street, a short, steep lane that was a few blocks west of the Hongkong and Shanghai Bank building and ran from Queen's Road up to Ice House Street. It was only about a ten-minute walk away, so I had plenty of time. My flight back to Bangkok wasn't until early evening and I really had no plans for the afternoon other than to pick up some cigars. The availability of a wide range of Cubans at remarkably low prices was for me the primary feature of any trip to Hong Kong.

I said my goodbyes to my fellow directors and slipped away from lunch as soon as decency allowed. Crossing Des Voeux Road, I walked through the Landmark, a ritzy shopping mall that joined the bases of two of Central's principal office towers, and emerged on Queen's Road. Across the street, just where Central began to slope sharply up toward Mid-Levels and ultimately the Peak, I spotted the blue and white metal sign on the side of the building. DUDDELL ST, it read, with a row of Chinese characters below.

Duddell Street was narrow and so steep that the sidewalks turned here and there into flights of stained concrete steps. I watched the street numbers carefully as I climbed and eventually found the building I was looking for almost at the end of the street, on the right just where it turned into a staircase that led up towards the old Governor's residence. It was an altogether unexceptional office building of no more than a dozen floors faced with yellow brick streaked with something black. An elderly Chinese man wearing a dirty undershirt and baggy gray trousers sat slumped on a folding metal chair next to the glass and metal entry door. He snorted and spat as I passed, but I didn't take it personally.

Inside the building the small lobby was dim and smelled faintly of urine. I examined the directory between the elevators and found a listing for the Asian Bank of Commerce on the ninth floor.

When I got out of the elevator, I found only three offices on the floor, and none of them looked much like a bank. One was a dentist's office, one seemed to be a sweatshop with an Indian tailor hovering hopefully just inside the open door, and the third was something called Hong Kong Directors Limited. When I spotted the large board at the end of the corridor with columns of small wooden signs hanging from brass hooks however, I realized that Hong Kong Directors had to be the place I was looking for after all.

Hong Kong Directors was obviously a corporate services office, one of dozens scattered around Hong Kong that catered to foreign companies too small or too unimportant to have local offices of their own, but who nevertheless needed an address and a formal place of business in Hong Kong for whatever reason. Corporate services companies existed all over the world, but they were most in demand in places like Hong Kong, Luxembourg, and the Cayman Islands where countless thousands of companies registered themselves as residents for the purpose of minimizing taxes or maintaining confidentiality while their real business was conducted elsewhere.

Companies being fronted by corporate services providers were often referred to as brass-plate companies since very little evidence of their existence could be found other than the brass plate a corporate services provider usually hung somewhere to identify itself as the registered address for each of its clients. Hong Kong Directors was probably operating in the modest end of the business. Its plates were wood.

I realized of course that my chances of finding out much about the ABC here were pretty slim. No corporate service company would give out any information about a company registered with it other than whatever local law required be made public, and in Hong Kong that wasn't much.

So, expecting very little I opened the door and went inside. Very little was exactly what I found.

The reception area was small. It appeared that Hong Kong Directors didn't receive very many people. Three folding metal chairs were lined up along the wall to the left and opposite them was a wooden desk piled high with stacks of paper. A young Chinese girl slumped at the desk, and along with all the indications of terminal sleeping sickness, she had badly permed hair, skin blotched with acne scars, and a dimple in her chin deep enough to hide Easter eggs. Perhaps she had a great personality, loved small children, and would make someone a wonderful wife, but I immediately doubted it. I got the feeling that her plainness was more than skin deep.

The girl ignored me as long as she possibly could, but I stood my ground and waited her out. Eventually she squinted up at me through a pair of glasses with lenses that looked like the bottoms of Coke bottles.

"You must wait," she said, and pointed to the stack of files closest to her on the desk.

"I only have one quick question."

"You must wait," she repeated emphatically, and started making small brushing movements with her right hand, the sort you would use to shoo a cat away.

I walked over to one of the straight chairs and sat down, folding my arms and fixing the girl with a stare that I hoped would be unsettling. Apparently it wasn't, as she took her time shuffling through the stack of files and never looked at me.

Once when she appeared puzzled she extracted a page from a folder and held it up to the light as if she was trying to see through it. Hoping she was about to glance my way again at least, I gave her my warmest smile and crinkled my eyes in a way that I hoped emphasized what an honest, open fellow I was, but I was wasting my time. She lowered the paper, returned it to the file without a glance at me, and went back to plowing slowly through the rest of the folders.

Eventually the girl ran out of other things to pretend she was doing and peered over at me.

"What you want?"

"I have a question about one of the companies registered with you, the Asian Bank of Commerce."

The girl looked puzzled, as if the request was a novel one, and made an odd noise.

"Whaaaa. . . ."

"I just need some general information about the company," I went on quickly, hoping for the best. "Who its directors are, where it's organized, that short of thing."

"No information," the girl immediately snapped and pulled another stack of files toward her.

"For Christ's sake," I muttered as I stood up and took a step toward her desk. "All I want to know is what's in the public filings. The company is licensed as a bank in Hong Kong and the registration information is public. I'm not asking you for the damned balance sheet."

The girl spun around in her swivel chair so hard that I thought she was about to corkscrew herself right through the floor. Reaching into a cabinet behind her she flipped through several piles of paper and then extracted a single sheet. She spun back around and wordlessly shoved it toward me.

I took the sheet and started to return to my chair to read it, but I needn't have bothered. There was nothing on it except the name Asian Bank of Commerce, the address of the building where I was, and one other sentence: "Contact Mr. Wang at Hong Kong Directors during business hours."

I turned back to the girl and tried my hard stare again.

"Is this all there is?"

"No information," she repeated without looking up.

"Is Mr. Wang here?"

"Not here."

"When will he be in?"

"Not here."

"Look, I'm not trying to be difficult, but. . . ."

The girl jerked up a telephone receiver, stabbed at a button, and began to bark something into the receiver in rapid-fire Cantonese, rotating her chair as she did until her back was to me.

I'd had enough. I dropped the piece of paper back onto the desk and left.

I stood out in the corridor for a moment wondering if I should have tried to push the girl a little rather than give up so easily. Maybe I could at least find a way to irritate her enough to force Mr. Wang to make an appearance. My eyes wandered over the rows of wooden plates hanging on the wall while I considered the possibilities, but then I noticed something that suddenly caused me to forget all about the dimple with ears.

Down near the bottom of the second column of plates, stuck among the generic names that sounded exactly like the empty corporate shells they were, was a company name I knew all too well from the Southeast Asian Investments board meeting that had just concluded — Cambodian Shrimp Farming Ltd.

That was quite a coincidence, I reflected. The same Hong Kong corporate services office that SAI had used to set up their shrimp farming deal in Cambodia was also fronting for the Asian Bank of Commerce. I couldn't offhand see what the significance of that odd happenstance might be, and no doubt several hundred other investment companies used Hong Kong Directors to form nominee vehicles for them, too, but still. . . .

"Ah, screw it," I murmured, burying the bones of the conspiracy theories that were rattling faintly in the back of my mind. It was just a coincidence. It had to be.

When I got back to the Mandarin, I stopped at the cigar shop in the lobby and bought a couple of boxes of Montecristos. I didn't really feel like going up to my room, so I went into the Captain's Bar and ordered a San Miguel draft. Since it was still early in the afternoon I had the place more or less to myself and I cracked one of the boxes and took out a cigar while I was waiting for my drink. The waiter noticed what I was doing and put a cutter and some matches on my table when he brought the draft. As I started into the ritual of lighting up, I started thinking about Barry Gale and the ABC again in spite of myself.

I couldn't quite make myself let it go. Until Sunday night I'd barely even heard of the Asian Bank of Commerce, but suddenly it was popping up everywhere. What the hell was going on here?

My personal policy for dealing with puzzling questions such as that had been honed over the years, but it was still pretty simple. There was always somebody who already knew what you needed to know, and if you asked him nicely, well . . . maybe he'd tell you. The only problem, of course, was how to find whoever it was who already knew what you needed to know.

That answer, too, was almost always the same. You had to know a guy.

I smoked the Montecristo and watched the tiny bubbles rising through the rich golden liquid in my glass.

I knew a guy.

The bubbles reached the surface, spread through the thin layer of white foam, and disappeared.

Even better, I knew a guy who was right here in Hong Kong.

I picked up the beer glass and compulsively straightened the cardboard coaster, then I knocked the column of ash off the tip of the Montecristo and straightened the ashtray as well for good measure.

The question was not how much the guy knew, but far more importantly than that, how much he'd tell me.

SIXTEEN

I WENT UP TO MY ROOM and stashed the cigars I'd bought. Then I pulled out my Filofax and got on the telephone.

My first call was to a direct line at the main office of the Hongkong and Shanghai Bank. The woman who answered told me that Archie Ward no longer worked there, but of course that had been more or less what I'd expected her to say. Brushing aside the woman's categorical insistence that she couldn't help me, I gave her my name and told her that I was at the Mandarin.

Archie Ward was a redheaded, pathologically profane Aussie I had first met about a year before. He told me then that he was a technology security specialist for HSBC and he had hired me to review a series of transactions that the bank thought had an unusually ripe odor to them. Large amounts of money had been moving back and forth between the bank's main office in Hong Kong and some of its branches in Europe and Asia, and the coordinated way the transfers had been occurring had caused Archie to suspect that the bank was unwittingly facilitating illicit transactions of some kind.

Archie told me he had tracked all of the transfers among HSBC's offices easily enough, but was having trouble understanding the movements of the funds once they had left the bank's own system. He said that was why he needed my help, but of course it wasn't. What he really wanted to know was exactly *who* was behind the transactions, and that was what he hadn't been able to find out on his own. I understood that, and he knew I understood that.

Archie never said exactly who had referred him to me, but he used the name of a Washington lawyer I had known for a long time. When I called the fellow he gave Archie the sort of vague endorsement that was the traditional indication of an official sanction of some sort, although the lawyer was unwilling to be more specific. The whole assignment had felt a little screwy, but I liked Archie, and I had no real doubt that he was one of the good guys, so I'd given him a hand without asking too many questions.

It hadn't taken me very long to figure out the corporate structure that HSBC's customer had been using to conceal the source of the funds. It was clever, but not that clever, and within a couple of weeks I knew that the instructions for the transfers had been coming from a Greek-born arms dealer who now operated out of Palm Beach, a ritzy beach resort about an hour north of Sydney. Somehow I got the impression Archie already knew that. He just hadn't been able to prove it until I did it for him.

Naturally the connection between what I had discovered was the source of the transfers and my friend Archie's colorful accent struck me as something less than pure coincidence. By that time it was pretty obvious to me that Archie wasn't actually employed by HSBC at all. To tell the truth, I had no doubt at all that Archie really worked for ASIS, the Australian intelligence service, but following accepted etiquette in such matters, I pretended not to know; and for his part, Archie pretended not to know that I knew.

Archie had called me a few times after that with some general questions about corporate finance, which happily I'd been able to answer for him. He always ended our conversations by saying that he owed me one. This seemed as good a time as any to collect on the accumulated debt.

I had a couple of other Hong Kong numbers in my diary for Archie, too, so I called those for good measure. One was a mobile that didn't even ring and had apparently been abandoned, but at the other number a woman's voice answered with a simple, "Yes?" I smiled at her Australian accent which was apparent even from the single word and asked for Archie. Before she could protest her ignorance I gave her my name, said I was at the Mandarin, and asked for Archie to call me there. Naturally she said she didn't know what I was talking about, so I thanked her and hung up.

One of the numbers must have worked, maybe all of them for what I knew, because about twenty minutes later the telephone in my room rang.

"You got your cell phone with you?" Archie spoke without preamble.

"I do."

"Then turn the fucking thing on, will you, mate?"

Before I even had a chance to give him the number, he hung up.

I seldom remembered to turn my cell phone on when I was out of Bangkok. Sometimes I didn't even bother to bring it. Inevitably when I did both some idiot would call me when I was in the toilet and then keep me on the phone for ten minutes professing his great amazement that I wasn't in Bangkok and how he'd never be able to tell from the wonderful connection we had.

I fished around in my briefcase until I found my phone, flipped it open, and pressed the power button. When it came on and located a Hong Kong network, I was relieved to see there was still enough left of the battery to last a while.

It was only a few seconds before it rang.

"Hello."

"Good on ya, mate. She'll be right now."

"I won't even bother to ask you how you got this number, Archie."

"Shit, mate. I wouldn't fucking tell you anyway."

"So. . . ." I hesitated a moment. "What's new?"

Archie started laughing so hard I thought he might hurt himself.

"*What's new?* Jack Shepherd, you are without a doubt the only bloke I've ever known who would have the nerve to ring me up and ask, 'What's new?' You Yank ratbags are too much. You really are."

"Just being friendly."

"Well, mate, I'm as busy as a one-legged bloke in an arse kicking contest, so let's have it. What's on your mind?"

"It's all probably just a lot of nothing, Archie, but something a little strange has come up and I thought you might be able to give me some background."

"Reckon I probably can if I want to. What's the subject?"

"The Asian Bank of Commerce. You ever heard of it?"

Then as suddenly as he had started laughing, Archie stopped.

"Bloody oath," he sighed. "What are you doing mixed up with those bodgie mongrels?"

"Well . . . it's a little hard to explain, but. . . ."

"Never mind. Can you meet me right now?"

"Yeah, I guess so. Sure."

"Then pay attention, Jacko. Do exactly what I tell you to do."

I paid attention, then following Archie's instructions I took the lift downstairs and left the Mandarin by the front entrance. I ducked down a short flight of stairs that was just on the other side of the hotel's service drive and walked through a wide, tiled pedestrian tunnel that passed under Connaught Road and emerged at the Star Ferry terminal.

The Star Ferry had been running back and forth across Victoria Harbour for over a century. The little green and white double-decked vessels crossed the harbor from the wharf on Hong Kong Island, docked at Tsim Sha Tsui at the tip of the Kowloon peninsula, and then traveled immediately back again, moving continuously along the same eight or ten minute route hundreds of times every day. All of the ferries were named for stars. There was the *Southern Star,* the

Morning Star, the *Twinkling Star,* and a dozen other stars, each bumping with practiced ease into its berth where a Chinese sailor in a blue uniform swung open an iron gate to allow boarding passengers to stream on even as disembarking passengers were still being funneled off in the opposite direction.

When the ferry was newly filled — and it happened very quickly, like everything else in Hong Kong — a loud bell rang, a large traffic signal hanging over the gate snapped first to yellow and then to red, and a sailor-suited man pushed the iron gate firmly shut, stemming if only for a moment the relentlessly advancing crowd. Of course there were always a last few stubborn stragglers determined to slip around the gate's closing edge and leap across to the deck of the ferry as the gangway was being hauled away, all that in spite of the fact that another green and white ferry would be slipping into the wharf almost as soon as the first one was clear and the whole process would begin again after only the slightest interruption. This was Hong Kong after all. Wasted time was wasted money.

By a few minutes after five I was standing in front of the Star Ferry terminal waiting for Archie. I glanced up at the big clock on the ferry building tower and contemplated my immediate future. The traffic to the airport would be horrible, and if I was going to make my flight to Bangkok, I probably had a half hour at the very most to get back to the hotel, grab my bag, and check out.

That looked pretty unlikely right then, and I realized that this unscheduled excursion would almost certainly cause me to be stuck in Hong Kong for another night. Anita was going to be less than thrilled about that. Actually, I was less than thrilled about that, too. I hadn't seen Anita since Monday, and particularly because things had been a little strained then as a result of my Sunday night rendezvous with Barry Gale, I was anxious to get home. Regardless, here I was waiting in front of the Star Ferry for Archie Ward, wasn't I? I began to polish the story I would be telling Anita a little later on the telephone.

The walkways of the ferry building were jammed with commuters on their way to Kowloon and the crowds shouldered past me as I shifted my weight from foot to foot. Finally I saw Archie coming from the direction of the Post Office building. He was easing through the throng in such a practiced way that there was hardly a ripple around him and I envied the evident deftness he had developed for living in a city as combative as Hong Kong.

Archie grinned as he eased up next to me and gave my shoulder a warm squeeze.

"G'day, mate. How you keeping?"

"I'm good, Archie."

"Still teaching in Bangkok?"

"Yeah, still teaching. You still with . . ."

I wasn't sure exactly how to put it, so I said the first thing that popped into my head.

". . . the bank?"

Archie chuckled.

"Nah. I've changed jobs."

He produced a pack of Marlboros from his shirt pocket and held them out to me. When I shook my head, he extracted one with his lips, lit it using a red Bic, and exhaled in a long, steady stream.

"Got no perks anymore, Jacko. No more promotions, no insurance, no pension. Just me, my shoeshine, and my smile."

"When did that happen?"

"A few months ago."

"Your idea?"

"Too bloody right. I'd been watching all those little ratfucks who used to be Mossad or Shin Bet quit and then use their contacts to make heaps in the arms or drug business. *Big* fucking bickies they were scoring, mate. And there was me without a brass razoo to me name."

The idea that my friend Archie had coolly set himself up in the business of dealing guns or smuggling drugs startled me, and my face must have shown it.

"No, Jacko, not me. I'm no drongo. I give all that crook shit the flick. But now a lot of your other blokes, they don't give a flying fuck. That mob's cunning as dunny rats and they make a few quid, I'll tell you. Problem is that a whole lot of those guys come a gutser. Most of them aren't around long enough to spend any of it."

"So what *are* you doing, Archie?"

He pulled at his cigarette, acting like he was thinking, maybe wondering if he ought to be saying what he was saying, but I knew better.

Archie Ward liked to play the cheery little Aussie larrikin who didn't really care about anything other than sinking a few tinnies with his mates down at the pub, but I seriously doubted he had ever uttered a word in his life that hadn't been carefully weighed in advance. Whatever he was about to tell me, Archie had decided there might be something in it for him somewhere.

"I'm completely independent now, Jacko. I sell my information to whoever I want, not just send it off to those arseholes back in Canberra who don't even kiss me after they give me a right rooting."

"What kind of information?"

"Ah, mate, you know. I've spent most of my life knocking around Asia. Everybody knows that I've got the good oil on just about everybody. Now I sell what I know to whoever offers me the best price. Sometimes it gets a little shonky, I got to admit, but bloody hell . . . the rest of the time it pays off like a busted pokie machine."

Archie paused and shifted his eyes around, sizing up the crowd. Finally he looked back at me and pointed to the ferry entrance.

"Let's go," he said. "Hanging around out here we stick out like a dog's balls."

SEVENTEEN

I FOLLOWED ARCHIE AS HE DROPPED some coins in a turnstile and we joined the river of humanity moving up the stairs and then down a ramp toward the ferry. Archie was in the lead, but when a loud bell started clattering and the green light flashed to yellow, the black iron gate at the bottom of the ramp began to close. The crowd surged forward, and I lost sight of him.

When the light snapped to red, a few people started to run as well as they could in the tight quarters. Bouncing on my toes to see over the crowd, I continued moving and I could tell that the gate was closing rapidly. I edged past an old woman who was carrying a stack of white food boxes from which drifted some pungent although unidentifiable smell, bounced off a very large and red-faced German tourist and, in the clear for a split second, took two fast side steps, twisted to my left and lunged through the last crack of open space as the gate clanged shut behind me. I trotted down the ramp and crossed the gangway just as the sailor began to haul on the rope that hoisted it away from the dock.

Archie was leaning on the rail, waiting for me, a half-smile flitting on his face.

"Still pretty good moves, least wise for an old guy," he said as I pushed in next to him.

"Is this all really necessary?" I asked.

"What?"

"The ferry ride. And by the way, where are we going?"

"Nowhere. We're just mucking around."

"Couldn't I have come to an office somewhere?"

"Nope."

I wasn't really as annoyed as I probably sounded. Riding the Star Ferry had always been one of my favorite things to do in Hong Kong anyway though I seldom took the time anymore. The ferry's engines throbbed and white water churned as we pushed away from the wharf with a slight shudder and began moving into the open water of the harbor.

"Friend of yours?" Archie asked.

"Who?"

"Over there, at the gate."

Archie gestured vaguely past me in the general direction of the wharf. The crowd had drifted back to wait for the next ferry, but there was a tall man who was still standing right up against the gate as if he was watching us go with some regret. He was wearing a dark raincoat and looked to be Chinese.

I shook my head.

"No. Don't know him."

"Didn't think you would."

Archie and I watched the man until the next ferry sliding into the berth blocked our view.

"Are saying this guy is following me, Archie?"

"Maybe. He was watching us before we got on. Not very professional. Either it's just a coincidence or you don't rate the real thing."

Before I could ask him what that was supposed to mean, Archie began walking toward the glass-enclosed cabin that walled off the fifty or so seats in the front of the ferry.

"Let's all go up here. We may have a lot to talk about."

Instead of sitting, Archie stood right in the bow, facing down the length of the ferry with his back to the stunning panorama of

Victoria Harbour. I wasn't sure what else to do, so I stood next to him. Over the heads of the crowd we watched the next ferry maneuvering into position at the wharf even while we were still pulling away.

My eyes sought out and eventually found the man in the dark raincoat again. He was still standing at the gate, both hands hooked through the bars, and still looking unhappy. Surely Archie's imagination was on overtime, I told myself.

"Look, Archie. . . ."

He waved me into silence.

"Let's give it a minute, huh, mate?"

I leaned back and folded my arms. While I waited for Archie to decide he was ready to talk, I passed the time studying the people who were packed into the ferry filling virtually every seat as well as standing along the rails. It had always seemed to me that every group of passengers on a Star Ferry was almost like an exhibition of Hong Kong life — a tableau in one of those amusement parks that were supposed to be educational for kids but usually ended up just being dull — and this bunch certainly fit the pattern.

A very old man sat in the row directly in front of us wearing a baggy, padded jacket and horn-rimmed glasses. He was holding a heavy-looking book close to his face that he was reading with rapt concentration. When I first started coming to Hong Kong, I had imagined that people like this man must be reading texts on Confucian ethics or Buddhist philosophy, but now I realized the man's book was most likely to be something about programming a PC to achieve quick profits from daily commodity price fluctuations. So much for the mysterious Orient. Welcome to the new China.

Just at the back of the cabin sat a bunch of school children carrying book bags and badminton rackets, looking very serious and uniform in green blazers still crisp at the end of their school day. Next to them two perspiring European tourists compared video cameras and just at the rail sat a pallid young couple, undoubtedly English and probably recently arrived and suffering badly from the humidity. Beyond them, out on the main deck beyond the enclosed cabin, the less distinguishable mass of the Chinese population hovered — mostly young, not at all sweaty, and everyone it seemed either unfailingly serious of expression or lost in dreams that I knew I could never fathom.

"Okay, I'm listening, Jacko."

The ferry had stabilized itself for the short crossing and Archie tilted his head slightly toward me while he continued scanning the crowd.

I told Archie most of what I knew about the Asian Bank of Commerce, but I adjusted the story on the fly so that I could talk around the resurrection of Barry Gale rather than bring all that up right away. Keep them guessing a little. That was my motto.

Archie remained expressionless throughout my tale, but the moment I stopped talking, he grinned at me.

"What is it you're not telling me?"

I sighed.

"I thought I was better than that."

"You're pretty good. But it's still London to a brick you wouldn't tell me the whole thing the first time."

"Well. . . ."

"Just lay out what you know, Jacko. Give me everything and I'll let you have a mate's rate on some good advice."

Figuring I had very little to lose, I told Archie the story again, this time including the part about the second coming of Barry Gale. By the time I'd finished, the ferry was bumping against the pier in Kowloon and the passengers were beginning to move toward the gangway. I started to join them, but Archie just shook his head and offered a little downward flutter of his left hand in a gesture that apparently meant we were to continue our voyage.

"Are we just going ride back and forth on this damned thing all night?" I asked.

Archie gave no sign that he had heard me and stood silently as once again the ferry filled with passengers and shoved off to begin its trip back across the harbor. I looked at the ferry that had been behind us and was now approaching our spot on the wharf and wondered if the man in the dark raincoat was vainly trailing in our wake, or if he was still somewhere back on the Central side waiting for us.

It wasn't until we had wallowed out into the harbor again that Archie finally spoke.

"Are you certain this man you met was really Gale?"

"No doubt at all."

Archie pursed his lips and made a little spitting sound.

"Well . . . *Christ,* mate."

The ferry slid into a trough left by a passing ship and floundered up the other side, forcing us to adjust our balance and lean into the roll of the ship.

"And he said he'd taken over the Asian Bank of Commerce using Russian mob money?"

"That's what he said."

"Did you believe him?"

"I can't imagine why anyone would lie about a thing like that."

"Yeah, but did you *believe* him?"

I tried to look as credible as possible, even though I wasn't entirely certain what constituted a look of credibility while riding a ferry back and forth across Victoria Harbour.

"He was scared to death, Archie."

"Maybe it wasn't Russian mobsters he was scared of."

"Then who?"

"The way I hear it, it wasn't the Russian mob behind the Asian Bank of Commerce. It was somebody . . . bigger."

It was the moment, a moment like the one when the airplane lifts slowly from the runway and seems just to hang there clawing at the air for lift, pulling against the overwhelming inevitability of gravity. The next few seconds would tell the story. The damned thing would either start to fly like a son of a gun, or it would fall back in a heap and explode right there in front of God and everybody. It would be one or the other. And it would be right now.

"Russian mobsters make for sexy stories, but the truth is that most of them are just jackasses. When it comes to these huge international conspiracies they always get blamed for, well . . . they'd be well and truly buggered, Jacko. Reckon they'd have Buckley's chance of making any of them work."

I kept quiet. Prodding Archie would get me nowhere. Either he was going to tell me what he knew, no doubt for reasons of his own that I was unlikely to understand, or he wasn't.

"It was Chinese money, Jacko."

"You mean the triads?" I asked.

"No, nothing like that."

"Then . . . what?"

Archie's head bobbed around on his shoulders as if it had become momentarily detached.

"Military?" I asked. "Government?"

"Not officially."

"You mean it was bribe money."

"Yeah, something like that."

I thought back to my midnight walk and talk in Bangkok with Barry Gale.

"If that's true, Archie, Barry Gale doesn't know it."

"So what?"

"But Barry Gale was *running* the ABC. If he didn't know it, how could it be true?"

Archie rolled his eyes and looked away.

"I think you've been in Asia too long for your own good, partner. Everything that happens out here looks like some huge conspiracy to you."

"Everything that happens out here *is* some huge conspiracy, Jacko."

The wharf in Central was coming up fast. I looked over what I could see of the walkways around it, but there was no sign of our friend in the dark coat. Archie's imagination had apparently gotten a little carried away about that. Maybe his tale of Chinese money being behind the ABC fell into the same category.

"Who was this bribe money supposed to be for?"

"The usual suspects. A bunch of generals, a couple of ministers. It even went as high as the Politburo, I hear."

"Who was paying? And what for?"

Archie didn't seem to notice I had asked him anything. He pulled out his pack of Marlboros again, then changed his mind and pushed them back into his shirt pocket.

The ferry's engines were churning into reverse as the pilot edged up to the wharf. A sailor stood by the gangway with the rope that would lower it wrapped around both his hands and a few people in the crowd were already beginning to rise and shuffle toward the exit.

"This is the end of the trip, Jacko." Archie's voice was flat. "That's all I'm giving you. We're square now."

"Just one more thing, Archie."

He shifted his eyes to mine and held my gaze.

"Did these Chinese generals and politicians get their money before the ABC collapsed?"

The ferry bumped the pilings and we stumbled slightly, but held our balance. Almost immediately I heard the sound of winches squealing followed by the crash of the metal gangway as it hit the concrete pier. The crowd surged forward and Archie turned away and began moving along everyone else, but I stuck to him as if we had been handcuffed together. When he finally spoke his voice was so low I could barely pick out the words through the rumble of shuffling feet and the bursts of Cantonese crashing around us like mortar shells.

"That's the funny part," he said without looking at me. "All that dosh disappeared without a trace."

That left only one more question to ask, so I asked it.

"Do you know where the money went?"

Archie turned his head slightly and shifted his eyes onto mine.

"You know how difficult it is to see anything when you look straight at it in the dark, Jacko? The harder you look, the harder it is to see. They tell me to see something clearly when the light's bad that you ought look at it out of the corner of your eye, like soldiers do when they're fighting at night."

"What in the hell are you talking about, Archie?"

Archie watched me as we shuffled forward with the crowd toward the gangway. He looked as if he was waiting for me to say something else, but I couldn't imagine what it was, and when I didn't, he slipped back into the rhythms of his Australian vernacular.

"Those Chinese blokes are as mean as cat's piss when it comes to money, you know. I figure they're about to spit the dummy, and I reckon that whoever did them is rooted. That's what I reckon."

"Rooted?"

"Fucked, Jacko. When they find whoever the poor wanker is who's got their bickies, it's a dead cert he'll be arse over tit before he knows what hit 'im."

Archie grinned at me then for second and, entirely unexpectedly, he winked.

"I just hope it wasn't you, matie."

And then he took three quick strides over the gangway and disappeared into the crowd as completely as if he'd never been there at all.

EIGHTEEN

When I'd finally gotten back to Bangkok on Friday morning Anita had pouted briefly so that her displeasure at the extra night I'd spent in Hong Kong would be officially noted. Nevertheless harmony had been fully restored by evening, and when we left for the Polo Club the night ahead was looking pretty promising.

Winter in Bangkok is a season that is usually unimpressed by the calendar, and with luck, our string of temperate days and chilly nights sometimes doesn't run out until March. This year we had been very lucky. The cool breezes were still drifting south from China, and the sweet, balmy air remained ripe with benevolence.

I had the Volvo's top down as we drove south on Soi Langsuan and Anita seemed besotted by the softness of the night. Her head was tilted back against the headrest and her eyes were closed. She was wearing a straight black dress that bared her shoulders, and I could hardly force myself to watch the road. My eyes kept drifting over every time the traffic thinned and I was on my third or fourth fix before I realized that she had opened her eyes and was looking straight back at me.

"What?" I asked.

"Nothing."

Not nothing. That much I was pretty sure of.

"Okay." She leaned over, knitted her hands together over my shoulder and rested her chin on them. "I like you in a tux, handsome, but remind me again why we're on our way to a stuffy club wearing these costumes."

"The Kingdom of Thailand has a new minister of finance and we are honoring him."

"We?"

"Well . . . Citibank and Standard Chartered Bank are honoring him. You and I are mostly along for the ride."

"And exactly why are they honoring him? Has he done something good?"

"Not yet. But we live in hope."

A red and cream bus suddenly changed lanes, cutting right in front of us. It was so jammed with people that it looked as if some of them were about to squirt out through the windows. I braked hard and muttered a curse, but Anita didn't seem to notice.

"Do we have any role in all this honoring?"

"Not really. I imagine they invited me because they thought I'd bring you. We're more or less decoration."

"Ah . . . decoration. I do so love being decoration."

Anita turned her head away and closed her eyes again.

"I'd bet my last baht you've got something else on your mind, Jack. Something that you haven't told me yet."

"Is it that obvious?"

"It is to me."

I hadn't said anything to Anita about Barry Gale's appeal to me to find the ABC's missing money and I had also of course omitted mentioning Jello's suspicions about Dollar as well. I had already decided that telling Anita either story would accomplish nothing other than to make her feel uneasy, yet somehow right now everything seemed different.

There was something about driving through the moist Bangkok night that seemed to transform the dime-novel tales Barry and Jello had spun me into narratives with an almost operatic quality to them, and impulsively I started recounting both stories to Anita in spite of my earlier resolution not to.

I tried to stick strictly to what I actually knew, leaving out Archie Ward and Hong Kong Directors because those were only things that I *thought* I knew, and it wasn't all that much so it didn't take all that long. I finished just as we got to the narrow *soi* that led to the Polo Club.

I slowed at the gate as a uniformed guard saluted and pushed aside his little red-and-white wheeled barrier, but Anita didn't speak again until I had pulled into an empty parking slot beneath a tall gum tree and shut off the engine.

"My God, Jack. What have you gotten yourself into?"

"I'm not into anything, Anita. I have absolutely no intention of being involved in any way with Barry Gale."

"But you're already involved with Dollar, and if he's . . ."

"Jello's wrong about that. Dollar's as straight as anybody I've ever known."

"I thought you told me that Jello knew everything that was worth knowing about what happened in Bangkok."

"He does, usually. But this time he's got it wrong," I repeated doggedly. "I know Dollar Dunne, and there's no way in hell he'd launder money for drug dealers. Absolutely no way."

Anita was still shaking her head as I walked around and opened her door, but she didn't say anything else. I pushed the Volvo's remote locking button and the answering chirp echoed across the big parking lot. We walked under the trees toward the club's entry in silence other than for the clicking sound of Anita's heels against the gray stone that paved the lot.

Just as we started up the short flight of brown brick steps, Anita looped her left arm through my right and squeezed my shoulder with her free hand.

"Hey, I'm just a painter. What do I know about stuff like this?"

I always figured she knew plenty.

"I'm sure you understand what you're doing, Jack. You always do."

I smiled and rubbed my right hand gently over her back. I hoped to hell she was right.

The Polo Club was the *nouveau* offshoot of the Royal Bangkok Sports Club — a notoriously exclusive, mid-city club famed for its decades-long waiting list, crummy golf course, and membership roster of old Thais who didn't much like foreigners. It was less than a half-mile away from its bigger brother in distance, but it was at least a century removed in attitude.

The main building was pleasant, although modest, and could have passed for a minor country club in a middle-class Dallas suburb. It was a low-slung, rambling structure of brown brick, set off with wooden trim and surrounded by lush tropical landscaping. Dark-tiled corridors — each with a peaked roof covered in cedar-shakes and open on the sides — linked the main building with the half-dozen or so other structures in the complex. There was a huge swimming pool, a half-dozen hard-surfaced tennis courts, several air-conditioned squash courts, and even a lawn bowling green so perfectly tended that you could almost imagine a corps of local gardeners down on their knees working it over with tweezers and eyebrow clippers. The Polo Club even sported a modest equestrian trail and a handful of horses, probably so the name of the place would make some kind of sense. Occupying as it did a prime block of real estate in the very heart of Central Bangkok, the Polo Club always appeared to me to rise from the city's haze like some sort of suburban mirage.

The club was occasionally used for private parties and tonight Citibank and Standard Chartered had no doubt selected it in order to make the biggest possible splash with their reception for the new minister of finance. After all, the new minister was an Oxford graduate who had done a brief turn at Harvard Business School. Even better, he was reported to like foreigners well enough, and by extension everyone hoped, foreign banks. He was the kind of Thai many other Thais referred to among themselves, at least when they were certain their voices weren't carrying too far, as a Brown Brit.

Ministers of finance came and went fairly rapidly in Thailand, and the next time around the foreign banks might not be so lucky. They were more likely to get a local politician from Ubon Ratchathani instead, someone who hadn't been able to stand foreigners since his daughter ran off to Brisbane and married a shoe salesman. That was why most of the foreign banks figured they'd better grab the chance to kiss this minister's butt while it was still around to be kissed.

As we mounted the steps a short gray-haired man in a dark suit stepped forward and pressed his hands together in a *wai,* the graceful Thai gesture of greeting that was nuanced in ways foreigners were helpless to unravel. I returned the *wai* in my normal clunky fashion and then offered my hand, too, just to make sure I was touching all of the cultural bases.

"Khun Teuk, may I introduce. . . ."

"Completely unnecessary, Jack." Teuk beamed like a man who had just won the lottery. "Everyone in Bangkok knows Anita."

"You are very generous, Khun Teuk." Anita tilted her head gracefully to one side and *waied.* She did it a lot better than I did, and Teuk beamed again.

"Please, this way." Teuk pointed up the walkway toward the gardens that flanked the swimming pool. "It was such a nice night that we decided to move everything outside."

"I wondered where everyone was."

"Well . . . the guest list is smaller than usual. Not the normal business of inviting every hanger-on in town this time. And almost everyone came early for some reason." He giggled slightly, a nervous high-pitched whinnying sound. "Don't know what Bangkok is coming to. People showing up on time? Next it's going to be locusts." He whinnied again. "Please, please. Go right on down to the gardens."

Anita and I were a dozen paces along the walkway when she leaned slightly toward me.

"Who the hell was that?" she stage-whispered without turning her head.

"A guy from Citibank. I'm not really sure what he does."

"So these are the kind of people you hang around with when I'm away, huh?"

I couldn't think of any answer to that, but a waiter with a tray of drinks intercepted us at just that moment and bailed me out. We each selected a Campari and soda, and then we stepped down off the walkway into the gardens and looked around.

A luxuriant, emerald-green lawn bordered with mango, oak, and gum trees stretched fifty yards or more from where we stood to the polo field on the south. To the east a thick grove of tall palms protected the deep lawn from the intrusion of the city. The trees were hung with white fairy lights, and wicker tables and chairs were set up under them in small groupings. Formally dressed people mingled on the lawn, while a string quartet played Mozart on a platform almost hidden under a bank of white orchids. It was a study in jade and auburn sprinkled with black and white.

"Jack!"

I heard the voice and looked around.

"Over here, Jack!"

A hand was flapping at us from a group of men standing near the center of the lawn so I took Anita's elbow and we started over. About halfway there the crowd parted and I saw that the hand belonged to a government official I saw around town occasionally.

Anita went back into her stage whisper.

"Do I know him?"

"I don't think so."

I kept my eyes on the group and tried to answer Anita without moving my lips.

"His name's Tammarat something, but everybody calls him Tommy."

"Another Citibank guy?"

"Nope. Officially he's a deputy to the spokesman for the Ministry of Foreign Affairs. But if you don't already know that he's really something or another at the NIA, he'll be happy to drop hints until you get the idea."

"NIA?"

"National Intelligence Agency."

Anita glanced over to see if I was joking.

"You mean he's a spy?"

"Yeah. Something like that, I guess."

"A Thai spy?" Anita was beginning to giggle. "Who does he spy on? Laos?"

"Jack, Jack!" Tommy rushed toward us before I could think what to say to that and clasped my right hand with both of his, like a politician working the crowd. "And this must be the famous Anita."

Anita couldn't hold back any longer. She burst out laughing, and Tommy's manner changed abruptly. His eyes went flat, examining first her and then me.

I improvised.

"There was this joke I heard yesterday in Hong Kong, Tommy, and I told it to Anita while we were walking in. I think she just got it."

"Ah. . . ." Tommy gave me a knowing look. "That would be why you're so late tonight. Telling funny jokes is very time-consuming."

"Waiting for Anita to get dressed is very time-consuming."

I felt Anita's hand brush my elbow.

"Jack, I see Laura over there. Would you excuse me?"

She favored Tommy with her most charming smile, *waied,* and slipped away. I didn't know anyone in Bangkok named Laura, of course, and I suspected that neither did Anita.

Tommy watched silently until Anita was well away from us and then he placed his hand in the small of my back and nudged me in the direction of the men he had been talking with before we arrived.

"Come over here a minute, Jack. I want you to meet some people."

Tommy made the usual introductions all around, and as usual for me, I missed almost everyone's names Actually, it wasn't until he got to the last man in the group that anything stuck.

"Jack, you know Manny Marcus, don't you?"

"Q Bar?" I asked as we shook hands, and the man nodded without saying anything.

It was the way Mango Manny had his double-breasted jacket buttoned over his paunch that contributed most to his gangster image. The yellow tie, black shirt, and outrageous diamond ring helped, too, of course, but the wide lapels of his jacket buckling outward from the point at which the buttons tugged at the fabric was what really did it. His thinning hair, unnaturally black, was slicked back against his skull and it glinted and glistened like he was still a Brylcreem man. Although it was nighttime, he wore gold Cartier sunglasses with very dark lenses. I knew the shades were Cartier because they said so on both earpieces.

"Some mutual friends of ours recently suggested I ought to call you."

I ventured the comment carefully, not sure how much I should say, but not wanting to pretend I'd never heard of Manny either.

Manny took off his Cartiers, folded them carefully, and pushed them into his breast pocket.

"Too bad you didn't."

"I didn't see any reason to bother you."

Manny let his eyes linger on mine and eventually he came up with a facial expression that was a rough approximation of a smile. I noticed that his teeth were even and white, but I also noticed that his eyes didn't match his smile.

"No, you probably wouldn't have."

While I was still trying to work out what that was supposed to mean, I felt Tommy's hand on my back again.

"Jack, I need to talk to you about a little business matter without bothering our friends here."

He made his mumbled apologies to the group and then nudged me away out of their earshot, Tommy draped one arm over my shoulders and lowered his voice.

"Do you know where the squash courts are?"

The question caught me flat-footed and I didn't answer right away.

"The squash courts, Jack. Are you listening to me?"

"I heard you. Why are you asking me about squash courts?"

Tommy looked at me levelly.

"They're out near the main entrance. Just on the other side of. . . ."

"I know where they are."

"Then why didn't you say so?"

"Even by your standards of *non sequitur,* Tommy, I thought you were kidding."

"This is no time for jokes, Jack. You are walking in deep shit, my friend and I'm trying to help you out."

He paused, but I stayed poker faced. What the hell was he talking about?

"I want you to go to the squash courts at exactly ten and wait there. Someone wants to talk to you."

"Who. . . ?"

"Just be there, Jack," Tommy interrupted. "And try to be discreet about it, would you?"

Then he shoved his hands deep into his pockets and walked away from me without a backward glance.

It was already a quarter to ten and I spent the next few minutes wondering what I was going to do. Once or twice I caught a glimpse of Anita across the garden, but I got a distinct impression she was keeping her distance. I wasn't sure I blamed her. So far the cast of characters she had encountered in my company tonight made that look like a smart choice.

An unnaturally thin German girl dressed all in arty black cornered me for a few moments against the rose bushes and gushed on about a television documentary she was making concerning female homosexuality among the hill tribes. Then two English stockbrokers I knew slightly spent a few minutes trying to convince me that the Thai stock market was just about to take off. It all added up to standard Thai cocktail party chatter. Nothing but sex and money.

At five minutes to ten I looked around for Tommy, but he was nowhere to be seen. Helpless to resist the intrigue, I abandoned my empty glass on a nearby table and headed toward the club's front entry. Anyone who saw me would probably assume I was going to the toilet, I thought, but instead of turning left, I turned right past the bowling green and entered the door to the squash courts.

Only a single dim light was burning, so I flipped on the big overheads and looked around. All three courts were empty of course, as were the wooden bleachers that rose a half-dozen tiers behind each of them. Feeling a little silly I sat down in the first row behind the court furthest from the door and waited. The bright lights glared off the white walls, throwing my reflection into high relief on the glass back wall of the courts. I thought I looked a little fuzzy, but that hardly surprised me.

After a short while the door opened and a young, well-dressed man stepped inside, quickly closing the door behind him. He was tall for a Thai and lanky, and he moved with a confidence that made him look a little dangerous. I had never seen him before, I was sure of that, and the expression on his face suggested that he had probably never seen me before either.

"You Khun Jay?"

The man's voice was polite, but he seemed a little twitchy. He had such a thick accent that I saw it was going to be heavy-going understanding whatever it was that he wanted to tell me.

"Jack. It's Jack Shepherd."

"Arai na krap?" What?

"I said I'm Jack Shepherd. Not Jay Shepherd."

There was a hint of puzzlement in the man's nod.

"Krap. You wait please."

The man stepped back outside, but just as I was standing up to follow him, the minister of finance walked in.

"Mr. Shepherd." He nodded pleasantly. "Sit down. Please."

I sat down again.

The minister stood in the doorway studying me for a moment, a half-smile on his face, and then he walked over and sat a few feet away on the same bleacher where I was. He settled himself comfortably, crossing his legs at the knee, and then he leaned forward slightly and laced his fingers together, resting his hands in his lap.

He was an average-sized man, probably in his sixties. His patent leather shoes gleamed even in the low light and he wore his tuxedo like a man who was accustomed to wearing tuxedos. He had a full head of silver-gray hair, hard black eyes, heavy-rimmed glasses, and the patient air of a traveler temporarily forced to camp out with barbarians.

"It is a very dull party, isn't it, Mr. Shepherd?"

"It was until about thirty seconds ago."

The minister chuckled appreciatively, then he reached into the inside pocket of his jacket and extracted a black leather Dunhill cigar case. Pulling off the top he held it out to me and I saw the brown and white bands even before he spoke.

"Cigar, Jack? Montecristos are your brand, aren't they?"

I glanced from the cigars to his face, but he was expressionless.

"No? Well . . . pity . . . you must have picked up all you needed when you were in Hong Kong."

The minister selected a cigar for himself, closed the case, and returned it to his jacket. Then he dipped into a side pocket and removed a cutter and a box of matches. He inspected the Montecristo, clipped the end, and lit it. He took his time about doing it, I noticed.

"I think I'm getting the message here, Minister," I said quietly as he drew on his cigar.

"No, Mr. Shepherd. We haven't got to the message yet. All I've done is to convey that we know a great deal about what everyone around here is doing. Including you."

"Who's we?"

The minister took another puff on his Montecristo, then resumed, ignoring my question.

"We know, for example, that you made some inquiries in Hong Kong concerning the Asian Bank of Commerce. Why were you pursuing that particular line of inquiry up there, Mr. Shepherd?"

"I thought you already knew what everyone around here was doing. Including me."

The minister laughed, apparently genuinely.

"We do, Mr. Shepherd. But sometimes we have a little trouble understanding why they do it."

I nodded, but I didn't say anything.

"Actually, Mr. Shepherd, I don't suppose it matters. My message to you tonight is the same regardless of your motives."

The minister took another puff on his Montecristo, but he kept his eyes locked on mine.

"You must stop asking questions about the ABC."

"And why is that, sir?"

"You might embarrass someone, Mr. Shepherd. If names happen to come up in the course of your inquiries — names of people who are, let us say, politically prominent and might have had some small, perhaps even accidental involvement with the ABC — you might cause them to lose face. You know Asia well, I am told. Surely you must know how bad a thing it is to lose face."

"Accidental involvement? I don't understand."

The bleachers squeaked as the minister shifted his weight.

"You Americans have become obsessed with what you insist on calling transparency in government, Mr. Shepherd. But those of us who actually do the work of governing understand that we must occasionally engage in undertakings that we would not particularly like to become public. Frequently those activities involve financial arrangements, and naturally those arrangements are generally routed through helpful banks like the ABC. It's just the way things get done in Asia, Mr. Shepherd. It has always been so, and it *will* always be so."

"Just for the sake of conversation, Minister, what do you suppose might happen if some of these arrangements you're talking about looked as if they might become public?"

"Oh, I don't really know, Mr. Shepherd."

The minister waved his Montecristo in a little zigzag motion.

"But we have a saying here in Thailand that you might do well to remember: When the elephants move, the grass is trampled."

The minister slowly stood, rolling his shoulders and stretching slightly.

"I always thought that was an African expression," I said, watching him.

His eyes flickered for a moment, met mine, and then looked away. With his left hand in the front pocket of his jacket and his head tilted down, he walked away from me toward the door. When he reached it, he took his hand out of his pocket, put it on the knob, and looked back over his shoulder.

"Actually, Jack, I think it's an old Icelandic proverb."

Then he pushed through the door and was gone.

NINETEEN

I DIDN'T SLEEP VERY WELL THAT NIGHT and predictably woke up too early on Saturday morning. I lay quietly for a while, one hand resting lightly on the smooth skin of Anita's thigh, replaying in my mind the way the feel of her body under my hands the night before had taken me outside myself for a while. Anita was still sleeping deeply and eventually I slipped quietly out of bed and padded into the kitchen to make some coffee.

My meeting with Dollar was looming only a few hours away and that raised a serious problem for me, so I pushed Barry Gale and the ABC into an unused corner of my mind while I dumped coffee into the filter and filled the coffeemaker with water. Before I saw Dollar I had a big decision to make. I had to make up my mind whether I was going to tell him about my conversation with Jello and the suspicions he had voiced concerning what Dollar and Howard might be doing together, or if I was just going to let the whole thing slide.

When the coffee started dripping I went back to the bedroom and pulled on some running shorts and a T-shirt and laced up my Nikes. Then after draining two mugs while flipping halfheartedly through the *Post* I drove over to Lumpini Park in the mood to do some serious thinking.

I parked the Volvo on Soi Sarasin just in front of a strip of bars shuttered tightly against the morning but still smelling vaguely of cigarettes and spilled beer. It was the beginning of another cool day, and while I did a few haphazard stretches leaning against the car for balance, I wondered vaguely if some kind of cosmic invoice for our pleasant weather was going to be presented to the city later in the year. If it ever arrived, I figured it would be a doozy.

Crossing the street and threading my way among the food venders who were already half blocking the park's north gate, I broke into a lope on the broad walkway just inside. Beyond the long curve of concrete in front of me and off through a gap in a grove of banyan trees, I could see patches of early morning sunlight glistening on the lake. A breeze rattled the fronds of the spindly palm trees that lined the walkway and they beat together with a rhythm like a marimba band gone mad.

I breathed steadily, adjusted my stride, and paced myself for a longer run than usual since I had a good deal to think about. It wasn't long before I reached the edge of the lake and I exchanged the hard surface of the concrete walkway for its grassy banks. Then I was ready for some somber pondering.

I knew I either had to tell Dollar immediately what Jello had said to me or I could never tell him at all. If I was going to bring it up, *ever,* I had to do it today. If I hesitated and then said something about it later, Dollar would read my hesitation as having at least half-believed Jello in the first place — and of course, he would be right.

My first instinct was to keep quiet. I didn't have the faintest idea where Jello's information had come from in spite of the fact that I had never known him to be careless about his sources. The more important consideration, it seemed to me, was that I had never seen anything myself that would suggest that either Howard or Dollar was involved in money laundering, and I had done a fair amount of work with Dollar and knew him pretty well. I just couldn't imagine myself sitting in his office and suddenly blurting out something like, "Oh, by the way, I hear you and Howard might be laundering money for a bunch of Burmese opium producers. Is that true?"

If on the other hand Dollar was about to ask me to do some more work for Howard — and the way Howard's name had been popping out every time Dollar opened his mouth recently that seemed at least a possibility — I didn't see how I could avoid raising the subject. Howard the Roach as the money-laundering front man for a crew of brutal international drug smugglers was hard for me to swallow, but then I didn't really know Howard all that well. I wasn't in the same position with him that I was in with Dollar and I could hardly claim I had an unconditional conviction that it was impossible for Howard to be involved in the drug business.

Jello had put me in a real bind. If what he said turned out to be true, and if I somehow ended up helping Howard do his wash no matter how inadvertent my participation might be, he would be able to point out that I had done it in spite of being on notice that something was up. That would, I readily recognized, put me a long way up my own personal shit cheek, and I would unquestionably be lacking the proverbial paddle.

Jello had known exactly what he was doing before we had our conversation at Anna's. That had been the point of the whole exercise, of course. I could see that now.

Although I doubted he knew about my meeting this morning with Dollar or about any of the frequent appearances Howard had been making in our conversations recently, still he would no doubt have surmised that Dollar would eventually ask me to help out with Howard's work again — and then I'd have no choice but to ask Dollar if there was anything behind the story Jello had told me. Jello had boxed me in with consummate skill. I had to give him that. I couldn't really see any path out of the trap he'd built except the one he obviously wanted me to take.

I was a little earlier than usual and I noticed as I circled the south side of the lake that Lumpini seemed a lot less crowded than it normally was. That was something of a mixed blessing. Actually, to be completely honest, it was a big disappointment.

One of the paramount attractions of running in Lumpini was that the usual pack of joggers included a significant throng of tanned and athletic-looking women pushing gracefully along with firm, confident strides. Every time I wondered if age might be creeping up on me and whether the time might have arrived for me to cut back a little on my distance, I would find some absolutely perfect little tail to tuck in behind and everything would somehow hang together for one more day. Running just behind a pair of tiny shorts that barely covered taunting buttocks, reveling in the sight of light brown, exquisitely turned legs gliding effortlessly around the park, unfailingly took me straight back to the stamina of my youth.

This morning however it looked like I might have to make it around on my own. The only other runners I could see as I looped around the lake were two local men pumping doggedly along without much enthusiasm. I passed them easily and a little later when I crossed a narrow metal bridge over a tiny sliver of water, I glanced back to see how the two were doing. It surprised me to see that they appeared to have disappeared altogether.

I was still wondering where they could have gone when a woman suddenly appeared from a stand of banyan trees near the edge of the lake and fell smoothly into stride right next to me. When I glanced over, I did a long, slow take.

It was the same woman who had been with Barry Gale at the Foodland.

She was wearing black shorts, a white halter-top, and a black baseball cap that said OAKLAND RAIDERS above the light gray bill. She ran easily, gracefully, her feet springing off the grass as if they were touching down on hot coals. She neither turned her head toward me nor spoke.

Other than describing her as Asian in a general way, I still couldn't put a specific place of origin to her features. The bone structure was too fine — high, wide cheekbones and a rounded European-looking nose — and now that I studied her closely, I could see that none of the separate parts of her face really looked Asian at all, except perhaps for the slightly tilted, deep brown eyes.

Running shoulder to shoulder as we were, I could see that she was actually a little taller than I was, and since I was an even six feet, that made her pretty tall for a woman. She was slim, but with distinct muscle definition, and she looked strong. Her complexion was the color of cinnamon, although her arms and legs were darker, burnished by strong sun to the color of *café au lait,* and her smooth skin glistened in the morning light as if it had been polished. She had pulled her shiny black hair back into a ponytail and in scale with the rest of her it was long, at least two feet long, and it rotated behind her head as she ran like a little propeller that was driving her forward.

"I was born in Hong Kong, Mr. Shepherd."

The woman's eyes stayed forward when she spoke.

"My mother was Chinese, but my father was American. He could never manage the tones in Cantonese, so we always spoke English at home."

She had said nothing at all when I met Barry at the Foodland, and hearing her speak now made me think back again to the voice that had left the message on my answering machine. Her accent was half British and half American, and her diction and phrasing were those of someone well born or well educated.

"Should I tell you the answer to the other question that everyone eventually gets around to asking?"

"Sure."

"It's, 'No, both of my parents were rather short actually.' "

I chuckled appropriately and waited for her to go on, but she fell silent again. We ran on like that for a while, not speaking, the rhythmic slapping of our shoes against the grass the only sound marking our progress.

Eventually my curiosity overcame me and I wiped the sweat from my face on the sleeve of my T-shirt.

"I gather this isn't just a coincidence."

She let a dozen strides go by.

"I thought this might be the best way for me to talk to you without attracting attention."

Off to our right, three boys who couldn't have been more than ten were practicing martial arts moves under the watchful eyes of an old man sitting on a folding stool, a straw hat pulled low over his eyes. Each boy was carefully turned out in a white robe with a belt tied around his waist, and they all stood facing the old man in a neat row, concentrating with remarkable intensity for such small boys.

"Then I figure you've got about nine minutes to say whatever it is you want to say."

I could feel raggedness creeping into my breathing.

"After five miles I generally fall over, and that lamppost we just passed was my four-mile mark."

One of the boys flung himself into the air and executed what looked to me to be a pretty nifty spinning kick, and as he did, he loosed an ear-splitting shout that caused my companion to swivel her head sharply toward him.

"Look, lady, if Barry thought sending you around would intimidate me somehow, you can tell him he doesn't remember me very well."

"My name's not 'lady.' "

"Oh? As I recall, you were a little hazy on that point when you introduced yourself."

Now I had my own eyes forward, too, waiting her out.

"My name is Elizabeth Staley. Most people call me Beth."

I stepped up my pace a bit, running faster as we passed a group of Japanese men who looked like a visiting sumo team, but who moved with remarkable grace and economy, gliding along as easily as marathoners. The woman effortlessly matched me stride for stride.

"No offense if I'm wrong here, Beth, but I get the feeling you're a cop of some kind."

"I work for a private company, Mr. Shepherd. We provide personal security for Mr. Gale."

"You're a bodyguard?"

"A private security officer."

I snorted, probably a little louder than I really had to.

We reached the southwest corner of the park and I started to turn toward my usual finish by the lake, but Beth pointed in the other direction, off across the park to where a green picnic table sat empty under a low-hanging tree.

"This way, if you don't mind."

She angled off toward the table without breaking stride, and I followed her — just out of sheer curiosity, I told myself.

In a few moments we were both settled, sitting on the top of the table with our feet resting on one of the benches and letting the perspiration flow. White puffs of cloud drifted slowly across an azure sky and a light breeze dried our faces while we tasted the air and smelled the distant odors of the city that was waiting beyond the tree line around the park.

"We've had a loose net on you ever since your meeting with Mr. Gale. We don't really expect to find anything, but we wanted to be sure."

That was the second time in a week someone had used the phrase "loose net" in connection with me, and I didn't like the sound of it now any more than I had the first time.

"It's no big deal, just our standard counter-surveillance procedure. Mr. Gale asked me to keep an eye out for a few days to see if anyone had tagged you."

"You're scaring me, Beth."

"Didn't mean to."

"Did Barry send you here this morning to tell me that?"

"No." She blinked back droplets of sweat. "I just thought you ought to know."

I turned my head and studied her, but she wouldn't meet my eyes.

"I guess I don't get it," I finally said.

"It's not very complicated. Barry is afraid the Russians may try to get to him through you. He asked me to keep an eye out to make sure that didn't happen."

Something behind me apparently caught Beth's attention and I turned to follow her eyes. Two men were walking toward us across the grass, the same two men who had disappeared earlier when I ran past them. I glanced at Beth and saw that she looked like she was expecting them. She must have been because we just sat there after that and waited until they got to us.

Both of the men were sweating badly, beginning to suffer as the morning temperature climbed. They looked even less like runners now than they had when I had passed them on the trail if that was possible, but then Thai men had never been particularly noted for expending energy in inessential pursuits like running.

Beth said something to them in a language I didn't recognize, so maybe they weren't locals after all. The language sounded vaguely like a Chinese dialect, but I didn't know a single word of any Chinese dialect so I couldn't be sure. She had something like a question in her voice — I was pretty sure of at least that much — and one of the men nodded quickly in response, a single crisp snap of his head. After that both men waited patiently while Beth looked off into space for a few moments.

"Okay," she finally said. Then she said something else in whatever language she was speaking and both men turned and walked away without another word.

Beth swung her legs around and pushed herself off the table.

"It looks like there may be somebody on you after all."

"You're joking."

"I never joke about that kind of thing."

"Who is it?"

"I don't know."

"Do you mean it's really possible that Jimmy Kicks. . . ."

Beth interrupted, waving my question away.

"I don't know yet. We'll keep you covered with a counter-surveillance team until I'm sure what's going on. Just keep on doing whatever you normally would and don't worry about it."

"Counter-surveillance team? Look, Beth, what the hell is going on here? All of a sudden you sound more like a spook than a bodyguard."

"I am not associated with any intelligence agency, Mr. Shepherd."

"Now wait just a damned minute. . . ."

"It's no concern of mine whether you believe me or not. Mr. Gale pays my company to provide security for him and we answer only to him. He asked me to check you for surveillance. Now it seems you may be tagged and I've got to tell you that I'm not real thrilled."

"Well, that makes two of us, Beth."

"The reason I'm not real thrilled," she continued, her tone neutral, "is that now I'm going to have to pull some people off Mr. Gale to cover you and that leaves me weak if anything goes down with him. I don't like to be weak."

She paused and looked at me to make sure I appreciated the point.

"You must not tell anyone about any of this, Mr. Shepherd. You would be putting yourself in danger, and possibly others as well. If you're under surveillance, this changes everything."

"Like what exactly?"

"It will be difficult for you to see Mr. Gale again."

"That's not a problem. I don't want to see Mr. Gale again."

"Don't make jokes, Mr. Shepherd. This isn't a game. You don't understand what you're up against here."

"I think I do, Beth. Horseshit always smells pretty much the same not matter how you try to dress it up."

The corners of Beth's lips lifted in a smile, but her eyes didn't join in.

"You Westerners look at Asians and you always laugh a little to yourselves, don't you? We're just not people you can take particularly seriously."

"Now wait a minute. . . ."

"It's risky to underestimate people you don't understand, Mr. Shepherd. That gives them the advantage, because they seldom underestimate you."

"Hold on, Beth."

I tried to put just the right tone of appeal into my voice without coming off like a wimp.

"Would you just lay it out? Can you just tell me what's going on here?"

"I'm only the hired help, Mr. Shepherd."

"But you *could* tell me, couldn't you?"

She hesitated, and for a moment I thought she might, but then she looked away.

"It's up to Mr. Gale what he wants to say. My job is just to make sure no one bothers you. We'll be around. Don't worry."

When she smiled at me there was something like an apology in her eyes, but I also saw that was all I was going to get.

"You really have nothing to worry about, Mr. Shepherd. In spite of what you may have assumed, I'm not just some bimbo. I did eight years with Special Branch Counterintelligence in Hong Kong. I'm very good at my job."

"I'm sure you are."

"I have expert ratings with a dozen kinds of firearms."

"Are you saying that you may have to *shoot* somebody to protect me?"

But I could have saved my breath. I was talking to Beth's back.

She had already slipped off the table and was walking rapidly away from me toward the park's main gates on Ratchadamri Road. She took a half-dozen strides and then broke into a run at an impressive pace. Within a short time she had blended in with the crowds of morning joggers and I lost track of her at together.

I shook my head as I pushed myself off the table and started back to the Volvo. There was only one sensible explanation for all this. Barry was trying to scare me. He must have concocted the whole ridiculous story and then sent this woman and her cohorts around to panic me. If Barry could get me to wet my pants in sheer terror, jump into his arms, and scream for help, then he'd have me right where he wanted me.

It was utterly inconceivable to me that there were people watching me at that very moment. I was just an unimportant lecturer at an insignificant business school in an inconsequential country in a non-influential part of the world. I couldn't believe that anyone — other than Anita, I at least hoped — gave even the most minuscule of damns about where I was going or what I was doing right then.

I had thought for a moment there that Beth might be about to tell me what was really going on. Had she really come to meet me without Barry knowing about it? There had been something, I thought, an instant in which she seemed to want to tell me everything — and I had almost been ready then to believe that she really was there on her own — but I was probably mistaken. Men in general tended to become unreasonably hopeful and stupidly optimistic in the company of beautiful women, and I was no different. That was probably all there had been to it.

When I got back to the Volvo, I happened to notice a man sitting behind the wheel of a blue Toyota van that was parked a short distance up Soi Sarasin and on the opposite side of the street. He looked like a Thai, but he was wearing a green baseball cap and dark glasses, and it was hard to tell for sure.

The man was probably just waiting for someone, I told myself. He really didn't seem to be paying any attention to me at all. There was nothing unusual about him or about what he was doing, but still . . . I found myself keeping a wary eye cocked in his direction while I started the Volvo, made a U-turn, and headed back toward my apartment.

The man in the baseball cap never moved — he never even looked at me as far as I could tell — and when I turned the corner onto Wireless Road, both he and his blue van slipped out of sight.

TWENTY

ANITA WAS STILL SLEEPING when I got back, so I showered and shaved as quietly as I could. I left a note reminding her of my meeting with Dollar and then went back downstairs to the garage and got the Volvo out again. I had nothing in particular to do before eleven o'clock, and I thought it might be pleasant to head on down toward the United Center, treat myself to a peaceful breakfast somewhere, and then just hang around the office until Dollar showed up.

The day was growing warmer and the sky turning milky from the thin layer of smog that was forming over the city. I drove south on Soi Chidlom, down to Central Department Store, and caught the light there.

As I sat waiting for it to change, I watched the army of sales clerks arriving for work streaming into the huge store through the employees' entrance. They were overwhelmingly young and mostly female. Although I had the Volvo's top down and was quite comfortable in a blue cotton shirt with the sleeves rolled up, most of the sales girls wore coats over the white blouses and black skirts of their uniforms — bulky nylon parkas in bright shades of red and yellow seemed to be the favored choice — and one tiny girl even sported a purple ski hat pulled all the way down over her ears. Clearly winter had arrived in the City of Angels.

When I got to Soi Sarasin and made a right in the direction of the financial district, I involuntarily glanced over my shoulder toward the spot where I had parked the Volvo when I was running in Lumpini Park. The blue van was gone.

I wondered briefly if I ought to take that as a good omen. Maybe it was even a sign that everything was going to start getting back to normal and in a few days I'd be laughing. No, that was going too fast. This morning I'd settle for just getting through breakfast without squinting suspiciously at the waitress.

After parking in the United Center garage I walked downstairs to the Délifrance. I went through the short line and selected a plate of hard rolls and cheese, picked up a *café au lait,* and then took everything to a table outside on the tiny front terrace. I busied myself watching the early morning traffic while I carved slivers of cheese onto the crusty bread and sipped at my coffee. When I was done with both, I went back inside, got a refill, and then sat quietly over it for a long time, thinking.

Jello's story still seemed to me to be ridiculous, but in an entirely different way, so was Dollar's tale about being mugged leaving his office with Howard the Roach.

I was sitting right where it had supposedly happened. The blue and white canvas umbrella under which I was drinking coffee might have been the very one Dollar claimed to have knocked over in the struggle. I could scarcely believe something like that had happened to them at all, let alone right here in the heart of Bangkok's financial district. What could their attackers have been after? More to the point, what was it that Dollar wasn't telling me?

As I thought about it all and sloshed the coffee around in my cup, a scene from an old movie suddenly popped into my head. *Three Days of the Condor* was one of those CIA conspiracy films that had been so popular right after Watergate, when a lot of Americans figured that now they could believe anything about the kind of people who were running the country. In the movie Robert Redford was the honorable man sucked by accident into an intricate government plot to do something that no one really understood, but that in any event required the killing of a bunch of other honorable people to achieve some obscure end for someone — maybe the CIA, and maybe not. Redford was the hero of the movie, of course. He was cool. He was steady. And he projected a steely determination not to let the bad guys get away with it. Whatever *it* was.

I had stumbled across the movie on HBO one night a couple of weeks earlier. Watching it again for the first time in more than twenty years, it was my own reaction that surprised me, not the film itself. Redford no longer seemed to me to be the hero of the story. On the contrary, his unyielding determination to do *right* even if it put him or the other people around him in danger seemed tired and dated.

The real star of the film for me now was a character actor named John Houseman, a sort of benighted Santa Claus figure wearing a rumpled blue suit and speaking with a British accent. Houseman's character was a lot older than Redford with a view of the world that was wearier, less hopeful that wrongs would be righted just by the conviction that they should be. He was the director of the CIA, and while you were pretty sure he wasn't one of the bad guys, you weren't absolutely sure — but then, I realized when I thought about it later, of course that was the point.

There was a moment in the movie when Houseman was reminiscing to one of his subordinates, a stiff-necked young bureaucrat played by Cliff Robertson, about the early days of the American intelligence community when he had been one of Alan Dulles' boys, a crusading young hotshot battling the Nazis in World War Two.

Robertson listened politely to Houseman's recollections, as we all do sometimes to old men who may have told the same stories a few too many times, and when Houseman was finished, he just sat there, not quite certain how he was supposed to respond. Finally, he asked politely, "So do you miss the action now, sir?"

Houseman seemed to consider that possibility as if for the first time, and slowly and deliberately he began to formulate a reply.

"No, I miss. . . ."

Houseman paused, searching for exactly the right word, and you hung there while the old man rolled the possibilities around in his mouth until he found just the word he was looking for.

"I miss . . . the clarity."

He drew the word out — "clar-i-tee" — and Robertson nodded, but you could tell he didn't understand what the hell Houseman was talking about. I wasn't sure that I understood either, then.

But now I did.

No, I didn't miss the action any more than Houseman did. Not one damned bit. But I missed the clarity.

Clarity was what had brought me to Bangkok in the first place, and clarity was what I had found. If I let it slip away, one day I knew I would end up just like that, living in the past, reminiscing to some young dunce who didn't know what I had lost or care much one way or the other how I'd lost it. I thought I'd managed to creep quietly out of the big ocean and slide undetected into my small pond without anyone really caring that I had gone, but now all of a sudden I was getting more attention than a Hezbollah float in the Rose Parade.

Oh Lord. I closed my eyes and shook my head. *Don't do this to me. Don't take it all away.*

I looked at my watch. It was a little before ten-thirty. Since Dollar and I weren't supposed to meet at the office until eleven, I had a half hour, maybe a little more if Dollar was late as usual.

If Howard and Dollar really were up to anything, there would almost certainly be some hint of it in Howard's files. I could probably find it if I looked carefully, at least I could now that I knew what I was looking for, and there was plenty of time to look through them before Dollar showed up. What could it hurt?

In the lobby of the United Center a gray half-light illuminated a sleepy-looking security guard flipping through a newspaper behind a wooden desk. No one else was in sight. I walked to the elevators and pushed the button, but the guard never even glanced at me. Like most Thai security guards he probably wouldn't have bothered to look up if I'd ridden an elephant into the building.

On the fifteenth floor I walked to the glass doors at the end of the hall where the big gold letters were dramatically backlit against a stark white wall. DUNNE, ANDERSON, LORD & AMPORNPHAKDI — INTERNATIONAL ATTORNEYS AND COUNSELORS AT LAW.

I did work fairly regularly for Dollar's firm and I kept a tiny cubbyhole of my own there to avoid dragging client files back and forth to my office at Sasin, so I had a key. I took it out, bent down, and turned it in the floor lock. When I did, for a moment I thought I heard voices coming from somewhere inside.

Lawyers in Bangkok, unlike their more ambitious brethren in serious places, didn't go to the office on Saturdays as a rule. It seemed unlikely anyone was there unless Dollar had shown up early after all, and that seemed really unlikely. When the lock snapped over I stood and pushed the door open and waited silently for a moment, listening, but I heard nothing else. I decided I must have been mistaken.

My office was the first door down the hallway to the left, just past the black marble counter manned during the work week by two receptionists. It was a tiny windowless cell situated in the inside portion of the hallway ring, an area mostly set aside for toilets, storage, and a kitchen. I flipped on the lights and settled into my chair, swiveling around and pulling open the bottom drawer of the big cabinet file behind my desk where I kept my most recent working files.

I flipped quickly through the drawer, and then I went back and checked it methodically again from front to back. At first I thought that perhaps I had just overlooked them, but I hadn't. All of Howard's files were gone.

Had I returned them to the file room? I was reasonably sure I hadn't, but then it had been quite a while since I had last looked at any of them and I supposed that was at least possible.

The main file room was a few doors down the corridor from my office, but when I turned the handle I discovered it was locked. I couldn't remember that happening before either. I pulled out my office master key and pushed it into the deadlock. It didn't turn. I jiggled it a couple of times, pulled it back out and put it in again, but clearly it wasn't going to open the door no matter how many times I tried.

I was certain that I had never found the file room door locked before, at least not during office hours, but then I never came in on weekends so I couldn't say for sure whether it was normally locked then. Regardless, my key was supposed to be a master — presumably it fit everything — so I made a mental note to ask someone on Monday why I couldn't get into the file room.

Walking back down the corridor I was just opening my office door when I heard a noise in the distance. This time I was certain. It was a voice.

I followed the sound across the darkened reception area and toward the opposite corner of the building until I came to Dollar's office. Dollar must have shown up early after all. That was out of character for him, I mused, so whatever our meeting was about, it had to be something that was making him anxious.

Dollar's door was standing slightly ajar and I had my hand on the knob before it registered that it wasn't his voice I heard inside. I stopped and listened quietly. I couldn't tell who it was or make out what the voice was saying, but it sure as hell wasn't Dollar. He must have someone else with him, I decided. With a sinking heart I realized that it was probably Howard the Roach. It appeared that Jello was going to get his way. His trap was about to snap shut on me with a bang.

I knocked lightly. Then I pushed the door open and stepped inside.

I was surprised to see that there was just one man in the office after all. I was even more surprised to see that the man was neither Howard the Roach nor Dollar Dunne. It was someone I'd never seen before, and he was sitting in the chair behind Dollar's desk, just hanging up the telephone.

The man was a well-built Westerner with big ears, the lean face of a chain-smoker, square shoulders, and an even squarer haircut. He was wearing an inexpensive-looking blue suit with a crisp white shirt and a red and blue striped tie neatly secured in a Windsor knot and he had an unblinking stare, rather like a stuffed owl it occurred to me.

"Who the fuck are you?" the man snapped in a resonant voice that seemed larger than his body. His accent was American, almost pure mid-Atlantic, but there was just a trace of a rural twang in it, too. The whole effect was something like Ross Perot on steroids.

"I work here," I said, feeling lame and defensive and not understanding why I should. "What are you doing in Dollar's office?"

The man studied me with obvious interest, but he didn't say anything.

"Okay," I said, turning to leave. "I'll call the police and they can straighten it out."

"Not necessary," he said, and held up something in his right hand. It was a small black folder with an ID card on one side and a gold badge on the other.

I stepped closer and read the card. SPECIAL AGENT FRANKLIN D. MORRISSEY. UNITED STATES FEDERAL BUREAU OF INVESTIGATION, it said.

I was still taking that in when I heard the sound of rapid footsteps in the hallway and Dollar burst into the office. He saw the man in his chair before he saw me and nodded slightly to him, but then he realized I was standing there and stopped dead, staring at me.

"What the hell are you doing here?"

I had never seen Dollar quite like that before. He looked awful, like a man who hadn't slept in days. His eyes were cloudy as if they couldn't quite focus properly, and he was pale underneath his golfer's tan. He looked badly shaken.

"You asked me to come in for a meeting at eleven."

"About what?"

"I have no idea. Probably something about Howard, if I had to guess."

"Howard?" Morrissey perked up. "Howard Kojinski?"

I looked at Dollar, not sure what to say, and I saw that he was staring steadily at Morrissey. Some color seemed to have returned to his face and his eyes were beginning to clear.

"What the hell is going on here?" I asked, but nobody answered me.

Dollar jammed his hands in his pockets and flopped down on a leather sofa off to one side of his desk. He swung his feet up onto the coffee table, crossing them at the ankle, and raised his eyebrows at Owl Eyes in a silent question.

"Makes no never mind to me," the man said.

"Then you may as well tell him," Dollar said.

Morrissey snorted slightly, like a man who didn't like to waste time blowing his nose.

"The local cops found Howard a little before seven this morning."

I sat down in one of the chrome and leather chairs in front of Dollar's desk. I did it slowly, since I had no doubt at all what was coming next.

Owl Eyes watched me, apparently evaluating my reaction to his announcement.

"He was hanging from a girder under a bridge."

I felt a drop-away sensation in my stomach.

"Oh, man," was all I could think of to say.

Nobody else said anything at all.

"Suicide?" I eventually asked when the silence became oppressive.

Owl Eyes blinked for what couldn't have been more than the second time since I'd found him sitting in Dollar's chair.

"Nope. Not unless the guy had a real slick way of getting up thirty feet or so over the Chao Praya all by himself."

"But you're saying he's. . . ."

"Yep," Morrissey finished for me. "Deader'n shit."

Dollar asked me to wait in the reception area while he talked to Morrissey, which seemed odd to me, but it was Dollar's office, so I did. After a few minutes Morrissey came out and sat down on the other couch opposite me.

"A guy in a longtail spotted the body just after dawn this morning and called the cops," he told me.

"When did it happen?"

"Could have been almost anytime last night. There's really nobody around that area after dark except a few security guards at the Pepsi plant."

"They didn't see anything?"

"Not as far as we know."

Then I twigged on what Owl Eyes had just said.

"Pepsi plant? What do you mean?"

"There's a Pepsi bottling plant just upriver from the bridge. Anybody who'd been watching from there could probably have seen who strung the little bastard up, but it was the middle of the night, so. . . ." Morrissey spread his hands.

As far as I knew there was only one Pepsi bottling plant in Bangkok, and it was located only a short distance upriver from the Taksin Bridge. Howard's body had been hung up not more than a hundred yards from the very spot where I had smoked a cigar and waited on Sunday night for Barry Gale to appear.

Could that really have been just a week ago, I wondered to myself? Christ, it felt to me like at least a generation or two must have passed since then.

I was still trying to get a grip on Morrissey's story when the glass doors from the hallway opened and Jello came in trailed by four cops in skin-tight brown uniforms with white Sam Browne belts and big guns riding high on their hips.

"What are you doing here, Jack?"

His rumbling voice had an edge in it, and right then it rubbed me the wrong way.

"Yeah, I'm real sorry to hear, too. Howard and his family thank you for your sympathy."

Jello's face softened. He looked embarrassed and for a moment I almost regretted being so harsh.

"I know," I said. "You're just doing your job."

Jello gave Morrissey a long look.

"Would you mind letting me have a minute here, Frank?"

Owl Eyes shook his head.

"No problem. He's all yours."

After Morrissey disappeared down the hallway in the direction of Dollar's office, Jello waved the uniformed cops outside and then he came over and sat down next to me. I looked at Jello when he didn't say anything right away. His hands rested on his thighs and rubbed back and forth, pushing the fabric of his pants into little mounds.

"Why the scout troop?" I asked, indicating the cops waiting beyond the glass.

Jello seemed strangely embarrassed again.

"I want to look around and see if there's anything here that might be connected with Howard's murder."

Now I could see *why* he looked embarrassed.

"Uh-huh," I said. "And maybe while you're at it you'll see if you can dig up anything on Dollar to prove that bullshit story you gave me about him laundering drug money for the Burmese. Is that what you had in mind?"

"Look, Jack. . . ."

I was on my feet and pointing toward the front doors before Jello could say anything else.

"To hell with you, man! Fuck you and the little elves who rode in with you! Get the hell out of here."

Then I turned and shouted down the hallway.

"Hey, you back there! Special Agent whoever-the-hell-you-are! You get out, too!"

Morrissey reappeared so quickly that I wondered later if he had been standing just around the corner listening to what Jello and I were saying. Dollar was right behind him.

"You've got no authority here," I snapped at Morrissey.

"Don't make any difference. I can get as much as I need."

"Then you just do that. It'll be good practice for you."

"What's this all about, Jack?" Dollar asked. "It won't do any harm to let them look around."

I thought about blurting out everything that Jello had told me right then, but I didn't. Dollar had no way of knowing that he was the real target of the search, and he seemed so shaken by Howard's murder that I couldn't bear to add to his burdens.

"Take my word for it, Dollar. It's a really lousy idea."

Dollar just nodded as if he hardly cared, then he sank down on a couch and stared off toward where the uniforms stood waiting outside. The unfocused look he had when he had first walked into his office had crept back into his eyes.

"Where's Just John, Dollar?" I asked, squatting down next to him.

"John?" Dollar raised his head slowly. "Just John?"

"Yeah. Can I call him? Do you know where he is?"

"I think he's. . . ." Dollar paused for a long time. "I don't know where he is. He's out of the country, I think."

Morrissey looked at Dollar as if he was going to say something, but I bounced up, thrusting out an open palm.

"Don't. Just get the hell out."

The cops out beyond the glass doors had stopped talking to each other and were now watching me standing there with my hand out, posing like some demented traffic cop. Eventually Morrissey shrugged slightly and started out the door.

"Come on, Jello," he said. "It's no big deal."

"Jack. . . ." Jello started to say something, but he trailed off as if he wasn't sure what it ought to be. Then with drooping shoulders he followed Morrissey through the glass doors. When they were all outside, Jello stopped and looked back at me again. I kept my face blank, and finally he gave a shrug and turned away, heading toward the elevators.

After they were all gone I walked around the office turning off lights to have something to do while I gave Dollar a chance to pull himself together, but when I returned to the reception area he was still sitting in the same position, just staring off into space. I watched Dollar for a while, but he never moved nor spoke. He continued to sit there in exactly the same lifeless way.

I had no doubt at all what I was seeing, no matter how hard I might try to explain it to myself in some other way.

It was fear that was written on Dollar's face and in the slump of his body, not surprise, and certainly not grief over Howard's murder. Dollar was a man who had been given a sign, and he was terrified by it.

As I stood there looking at Dollar, I wondered why I had been so fiercely protective of him. I really didn't have the slightest idea what his real connections with Howard might have been, or for that matter, even who Howard the Roach really was. When I couldn't decide, I figured it was time for me to go home.

I turned away, pushed through the glass doors, and walked down the corridor to the elevator.

TWENTY-ONE

THE REST OF SATURDAY I just hung around the apartment with the telephone unplugged and the answering machine shut off. Anita had gone to her studio to paint and I didn't do much except look out the window and think about Dollar and Howard.

I had hardly known Howard, and I really hadn't been all that close to Dollar either, so I knew it wasn't grief over Howard's death or dismay that Dollar may have been involved in some bent deals that had suddenly drained the life out of me. The more I thought about it, the more certain I was the chill was coming from someplace a lot closer to home.

All of this had something to do with me. I was sure of it. I just couldn't figure out what it was.

After breakfast on Sunday, Anita went off to her studio again, and I sat drinking coffee and looking out the window some more. Another unseasonable rainstorm was coming in from the west and it made me think of the night I'd gone out to the river in answer to the message from Barry Gale, which naturally caused me to picture Howard the Roach hanging underneath the Taksin Bridge.

I sat there watching the storm gather itself until the thick swirls of gray roofed the city and fat drops of rain were thudding against the window like berries being thrown by little boys. For a while I fidgeted with the Sunday *Bangkok Post,* looking through it more than reading it, then I made another pot of coffee which I really didn't want, turned the television on to watch CNN, and then turned it back off again. Eventually I decided that what I needed to do was to get out of the apartment, so I put on some jeans and a polo shirt, slipped into a pair of old Topsiders, and went down to the Volvo.

By the time I got on the road most of the rain had retreated across the river, but I kept the top up anyway since the winds from the west were still shoving clouds of fine mist over the city. I got on the expressway and chasing the rain I followed it south all the way to the glittering steel spider web from which the Rama IX Bridge hung suspended high above the Chao Praya.

The river lay gun-metal gray in the sodden, morning light, winding lazily over the featureless flood plains like the tail of a huge sleeping cat. Bangkok was strewn haphazardly on both sides, towers of steel and concrete flung chaotically here and there as if they were plastic models hurled from a toy box by an angry child. The sun was lost somewhere in the churning dampness, and the light was a flat, sourceless glow.

On the other side of the bridge the road led south to the old seaside resort of Hua Hin, and Hua Hin always made me think of Lyndon Merchant, the poor bastard whose stupidity and misfortune had first brought me to Bangkok. We all had known that Lyndon was into something way over his head, but no one ever figured out exactly what it was. I wondered how he had felt at the end, at the very moment both big barrels of the Remington were stuffed into his mouth on that lonely beach and he swallowed the sour bile that surely rose in his throat from the taste of the metal and the knowledge of what was about to come. I wondered if at that moment even *he* had known out what he was actually involved in.

Across the bridge I turned onto Ratburana Road and drove aimlessly, following it as it traced the meandering curves of the Chao Praya north toward Thonburi, Bangkok's left bank. By the time I passed the Marriott the rain was far out over the fields to the south and the sky had turned so blue above that it was hard to imagine that any rain ever fell on Bangkok at all.

The extravagant peacefulness of Bangkok on a Sunday morning was beginning to work its magic on me and I could feel myself coming back to life.

A few miles further on the right, between Ratburana Road and the river, a huge complex of Buddhist temples came into view, and in the new warmth of the morning sun their fragile, gilded spires glittered like golden flares against the cobalt sky. Beyond them, about a half-mile further upriver, I suddenly saw the gray bulk of the Taksin Bridge.

I had thought all morning that I was going nowhere in particular, but now I knew better. I had come to the place toward which I'd been unconsciously driving ever since I'd left the apartment.

There was a shopping mall in a bend of the river just below the bridge, one of those desolate, mostly vacant commercial structures with which the city had been littered ever since the currency collapsed in 1997 and dragged the rest of the economy with it. I parked in the empty lot and walked slowly across the pitted concrete toward the river, my thumbs hooked in the pockets of my jeans. There were some benches just along the riverbank, and I sat down on one. With my back to the parking lot, I looked at the bridge, trying to imagine Howard's body dangling underneath it at the end of a rope.

It was disconcertingly easy. Howard had been that kind of guy.

But then what kind of guy did that make Dollar? It was still difficult for me to imagine Dollar as a crony of drug barons. If it was really true, what was it that had turned him? Just greed, or could there have been another motive, something subtler? Dollar had always been a risk junkie, I knew. Maybe whatever he had done was a part of that. Maybe it was just his way of upping the ante when things got dull.

Thinking about it that way made me feel a little better. Greed was never anything other than ugly, while risk-taking had a sort of raffish spin to it, even a touch of old-fashioned romance. That was probably torturing the language, I understood, but distance had given every foreigner in Bangkok a license of sorts and each of us had chosen to use it in our own way. The problem of course was that the real world didn't have a whole lot of respect for distance anymore. It had an unnerving habit of showing up at the most awkward times, even way out here, in a place where most of us never really expected to see it again.

There was a line of bare flagpoles along the edge of the shopping mall next to the riverbank. A light breeze rose from the water and the empty pulley ropes began to swing against the aluminum poles. The impacts clanked out mournful little chords, hollow chords, like tin drums tapping out a clumsy cadence for Howard's passage to the other side.

I sat there staring at the bridge until I suddenly realized I was very hungry. I took that as a good sign. It seemed like an ordinary enough feeling, and right then ordinary was pretty welcome. I stood up, turned my back on the Taksin Bridge, and headed off to find some lunch.

I didn't know that part of town very well and the only place to eat that came readily to mind was the Marriott I had passed a few miles to the south. I hadn't ever eaten there before and wasn't sure whether I wanted to, but this was a clear case of any port in a storm and I turned the Volvo in that direction.

It was early afternoon when I parked in the hotel's garage. When I got inside I wandered around both levels of the vast, dimly lit lobby without finding the coffee shop, but then I heard an alto sax somewhere in the distance playing a creamy version of *Green Dolphin Street.* I followed the sound to the back of the hotel where in a large, sunny room with big windows that overlooked the river I discovered a four-man jazz combo and the biggest Sunday brunch buffet I had ever seen. The place was only about half full and the band sounded pretty good, so I settled in at an empty table by a window and ordered a Heineken.

While I was waiting for the beer, I got a plate and helped myself to some *mee krob* and *peek kai* from the salad table, then loaded on a couple of pieces of tuna sashimi and two sticks of chicken satay for good measure. I got back to my table just as a slight young girl in a black uniform and a white apron was pouring my Heineken.

"Korp khun krap," I said. Thank you.

The girl gave me a shy smile, bobbed her head, and slipped quietly away.

I had polished off most of the plate of salad and was halfway through the Heineken when I glanced up and spotted a familiar face across the room. Bar Phillips was a columnist for the *Bangkok Post,* and probably had been since just after the invention of moveable type. His column was called "Bar By Bar" and it had been a weekly staple in Bangkok for longer than anyone now alive could remember.

The kind of stuff Bar kept prattling on about was badly out of style now, even a little distasteful to some people, but that apparently had had no effect on him at all. He merely continued doing what he had done for decades — chronicling his rounds through the city's go-go bars and massage parlors, espousing his theories of bargirl psychology, reporting the comings and goings of the city's legion of foreign saloon keepers, and generally holding forth on anything else that took his fancy about Bangkok's legendary nightlife.

The newer generation of Bangkok's foreign residents regularly engaged in spasms of self-righteousness over the *Post* continuing to publish Bar's column, probably as much as anything because he utterly ignored the scorn that they heaped on it. Regardless, I had always suspected their indignation might have less to do with any genuine contempt for Bar's travesty of journalism than it did with their own need to exhibit as publicly as possible their own personal standards of high-mindedness.

Bar and I had first met not long after I'd joined the faculty at Chula. He had apparently come into a bit of money somehow and since we had some friends in common — not surprisingly, since Bar seemed to know everybody in Bangkok — he had approached me for help with setting up and operating a string of bank accounts outside Thailand.

I never really knew where his money came from or exactly how much there was. Bar offered vague explanations, mostly starring the usual panoply of dead relatives, but I didn't believe him and I don't think he expected me to. On the other hand I didn't sense anything ominous about his money's origins either, so I had been happy enough to help him out.

After I got his bank accounts working, that was the last I heard from Bar about money; and as far as I could tell nothing about his life or attitudes changed after that, regardless of what he had socked away. I didn't really see that much of him anymore, but I was always happy to run into him. He loved me like a son.

When I walked over to his table carrying what was left of my Heineken, he glanced up without expression.

"What the fuck do you want? Can't you see I'm trying to eat?"

Loved me like a son, he did.

Between trips back and forth to the buffet tables over the next hour, Bar and I made disjointed small talk and listened to the band. Eventually Bar polished off the last of a large bowl of bread pudding, then bent down and took a package of tobacco and a pipe out of a plastic shopping bag he had on the floor by his feet. Packing the bowl of the pipe, he tapped the tobacco down with a metal tool, then struck a match and puffed away until he got it going. It all looked like an awful lot of trouble to me. Maybe that's why I smoked cigars.

Slumping forward on his forearms, Bar took several long draws on his pipe and the aroma of cherry wood blended with the odor of garlic, fish sauce, and chilies. It smelled better than it sounds.

"You got a lot on your mind other than food, don't you, pal?"

Bar drew on his pipe again and exhaled an enormous cloud of smoke. He didn't leave an impression that he cared much one way or the other whether I was going to tell him about whatever it was, but of course he assumed that I probably would, and I did.

"You heard about the man they found hanging under the Taksin Bridge?"

"Yep." Bar sucked on his pipe. "Friend of yours?"

"Not really. He was a client of Dollar's. I helped out with some work for him a few times. That's all."

"Why did he hang himself?"

"He didn't."

I hadn't really intended to go through all this with Bar, but there it was.

"Somebody killed him."

I told Bar about my encounter at Dollar's office with Jello and the FBI agent and he listened without expression. When I finished he raised his right hand and crooked a finger toward a passing busboy, muttering something to him that I missed, then folded his arms and went back to puffing on his pipe as if he were sitting all alone at the table.

I was just on the verge of asking him what that had all been about when the boy reappeared with a copy of the *Bangkok Post* and handed it to Bar. He flipped through it quickly, then finding what he was looking for, he folded the paper over and laid it right in front of me, tapping on it with his forefinger.

The story he was pointing to was short, not more than six column inches, and it had been played small down at the bottom of an inside page. The headline was AMERICAN TOURIST FOUND DEAD. But it was the subheading that got my attention. In smaller type that read, SUICIDE POLICE SAY.

"The reporter must have gotten the story screwed up," I said when I glanced up. "Howard was certainly no tourist, and the FBI agent said it was a murder. He said it would have been impossible for Howard to have hung himself."

"Who was this FBI man? One of the embassy legats?" Bar asked.

Most American embassies had at least one FBI agent assigned to them, sometimes more if it was in a country like Thailand where criminal investigators could find a lot to do. To keep from offending the host country, FBI agents were always technically referred to as legal attaches, legats in State Department talk.

"I guess . . . well, I don't know for sure. I assumed he was with the embassy. What else would he be doing here?"

"What was the guy's name?"

"Frank something." I thought back. "Frank Morrissey. That was it."

Bar stood up and pointed to the folded *Post* lying on the table. "I'm going to take a leak. I think you'd better read that before I get back."

I skimmed the story with growing astonishment and then I read through it twice more, taking it carefully and deliberately.

"This is completely wrong," I told Bar when he returned. "Everybody told me it was a murder, not a suicide. Even Jello."

Bar retrieved his pipe from the ashtray and poked tentatively at the bowl with one finger.

"You sure of this FBI agent's name?"

"I saw his ID myself."

Bar dipped back down into the plastic shopping bag and produced a mobile phone, one of those old green Motorolas that was about the size of a World War Two walkie-talkie.

"Who are you calling?" I asked him.

"The American Embassy."

"Isn't it closed on Sunday?"

"Not to me."

I watched as he finished dialing and hoisted the huge handset to his ear.

"Duty officer, please," he said after a moment.

There was a wait, apparently first for his call to be switched and then for it to be answered.

"Hey, Barney. It's Bar Phillips."

Bar listened a couple of beats.

"Uh-huh."

As Bar listened some more, I studied his expression, but it gave nothing away.

"You got it, pal," he finally said to whoever was on the other end. "But I need a favor in return. There's an FBI guy named Morrissey who's either attached to the embassy or in town temporarily on some kind of investigation. You know him?"

The band swung into *One for My Baby* and I watched the trumpet player, a short man with wide shoulders and slicked back black hair.

"Yeah, it's Frank," Bar said into the telephone after a moment.

He glanced at me and I nodded quickly.

"Yeah. Frank Morrissey."

There was a pause, then he said, "No shit," followed by a long, low whistle. "Hang on a second Barney."

Bar lowered the telephone, slipped his hand over the mouthpiece, and looked at me.

"He says Frank Morrissey used to be one of the legats all right, but he's been retired for three or four years. Lives somewhere in Florida, he thinks."

"So what's he doing back out here now?"

Instead of answering my question, Bar asked me one of his own. "What did this man in Dollar's office look like?"

I made a guess as to the guy's age and size, and I described his natty dress and cool demeanor.

Bar lifted the headset back to his ear.

"Barney, let me ask you something. Is Frank Morrissey a middle-aged guy of average size and a sharp dresser who comes across as serious and intense?"

I could hear the laughter from the other end of the telephone without Bar taking it away from his ear.

"I see," he said after listening for a moment longer. "Well, I'm sure it's all some kind of mistake. I'll get that stuff to you tomorrow. Thanks a lot, Barney."

Bar pushed the disconnect button and lowered the heavy headset to the table.

"He says Frank Morrissey is probably older than I am. He also says he's a fat slob who usually looks like an unmade bed and never stops talking shit."

"I don't get it," I said. "This guy showed me his ID, and it must have been real since both Jello and Dollar knew him."

Bar sat impassively, saying nothing.

I pointed to the telephone.

"You've probably got a secret weekend number for Jello, too. Call him. He'll tell you."

Bar shook his head.

"Not a good idea."

"Why not?"

Bar shook his head again and looked away.

"Oh, come on, Bar," I said. "Tell me you're not about to say there was a conspiracy between Dollar and Jello to pass this fellow off as an FBI agent just to fool me."

"Okay. Then I won't say that."

I was starting to get a headache.

"Look, Jack, think about it. Somebody doesn't just kill this poor bastard, they dangle him off a prominent landmark where all sorts of people can see him twisting up there in the wind. Now doesn't it strike you as a pretty clear message of some kind?"

"Yeah, but. . . ."

"Then some guy masquerading as an FBI agent shows up inside Dollar's locked offices before the body's cold," Bar interrupted. "And a few minutes later, Jello walks in with enough manpower to turn the whole place over."

"But then Jello just left. He didn't do anything."

"You scared them off when you threw your fit."

I thought back to the empty look in Dollar's eyes on Saturday morning and wondered again why I had been so instinctively protective of him.

"But doesn't that mean that Jello and Dollar probably know who killed Howard?"

"Sharp as a fucking cue ball, aren't you, pal?"

The busboy materialized and began quietly gathering dirty dishes. Neither of us said anything else until he had wiped down the table and withdrawn.

"You sure you're not a player here, Jack?" Bar asked quietly when the boy was well out of earshot.

Bar produced the metal tool again and started poking at the bowl of his pipe, narrowing his eyes in concentration. He looked like a plumber examining a jammed toilet and unhappily contemplating what had to be done next.

"Look, Bar. I'm just a teacher now. I'm not a player in anything anymore."

"They don't always ask you if you *want* to play, Jack. Sometimes they just stick you in the game."

The silence stretched on after that and Bar's gaze drifted away from me and off toward the band. The trumpet player was just launching into *How Long Has This Been Going On.* He shut his eyes as he played and swayed back and forth, and the notes emerged from his horn with what seemed almost like reluctance. Their sound left a deep sense of melancholy floating in the air.

I sat at the table and looked out across the room at the families gathered together there to share a Sunday lunch and at the hustling businessmen cutting deals. I had been part of both groups once, but now I wasn't really part of either, and I watched them all acting out the half-remembered rituals with a faint pang of nostalgia.

It was early afternoon and the dazzling shimmer of the sunlight on the river just beyond the windows made the table where I sat seem like a good place to be still and let some time pass. A noisy crowd packed the room and the sounds of their voices and their laughter washed over me while the bandleader's trumpet wailed a baleful counterpoint to the brightness of the day.

The beer was rich and thick on my tongue, and time and possibilities swirled around me as if I were no more than a stone in the river, and they passed and were gone.

TWENTY-TWO

THERE WERE A LOT OF THINGS I could have done after that. I could have gone to my office and prepared my lectures for next week's classes. I could have headed over to Lumpini Park and pounded around the lake until I sweated out my rapidly growing sense of foreboding. I could have retreated to my apartment, locked the door, and gone back to bed. That's probably what I should have done.

Instead I drove out to Dollar's house. It wasn't that I particularly wanted to, but he and I were going to have a serious conversation pretty soon — that appeared inevitable — and I figured there was nothing to be gained by putting it off. I could have called first to see if he was at home, of course, but it seemed to me that catching Dollar by surprise might make for a more compelling conversation.

Dollar lived on the river north of the city, not far from the international school where a lot of Western residents and a few wealthy Thais with pretensions sent their children. I had been there four or five times for parties over the past couple of years, but had never actually been inside the house. Dollar's parties always took place on the lawn, a sprawling, close-cropped expanse of grass that was impenetrably walled with towering banyan trees and rolled as smoothly as a putting green down a gentle slope to the Chao Praya River.

On party nights the lawn was bathed in white light from powerful floods tucked discreetly in the trees and a string quartet from the university was usually out there floating Mozart and Bach off on the heavy night air. Dollar's smartly-dressed guests generally represented more nationalities than I could name, and as they wandered among linen-draped tables engaging in pleasantly ambiguous conversation, they generally made certain that they were noticed by everyone else who was there. The first time I had gone to one of Dollar's parties I remembered standing quietly at the top of the slope and looking down across the lawn for a long time. Because the illumination was so white, so flat and colorless, and the people and the table settings looked so faultless, so perfectly formed, the whole scene made me think of a tiny diorama atop a particularly expensive wedding cake.

The house was a rambling two-story affair of no particular style, but it was large and comfortable looking, the kind of a place in which you had no difficulty imagining a man living. The story around town was that Dollar had been married three times — once to a Japanese woman, once to a Chinese, and once to an Indonesian — and each woman had in turn left him. So much for the myths about submissive Asian women with which Western men liked to entertain themselves. Dollar had no children, none that anyone had heard about anyway, and as far as I knew he lived alone except for the Thai couple that cooked and cleaned for him.

I pulled the Volvo to the side of the *soi* and parked close to the high concrete wall that pinned Dollar's house against the river. You couldn't see the house from the street because there was only one opening in the wall, a black metal drive gate that slid open like a huge peephole. Set into the larger gate was a door for callers on foot.

I'm not sure exactly how long I sat there looking at the gate wondering if I really wanted to go in. Eventually I decided that I didn't, but that I was going to anyway. I got out of the car quickly and pressed the intercom button before I had a chance to change my mind.

While I was waiting for someone to respond, I reached down and rested my hand on the handle of the little door within the drive gate. As I touched it, the door drifted open slightly, propelled by nothing more than the weight of my hand. The motion was so smooth and silent that it was a little eerie, but still I pushed the door the rest of the way and stepped inside.

The front of Dollar's house was a solid wash of white stucco without a single window or opening other than a big pair of dark teak doors that Dollar swore he had personally taken from a Khmer temple near Angkor Wat. Naturally I had never believed that for a moment and I doubted anyone else had either.

I knew that the other side of the house, the side that faced the river, was exactly the opposite in style. It was an unbroken curtain of glass that opened the whole house to a spectacular view of the Chao Praya and its constant traffic of longtails, rice barges, tourist boats, ferries, and ambiguous vessels whose real tasks one could only surmise.

I started up the walkway to the front, but finding the door in the gate open and seeing no sign of life made the whole scene feel a little spooky. On impulse I angled off across the grass around the back. It wouldn't hurt to have a quick look around before I just blundered up and rang the bell.

As I rounded the northeast corner of the house, Dollar's spectacular view of the river captured me just as it always did. For a moment I stood absolutely still and watched a long train of teak rice barges that were tethered nose to tail like a column of elderly circus elephants wallow noiselessly downriver toward the Gulf of Thailand. So peaceful was the sight that when I finally turned back toward the house and glanced through the glass curtain wall, what I saw didn't quite register at first.

The entire living room was in shambles, as completely devastated as if a bulldozer had run through it from one end to the other.

Lamps were broken, chairs overturned, tables smashed, and every book had been pulled from the long shelves flanking both sides of the fireplace and dumped into piles on the floor. Two once-plush couches lay on their backs with their bases turned toward the windows. The rich blue of their silk upholstery had been slit into wrappings of ribbons as if some maniac had attacked them with a broadsword.

I stood and stared, rooted to the spot by the appalling and yet still somehow mesmerizing magnitude of the destruction.

"Looks like a real messy burglary, doesn't it?"

Startled, I jerked my heard toward the sound of the voice and was confounded to see Bar Phillips standing off to my left with his arms folded across his chest, looking back and forth between Dollar's house and me.

"What are you doing here?" I asked.

Bar's eyes searched around briefly as if he might find the answer inscribed on the sky.

"I figured you might be coming out to see Dollar," he finally said.

Then he lifted his arms and let them flop back to his sides in a gesture that combined bewilderment with exasperation.

"Something's not right, pal. Not right at all."

"What's that got to do with you?"

"Well . . . I thought maybe someone ought to watch your back."

"The hell you did. You're a reporter and you smelled a story."

Bar made a face at that and fished his pipe out of his shirt pocket.

"You flatter me, boy. All I write anymore is a load of shit. Nobody's thought of me as a real reporter in thirty years."

"Then why the sudden concern about my welfare? If you thought I was walking into trouble, you could have just told me back at the Marriott. You didn't have to follow me all the way out here."

Bar stuck the pipe in the corner of his mouth and chewed on it without an indication that he planned to light it anytime soon.

"You're my friend. I always do what I can for my friends. But I *only* do what I can. Not what I can't."

I took a long breath and let it out slowly.

"That sounds good. Does it mean anything?"

"Nope. Thailand's made me a happy convert to the church of creative ambiguity."

Bar walked up to the glass, put his hands around his face to block the glare, and briefly studied the interior of Dollar's house.

"Man." He puckered his lips as if he were lining up a particularly difficult putt. "They did a good job of making it look like a burglary, didn't they?"

"What else would it be?" I asked.

Bar glanced at me. It was plain he relished my puzzlement. Then he started back around the house toward the front. Not having any better idea, I followed. When he got to the big teak doors, he rattled the brass handles with both hands, but the doors seemed securely locked. I reached past him toward the doorbell, but Bar gave me such a look of disdain that I pulled my hand back without touching it.

He dug in his trouser pocket and pulled out his pipe tool, flipping from it what looked like a stainless steel toothpick about three inches long. Bar slid the pick into the keyhole above the handle on the right hand door, bent forward slightly from the waist, and began to jiggle it gently between the thumb and forefinger of his right hand, chewing in concentration on his lower lip.

I burst out laughing. "You've got to be joking."

Bar didn't answer, but after a few seconds I heard a soft click and he didn't have to. He straightened up and turned the knob with his left hand while retracting the pick and pocketing the silver tool with his right.

"Okay," I said. "Maybe you weren't."

As soon as we walked inside, it was obvious that the whole house had gotten the same treatment as the living room. Whoever had turned the place over had clearly done a thorough job of it. I followed Bar silently from room to room. Nothing seemed to have escaped unscathed.

"Very professional," Bar said with a note of something like admiration in his voice. "Really very professional."

I didn't know what to say. The house just looked like a mess to me. I would have to take Bar's word for the fact that it was a professional mess.

"What makes you think it wasn't just a burglary?" I asked.

Bar gave me a disgusted look and started down a hallway that looked like it led to the bedrooms.

"Holy Christ," I murmured softly when I got to the end of it and looked around.

The master suite consisted of a huge bedroom with a line of walk-in closets on one side and a small study with floor-to-ceiling bookshelves on the other. The king-sized bed, now half obscured by a mound of debris, was in the middle of the room, its headboard a futuristic-looking rack of reading lights and telephones shuffled together with an elaborate collection of video and sound equipment. The whole setup faced a curtain of glass that overlooked the river and I glanced involuntarily toward the ceiling. I was a little surprised not to find a mirror up there.

The room had been spectacular once, but now it looked like a garbage dump. Clothes, shoes, papers, framed pictures, files, and books were heaped in a massive pile at the center of the room. The place looked like someone had begun to build a bonfire, but had been interrupted before they could ignite it.

Bar crossed the room to the walk-in closets and shoved aside a long chrome and glass table that was overturned in front of them. He checked the first closet, then pushed his head into each of the others and examined them as well. When he had finished, he turned to me and delivered his verdict.

"Dollar's on the run."

"Christ, Bar. I'd be halfway to Madagascar by now if I came home and found that someone had worked my place over like this."

"No, that's not it. I'm pretty sure he took off before any of this happened."

"And this you know exactly how, Sherlock?"

"His luggage is gone."

Dollar was a big fan of Haliburton bags, those outrageously expensive suitcases of silver-colored magnesium that were favored by airline pilots, people in the oil and gas business, and guys who delivered drug money in old episodes of *Miami Vice.* Dollar even carried a Haliburton briefcase, a flashy companion that had no doubt cost him more than the university paid me every month. He always said his Haliburtons were indestructible, but it never even occurred to me that he carried them because they were practical and long lasting. Dollar just liked their style.

"Maybe whoever hit the place took the luggage," I said, surveying the mess again.

Bar shook his head.

"This wasn't just some kids cored on amphetamines. Anyway, they'd take pillow cases, not a matched set of expensive luggage that's easy to ID and hard to get rid of."

"Yeah, the stuff is indestructible," I said.

"What?"

"Never mind."

While Bar squatted and probed at the papers and clothing piled in the middle of the bedroom, I walked into the study area and righted a black leather swivel chair that had been pushed onto its side. I wheeled it around behind Dollar's desk and sat down.

The desk had been thoroughly ransacked, too, yet whoever had done it had left it looking a little neater than the other things in the room. Dollar's computer had been pushed off to one side, but it looked intact and all the pieces seemed to be connected in the usual way, so I hit the power-on button to see what would happen. I heard a musical chord and a light blue background appeared on the screen.

Dollar's computer was a Mac, not the Windows PC I would have expected him to have. I wasn't much of a computer guy, and I knew absolutely nothing at all about Apple stuff, so I just sat and watched the screen while it filled with icons and windows popped open displaying file names and application titles that meant nothing at all to me.

Bar heard the chord and came over and stood behind me where he could see the screen.

"We've got Macs at the *Post,*" he said. "I can probably figure this out."

When the computer's start-up routine was done he leaned across me, cupped his right hand over the mouse and scooted it around, selecting something from the bar of commands that ran across the top of the screen. He clicked the mouse button and all the icons immediately changed. Then he clicked it for a second time, and they changed again. Although the names of the files remained the same, each little folder now had on top of it a small cartoon figure which was decked out in the uniform of a Hollywood-style spy — dark glasses, fedora pulled down low, and a belted trench coat that was an odd electric blue color.

"Crypto shit," Bar snorted. "PGP, I think."

Bar might well have lapsed into Turkish.

"What does that mean?" I asked.

"Dollar's encrypted all his files, probably using a program called PGP. It's supposed to be uncrackable. Without his password, you can't read anything."

Bar abruptly lost interest in the computer and began examining an answering machine that was near it on the desk.

"Why would Dollar encrypt the files on his home computer?" I asked, not ready to give up yet. "Doesn't that mean he's got something pretty important on it?"

Bar grunted.

"It's no big deal. Any ten-year-old can get PGP on the Internet for nothing, and they say it's almost as good as what the CIA has. Anyway, Dollar's too smart to leave anything that really matters just lying around on a computer in his bedroom, even if it is encrypted."

Without taking his eyes off the answering machine, Bar gestured vaguely in the direction of the computer.

"All that's probably nothing. Anyway, forget it. Without knowing the password, you'll never get in."

The answering machine was a digital model without any tapes in it. Bar put it down on the floor, plugged it in, and turned it on. When he pressed the play button, there was a brief silence, the sound of a dial tone, and then a beep.

"Hang up," Bar observed.

After a few moments, a disembodied voice issued from the machine in a slightly spooky cadence.

"That . . . was . . . your . . . last . . . message," the voice intoned.

Then the machine clicked off.

"I hate it when answering machines do that," Bar said. "It sounds like they're telling your fortune"

I looked at Bar without saying anything. Then he realized what he had said and quietly returned to sorting through the pile of papers and clothes mounded in the center of Dollar's bedroom.

"You're not going to find anything there, Bar," I said.

Bar straightened up and poked at the mound of debris with one foot, but he didn't turn around.

"Whoever tossed this place either took what he was looking for or he didn't find it," I said. "Whichever it was, that still doesn't leave anything for us to find."

Bar nodded. "You're probably right."

I stood up from behind the desk and dusted my hands off on my jeans.

"I guess we probably ought to call the cops."

Bar twisted his head around and looked at me as if I had suddenly begun to speak in tongues.

"Don't be a jerk, pal. Why in Christ's name would you want to get the cops involved?"

"Dollar might be in some kind of danger."

"Bullshit, Jack. He's probably shacked up in Monte Carlo with a couple of French chickadees by now. Besides, Thai cops couldn't find Santa Claus at the north pole."

He was right about that, of course, but then I thought back to the look I'd seen on Dollar's face the morning after Howard's body had been found and I was less sure that Bar had the Monte Carlo part right.

Regardless, the thought about calling the cops had been an American's reflex. In Thailand nobody ever called the cops. The driver always fled the scene, and when he didn't, all he did was disrupt the natural course of life and make a nuisance of himself. So I just nodded and let it go.

When we left I made sure the button on the back of the front door handle was pushed in so that the doors would lock behind us. It was a silly gesture perhaps, but it just didn't seem right to walk out and leave Dollar's house unlocked no matter what condition it was in.

Out on the street Bar and I made vague promises to keep in touch and then Bar got into his old Toyota and drove away. I started to get into my car, too, but then the thought occurred to me that I ought to check out the wall surrounding the house. It was an entirely pointless gesture since the damage had already been done, but it just seemed to me to be the least I could do for Dollar under the circumstances.

About a hundred feet south of the big gate Dollar's whitewashed wall joined the black stone of the house next door and that left me nothing much to see in that direction, so I turned around and walked back the other way. At the north end of the property I found something considerably more interesting.

Here a narrow gap had been left between Dollar's wall and his neighbor's. It was a small area where both houses stored their trashcans, and all of the cans were the aluminum kind with rigid sides and heavy lids that you hardly ever saw anymore. The way the cans were arranged told an obvious story.

Two small cans had been drawn up against two large ones to form a staircase right up the side of Dollar's whitewashed wall. I stepped up on the first can, climbed onto the second, and found myself standing with the top of the wall just above my waist. From there, swinging up on to it and dropping down the other side would have been a piece of cake. I had no doubt at all now that Dollar's visitors had come in this way and then left by opening the gate from the inside.

When I turned around to climb down, the lid on one of the larger cans popped loose and I could see inside. The can was filled with papers and files that looked just like the ones that Bar and I had found scattered over the floor of Dollar's bedroom.

But why would whoever had ransacked Dollar's place have stopped to put some files in a trashcan? Plainly they wouldn't, it seemed to me, so that could only mean that Dollar must have thrown out all this stuff sometime *before* his unexpected visitors arrived.

That could be pretty interesting, I realized, so I pulled the lids off the other cans as well to see what else I could find. All of those appeared to contain nothing but the usual kind of household garbage — wadded up advertising circulars, old newspapers, crushed bottles of washing machine detergent, empty Coke cans, plastic milk bottles, and unidentifiable organic matter emitting various unappetizing odors. None of those things looked nearly as interesting as the papers in the first can had, so I closed up the other trashcans and gave my full attention to the one that had caught my eye in the first place.

I dumped it out onto the ground and used my foot to stir through the contents. At a glance it seemed to be nothing more than the usual accumulation of office trash, but since I'd come this far I squatted down and began to sift methodically through everything.

There were piles of American Express vouchers, a lot of mobile phone bills, receipts for electrical service, statements from several different banks, and bundles of letters that all looked routine. Opening one of the bundles, I sat on the ground and began to read. After five minutes I knew what I'd found.

Nothing.

The stuff was just a bunch of correspondence going back years between Dollar and some investment managers in London. Other than confirming that he had a bit of money put away — which I already assumed — and that he kept a close eye on it — which I could have guessed — none of it told me anything at all.

I flipped through a second bundle and found more of the same. The third was mostly contract notes confirming securities trades as well as a few monthly position statements for several brokerage accounts. I had given up and started tossing everything back into the trashcan when a shiny disk slid out of one of the bundles I hadn't looked through and fell to the ground.

I picked it up and examined it closely. It was a compact disk that looked new, but there was no label on it. I thought back to the Mac in Dollar's bedroom. Did it have a CD burner in it? I couldn't remember.

I turned the disk around in my hands. Was it a copy of Dollar's personal files? Or was it just a pirate copy of Quake he'd bought in some night market and then discovered didn't work? There was obviously only one way to find out, so I set the disk carefully to one side and started piling everything else back in the trashcan.

When I'd finished cleaning up I collected the disk again, holding it gently by its edges. Then on impulse I grabbed the handle of the trashcan with my free hand and carried both of them around to the front of the house. I placed the CD gently on the Volvo's front seat while I dumped the entire contents of the can into the trunk.

Howard the Roach was dead and Dollar Dunne was on the run. I still had absolutely no idea why that was, or what might be coming next, but there was no doubt in my mind that I was involved in it all somehow. I had better find out exactly *how* before some asshole showed up at my door one day tidying up loose ends that I hadn't even known existed.

I would have hoped for a more dignified way to do that than digging through Dollar's garbage, but . . . I had to start somewhere, didn't I?

TWENTY-THREE

WHEN I GOT HOME Anita was still at her studio so the apartment was empty. I found a big trash bag under the kitchen sink, took it down to the garage, and scooped all of Dollar's garbage out of my trunk. After I had lugged everything back upstairs to the apartment, I got out my laptop and settled down in one of the leather chairs in front of the windows to look at the CD I'd found in Dollar's garbage can.

Sure enough it was a computer disk as I had suspected, and I enjoyed a small, smile at the hum of the laptop's CD-ROM drive spinning up. After the drive was ticking along nicely, I double clicked on its icon and the computer displayed an index of the disk's contents.

There was only a single file on the CD, one called BACKUP. That was pretty encouraging, so I double clicked on the Windows icon next to the file name to see what was in it. I was surprised and disappointed when nothing appeared on my screen other than a dialogue box inviting me to tell Windows what program it should use to open the file.

"If I knew what program to use, I'd have used it in the first place, wouldn't I, you moron?" I muttered at the laptop. "You're supposed to be the computer here. You tell *me.*"

The laptop didn't say anything, of course, so more or less at random I tried a few of the programs that the dialogue box suggested

—Word, Excel, even Internet Explorer—but nothing worked. That pretty much brought me to the limits of my technical expertise, and I just sat there staring at the useless little icon for a while. All at once, however, it dawned on me what the problem was.

The computer I had seen in Dollar's bedroom had been a Mac, hadn't it? So if this CD actually *did* contain a backup of documents that Dollar had copied off his home computer, then what I had here was a Mac file and that was a format that Windows couldn't read at all. The utter incompatibility between Macs and PCs had always struck me as one of the more peculiar idiocies of what was supposed to be a brave new high-tech world, but regardless, I was now left with absolutely no idea what to do next.

I fidgeted for a while, but when no course of action likely to resolve the technical conundrum occurred to me, I closed the laptop and turned my attention to the garbage bag instead. At least garbage seemed like something I ought to be able to handle. Pulling it around in front of me, I emptied the contents out onto the floor.

The first thing I did was to arrange everything by categories: Amex receipts in one pile, telephone and utility bills in another, and then securities trading confirmations, brokerage account statements, and correspondence each in their own piles. I also found a bunch of documents that I hadn't noticed before. They looked very official, but I couldn't be certain what they were since they were written entirely in Thai, which I couldn't read a word of. I set all those aside in a separate stack, and then I pushed back in the chair, folded my arms, and contemplated where to begin.

The Amex receipts looked easiest, and so I gathered them up and shuffled through them, looking for patterns. At a glance, they covered exactly the sort of travel and entertainment expenses that I would have imagined Dollar had been incurring for decades. About half of them were for charges in Thai baht, and the rest were in an assortment of United States dollars, Japanese yen, Hong Kong dollars, UK pounds, and Australian and Singapore dollars. It looked to me like Dollar had just been cleaning out some old files and had decided to toss his out-of-date receipts like most all of us did from time to time.

Taking it another way, I sorted all the receipts into their own separate categories — restaurants, hotels, airlines, merchandise, and those I couldn't figure out — but that didn't suggest any pattern either. Then I tried sorting them by currencies and had a look at them that way. Still nothing.

Then, just to touch all the bases, I sorted the receipts by the localities where the purchases took place. The Bangkok stack was the largest, closely followed by a stack for Phuket, then a much smaller one for Hong Kong. After that, the receipts were all over the place, so I gave up.

Okay, so Dollar lived in Bangkok — I knew that, of course — and he liked to get away to Phuket as often as he could. Didn't we all? What did that prove?

With a sigh I pushed the Amex receipts aside and began to work my way through the telephone bills, the utility bills, the confirmations of the securities trades, and the brokerage statements.

Thai telephone bills contained no details about numbers that had been called, so that was a dead end, but I got a pad and made notes of the names of the securities firms on the statements and the people with whom Dollar had been corresponding. Then for good measure I went back over the Amex receipts again and made lists of the hotels and restaurants were Dollar had been doing most of his charging. It was probably all a waste of time, but if Dollar didn't turn up pretty soon, I was going to have to start looking for him *somewhere.*

When Anita eventually came in around ten, the living room of our apartment was largely buried under a layer of receipts, documents, letters, and notes.

"Good, God, Jack! What in the world are you doing?"

I tried to tell her, but since I wasn't altogether certain, it wasn't easy.

Anita gently lowered herself into an empty space on one of the couches. Her face reflected a perfectly understandable degree of bewilderment.

"And you think this stuff will tell you were Dollar's gone?"

"Well . . . maybe."

"But why does it matter? Dollar's a grown man. Surely he's entitled to go anywhere he wants without you snooping through his garbage to try and figure out where he is."

"Something's wrong here, Anita. One of Dollar's clients has been murdered in a very public way; he's apparently gone into hiding himself; and his house has been turned over by somebody who wanted to find something pretty badly."

"Even if that's all true, Jack, it's got nothing to do with *you.*"

"Yes, it does."

"What?"

"I . . . don't know yet. That's why I'm looking through all this crap. I'm trying to find out."

"Well, have you allowed for the possibility that you're *not* involved in whatever Dollar is up to. That you might be *wrong?*"

"I am involved somehow, Anita, I'm absolutely sure of it. I can feel it."

"Maybe it's only gas, my darling. What did you have for lunch?"

"That wasn't very helpful," I said.

"I wasn't *trying* to be helpful. I was trying to tell you how ridiculous all of this looks. Dollar may well be doing something that you don't understand, but why *must* you understand it?"

I raised my eyebrows and waited.

"You have absolutely no business getting involved in any of this, Jack. No business at all."

Anita's hands motioned vaguely in the air.

"You never think of how these upheavals you're always getting yourself involved in affect *me,* do you? We're trying to be a sort of a family here, and yet you still act like you're a man without a responsibility in the world except for yourself. You go careening off on your little crusades without giving the first thought to me."

She turned to look out the window and then almost immediately glanced back.

"Your stupid curiosity is going to be the end of us some day."

I took a long breath and slowly let it out.

"I'm sorry you feel that way."

"So am I, Jack. So am I."

"This really isn't fair."

"No, I suppose from your point of view it isn't, but as a great man once said, '*Fuck* fair.' I'm going to bed now. Feel free to play with your little scraps of paper as long as you like."

As Anita left the room I turned toward the window so I wouldn't have to watch her go. After that I sat for a long time with my arms folded and stared out at the lights of the city.

I should have dismissed everything Anita had said as mere petulance. Maybe she'd had a bad day at her studio and was just taking it out on me. Nevertheless something she'd said had touched a nerve and I couldn't easily shake it off.

Some part of me had always wondered if I wasn't just the wrong kind of guy for anyone to try and share a life with. Maybe that sort of thing was a God-given talent — something like singing opera or throwing a ball through a hoop — and that it was a talent I just didn't have. Anita didn't seem to think I had it, and I supposed she knew me about as well as anyone.

After a while I decided that there wasn't anything I could do about that right then anyway, even if it were true, but as I was thinking about what Anita said another idea popped unbidden into my head. There was something that I *could* do about everything else that was bothering me, I suddenly realized, and maybe I'd be better off focusing on what I *could* do than fidgeting over what I couldn't.

I collected all of the stuff I'd gotten out of Dollar's garbage except for the Thai-language documents that I had set aside earlier and dumped it back in the garbage bag. Then I removed the CD from the drive in my laptop, put it in a padded manila envelope together with the Thai documents, and took everything down to the Volvo. The envelope went on the front seat and the garbage bag into the trunk.

After that I started the car and drove to Arlene's place. I had no doubt that Arlene and Nata could tell me what was on the disk and in the documents and I had a feeling that both were important somehow.

I needed to know what they said.

Yes, Anita, I admit it. I *wanted* to know.

I had left the envelope with Arlene and Nata on Sunday night and slipped away quickly, pleading fatigue. I was in my office early on Monday morning but was still barely halfway through my first cup of coffee when Arlene called.

"Nothing all that dramatic after all," she said when I answered the telephone.

It was unnecessary of course for her to tell me what she was referring to.

"I've emailed you a copy of what was on the disk, but you're probably going to be disappointed. It was a backup all right, but it was just an address book. Nothing else. Might be something there for you, but. . . ." Arlene trailed off.

"Was it encrypted?"

"Uh-huh."

"So how'd you open it?"

"I used the password."

"But how did you know what Dollar's password was?"

"It was no big deal, doll. People are pretty predictable. When they pick a password, they always use something they won't have any trouble remembering. That's why nearly everyone picks just some ordinary word, or maybe a phrase that's pretty well known. Either that, or they pick a combination of numbers that represent a date or something they can easily remember."

I just listened, making a mental note to change my ATM code as soon as we hung up.

"First we tried a random number crack of four through eight digits. When that didn't work, we ran the file against English, Thai, French, Spanish, and Italian dictionaries and then for good measure against a database of a few hundred thousand proper names, places, and phrases that people sometimes use for passwords. It only took about twenty minutes to crack Dollar's password."

"What was it?" I asked.

"*Berchtesgaden.* That mean anything to you?"

I thought about it briefly.

"Wasn't that the name of Hitler's mountain retreat in World War Two? A place somewhere up in the Bavarian Alps?"

"Yeah, that's right. Still that seems an odd choice of a password for Dollar. Was he a World War Two fanatic?"

"Beats me. How about those documents, the ones in Thai?"

"Now what we've got there might be a little more useful to you, doll. They were all title deeds and property transfers."

"For what? Dollar's house?"

Arlene hesitated, and from something in the way she did it I knew I wasn't going to like whatever it was she was going to say next.

"No, I don't think so. You really can't tell very much from a Thai title deed until you compare the property description with a detailed map of the area where the transfer took place, but as near as I can tell, these transfers all involved large tracks of land in Phuket."

That would probably explain all those American Express receipts Dollar had from Phuket, it occurred to me.

"Maybe Dollar was working on a hotel development there," I said. "Who were the transfers made to?"

"They were all corporate, and they all looked to me like shelf company nominees. It'll take a while to find out who's really behind the companies. You know that better than I do."

"But I still don't see why Dollar would throw title deeds away. Whoever the property was transferred to, the title deeds themselves are still important documents in Thailand."

"These weren't originals, doll. They weren't even complete. My guess is that they were just copies that were attached to something else he was working on, probably as exhibits of some kind just to prove that the transfers had actually taken place."

"I still don't see it, Arlene. A man who'd go to the trouble of encrypting his address book wouldn't just toss copies of transfers like that into the trash. There's too much information on them. He'd shred them first."

"He would if they were real."

That stopped me.

"What do you mean?"

"Now I'm not real sure about this, doll, but I think these are all forgeries."

I blinked at that.

"Not even particularly good ones," Arlene continued. "My guess is that your man had a pressing need to show somebody that he'd purchased a whole hell of a lot of property that he hadn't, so he manufactured these title deeds real quickly to show where a whole bunch of money had gone."

"I just don't know what to say, Arlene."

"I knew you wouldn't, doll. Look, I got some real hot stuff running today, so I'm afraid I've got to leave all this with you for now. Why don't you have a look at that address book and see if anything jumps out at you, then we'll talk again in a few days. Maybe by then it will all have come together for you and it won't look so bad."

I thanked Arlene and we hung up. After going down and refilling my coffee mug, I logged onto the university email system and retrieved the address book Arlene had sent me which turned out to be a single file that she had converted to plain text. I opened it easily enough and started reading though it, although my mind was still back on those title deeds and I figured it was probably a waste of time.

I didn't get any further than the second screen before I realized just how wrong I was.

The fifth entry down the second page was on a single line. Neatly typed all in capitals it read, ASIAN BANK OF COMMERCE.

Next to the name there was a number — a phone number, I assumed, since it had seven digits — but there was no address and no country or city code. It could have been a Bangkok number, but it just as easily could have been one in Teaneck, New Jersey. Far more thought provoking, however, was what appeared in parentheses immediately following the telephone number.

It was a name.

Arthur Daley.

There was nothing else included in the entry. Not one single thing.

My mind clicked straight back to Took Lae Dee when I'd been perched on a stool studying the Hong Kong ID that Barry Gale had handed me. The name on the card — Arthur Daley — had meant nothing at all to me then. Now it did.

Christ, Jimmy Kicks' gangster bank and the name on Barry Gale's phony Hong Kong Identity Card were both right here in Dollar's computer address book.

What could *that* possibly mean? As I fumbled for an answer to my own question, I felt a cool chill pass over me, a charged foreboding of . . . *of what?*

Okay, don't jump to any conclusions here, I lectured myself in a stern voice. *Think this through clearly.*

So there might be some kind of connection between Dollar Dunne and Barry Gale. That was all Dollar's address book really said, wasn't it? It didn't prove that there was also a connection between Barry Gale and Howard Kojinski's body twirling away under the Taksin Bridge. And it certainly didn't prove there was any connection between whatever might be going on here and my own relatively minor involvement with Howard and Dollar or with the recent resurrection of Barry Gale. Right?

Horseshit. Who was I trying to kid?

Exactly how much longer was I going to sit there looking at Barry Gale's cover name in Dollar's computer address book and tell myself that it might only be a coincidence? How long was I going to try and convince myself that it really meant nothing, and more crucially, that it certainly had nothing to do with me?

For the last few days two big trains had been rumbling through my life — one carrying Barry Gale and Jimmy Kicks, and the other carrying Dollar Dunne and Howard the Roach. I had felt both of them gathering speed, relentlessly building momentum toward something, although I had never had the slightest idea where either one was headed.

But now I knew. The whole time they had both been barreling right down the same track, and they had both been aiming straight at each other.

Somehow I made it to my eleven o'clock class and got through it, but I had also agreed to deliver a lecture to an alumni luncheon that day and it was too late to cancel. Someone had hung a particularly dizzying moniker on my otherwise harmless luncheon spiel — *The Creation of Public Securities Markets and their Regulation in the*

Developing Countries of Southeast Asia with an Emphasis on Malaysia, Indonesia, Thailand, Cambodia and Vietnam. I couldn't see why anyone would show up for lunch if they knew they'd have to sit through a speech with a title like that. I couldn't even figure out what the hell it was supposed to be about.

Regardless, a lot of people did show up and I rambled through my notes as well as I could under the circumstances, but my mind was a long way away from the enforcement mechanisms for insider trading regulations in Malaysia and I'm not sure how much sense I made. Still, the audience either didn't notice, or pretended not to. Somehow I got to the end of the hour without anyone asking me if I had the slightest idea what I was talking about.

After the lecture all of the audience mercifully disappeared without anybody staying behind to try and suck up a little by asking me obscure questions designed to suggest the careful reflection they had given to the subject matter of the talk, and afterwards I bolted straight back to my office. Closing the door I switched my computer back on and reopened the file Arlene had sent. I looked at it for a long time, reading and rereading the entry for the Asian Bank of Commerce, but nothing particularly useful came to me.

I didn't like calling for help unless I was absolutely certain why I needed it, but trying to work out what was going on all by myself just didn't look very promising anymore. I was getting my butt kicked here. It was clearly time to send up a couple of flares.

Stanley Ratikun was the only guy I could think of to go to with something like this, but I'd probably have gone to Stanley even if there had been a lot of other choices as well. I hadn't really known him all that well back when he persuaded me to abandon the real world for Bangkok, but I had since come to know and respect the old-fashioned sense of righteousness against which Stanley seemed to test everything he did.

We'd never exactly been pals, of course. Stanley was hardly the sort of guy you could imagine slumped over the bar at the Titty Twister ogling the go-go dancers while he chugged back the Singha. Still, I was pretty sure the mutual respect we had accumulated would survive the questions I had to ask him about Dollar. He wouldn't necessarily tell me what he knew just because I asked him to, but I didn't think he would exactly lie to me either.

When I went up to two floors to Stanley's office, his secretary's desk was empty and I could see through his half-open door that he was on the telephone. I leaned against the wall outside until he finished his conversation, admiring the brass plaque that said, STANLEY RATIKUN, DIRECTOR, SASIN INSTITUTE OF BUSINESS ADMINISTRATION.

After he hung up the telephone, he smiled broadly and waved me in.

TWENTY-FOUR

I TOLD STANLEY WHAT HAD HAPPENED after I got that telephone call from Barry Gale, but I couldn't help noticing that nothing I said seemed to surprise him very much. He did lean forward once and steeple his fingers. The gesture came about the time I was describing the man in Dollar's office who had claimed to be an FBI agent named Frank Morrissey, and I thought I saw a flicker of something like dismay cross his face then, but I might have been mistaken.

I told Stanley almost everything. All I left out was the part about my ferry ride with Archie Ward in Hong Kong and Archie's intimations that the Asian Bank of Commerce had been a front for Chinese bribe money rather than the Russian mob operation that Barry had claimed it was. I didn't think I had the right to drag Archie's name into whatever was going on here, and even more to the point, I wasn't really sure that I really believed what he'd told me. To do that I would also have had to believe that Barry either didn't know the Chinese were involved with the ABC or had made up the whole business about Jimmy Kicks just to mislead me, and neither of those possibilities made any sense at all.

I wound up by telling Stanley about the reference I'd found in Dollar's address book to the Asian Bank of Commerce and the name on Barry's phony Hong Kong ID, then I fell silent.

Stanley's only response was to purse his lips slightly.

"That's it?" he asked.

"Yeah," I said, not bothering to hide my disappointment.

I had just told him what I thought was one hell of a story and Stanley was sitting there like I had strolled into his office and asked to borrow a cup of Nescafé.

"Whatever it all adds up to, Howard Kojinski's dead and Dollar's on the run because of it," I pointed out. "You can't just shrug it all off, Stanley."

Stanley got up and walked to the window and stood with his back to me for a time. Eventually he turned around and leaned against the sill, his arms folded.

"I don't see how any of it explains why Howard was killed, even if everything you say is true, Jack."

"I think Howard stumbled over something he shouldn't have. Maybe it involved the ABC and maybe it didn't, but I think whatever it was scared him badly enough to make him tell someone about it. And I think the person he told was Dollar."

Stanley's face was impassive.

"If Howard started talking to Dollar," I went on theorizing, "maybe that's why he was killed. It would certainly explain why Dollar looked so shaken up when Howard's body was found and why he went to ground so fast after that."

"So you're saying that Jello was right, Jack? That Howard was laundering money for the Burmese and that Dollar knew it, or perhaps was even helping him?"

"Howard might have been doing something like that, but not Dollar. Dollar plays it fast and loose, but he's not a man who'd carry water for a bunch of opium producers just for money. If Dollar was involved, there's got to be something else."

"Such as what?"

"Look, I know this may sound a little nuts to you, Stanley, but just follow me through it. What if the Asian Bank of Commerce was being used in some kind of intelligence operation. Say the FBI was working through the ABC, maybe using it to cover up something they didn't want to be caught doing, and *that* was what Howard stumbled over? What if that's what he told Dollar about?"

"Are you saying that the FBI killed Howard Kojinski to shut him up about their offshore banking activities, Jack?"

"No, I'm . . . well, I don't know. Somebody killed him."

That sounded awfully lame, even to me, but there it was.

Stanley returned to his desk and settled himself behind it, knitting his hands behind his head.

"Even assuming this theory of yours has any substance to it at all, Jack, what does it have to do with you?"

"Howard was carrying my home telephone number and Dollar was doing a funny kind of dance all around me that had something to do with Howard. My guess is that they had a problem and they were edging toward asking me to help them out somehow. Maybe the problem even involved the ABC, but I can't be sure of that. Anyway, then Barry Gale comes back from the dead and starts chatting me up in strange places in the middle of the night."

"I still don't see what you're getting at."

"Look, Stanley, think of it this way. If somebody thought that Howard was talking too much about the ABC — and maybe they even killed him because of that — and this same somebody thought that not only Dollar and Howard, but also Barry Gale might be talking to Jack Shepherd, what kind of conclusion do you think they would draw? Don't you think they would probably guess that I'm right in the middle of everything?"

"Why are you telling me all this, Jack?"

"You're a pretty plugged-in guy, Stanley. You know who's who around here, and you know pretty much what they're up to and what they're saying."

"I've been away from the firm a long time."

"But you're still a player, Stanley. We both know that."

"You're giving me way too much credit, Jack. These days I'm just another retired old fart living out his golden years doing things that nobody cares very much about."

This wasn't getting me anywhere. It was time to chuck one across Stanley's bow and see if I could get his attention that way.

"I'm only trying to find a safe place to get out of the way, Stanley. If while doing that I stumble over something I shouldn't, or if I mess up things I didn't even know were there, you're going to think back to this afternoon and know that this was the day you blew your chance to prevent it."

Stanley swiveled his chair slightly away from me. He studied his left hand briefly as if he had just realized how interesting it really was.

"I think you should have a little history here, Jack. There are a few things you probably ought to know."

I nodded, but Stanley was still looking off toward the other side of the office and couldn't have seen me. Nevertheless, after a short pause, he started talking, choosing his words with obvious care.

"It is true that my firm has done work over the years for various branches of the American government, the kind of work which requires a special form of trust. It makes exotic copy in the press to talk about front companies and foreign banks, but the plain fact is that the world is a complicated and dangerous place. As we all understand that domestic law enforcement cannot be done solely by uniformed officers cruising the streets in brightly painted cars, we must also come to understand that a nation's international affairs cannot always be conducted by announcing one's undertakings publicly."

Stanley had consciously or unconsciously slipped into his business-school lecturer's cadence.

"Consequently, when national interests require a country to work beyond its own borders to defend its security, it is commonly accepted that such work is frequently done through the structure of apparently private businesses. That is a convenient arrangement for both the country that is pursuing its interests and the country in which those interests are located. It gives both of them the security of deniability, something essential to the conduct of modern foreign policy. In any event, these private businesses require organization and administration which obviously cannot be done by the governments working through them, and such tasks are frequently undertaken by discreet, well-connected law firms who are experienced in such matters."

I liked Stanley, and I usually enjoyed his lectures, but this time I wasn't in the mood to learn how to make a watch. I just wanted to know what the hell time it was.

"Are you saying your firm is in the business of camouflaging the FBI behind corporate front companies, Stanley? How about the CIA? You got a few of theirs in your client files, too?"

Stanley sighed deeply.

"I am trying to communicate to you the subtlety of such an undertaking in all its forms, Jack, but — if you must put it so crudely — I guess the answer is yes. Yes, my former firm has had a long-standing relationship with the government of the United States. And, yes, from time to time it has represented companies through which the FBI, the CIA, the DEA, and even quite a few agencies you've almost certainly never heard of have conducted their affairs here in Asia."

My first reaction was to laugh out loud.

"You mean In The Pink Inc. really belongs to George Bush?"

Stanley didn't smile, not even a little.

"What did Howard the Roach have to do with these operations of yours, Stanley?" I asked.

"I must remind you again, Jack, that I retired several years ago. The firm's current activities are entirely out of my hands."

"Yeah, sure."

"You don't have to believe me, but it *is* true."

Stanley sounded genuinely wounded that I wasn't taking him at his word and he sat silently for a while after that, but I figured mostly he was weighing just how much he was actually going to have to tell me to keep me happy, and quiet.

"Howard once laundered money for a variety of people in which the American government had an interest," he eventually resumed. "The short answer is that ultimately he got caught doing it. He was then persuaded to turn his talents to the public good rather than face prosecution."

I figured I'd better push Stanley's narrative along before old age overtook us both.

"You're telling me that Jello was right, aren't you, Stanley? Howard and Dollar *were* laundering money for someone, but it wasn't for Burmese drug dealers. It was for an American intelligence operation."

"No, Jello was only half right at best. Howard and Dollar did manipulate large sums of money from time to time, it is true, but they always did it with the full knowledge of the United States government and only in support of legitimate American interests. You can't call that money laundering."

Stanley shook his head firmly. I wondered if that was entirely for my benefit or if some of the effort was going into convincing himself.

"No," he repeated, "you really can't call what Howard and Dollar were doing money laundering."

I didn't bother to argue with Stanley and instead pressed the more important point.

"So who were they working for? Was it the FBI?"

"It would be better, Jack, if we just left it. . . ."

"Oh Jesus. I get it now."

"I doubt. . . ." Stanley began, but I cut him off before he could get wound up again.

"Stanley, let's be absolutely clear about this. Are you telling me Howard was laundering money for some cockamamie CIA operation and Dollar was helping him do it? Is *that* what they were going to ask me to get involved in?"

"You've been watching too many movies, Jack."

Stanley's voice was level, but I could tell that an edge had crept into it.

"Don't try to reduce the real world to something simple enough for teenagers to understand, Jack. You'll look like an idiot every time."

"And don't jerk me around like some dim-witted student, Stanley. You and your little buddies were having a great time playing spook until somebody took it all too seriously and killed Howard. That scared the shit out of Dollar because he knew he might be next on the list, and so he took off. How am I doing so far?"

"That is *not* right!"

Stanley sounded seriously angry now.

"And I will not say that because it is *not* true!"

"Then you can explain it however you think you should," I said.

"What makes you think that I have to explain anything to you, Jack?"

"Because you don't want me to mess anything up, Stanley. You're up to your neck in some deep shit here and you know I *might* mess it up if I keep asking questions."

"*Will* you keep asking questions?"

"You bet your ass I will. I will keep asking questions until I understand exactly what the hell I'm involved in here. Am I coming through loud and clear?"

Stanley gave a heavy sigh as if all the air had suddenly been let out of him and then his eyes went as dead as the moon. A stillness settled over the office after that and we both sat for a while without saying anything else, looking out the windows to where the sun hung just above a thin wisp of clouds that streaked the horizon beyond the river. While we watched, the setting edge of the sun touched the clouds, the room darkened slightly, and the grayness filtered over us like a fine mist.

Eventually Stanley turned back toward me and leaned forward on his elbows, his eyes seeking mine.

"The loss of British control over Hong Kong was a tremendous problem for the West. We tried to pass it off as inconsequential, but that was not the case. Hong Kong had been our only real window on China since the end of World War Two. It provided our best, sometimes our only access. In one stroke we were cut off from the few assets we had in China and largely lost our ability to collect and evaluate intelligence data from there."

I had a sudden flash of memory, a vivid image of balancing in the bow of the Star Ferry with Archie Ward as we wallowed through the oily swells of Victoria Harbour.

"Everything in the biggest nation on earth, developments that ranged from stepped-up drug smuggling operations by the Chinese army to the production status of intercontinental missiles capable of delivering nuclear warheads anywhere in the world, would soon be a complete mystery to us. The West had almost no human intelligence sources in China anymore, but those few we had, we had to keep supporting in spite of the loss of Hong Kong as a point of access. We *had* to find a way to keep supplying our assets with the resources they needed in order to keep operating."

Archie had been scanning the crowd around us with obvious wariness while he hinted at a variety of connections between the Asian Bank of Commerce and bribe money meant for China. None of it had really made a lot of sense to me then — to tell the truth, it still didn't — but I had a feeling it was all about to.

"Howard Kojinski had connections with several different agencies of the United States government and in working on their behalf he utilized a great many banks and front companies for his operations.

His role was to assist with re-establishing and resupplying the points of access in China that we needed to maintain in order to keep the information flowing."

"Who exactly were we renewing access to in China, Stanley? Who were we resupplying?"

"I would presume, Jack, that we were resupplying the guys on *our* side. That's the way it usually works."

"You mean the dissidents? The democracy activists?"

"Yes." Stanley measured his words. "And some others."

Thinking back on my conversation with Archie Ward, I didn't recall him including any democracy activists or political dissidents among the people who were unhappy about the money that was missing in the collapse of the Asian Bank of Commerce. As I remembered it, he had fingered a long list of Chinese generals and government ministers instead.

"What did Dollar and Howard have to do with this resupplying, Stanley?"

"My former firm was working with Howard and these government agencies to establish the mechanisms that were required for his operations."

"What agencies?"

"You wouldn't know them if I gave you their names and addresses, Jack."

"Try me."

Stanley looked for a moment as if he might, but then he abruptly leaned back and folded his arms.

"Dollar directed the legal work involved in organizing and operating the companies that were used to mask the funds involved in these operations. He was the man who was ultimately responsible for the money. Howard was just the bagman."

I noticed that Stanley had begun referring to *both* Howard and Dollar in the past tense and wondered if that had any significance.

"That's all I know, Jack. If I knew more than that, I probably wouldn't tell you anyway, but I don't. That's it."

"Do you know who killed Howard, Stanley?"

He shook his head slowly.

"Do you know *why* he was killed?"

Stanley shook his head again.

"Do you think it might have been because somebody neglected to tell Howard what he was really being used for?" I asked. "That when he found out somehow, it scared the crap out of him and he started shooting off his mouth? Could that have been the reason?"

"I'll bet you're one of those people who think that the CIA killed Marilyn Monroe, aren't you, Jack?"

"Didn't they?"

Stanley had about half a smile on his face.

"Are you saying, Jack, that Howard's murder was organized and directed by some shadowy operatives of the American intelligence community in order to keep him quiet about these China operations?"

"You don't think it's possible?"

Stanley shook his head.

"No. I don't think it's possible. For two reasons. First, no matter how endlessly fascinating the tales to the contrary may be, the government of the United States does *not* in my experience kill its own citizens in order to advance vast and obscure conspiracies. The real nuts aren't in Washington, Jack. They're in Hollywood."

"And the second reason?"

"Let me suggest to you a rule of thumb to apply when you deal with agencies of the United States government. Never forget, on the whole these are exactly the same kind of people who couldn't convict OJ."

"Then who did kill Howard, and why is Dollar on the run?"

"I don't know, Jack. That's the God's truth. I just don't know."

I held Stanley's eyes and we sat like that, hooked together, until he glanced away again. There was another silence and we both hid in it for a while.

"There's something else I want to know, Stanley."

He raised his eyebrows and waited.

"Who is Just John?"

"He's a good man, Jack."

"That's not exactly what I meant."

"I know," Stanley said, "but I think it's important to say that first."

"He's not just some retired old duffer who runs errands and pours drinks, is he, Stanley? What's John's connection? Is he the firm's CIA man in residence?"

"Would you believe me if I told you John was retired from the State Department?"

"No."

"Well," Stanley said, spreading his hands, "there you go."

We looked steadily at each other, neither of us blinking.

"How did he get hooked up with Dollar?"

"We were asked by a National Security Council staff member to provide a local cover for John about two years ago. The whole operation of re-establishing our access channels into China was a big, complicated undertaking with a lot of pieces that could come unstuck and cause considerable embarrassment all around. Having someone around whose job it was to prevent that from happening seemed sensible. It also sounded reasonable that the firm might take someone on for security purposes, so we readily agreed to the request."

"Then Just John's not CIA? He's with the NSC?"

I briefly considered the implications of that.

"Doesn't that mean he works for the White House?" I asked.

Stanley just shook his head.

"Don't be naïve, Jack. Who the hell knows who John really is or where he really works. And frankly, who cares? John Hanratty, or whatever his name really is, is one of the good guys. He represents the highest levels of American authority and he's doing work that is essential to the preservation of national security. Isn't that good enough for you?"

"Not really. Not with Howard Kojinski swinging off the Taksin Bridge, Dollar on the run, and somebody stalking me around Bangkok. No, it isn't nearly good enough."

"Well, it's going to have to be good enough, Jack." Stanley's voice was tight.

I had one really big question left to ask, and I decided I'd better get to it before whatever goodwill I had with Stanley was entirely exhausted.

"What is Barry Gale trying to get me involved in here, Stanley? Is it something to do with these spy games you guys are playing with the Chinese?"

Stanley met my eyes squarely and he didn't blink. I was sure that he wanted me to know that he was telling me the whole truth, at least as far as he knew what the whole truth was.

"I have no idea what this man Gale wants with you, Jack. I never heard of him until you told me about him today. But none of the rest of this has anything at all to do with you. That I can promise you."

"How can you be so sure?"

"Look, even if Howard or Dollar really was going to ask for your advice on some technical details concerning the work they were doing, as you suspect, I'm certain they had no intention at all of cutting you in on the whole picture. Besides, they never got around to asking or telling you anything at all, did they? You are clearly not involved in this in any way, and I can't see how anyone could think otherwise."

"Then why am I being followed?"

"I doubt you are. But *if* you are, it must have something to do with Gale or his gangster buddies."

"It's not Just John?"

Stanley smiled for the first time in what seemed to be hours.

"You're not that interesting, Jack. John Hanratty moves in higher circles than either of us."

"Let's put this plainly, Stanley. Just for the record. As far as you know, does any agency of the United States government have any interest in me at all?"

"Not unless it's the IRS, Jack."

Our conversation went on for a while after that, as conversations frequently do even after they're really over, but nothing else of any real importance was said by either of us. By the time I left Stanley it was dark, and I went back downstairs to my own office and sat there a while, thinking, without turning on the lights.

Although there were still some missing pieces, on the whole I felt a lot better.

In real life coincidences really *did* occur. When I thought about what Stanley had told me, I could see now why the Asian Bank of Commerce might have been in Dollar's address book. Barry Gale was in the business of facilitating shady dealings for foreigners in Asia by providing them access to compliant banking facilities and bankers who didn't ask too many questions. That would have been just the ticket for Howard and Dollar in setting up their Chinese money runs. Maybe there really wasn't any more to it than that.

It made sense that Barry Gale would have known nothing about how Dollar and Howard had been using the ABC, so his sudden appearance in my life almost certainly had nothing to do with them at all. While Barry Gale might still want me to bail him out of his personal predicament with Jimmy Kicks, the probability that anyone more substantial might be gunning for me was diminishing pretty fast.

The question of who killed Howard was still unanswered, of course, and exactly what Dollar was hiding from remained a mystery, but I decided that Stanley had to be right. I had never actually been involved in anything myself, and regardless of what the answers to those questions ultimately turned out to be, they would have nothing to do with me.

I stood up, turned on the lights, and flipped through the messages Bun had left on my desk when she went home. None of them was important, so I collected my briefcase and locked up.

Yeah, I was pretty much in the clear, I thought to myself again as the elevator whirred down and bumped to a stop at the garage. Now if I could only find some way to get rid of Barry Gale, my life would be on its way back to normal.

Then I climbed into the Volvo and drove home, holding onto that thought the entire way, and enjoying it well beyond all reason.

TWENTY-FIVE

WHEN I GOT HOME AND TOOK the elevator upstairs the first thing I noticed after the door opened at my floor was the faint odor of cigar smoke.

I reminded myself again that I was either going to have to clean up my act or at least get the apartment aired out every now and then. It was a minor wonder to me in this age of advanced self-righteousness that one of my neighbors hadn't already complained to the residents' committee and started a movement to get me thrown out of the building.

It wasn't until I had opened the door to my apartment, dumped my briefcase, and crossed the entry hall into the living room that I realized the smoke I smelled wasn't quite as stale as I had first thought.

"These are pretty good." Tommy gestured with the lighted cigar in his hand. "I generally prefer Cohibas, but Montecristos were all I could find around here and — like you Americans say — don't look in the mouth of a horse that is a gift from somebody."

"It's, 'Don't look a gift horse in the mouth'."

"Sure. Whatever."

Tommy took a long draw on the Montecristo.

"My English may be a little rusty. Maybe you ought to help me with it, Jack."

Tommy seemed to have made himself entirely at home there in my apartment. Although the living room was dim and he hadn't turned on any lights, he looked comfortable enough settled as he was into one of the two low-slung black leather chairs that were turned at right angles to each other in front of the big front window. The cigar he was holding was about half-smoked, so I gathered he had probably been there for a while.

"Don't just stand there, Jack. This is your apartment. Come in, come in."

Tommy's tone was so avuncular that for a moment I wondered if I had forgotten some arrangement we'd made for him to be waiting there for me. I hadn't, of course, and I stood looking at him as he took another long pull on the cigar and exhaled in a steady stream.

"Where's your girlfriend, Jack?"

"She's out. Somebody's having a birthday party at the Oriental."

My response was automatic and I immediately regretted it. Why did I owe Tommy an explanation of anything? After all, he had gotten into my apartment somehow and was lurking there in the dark waiting to ambush me when I came home. In my book, that hardly entitled him to start asking questions, much less to getting any answers.

"Okay, fine." Tommy's voice filled the room with a hearty, good-natured boom. "That's good."

I wondered what was good about it from Tommy's point of view.

"How did you get in here?" I asked.

"You ought to be more concerned about how I'm going to get *out* of here, Jack. That's what I'd be worried about if I were you."

What the hell was that supposed to mean? Was Tommy threatening me?

"Why don't you just sit down? This won't take long."

Tommy tapped the Montecristo against a green celadon bowl he'd put on the floor by the chair to use as an ashtray. He smiled slowly in what I gathered he thought was a reassuring way.

Other than grabbing Tommy and flinging him bodily through the living room window, I didn't see what else I could do. And that didn't seem like too hot an idea, so I sat down.

I watched Tommy as he smoked quietly, smiling in a vague sort of way and looking off in the direction of the lights along Ploenchit Road. He had a soft, almost pink face, and he wore plain, black-rimmed glasses. His dark hair was neatly cut and he was conservatively dressed in a dark suit that was neither snappy nor expensive, a white shirt, and a plain tie with a muted pattern. He didn't seem to notice that I was looking him over or, if he did, to care very much.

"You weren't expecting me tonight, were you, Jack?" he asked, still looking out the window.

"I wasn't expecting anybody."

"But you should have been, Jack. You should have been."

He took a quick draw on his cigar and twisted his head toward me when he exhaled, pointing his free hand toward the humidor that was sitting on a desk across the room.

"You want a cigar or something?"

"It's my apartment, Tommy. If I want anything, I'll get it myself."

He nodded slowly at that, and that was when I noticed that he had stopped smiling.

"Okay, here it is," he said.

Tommy tapped the arm of the chair lightly with his fingers.

"We asked you to stay away from the Asian Bank of Commerce, Jack. We asked you nicely. Then we find out that you're still asking all kinds of questions about the ABC; you're searching through people's houses and looking at their personal papers; and you're pitching all these crazy conspiracy theories. Why would you do things like that, Jack? Are you trying to fuck with us?"

"Well," I said, "I guess that qualifies as getting straight to the point."

Tommy started smiling again, but this time it was in a way I didn't much like. I thought about asking him how he knew all that, but decided it would be pretty much a waste of time.

"You see, Jack, this is the way it works around here. I'm responsible for looking after some things."

"Things like what?"

"Money. Banking. Investments."

Tommy puffed at the Montecristo again and I started wishing I had taken him up on his suggestion that I have one, too.

"You know the things I'm talking about."

I didn't know, but I nodded anyway.

"Those things get fucked up and some people start thinking that *I* fucked up. Suddenly that would make me a problem for them. And I don't want anything like that to happen. You can understand that, can't you?"

"I can understand that," I said.

I still didn't have the slightest idea what Tommy was talking about, but I figured that if I let him keep talking, eventually he'd tell me.

"Good, good." Tommy rolled the Montecristo in his fingers. "When Barry told me that he'd brought you in, that was when I started worrying."

Caught completely off guard, I almost laughed.

"Barry Gale?"

Tommy nodded.

"He told you *what?*"

"That he'd brought you in to help with some problems at the ABC."

"Look, Tommy, I've seen Barry Gale exactly once in the last two years, and I promise you that he didn't bring me into *anything.*"

"Is that so?"

"Yeah, Tommy. That's so."

"Well, Jack." Tommy pulled a face. "I'm having a little trouble there."

"Why is that?"

"Because Barry also told me something else."

"Yeah?"

"He told me you were looking into how the ABC had been disbursing its funds recently, that you were looking for some assets of theirs that had gone missing."

"Well, if you believed him, Tommy, you're shit out of luck."

Tommy took another puff and then he turned the cigar around and examined the long ash that had built up at its tip as if he was looking for something that might be hidden in it.

I waited, but Tommy didn't say anything else. The longer the silence went on, the more threatening it felt, so I started talking again, mostly just to break it.

"Look, Barry Gale showed up here in Bangkok right out of the blue last week. He told me. . . ."

"I know what he told you," Tommy interrupted.

Tommy went silently back to his cigar, leaving the conversation entirely up to me again. I wouldn't have minded so much, but not knowing what we were talking about was a considerable handicap. Finally I decided to give him a little jab, just to see what might develop.

"So then I guess it was your people who swung Howard off the Taksin Bridge, huh? And that would also no doubt be your people following me around town. Not the FBI or the CIA."

I thought Tommy looked startled for an instant and then tried to cover it by drawing slowly on the cigar and carefully tapping off the ash against the bowl at his feet. It was a technique I had used on a few occasions myself when I wasn't sure what was happening, so I readily recognized the signs of a slight opening. I pressed him before he could regroup.

"Didn't know I'd picked up on your flunkies, did you, Tommy? Maybe you'd better find yourself some higher quality guys."

Then he glanced over at me and I could see clearly how surprised he was. I figured I was on a roll and kept going.

"The real question, of course, is why you've got guys tailing me in the first place. It wouldn't be that you've lost Barry Gale, would it? That you think by sticking with me, you can find him again? Because if it is, you're shit out of luck there, too. I have no idea where Barry Gale is."

Now Tommy was staring at me as if I had suddenly gone mad.

"What the fuck you talking about?" he snapped.

"I'm talking about you having me followed."

Tommy looked disgusted.

"What do you take me for, Jack? I'm not some cheap criminal. I'm an official of the Thai government. If I cared where you were, I'd just stick a bug up your ass."

He snorted and started to turn away, but then he stopped.

"What's this shit about the CIA?"

I tossed out a hapless-looking gesture to buy some time while I worked out what was really going on here. Under the circumstances, it came naturally.

"It was just a figure of speech," I said after a moment. "I've had a feeling that someone is following me, but I don't know who it is. I guess I'm still just spooked about Barry Gale showing up like he did."

"Yeah, well." Tommy nodded. "He's a spooky kind of guy."

I could see that my mention of the CIA was still turning in Tommy's head, so I pushed on without giving him any more time to think about it.

"I'm really enjoying your little visit, Tommy, but are you going to tell me what you want any time soon?"

"Yeah, Jack, I'll tell you right now."

Tommy bent over and punched out his cigar in the celadon bowl with a half-dozen stabs that looked just as harsh and brutal as he had wanted them to. Then he took a handkerchief from his pocket, wiped his hands, and stood up.

"Forget about the ABC, Jack. Back off. Do you understand me?"

"I'm not involved with the ABC, Tommy, and I'm not helping Barry Gale. You have my word on that."

Tommy turned and walked out of the living room, and I followed him into as the entry hall. He opened the front door, but then he stopped and looked back at me over his shoulder.

"That's not the way I hear it, Jack, and I usually hear things right. I've warned you to back off, and I'm not going to warn you again. Get as far away from the ABC as you can. Believe me, it's the only thing you can do now."

I was playing in some kind of game that nobody would tell me the rules for, and suddenly a piece of advice usually associated with poker popped into my mind: *Look around the table,* went the maxim. *See if you can figure out who the sucker is. If you can't, it's you.*

I didn't like being a sucker, and something in Tommy's tone made me angry.

"Yeah? And what are you going to do if I don't back off, Tommy? Kill me?"

"You know better than that, Jack. Thais are gentle people with peaceful hearts. We're not violent like you Americans are."

"I'm glad to hear it."

"Then, on the other hand, you know Bangkok, too, Jack."

Tommy let his eyes hang on me through the pale blue haze of cigar smoke that was drifting in the apartment.

"It's tough to get much done without occasionally having somebody shot."

In the dim light and still air the cigar smoke began breaking into long, spiraling wisps, elegant little whorls that floated gracefully away into the darkness at the ceiling.

"Good night, Jack. Thanks for the cigar."

TWENTY-SIX

I WENT BACK INTO THE LIVING ROOM and took a Montecristo out of my humidor. After cutting it and lighting it, I dropped down in the same chair where Tommy had made himself at home, crossed my legs, and sat staring out at the city.

Once in a while, I had to admit to myself, I really did wonder what I was doing in this place.

Bangkok was an enigmatic city at the best of times, a place where the mystery of what you couldn't see was surpassed only by the ambiguity of what you could. But it was also a place of sensual immediacy, and lush, transporting power. Something magical always seemed to be dangling just out of reach.

Living in Bangkok, I sometimes felt like I was playing a scene from *The Third Man* — lurking warily in the shadows; picking my way through markets, temples, and bars; dodging gangsters, conmen, and terrorists; trolling the streets of the city like Holly Martins searching the back alleys of Vienna for Harry Lime in 1945. Holly Martins did have one thing on me, however. At least he knew what he was trying to find.

The Kingdom of Thailand thrived on contradictions, and it was with them that it eventually seduced you. Thai people were generally placid and charming, and somehow they had contrived to combine Buddhist stoicism and the upheavals of modern life into a brew of ambivalence that beguiled the Western soul. *Mai pen rai* — never mind — was the national motto. Who could resist that?

Still, I knew I would always be a foreigner here, and I was constantly reminded of it. Sometimes I felt like a guest at a dinner party being hosted by a secret lodge that didn't want me for a member. Every spoken word contained a nuance I couldn't hope to decode; every look included a social commentary worthy of Dickens; every silence concealed an entire conversation.

Why, I questioned myself sometimes, would any man voluntarily choose to live in a country in which he would always be an outsider, a place where he would never even be able to read the signs. Stanley had offered me the position at Sasin. That was the obvious reason I was in Bangkok, but of course that was no answer at all, and it begged the real question: Why had I accepted so readily?

I had told myself back then that it was because of the never-ending contentiousness that had become the lot of my profession and the theme my life. Perhaps that was just a lawyer's natural plight, but still, sometimes it was genuinely scary being surrounded day after day by all those angry, self-righteous people screaming insults at each other. Often I got the feeling that the slightest spark could ignite something ugly and painful. It felt like living in the midst of a sprawling trash novel come to life.

I'd known in my heart then that I'd better lay me down my sword and shield before I awoke one morning and was too old and too tired to lift them anymore. The academic life appeared to be just the ticket. Even better, Bangkok was about as far away from Washington I could get.

Yet now Barry Gale's resurrection had set off something like a landslide inside me. The force of it should have been unsettling. It should have made me run a mile. But it wasn't, and I hadn't.

Instead the feel of it was energizing and tantalizing. Actually it was nothing less than irresistible. I felt like a man waking from a coma, cautiously testing his body parts and perceptions, vaguely surprised to find that everything was still working. I started wondering if I had ever really wanted out at all, or if I had already sensed back then that Bangkok would eventually change the game into something even more exhilarating.

After I had smoked the cigar down to a butt, I let it lie in the ashtray until it went out and then I got up and went into the kitchen to see what I could find to eat. When Anita was out I reverted effortlessly to my old bachelor routines so I grabbed a Heineken from the refrigerator and a bag of pretzels from the pantry, carried them both back into the living room, and turned on CNN.

I sipped at the beer and watched Larry King for a while as he interviewed Harrison Ford. The two men were talking about the Christmas holidays just passed, and they chuckled together about how much they had overindulged and how hard they had to exercise now to make up for it. Was that the way it was back in America now? Overindulgence was an extra slice of pie at Christmas? It was all so depressingly earnest, I couldn't bear to listen any longer. I hit the mute button and the screen flickered in silence while I finished my Heineken and ate the rest of the pretzels.

I had lived in Bangkok long enough that watching CNN made me feel like Jay Gatsby standing on his lawn in the darkness and watching that green light blinking across the water at the end of Daisy's dock. CNN had become a beacon marking the existence of an entirely different world from the one in which I lived. That world seemed vaguely recognizable and almost close enough to touch, but now so strange and far away that I knew I could never be part of it again. Here I was pondering death threats from a Thai intelligence officer because of vast sums of Chinese bribe money that were missing from a Russian mob bank in the Philippines, and Larry King was worried about eating too much pie at Christmas.

How the hell could I ever go back to *that?*

Anita still hadn't gotten home and eventually I gave up thinking about it all and went to bed, but I lay there wide-awake, helpless to turn off the conversation with Tommy. There was something in it I had missed the first time by, but I couldn't put my finger on whatever it was no matter how often I ran it back.

There was at least one thing that was clear enough, however. Whatever I had gotten sucked into, I was pretty sure that only Dollar or Barry Gale could explain it to me. Other people might have part of it — people like Stanley and Beth and Tommy — but I was certain now that only Dollar and Barry had all of it. I had to find at least one of them, but which one? Maybe it didn't even matter what I decided. After all, I had no better idea where to start looking for one than I did the other.

Actually my prospects of finding either of them didn't seem all that great. I noticed Barry hadn't bothered to leave his number with me when we'd met at Took Lae Dee, and what with him being dead and all, I doubted he would be in the book. And as for Dollar, from the looks of his house I didn't think he'd left a forwarding address anywhere either.

There had been something in the way Tommy spoke about Barry Gale that left me with the feeling he knew *exactly* where Barry was, but from the message he had delivered that evening, I also knew he wasn't going to tell me. After all, how could he *not* know where Barry was? Surely Tommy was able to keep track of just about anybody. What was that he said? *If I wanted to know where you were, I'd just stick a bug up your ass.*

That was a pretty funny line. At least it was for a Thai spy.

I tried again to get to sleep, but there was still something Tommy had said that worked at me. I just couldn't get my hands around whatever it was long enough to grab on.

A few minutes later, thinking again what a funny crack that had been, there it was. *I'd stick a bug up your ass.*

I jumped out of bed, pulled on some shorts and a T-shirt, slipped into a pair of loafers, and went straight down to the garage.

I got into the Volvo and lowered the top, and then I got out again, trying to stand exactly where I had seen the man in the dark blue suit leaning over my car in the faculty garage. I bent forward in just the way I had seen him bend forward. My hands fell near where the steering column passed underneath the dashboard and I ran them carefully over the bottom of the column and up under the dash.

Now that I knew what I was looking for, it didn't take me long to find it.

The man had hidden the device behind the ignition wiring. I carefully pulled it loose and stood there weighing it in my hand. It was no bigger than a credit card, and at a glance it looked as if it might even be a part of the car. The thin rectangular case was black plastic and it had a small magnet attached that held it firmly to a bracket on the back of the dashboard.

I examined the little box, wondering what its range was. That was probably why I'd never seen anybody following me. They didn't have to stay close enough to me to be seen. Whoever had planted it was probably just holed up somewhere with their feet on a desk, drinking lousy coffee, and watching a little red dot crawl around a big wall map.

Tommy had seemed genuinely puzzled when I accused him of having me followed and now I understood why. Hidden transponders working off GPS satellites were way too sophisticated for the locals. This little baby was major league.

I stood there in the silent garage holding the gadget for a while, then I walked down a few parking slots, squatted behind a big, black Mercedes with heavily tinted windows, and snapped the thing up into a hollow in its rear bumper. I rattled it a couple of times to make certain it was secure, then I stood up and wiped my hands on my T-shirt.

The Mercedes belonged to an elderly man who owned the building. I didn't really know him, but rumor had it that he was a local godfather who controlled a lot of the underground casino action in Bangkok and there was also a widely-held view that he had a great many interesting political and military connections.

My neighbor's travels would probably prove highly entertaining for whoever it was sitting out there watching that little red dot. I really enjoyed thinking about that all the way back upstairs in the elevator.

Tuesday was my busiest teaching day. Two lectures, a seminar on developing effective financial plans for start-up companies, and scheduled office hours for students who wanted to come in and suck up a little. I threw myself energetically into all of it, hoping that it might help me to clear my head, but naturally my thoughts kept turning back to the problem of finding either Barry or Dollar.

Talking to Stanley had been interesting, and listening to Tommy's threats had been a real kick, but I seemed to have been doing very little recently other than talking and listening. Something a lot more energetic was clearly called for if I really wanted to get this monkey off my back. And I really did.

I made up my mind what to do somewhere between discoursing learnedly on the regulation of finance companies in Hong Kong and listening patiently to a tall Japanese-looking student with very long hair complain about his grades. Barry Gale had come to Bangkok because he wanted something from me. Since he hadn't gotten it yet, he would probably still be somewhere close by. Dollar, on the other hand, could have gone almost anywhere. That clearly made Barry the missing person to focus on.

Moreover, the time had clearly come to hit the streets if I actually intended to find anyone, although I had to admit that I really had no idea how to go about finding somebody who didn't want to be found. Fortunately, however, someone came to mind who was no doubt a lot better at that sort of thing than I was.

Mango Manny probably had eyes and ears in places most people didn't even know were places. I didn't know what Arlene had told Manny about me and I couldn't guess what he might be prepared to do to help me out, but I figured there was only one way to find out for sure.

When my last appointment of the day was over, I went home and made myself a tuna sandwich and some iced tea. Anita was at her studio and so I polished both of them off sitting alone at the kitchen table and flipping through the *International Herald Tribune.* After that I showered and changed into khaki slacks, a white shirt with a button-down collar, and a blue blazer, then I got out the Volvo and drove over to Q Bar.

It might be a little early to check out the action, but it was exactly the right time to find out if a semi-retired British hitman was willing to do me a little favor.

TWENTY-SEVEN

Q BAR WAS A STYLISH TWO-STORY STRUCTURE of raw concrete and black glass that was set off by itself on a quiet back *soi* in Bangkok's fashionable Sukhumvit district. Half obscured by groves of gum trees and tall stands of spindly bamboo, it looked less like a bar than it did the home of a very hip witch nestled away deep in a cartoon forest.

Nevertheless a bar it was, although hardly just another pedestrian saloon. The place was a shifting kaleidoscope of gorgeous Thai women and flamboyant gay men, flat-eyed Chinese millionaires and hard-hitting Israeli hustlers, chubby Arab conmen and twitchy German smugglers, eager American drug runners and expressionless Japanese gangsters.

Q Bar was nothing less than a Whitman's sampler of the assorted international riffraff that Bangkok sucked up like a vacuum cleaner, and by eleven every night it was crammed top to bottom with the beautiful people. Everyone who was chichi enough to count for anything in Bangkok had to turn up at least once a week or risk losing his standing.

It wasn't quite eight o'clock yet when I handed over a hundred baht to a skinny kid at the driveway and bumped the Volvo over the gravel of the parking lot across the street. The lot was almost empty, so I pulled into the shadows of a corner away from the street to avoid advertising my presence too blatantly. It probably didn't really matter, but there weren't that many Volvo convertibles around Bangkok and parking mine where anyone who happened to be passing could guess I was inside Mango Manny's place didn't seem to me to be a particularly good idea right then.

After I locked the car I walked across the narrow *soi* and over the concrete bridge that led past a parked rickshaw to Q Bar's improbably turreted entry. I made my way up the narrow staircase just behind the bar and found a table to myself off on one side of the large outdoor terrace on the second floor. I remembered that the last time I had been there everybody had been puffing cigarettes like it was an entrance requirement and by eleven the interior had become one huge blue cloud. Most of the year sitting outside in Bangkok's humid night air wasn't most people's idea of a good time, but at Q Bar it might beat the alternative.

I ordered a beer and waited. Sure enough in a couple of minutes Mango Manny slid into the chair opposite mine.

He was dressed quite differently from the way he had been at the Polo Club and I wondered if he might have been tweaking the cheeks of the local high-society types a bit then. Tonight he wore a dark gray tropical-weight wool suit that must have cost at least three thousand dollars and a crisp, white-on-white dress shirt without a tie. On the other hand, when I registered the thick gel coating his hair and the diamond ring on his left pinkie, I decided that Manny still left the same general impression that he had at the Polo Club, something like a low-fat Marlon Brando with a good tailor.

"What you drinking that Singha shit for?" he muttered as he sat down. "Tastes like fooking horse piss."

Manny snapped out something to a hovering busboy. I'd never heard Thai spoken with a cockney accent before and the combination produced an interesting if utterly unintelligible sound.

I missed what Manny said, but the boy apparently had no trouble understanding because he nodded and disappeared. Moments later a waiter materialized. He poured Manny a cup of tea — white, no sugar, in a china cup that looked to me like Wedgwood — and then whisked away my Singha. He replaced it with a Corona that had a dewy slice of lime tucked into its long neck. The bottle was so cold that the condensation began forming a little pool on the metal table before I even touched it.

Manny took a pack of Marlboros out of the inside pocket of his jacket and I sipped at my beer while he lit one. When I was certain I had his full attention, I put the Corona down and folded my forearms on the table.

"Arlene told me to come see you if I ever needed help, Manny," I said. "I need some now."

He nodded, drawing on his cigarette, then he sipped tentatively at his tea and nodded again in what I took to be a gesture of permission for me to continue.

While I told the story of Barry Gale and the Asian Bank of Commerce, Manny sat quietly and puffed on his Marlboro, taking an occasional sip of tea. At the mention of Tommy's nocturnal appearance in my apartment and his parting threat, Manny raised his eyebrows slightly, but he didn't say anything.

I had intended to tell Manny everything. I assumed he knew Dollar since everyone seemed to, and I was even going to tell him about the apparent connections that I had stumbled on between Dollar and Barry Gale, but somewhere in the middle of the telling, I changed my mind. It wasn't that I didn't trust Manny — frankly I wasn't absolutely sure whether I could or not in spite of the weight that Arlene's endorsement carried — it just seemed to me that keeping a few cards in my hand wouldn't really hurt anything.

I wound up my tale with a description of the tracking device I had found in my car, and I finished talking at the same time Manny finished his Marlboro. He had left the pack lying on the table next to his cup and he shook out another, tapping it against the table a couple of times before lighting it.

"All this shit got anything to do with that geezer they found under the bridge?"

"No." I bit my lip slightly. "At least not as far as I can see right now."

I was prepared to edit the truth a little, but I hated flat out lying to a man whose help I was asking for.

Manny stared directly at me, his face as flat as a dinner plate, and he continued to watch me while he took a long hit on the fresh Marlboro. He almost looked to me like he was sniffing the air, checking for the scent of danger, and I wondered briefly if he had found it. Apparently not, because before long he shifted his eyes away from my face and focused somewhere out over my shoulder.

"So what you want from me, mate?"

"I need to find Barry Gale. Arlene says your people have the whole country wired. I was hoping you'd be willing to help me."

"I thought you said you weren't going to do anything for the bugger. Now you wanna find him?"

"Look, Manny, think about it. I'm right in the middle of something here and I don't know what it is or how to get out of it. When you start discovering surveillance transmitters in your car, you know you're on *somebody's* shit list. I think Barry Gale's the only guy who can tell me whose and why."

Manny looked doubtful. The tea had grown cold and he pushed it aside with the back of his hand.

"Where's this geezer gone?"

"Nobody knows."

"Somebody *always* knows."

"It's not me. That's why I'm here."

"You saying you got no idea at all?"

"Well. . . ."

Many leaned back, folded his arms and waited.

"There's some other stuff I didn't tell you about," I finally said.

"That sounds right."

"I've got a hunch — and this is just a hunch, Manny — that Barry might be somewhere in Phuket."

"Little birdie must 'a told you that, huh?"

I sighed. So much for keeping a few cards in my hand.

"Do you know Dollar Dunne?"

"Heard of him."

"I think he was doing some work with Barry."

I explained to Manny the connection I had found between Dollar and Barry Gale, and I told him what I'd heard about Dollar laundering money for American intelligence. I didn't tell him where I'd heard it or what Stanley had said the money was going to be used for, and I noticed that he didn't ask.

Manny was a smart guy, all right. There were some things that smart guys didn't really *want* to know.

But I did tell him about all the American Express receipts from Phuket I'd found in Dollar's garbage and the package of property transfers that Arlene thought were fakes.

"It might mean that Dollar was using a property development scam in Phuket to launder money through the Asian Bank of Commerce and that Barry was hooked into it," I said. "So maybe he's gone to ground somewhere down there."

Manny didn't say anything right away.

I cleared my throat unnecessarily.

"It's pretty thin," I admitted.

"Bugger thin. It's fooking transparent."

"Yeah, well. It's all I got."

Manny's eyes shifted off mine and were still for a long moment before he spoke again.

"You know, you're the second bloke today who's come around asking me about this tosser," he said, still not looking at me.

"You're kidding."

"I look like Mr. Bean to you or what, mate?"

"Sorry, Manny. Just a figure of speech."

I waited for him to go on, but he didn't. He appeared to be lost in his cigarette.

"So who else was looking for Barry Gale?" I eventually prompted.

Manny shrugged elaborately.

I gathered I was asking Manny to break his personal code of ethics, and I also gathered that he wouldn't.

"Then what *can* you tell me?"

Manny's brow furrowed and he looked pained. His eyes narrowed, a wary shadow appearing at their corners.

"I hear there's a shooter looking for your boy."

Somebody was looking to kill Barry? Who? Jimmy Kicks? It seemed unlikely that Jimmy would want Barry dead, at least not yet. He hadn't found out where the ABC's money had gone yet and Jimmy would certainly want to know *that* before he said good-bye to Barry.

It seemed just as unlikely to be the Chinese. Archie Ward had said they were mighty unhappy that their money had disappeared, of course, but they probably wouldn't be trying to kill Barry yet either. With Howard already dead and Dollar among the missing, if Barry was killed, then the only person left alive they might figure could find their money for them was. . . .

Oh, shit.

"Son of a bitch," I muttered.

Manny tilted his head slightly to one side, but he didn't say anything.

"So you don't know anything else about Barry Gale?" I asked after a pause. "At least nothing you're going to tell me."

Manny took another long pull on his cigarette and scratched at his nose, but he still didn't say anything.

I popped my lips and made a palms-up gesture of exasperation.

"Okay, I can take a hint. But can I ask you another question about something else, Manny?"

He looked at me and raised his eyebrows.

"Did you really go to Cambridge?"

A look of discomfort crossed Manny's face before he could chase it away.

"Look, mate, I'm just a cockney cowboy who owns a Bangkok boozer."

"You didn't answer the question, Manny."

"Okay, mate. I really went to Cambridge. You happy now?"

Manny took a last puff on his Marlboro, dropped it to the terrace, and stabbed at it with his foot.

"They thought I was a fooking idiot."

Abruptly he scraped back his chair and stood up.

"You had your dinner yet, mate?"

Without waiting for me to answer, he turned and walked away.

Shortly after that the waiter brought me another Corona, a plate of rice, and a pungent dish of garlic squid in a rich, black bean sauce. I gathered that was going to be the last I would see of Manny that the evening, and it was.

A half hour and another Corona later Q Bar had gotten a good deal more crowded and I had already grown bored with watching the beautiful people preen for each other. All the women were too dazzling and blasé for me, and all the men were too gay. Or maybe it was the other way around. I couldn't decide for sure.

I worked my way down to the first floor, pushed outside through the thick crowds, and walked back across the street to where I'd parked the Volvo.

Maybe Manny would decide to help me find Barry Gale. Or maybe not. Maybe I was right and Barry was holed up in Phuket. Or maybe not.

Bits of an old Pete Seeger folk song from the seventies came back to me as I walked across the parking lot. I whistled tunelessly, searching for the melody, but all I really remembered was part of the lyric, a few lines declaring that you could sum up all the wisdom in the world in a single word — *maybe.*

Wherever Barry Gale had gone to ground, I'd bet my last dollar he was close by. Dollar, on the other hand, might be another matter altogether. If I ever found him, I was certain he would turn out to be an awful lot further away.

I threaded my way among the Mercedes and BMWs crammed into Q Bar's parking lot. It was a nice night, clear and comfortable, and I was just thinking about whether I ought to put the top down when a car's headlights swept over the lot and I saw the silhouette of somebody sitting in the Volvo's front passenger seat.

I slid into the shadow of a van that was parked at the end of a long row of Mercedes and watched for several minutes, but it was too dark to see anything very clearly and no other lights hit the Volvo at just the right angle to light up the interior again. Eventually my curiosity overcame my caution. I edged away from the van and worked my way toward the Volvo, keeping in what I hoped was the car's blind spot. I moved around to the passenger side and crept toward the door in a half crouch.

It never occurred to me that it might be Dollar there in the front seat until I got up to the door and got a good look through the window.

And it certainly never occurred to me that Dollar might be dead until I opened the passenger door and his corpse shifted and fell out onto the ground.

There were no visible wounds that I could see as I bent over him, no blood at all, and that made him look even spookier lying there. I touched his throat without expecting to find a pulse, and there wasn't one. While I was certainly no expert on such things, I guessed he must have been dead for quite a while. He was very pale, his skin almost transparent, and the body was cold.

It seemed obvious that Dollar had been killed somewhere else and then deposited in the front seat of my locked car as a message, just as leaving Howard dangling underneath the Taksin Bridge had undoubtedly been a message, too. When Howard had been found, I had no idea who the message might have been for. With Dollar, however — try as I might to conjure up some comforting ambiguity — the intended recipient was obviously me. The problem was that I still wasn't certain what the message actually *was,* although I was beginning to get a pretty good idea.

I was a little disappointed in myself later when I remembered what I had been thinking right at that moment. After all, there I was squatting on the gravel of the parking lot at Q Bar with one hand resting on Dollar's dead body sprawled in front of me and I had been essentially looking at his murder as a shortening of my to-do list.

Still, finding Dollar's body in the front seat of my Volvo had made at least one thing absolutely clear.

Okay, so now that leaves just one guy I've still got to find.

TWENTY-EIGHT

I HAD NEVER REALIZED HOW MUCH crime scenes in real life looked like the ones on television. Of course, I couldn't remember ever being at a real crime scene before, and maybe the Thais watched a lot of television, so perhaps that explained it.

Yellow tape had been strung across the parking lot's entrance and bubble lights rotated lazily on the roofs of two police cars parked just outside. Tongues of blue light whipped over the little knots of people who had gathered in the street to watch the action and every so often one would illuminate a whole face, leaving its image hovering in the night air for a moment, shimmering with otherworldly phosphorescence.

A few policemen in tight brown uniforms, high boots, and white helmets stood here and there like men who were accustomed to standing sentry against God-only-knew what imagined intervention. A half-dozen other people in civilian clothes, mostly short-sleeved shirts and dark trousers, were bunched up around Dollar's body peering down at it. One woman in a brown uniform with a very short skirt kept walking back and forth between the body and the street where a collection of vehicles had been abandoned in haste as each new wave of arrivals had washed up at the parking lot.

Radios crackled and muffled voices muttered briefly before disappearing in little pops. Occasionally there was the unintelligible murmur of a voice, but other than that, it seemed to me oddly quiet.

Someone had set up three mercury-vapor floodlights on tall aluminum stands and their illumination made everyone in the parking lot look waxy and artificial, almost dead. Everyone, strangely enough, except Dollar. The wan, yellowish light made him look more alive somehow, and I almost expected that any minute he was going to get up from the ground, brush off his suit, and walk over to ask me for a cigar.

Instead it was Jello who walked over to where I was leaning on a concrete-block wall at the back of the parking lot. I hadn't seen him since that Saturday morning at Dollar's office, but our conversation then made it entirely unsurprising to me that he would be here now.

Jello was wearing rumpled jeans and a Hawaiian shirt but in a muted variation of the usual style. Maybe it was one he kept around for visiting murder scenes. The shirt had a very dark blue background against which little yellow waves were etched in endless coils, and as he lumbered toward me the rolling of his big belly caused the waves to stretch and ripple so frantically that I wouldn't have been surprised to see a tiny surfer suddenly whiz from one side of his body to the other.

Jello leaned against the wall next to me and nodded slightly. I nodded back, but both of us kept our eyes on the parking lot.

"I don't know what to say, Jack."

We stood quietly a while longer, watching people I didn't know walk around doing things I didn't understand.

"Neither do I," I finally said.

A tall, young-looking woman in a dark brown uniform was circling Dollar's body firing off photographs from various angles. When a flash of her strobe light caught me squarely in the eyes, I blinked and looked away.

"How did it happen?" I asked Jello without looking at him.

"Broken neck, they think."

Just like Howard. Why wasn't I surprised?

"How long ago?"

"Probably four to six hours."

While I watched the tall woman circle Dollar's body again, I did the math. I had parked in the lot around eight and come back to the car just before ten. It was now almost eleven. If Jello was right, that meant Dollar had been killed about the time I was deciding to drop in on Manny.

I hadn't even known where the Volvo was going to be until nearly eight. Had someone been following me, just hauling Dollar's body around town and looking for a chance to stuff it into my car? Or was there another locator device somewhere in the Volvo? Maybe I'd only found the one they meant for me to find. If that was the case, then whoever was watching me could just have sent somebody over to where the little red dot had stopped on their map, pop open the passenger door, and jam Dollar's corpse inside. I felt sick just running through the possibilities.

"I want to find out who did this, Jack."

I looked at Jello's eyes and saw something else.

"No, you don't. You just want to find out what Dollar was up to because you think it would look good in your intelligence files."

"I don't have to find out. I know exactly what he was up to."

"Bullshit you do."

A stout, middle-aged Thai in a long-sleeved white shirt buttoned at the cuffs stood looking down at Dollar's body, his hands on his hips. Then he glanced up abruptly, staring straight at my face almost as if he was comparing it with Dollar's and trying to decide why Dollar was lying there on the ground instead of me. Finally the man jammed his hands in his pockets, turned, and walked away in the direction of the yellow tape.

"Dollar and Howard were laundering money all right, Jack. That much of what I told you was true. But it wasn't drug money."

Jello's voice was low and I watched his eyes flicking around the parking lot as he talked.

"So what was that crap you gave me about the Burmese?"

"I was afraid they were going to ask you to help them without telling you what they were really doing. I thought if I gave you the drug-money story, it would scare you off."

"So what were they really doing?"

"I can't tell you that, Jack."

I shook my head and looked away, but Jello kept talking anyway.

"I imagine you know by now that the guy you found in Dollar's office wasn't really FBI."

I smiled tightly.

"He works out of the American Embassy. We've met a few times, but I don't know who he really is. He carries FBI ID, but I think he's probably CIA."

"No shit, Sherlock."

"Look, Jack, you weren't supposed to be there so what the hell did you expect me to do?" Jello sounded exasperated. "Say, 'Hey, Jack, let me introduce you to a man I think is a CIA case officer investigating the murder of the chief money launderer for an American intelligence operation?' You think I should have done something like that?"

"Maybe."

Then I realized what Jello had just said.

"What kind of intelligence operation?"

Jello looked very tired and, I thought, suddenly a little pale.

"Fuck, Jack, just forget I ever said it. Shit rolls downhill here like every place else. Local boys like me are nothing in this kind of deal. I fetch files, I get coffee, and I pass along native wisdom. They don't tell me anything. You think I like that, man?"

"Nobody makes you do it."

"You don't think so?" Jello's anger sounded genuine. "If you think nobody makes me do it, you've got a lot to learn about power, Jack."

We went back to watching the festivities in the parking lot and let the undertone of anger and resentment that had taken over the conversation dissipate.

"There's something else," Jello said quietly, and somehow I wasn't surprised. "Some of the money Dollar and Howard were moving is missing."

"Yeah?"

I made an effort to sound disinterested and found it wasn't all that hard.

"The rumor is that fifty or sixty million dollars is unaccounted for."

If Jello expected me to be impressed, he must have been surprised. I'd dealt with numbers like that too long to wet my pants just because somebody mentioned a huge amount of money.

"Is that what this is really about, Jello? The money?"

"Shit, Jack." Jello sounded disgusted, although whether at my question or at himself I wasn't sure. "That's what it's *always* about, isn't it?"

There was a rustle of movement near the street and several uniforms trotted toward the opposite side of the police cars that were parked across the driveway. When Jello saw the activity, he pushed himself away from the wall.

"Be right back," he said.

I watched the yellow waves ripple across his Hawaiian shirt as he walked away.

How much did Jello really know, I wondered? He'd just admitted to a few tidbits, of course, but confessing to what you think someone else already knows hardly amounts to a particularly impressive demonstration of candor, even if people who did it usually tried to make it look that way. On the other hand, maybe he was actually stumbling around in the dark just as much as I was.

Across the parking lot Jello talked briefly to one of the uniforms, and then he reached down with one big hand and lifted the yellow tape for someone. When he turned around and started back to where I was waiting, I saw Just John next to him, his hands jammed deep in his pockets.

"Well now," I said when they got to where I stood in the shadows against the wall. "Been away, John? Incidentally, have I told you what a bang-up security job you're doing here for Dollar? Keep up the good work, man."

"Why are you so cranky, Jack?" Jello asked, the tired note back in his voice.

"I can't imagine."

John settled into a comfortable lean against the wall next to me.

"Maybe there's nothing I can do for Dollar anymore, Jack, but there's something I can do for you," he said.

I looked from John to Jello.

"Oh please. Tell me you're not about to run the good-cop-bad-cop routine on me."

"Look, Jack," Just John said, "I'd be happy to spell it all out for you. You want to hear it?"

I looked away from both of them, but I nodded slightly.

"Two guys bagging money for a major national security operation both get whacked and the only live connection either of us . . ." Just John waggled a finger back and forth between himself and Jello ". . . can find between them is a business school professor whose hands are so clean you could lick sugar off them. That doesn't make any sense to us. That make any sense to you, Jack?"

"I'm not the only guy around who knew both Howard and Dollar."

"That's not the connection we're talking about and you know it."

Just John shook his head. I thought he was trying way too hard to get something like regret and even a little sadness into the gesture, and it ended up looking silly.

"We're here to help you work this thing out, Jack," John went on, "but you keep feeding us dog turds and calling them Twinkies."

I took a breath and looked toward where two elderly men, one very short and the other very tall, were wheeling a metal gurney in the direction of Dollar's body. As it rattled and knocked across the gravel, the background murmur of voices gradually faded and several dozen pairs of eyes silently tracked its progress toward where Dollar sprawled just outside the open door of my Volvo.

"We know about Barry Gale." Just John's voice was flat. "We just don't know what your connection with him is, Jack."

"We were partners in the same law firm once. Other than that, I don't have a connection with him."

"Under the circumstances, that's pretty hard for us to swallow."

"Yeah? And what circumstances are those?"

"Look at it from our point of view, Jack. Barry Gale shows up here in Bangkok. He has a quiet little meeting with you. A week later, two guys who were using the ABC to front a major intelligence operation are dead and the money they were responsible for is gone. I suppose that's just a coincidence, is it?"

"What are you saying, John?" I snapped. "That I helped Barry Gale set up Dollar and Howard in order to steal the money? Or maybe you're saying *I* killed them and took the money all by myself."

Neither Jello nor John answered me, but then I hadn't really expected them to.

When the gurney clattered to a stop next to my Volvo the men who had been grouped around the body began to drift away, leaving what was left of Dollar Dunne to the two old men.

"Who do you work for, John?" I asked, keeping my eyes on the gurney. "Are you NSC? Do you really work for the White House? Or maybe you're just some bored little spook with a cubicle in Langley who's way over his head in something he doesn't understand."

One of the men spread a bright orange body bag on the ground next to Dollar and pulled open the zipper. The sound scraped across the parking lot like a sharp object being pulled over glass.

"Ultimately we all work for the White House, Jack."

I started to say something, but John held up one big hand.

"Let's get back to the main point here, can we? Neither Jello nor I can figure out how you got in the middle of all this, Jack. We need to know exactly what your role really is. We really need to know right now."

"I don't have a role."

"Yes, you do, Jack. Yes, you do."

I expected the two men to lift Dollar's body into the bag, one holding the shoulders and the other the legs, but they didn't. Instead they went around to the same side of the body, gave it a push, and rolled it over on top of the bag. Then one of the men bent down and yanked the sides of the bag up around the body, wiggling it until Dollar was completely inside. The other man grasped the zipper and walked it closed, causing the same awful scraping sound to echo across the parking lot for a second time.

"This happened because of some bullshit CIA scheme you're running, didn't it, John? This happened because the CIA was using Dollar and Howard to funnel tens of millions of dollars to corrupt Chinese officials to keep them spying for you, didn't it?"

Just John looked surprised in spite of what I gathered was his best effort not to.

I winked at him.

"Gotcha."

John gave a little snort and looked down at his shoes.

"Stanley Ratikun must have told you about the NSC thing. Did he tell you the Chinese story, too?"

I didn't say anything, but of course I didn't have to. Just John knew he was right.

"What else did he tell you?" John asked me after a moment.

"Not much."

I thought back briefly over the conversation I'd had with Stanley.

"Not anything really."

All three of us watched silently as the gurney rattled away toward the street. When it reached the edge of the parking lot, one of the brown uniforms lifted the crime-scene tape and the two attendants wheeled the gurney under it. Then they turned left behind a white Toyota van and disappeared from sight.

Just John pushed at the gravel with the toe of his shoe.

"This happened, Jack, because there's forty-three million six hundred thousand dollars unaccounted for. Plus change."

"Christ, you guys go first class, don't you? What did you think you could get for forty million dollars? Mao's body?"

Just John gave me an imitation of a smile.

"That's not my point."

"Then what *is* your point?"

"Dollar and Howard knew where that money went."

"Well, I think you're going to have one hell of a time sweating it out of them now."

"You still don't get it, do you, Jack? That's why somebody stuck Dollar's body in your car. They think you know where the money is."

John leaned closer to my ear.

"And they wanted to remind you that they know where *you* are."

"For Christ's sakes, John, I'm just a college teacher!"

I pointed angrily toward where Dollar's body had disappeared behind the white Toyota van.

"*He* was just a lawyer. Guys like us push papers around when somebody tells us to. That's all we do. It's guys like you who screw around with stupid schemes that get people killed, not us. I *don't know* where any money is, and I've got *nothing* to do with whatever is going on here. How many times do you want to hear it?"

John's sigh was long and deep.

"Let me run it down one more time for you, Jack. Dollar and Howard were using the ABC to handle enough black money that somebody is willing to kill people to get at it. Barry Gale fronts the ABC. Gale disappears one day, then he turns up in Bangkok and goes straight to you. You get curious and start sniffing around the ABC and that idiot Tommy turns up in your apartment and tells you to back off."

John saw me blink.

"Gotcha," he grinned.

Jello and John were both looking at me, but I wasn't looking at them.

"Yeah, sure we know about Tommy going to your apartment, but that's not what you should be focusing on here, Jack. Focus on what this looks like to us when we put it all together. Focus on how it looks to anybody wondering where you fit in. How do you think it adds up?"

Just John waited patiently for me to meet his eyes before he finished.

"It adds up to you being the link between Howard and Dollar's operation and the ABC, Jack. That's how it adds up."

"That's not how it *is,*" I said.

The people who had been in the parking lot began to drift away and first one then the other of the mercury vapor lights snapped off. As hard as I tried, I couldn't get that orange bag out of my mind and the darkness only made it more vivid. It was almost as if the bag had left behind a vapor trail where it crossed the lot, a luminescent orange wake that still hung in the air all the way from the door of my Volvo out into the street, and then around the corner.

"Look, I can't help you," I finally said, not knowing what else to say. "Why don't you just go find Barry and ask him what's going on?"

"Well, Jack," Just John said, "Jello and I sort of thought you might do that for us."

"I don't know where he is."

"Oh, *fuck,* Jack."

Just John sounded genuinely disgusted.

"When are you going to show us some respect, man? You figure we think you're down here in Bangkok's favorite hot-spot to check out the action? Or maybe just because you were dying for a beer?"

"An unfortunate choice of words."

"Not for me, Jack."

"You know a lot of people, Jack," Jello said. "And you're not the kind of guy to sit around and wait for something to happen. We figure you either know where Barry Gale is or you have some way to contact him."

"Somebody's been following me around town for weeks already, John, and we both know who it is. So what's the problem? You've already found out who I know and where I go. And you know I'm not hanging out with Barry Gale."

I had no doubt at all now that it was John's people who'd been on my tail — that would certainly account for the high-tech tracking device — although I'd bet dollars to donuts that nobody had let Jello in on the plan.

That immediately raised an even thornier question, however, one I wasn't sure I was too keen on answering for myself right then.

If it really *was* Just John's people following me, were they the people who killed Dollar and left his body in my car? Or, at the very least, wouldn't they know who did?

I thought back for a moment on my conversation with Stanley.

In my experience, he had said, *the CIA does not go around killing American citizens in order to advance vast and shadowy conspiracies.*

Maybe not, it suddenly occurred to me, but how about in order to hide small and fucked-up ones?

"I've got nothing to do with any of this," I repeated stubbornly.

"Then, Jack, you're going to have to give us something," Just John said. "Something that might make us believe you."

"Like what?"

"Like Barry Gale."

"I don't have Barry Gale."

"Get him."

A patrolman started rolling up the yellow tape and the vehicles and people continued to thin out. In another few minutes the parking lot would be empty, as empty as if nothing had ever happened there at all.

Some son of a bitch is going to kill me if I don't get out of this, I thought to myself. *Sure as hell, some son of a bitch is going to kill me just like he did Dollar and Howard, and I'm not even going to know why.*

"Barry Gale told me that the ABC was tapped by somebody and lost a lot of money," I finally told John and Jello. "He's scared shitless that the Russian mobsters who set the whole deal up in the first place will think that he scammed the bank himself."

"So why did he come looking for you?"

I thought Just John asked the question like a man who already knew the answer and just wanted to see if I would tell him the truth.

"He asked me to help him find the money and get it back."

"What did you tell him?"

"I said I wouldn't get involved, and I haven't seen him since. That's all I know. I can't help you find him."

Just John's eyes were locked on mine.

"Yes, you can, Jack. And I got to tell you this. I'm absolutely sure that you will."

I didn't respond, but I could feel John continuing to watch me as my eyes drifted away from his and back across the parking lot.

The Volvo's passenger door was still hanging open and the car's interior light was shining out like a beacon in the darkness. It was the only indication of the spot where Dollar's body had been lying until two men had zipped it into a bag and hauled it away.

TWENTY-NINE

ANITA WAS PACKING FOR A TRIP to an art show in Hong Kong when I got home. She had so much stuff spread around the bedroom that I could hardly find a place to walk much less sit down, but boy was I glad to see her. Actually I would have probably been glad to see almost anybody about then who had no interest in killing me, and as far as I knew, Anita didn't. At least not right at the moment.

She asked me what I'd been up to that evening. I didn't want her to worry, so I kept things simple.

I lied.

My reward was that we went to bed early.

When I woke the next morning, I lay still for a while, keeping my mind as empty as I could. Eventually however a fresh surge of foreboding overwhelmed me and I got up, being careful not to wake Anita, pulled on some old running shorts and a Jerry Garcia T-shirt, and I padded out to the front door to pick up the *Bangkok Post.*

I put on coffee, and while it was dripping I flipped through the *Post* looking for the story about Dollar having been found dead in my car outside Q Bar the night before. I didn't immediately see it, so I fixed a bowl of bran flakes, poured a mug of black coffee, and took everything over to the kitchen table so I could read while I ate. I was finishing the bran flakes and was halfway through my second cup of coffee when I realized why I hadn't noticed the story the first time I looked.

It wasn't there.

Maybe the *Post* was just trying to avoid scaring the tourists, but naturally I was suspicious that there was more to it than that. First there had been that odd little story they'd run passing off Howard's death as a suicide, and now there was no mention at all of Dollar's murder. The killing of a prominent member of Bangkok's foreign community was a newsworthy enough event, so why was the *Post* ignoring it?

Maybe they were just lazy and printed whatever was given to them and not much else. Maybe whoever was involved in both their murders had enough local leverage to tell the *Post* what they could print and what they couldn't.

Maybe I was getting paranoid.

A hard run in Lumpini Park and a little honest sweat would probably clear my head, I decided, so I slipped back into the bedroom, put on my running shoes, and took the stairs down to loosen up. When I pushed open the metal door at the bottom of the stairwell, I looked glumly at the empty space in the garage where my car was normally parked.

It hadn't been until the tow truck backed into the parking lot the night before and began hooking up to the Volvo's bumper that it had occurred to me I wouldn't be getting in it and driving home after the cops were done. When the driver had brought over the clipboard for my signature, the form on it had been in Thai of course and I hadn't been able to read a word of it.

The fellow hadn't been much help. His English was limited and my Thai didn't include the vocabulary for having my car towed after a dead body was removed from it. One English word the guy seemed to know well enough however was *impounded.* He used it several times, like he thought it was really a lot of fun to say.

As I had been watching the men from the tow truck fussing with their equipment it suddenly occurred to me that the garbage bag full of stuff from Dollar's house was still in the trunk. If the Thai cops found *that,* I figured the fun would just be beginning. With Jello and John both still standing around, retrieving the bag would have made me pretty conspicuous, so I decided just to leave it where it was and hope for the best. After all, a couple of years back the local cops had impounded a truck and never even noticed a dead body in the back until the smell became impossible to ignore any longer. I always had that going for me.

Jello promised to get the Volvo back in a day or two and had offered to drive me home, but I waved down a taxi instead. I had had more than enough of Jello for one night.

I walked briskly down the driveway wheeling my arms in my usual ineffectual warm-up gestures, crossed Soi Chidlom, and jogged slowly toward the back of the Hilton.

I needed to think for a while, to try and pull things together for myself before I did any more talking to anyone. Maybe it was part of being a lawyer to brood about how to make sense out of the senseless, but if that was a disease, then I guessed I was incurable.

Turning south on a narrow *soi* that ran along a shaded canal, one of the few that still remained as a reminder of the city's waterborne past, I followed the wall along the western edge of the British Embassy compound until I reached Ploenchit Road. Early morning traffic was still light, so I ignored the pedestrian bridge, risked a sprint across Ploenchit's six lanes, and climbed the center barrier right over the sign that read, JAYWALKER FINE B200. On the other side I crossed the driveway of a still-dark office tower, turned south on Soi Tonson, and headed down behind the American ambassador's residence.

Since my runs usually involved parking near Lumpini and making circuits on tree-shaded pathways, running the streets of Bangkok was an unusual experience for me. The morning air was still fresh and the slight breeze blowing from the north kept the humidity in hand, so before long I was telling myself that I would have to hit the streets more often.

The waters of the little *klong* that paralleled Soi Tonson looked fresh and blue, and the grassy bank was lined with tall trees that knitted at their upper branches into an almost continuous canopy. The softly shifting mottle of morning light through the branches dappled the *klong* in a way that made me think of Monet, and it wasn't often that anything in Bangkok made me think of Monet.

I cut over to Wireless Road and turned right. I was enjoying the change from my usual routine so much that on impulse I angled away from the park and darted across Wireless through a break in the traffic. Sticking to the streets, I ran up a back *soi* in the general direction of the Polo Club.

It was still too early for the gate attendants to be paying much attention so when I reached the entrance to the parking lot I dodged past the barrier, tossed the uniformed guard a quick salute, and ran inside before he could stop me. Of course it was unlikely he would have anyway. Thai security guards seldom challenged foreigners regardless of where they were going, and a foreigner mad enough to be running the streets of Bangkok in a Jerry Garcia T-shirt before seven o'clock in the morning would have been one to avoid in particular.

I ran across the parking lot and on a whim turned in through the main entry to the club itself. I loped down the wide, brown-tiled walkway between the tennis courts and the bar, passed the swimming pool, and emerged onto a large field of neatly clipped grass. Circling it between white railings was a sand track about fifteen feet wide with a yellow sign that warned, WATCH OUT FOR PASSING HORSES.

Although it was obvious that the track wasn't meant for human runners, my ankles were starting to ache from the hard surfaces of the streets and so I settled into a comfortable jog circling the club grounds on the loosely packed sand. I felt my mind begin to empty, and soon I began seeing my predicament with new clarity.

I had told Just John in the parking lot at Q Bar that I didn't know what I was going to do, but that hadn't been true. I *did* know. As far as I could see I had no real alternative.

I was going to find Barry Gale. I *had* to find Barry Gale.

With Howard and Dollar both dead and an awful lot of people starting to look at me as the only remaining link to the ABC's missing money, Barry was probably the only person left alive who knew how to call off the dogs.

Before I'd finished even two full circuits of the sand track, I felt my confidence growing. I could handle this. I was certain of it now.

When I passed behind the club's huge swimming pool for the second time, I left the track, taking the steps up to the pool area two at a time and flopped down in one of the blue lounge chairs that were scattered around the gleaming water. As I fell back against the cool, cotton-duck cover I gave in to my exhaustion and sucked down great gulps of air, letting my chest rise and fall in deep heaves until my pulse rate began to return to normal. Then, pushing myself into a sitting position, I pulled up my knees and clasped my arms around them as I checked out the early arrivals filtering into the club.

There weren't many. A portly, middle-aged Thai with an ancient-looking wooden tennis racket was patting balls gently against the backboard on one of the tennis courts. In the pool, two elderly foreigners who I took to be husband and wife were swimming together, stroking slowly but methodically back and forth from one end to the other, staying side by side as they swam. I liked the look of that, and I wondered briefly if some day Anita and I would grow old like that, staying together, just stroking methodically along side by side. I hoped so, but I supposed that was all pretty much up to her.

It was while I was watching the old couple that I noticed the man in mirrored sunglasses. He was sitting alone at a table back away from the pool in the deep shadows at the front edge of the tennis pavilion. The man looked familiar, but the distance and the sunglasses made him difficult to place. I was about to decide that I was mistaken when he raised his hand and waved me over. Something about the gesture caused my memory to click.

It was Mango Manny.

"I didn't know you were a member of the Polo Club, Manny," I said after I had walked over and dropped into the chair opposite him.

"Too bloody right I'm not. You high society fuckers would never let a working-class boy like me into a place like this, even if I did go to Cambridge."

"Hey," I protested, lifting up my T-shirt and wiping sweat from my face. "Leave me out of this. I'm not a member either. I'm just passing through."

Manny was wearing sharply-creased pearl-gray slacks and a matching silk shirt. He looked liked he might have come straight from Caesars Palace, and for all I knew, he had.

"So what are you doing here so early this morning?" I eventually asked when he didn't say anything else.

"Waiting to talk to you."

I looked closely at Manny. He had to be kidding, although he didn't give that impression.

"Why would you wait at the Polo Club for me? I didn't know I was going to be here until a half hour ago."

"I know things, mate. Just like you know things."

"Yeah? Well, I only know things *after* they happen. Knowing things *before* they happen is pretty spooky in my book."

Manny just shrugged.

Foreigners in Bangkok, even long-time residents, frequently forgot how conspicuous they actually were. Since most Thais politely pretended not to notice us, most of us drifted into the agreeable sensation that we were going about our lives almost invisibly, although nothing could be further from the truth. Everywhere a foreigner went in Bangkok, there was someone who saw him go there. Everywhere a foreigner was in Bangkok, there was someone who knew he was there. And that information was always available — for a price — to someone.

I looked at myself in Manny's mirrored sunglasses. Patches of sweat had soaked through my shirt and droplets from my hair rolled down my face like silver balls bouncing through a pinball machine.

"Would you take those damned glasses off, Manny?" I asked when I was through admiring myself. "You trying to look like a hard guy or something?"

I watched the muscles of Manny's face bend and twist around the edges of the silver mirrors covering his eyes, and I tried to decide whether or not he was smiling. Then he took the glasses off. He wasn't.

"Sorry about Dollar," he said.

"Yeah. Me, too."

"A good bloke, he was."

I nodded.

"But over his head," Manny added. "Way over."

"Maybe."

"I think maybe you're over your head here too mate."

"That could be."

Manny nodded. "So, you want some help?"

"I've already asked. You didn't offer any."

Manny let that pass.

"You still want to find this geezer, mate? This Barry Gale?"

"I do."

"How you going to do that?"

"You found me this morning when *I* didn't even know where I was going. How tough can it be to find a bald American who's hiding out with a six-foot Chinese woman?"

Manny picked up his glasses and twirled them in his fingers, first one way then the other.

"Not tough for me. But a lot tougher for you, I reckon."

"Maybe you're underestimating me."

"Maybe not."

He had me there.

"You already know where he is, don't you, Manny?"

"Yeah."

"Thailand?"

Manny nodded.

"But not in Bangkok."

"No."

"Is this going to be one of those conversations where if I don't ask the right questions I don't get the right answers?" I asked.

Manny looked at his watch and folded his hands, but he didn't say anything.

"Why are we playing this stupid game, Manny? You said you wanted to help. If you know where Barry is, just tell me for Christ's sake."

"Let's just say I *do* tell you where this bugger is, mate. What you gonna do then?"

"I'm just going to talk to him, Manny. Just talk. That's all."

"You want me to have somebody torture him a little first, maybe loosen him up?"

I examined Manny's face for some sign he was kidding. I didn't see any.

"Not right away, but I'll certainly keep your offer in mind."

Manny nodded as if that sounded reasonable enough to him.

"So after you talk to this wanker, then what?" he asked.

"I'm not sure."

Manny put his glasses back on and turned his head away.

"You might end up like Dollar and that other guy if you keep fucking around. You ever think of that?"

"I can handle myself."

"You're pretty cocky, mate. A lot of shit's going down you know fuck all about."

"Meaning?"

Manny looked toward the elderly couple climbing out of the pool. The old man lifted a towel and began wiping the woman's back.

"These bastards are mental. I've done some shit for them once or twice, but I won't touch them now. They're out of control."

"*Who's* out of control, Manny?"

He slowly turned his head until he was looking me full in the eye. I watched myself in his glasses.

"I used to think they were Yank coppers, maybe even CIA, but I'm not sure anymore. For fuck's sake, mate, even *I* don't know who these arseholes really are. Shit, some of *them* may not know who they are."

"Are you talking about Just John?"

"Yeah." Manny nodded. "And . . . others."

We sat for a while after that without saying anything else. The old man finished drying the woman's back, and then she picked up a fresh towel and began gently rubbing down his chest and stomach. The whole concept still looked pretty good to me.

"I want to know where Barry Gale is, Manny."

"I understand that."

"And I want something else. I want to get to him without a whole goddamned parade behind me. Can you do that for me? Get me to him without anybody knowing where I'm going?"

"They want Barry Gale, not you, mate. So why don't you just let me give him to them?"

"I don't understand what's really going on here, Manny, and I'm not going to start giving up anybody until I'm sure I do."

Manny turned away, watching four middle-aged foreign women swatting a tennis ball lightly back and forth on one of the courts. They shrieked and giggled like young girls, bouncing around the court without much apparent interest in playing well. The sunlight made long glistening streaks through the thin sheens of perspiration that coated their smoothly tanned arms and legs.

"Why do you have to do this, mate?"

"Because whatever is happening has gotten two people killed already, Manny, and I don't want to be responsible for anyone else ending up dead. Least of all me."

"But you want me to tell you where this guy is. What if you're the next one to get topped? I'm not responsible for you then?"

"I'm going to go looking for Barry Gale with or without your help. You can't do anything to change that. You can just make it easier for me, or you can make it harder."

Manny leaned forward on his elbows, taking off his sunglasses again. He folded the glasses and clasped his hands together in front of him.

"I was right about Phuket, wasn't I?" I said. "That's where he is."

I watched and waited. Finally Manny sighed heavily and tapped the table firmly with his forefinger.

"You not gonna top him?"

"I already told you, Manny. I'm just going to talk to him."

"And then just leave him and walk away?"

"Unless he had anything to do with killing Dollar. Then I'll blow the whistle."

Manny's expression hardened and his eyes narrowed almost out of existence.

"Do it, mate. Find him and fuck him."

He looked sideways for a while after that and I waited for him to go on, knowing now that he would. Finally he shifted his eyes back and stared hard at me.

"I'll get you where he is without anyone knowing about it, but after I do that, I'm out of it and you're on your own. I've got people to protect and I'm not going to fuck around with a bunch of crazy wankers just so you can satisfy your curiosity, mate. That's the deal. Take it or leave it."

"I'll take it. Where is he?"

Manny ignored my question.

"Can you leave now?" he asked instead.

"The sooner the better."

"Okay. Let's go."

I glanced at my watch.

"Sure. I haven't got any classes today. Give me a chance to change, and. . . ."

"Forget it," Manny interrupted. "Now means now. They know you came to see me last night. I'm not going to fuck around, let them get set up, then put my lot in danger."

"I can't go anywhere in these sweaty jogging clothes, Manny. And Anita was still asleep when I left. I've got to at least tell her where I'm going."

"You tell her nothing. The less she knows, the better off she is."

Manny produced a cell phone from somewhere.

"I'll get clothes for you."

"I've got to talk to Anita," I said. "I can't just disappear."

Manny shook his head.

"I'll get a message to her that there's some kind of business emergency. Now go take a piss or something while I get the rest of this shit fixed for you. I'll be out front in five minutes. You're not there, I'm gone."

THIRTY

I WASHED MY FACE AND DRIED OFF as well as I could in a men's toilet and ten minutes later I was under the portico at the main entrance to the Polo Club buckling myself into the passenger seat of Manny's lemon-yellow Porsche. Before I was entirely done, he accelerated out the main gate past the poker-faced security guard, and still in second gear, turned south on Wireless Road.

"Why are you doing this, Manny?" I asked.

Manny didn't answer, didn't even seem to have heard the question, so I let the question slide.

"Anyway, I want you to know that I really appreciate it," I said.

"Wait till you see what happens to you, mate. Then decide how much you appreciate it."

A blue and white city bus chugged away from the curb in front of us and Manny corkscrewed around it with two practiced flicks of his wrists. He downshifted, pulled a hard left into Rama IV Road, and headed east. Since Manny didn't seem inclined to offer any indication as to what we were doing, I sat back and awaited developments.

"I've set everything up to get you to Phuket on the quiet," he eventually said without looking at me. "You were right about that. He's holed up down there."

"Okay."

"After that some of my people will show you where this wanker is, but that's *all* I'm going to do."

"Fine."

"Even then, if there's some kind of a cock up. . . ."

Manny didn't finish the thought, but I got the point anyway.

"I understand."

"You've got to do every fucking thing my people tell you to do while you're with them. Every fucking thing. We clear on that, mate?"

"We're clear," I said.

I settled back and folded my arms, placing myself entirely in Manny's hands. Strangely that felt like a completely sensible thing to do.

It was Monte Carlo that Somerset Maugham had been describing when he referred to "a sunny place for shady people," but I figured he could just as easily have been thinking of Phuket. An island resort off the coast of Thailand about five hundred miles to the south of Bangkok, Phuket was set in the turquoise splendor of the Andaman Sea and soaked by sunshine nearly year round. It was a glamorous, alluring vacation hideaway that had become justly famed among sailors, golfers, skin divers, and social glitterati all over the world.

Phuket had also attained a certain kind of fame among quite a different group — international criminals on the lam. The weather was good, the living was easy, the food was terrific, and the women were . . . well, Thai. Best of all, if the local police unaccountably noticed them at all, rascals on the run were generally offered the option of making a modest contribution to the local authorities to renew their invisibility. A lot of people seemed to think of Thailand as not much more than an asylum for thrill seekers and the morally impaired anyway — it was the cuisine and the sex, the theory went — so what better place could there be for a scoundrel to lie low?

Every now and then I'd see a small piece in the *Bangkok Post* about a German bank robber or an American con artist who'd suddenly been discovered living quietly in Phuket and bundled off home for trial. These intermittent demonstrations of Thai co-operation with international law enforcement were very impressive, and it was doubtless a coincidence that they usually occurred just after the fugitive had been living in Phuket long enough to have exhausted the booty from his misdemeanors, but I never got the feeling that the total population of villains hiding out in Phuket was ever significantly diminished.

Morning traffic was building as we turned into the ramp to the airport expressway. Still rolling, Manny flipped a note toward the toll booth, downshifted, and accelerated away. I tilted my head back and listened to the distinctive, high-pitched whine of a Porsche stepping up through its gearbox. Manny cradled the black, leather-covered steering wheel in his palms, elbows slightly bent, hands in the approved racing positions of ten o'clock and two o'clock, snapping his elbows as he dodged from lane to lane.

Manny was in the far right lane as we took the long curve just past the Din Daeng intersection and turned north toward the airport, but I wasn't particularly surprised when he abruptly shot across three lanes of traffic and roared off onto an unmarked connector road that I knew would eventually lead back to the new south-bound expressway link. We weren't just driving out to the airport. I'd been pretty certain of that from the beginning.

"I'm only fucking around," Manny said, reading my mind.

The tall limestone column of the Victory Monument flashed by on our left and Manny loosed a blast from the Porsche's air horn at a motorcyclist who started to cross in front of us.

"These guys are pros. If they're on you, we won't lose them like this, but it'll look like we're bloody well trying." Manny patted the dashboard of the Porsche with affection. "We'll keep their attention right here for a while."

Call me crazy, but I'd always thought that when you were trying to lose somebody, the last thing you wanted was to keep their attention on you. On the other hand, what did I know about such things compared to a guy like Manny?

"Fuck you, you cocksuckers!" he screamed, slamming both big hands against the wheel so hard I was afraid he would break it off the column. "I'm too good for any of you bleedin' wankers!"

He slammed his hands down again, harder, and this time the whole car rocked. A blue Toyota pickup with a half-dozen kids sliding around in the bed began to drift slowly into the middle lane, veering right at us with its exhaust pipe burping puffs of purple-black smoke. I involuntarily leaned back in my seat, but Manny flicked his elbows and blew right by the truck without even slowing down.

He turned north on Rama VI Road, made a U-turn through the parking lot in front of the Ministry of Finance, then took Sawankhalok Road south past Chitrlada Palace. Just across from the Royal Turf Club, he swung into the garage reserved for officials of the Ministry of Foreign Affairs, fished a laminated card out of the glove box, and thrust it at one of the two unsmiling, battle-dressed soldiers blocking the entrance. While they examined the card, I examined the M-16s hanging across their chests.

After only a second or two the guard handed the card back to Manny. He took a couple of quick steps away from the Porsche while muttering something under his breath to the other guard, then both of them cracked to attention and snapped their right hands to their helmets in salute.

Manny ignored them and roared into the garage. He cut straight across the bottom floor to the exit, and accompanied by another flurry of salutes from another pair of heavily-armed sentries, shot out of the garage again into Sri Ayutthaya Road. I started to ask him why he had a pass to the Ministry of Foreign Affairs' garage, particularly one that seemed to merit such deference from two guys with big guns, but then decided I really didn't want to know.

Manny bumped in and out of a couple of other parking garages, tooled around the Parliament building a couple of times, and after checking his watch, headed south through the tree-lined residential streets of the oldest part of the city.

Soon after that the Grand Palace came into view beyond the grassy expanse of Sanam Luang, shimmering like a mirage in the wispy morning sun. The red and green rooflines of its fairy-tale structures undulated wildly beyond the high battlements, and the fragments of colored glass embedded in the walls glinted as fiercely as if they actually were the precious stones they appeared to be.

Inside those parapets had once been the mysterious core of the fabled Siamese empire, but these days there were only mobs of foot-sore tourists wilting in Bangkok's customary heat and humidity. Regardless, narrow pathways unchanged for a century still twisted among fanciful pavilions and the same stone giants, half human and half animal, still guarded a royal temple where thousands of candle flames flickered endlessly under the unsmiling gaze of the Emerald Buddha.

"Okay," Manny said to me as we turned suddenly into the road leading to the main gates of the Grand Palace, the place where the tour groups entered. "You see all these buses?"

I did. They were lined up nose to tail along both sides of the road like two freight trains parked in a rail yard.

"We'll be out of sight as long as we're between them," he said.

Manny took one hand off the wheel and pointed up ahead to the left. "I'm going to dump you out just before the last bus. You'll see a bunch of Japanese. Get on their bus with them. I'll keep going back to the expressway and out toward the airport."

"You're joking."

"Dead serious, mate."

The Porsche slammed to a stop. Manny reached across my lap and shoved the door open. A large bus painted pink with giant yellow flowers idled next to us, and just as Manny had said, a group of middle-aged Japanese was milling around near its open door.

"The driver's a very reliable bloke. Trust him. Good luck, mate."

Manny put both hands on the wheel and looked away. He didn't offer to shake, so neither did I. I got out and closed the door.

I was still standing in the street with my hands on my hips watching the Porsche disappear when I heard the tapping sound behind me. The round-faced Thai at the wheel of the bus was beckoning through the window at me with his left hand and rapping on the glass with his right index finger.

I circled around to the door and the Japanese all politely stepped back. There were about a dozen of them and they were carrying a collection of cameras, backpacks, and water bottles exactly like every other group of Japanese tourists I had ever seen. An elderly woman in a brown golf hat smiled and made little pushing gestures toward the open door of the bus.

"Arigato," I said, stifling the urge to bow.

"Gud ruck," she whispered as I passed.

The bus driver smiled when I mounted the steps.

"Sawadee krap, Ajarn. My name Thavee. I be driver today."

I looked around and saw that the bus was completely empty. The Japanese had been carefully arranged to make them appear to be a much larger crowd than they actually were, but the windows of the bus were very dark and from the outside no one would know that it wasn't chock full of camera-wielding tourists trying to get just one more shot of the Grand Palace before flying back to the factory in Yokohama.

Although Thavee had the typically small build of a local lad, he was well fleshed out and his belly jiggled when he twisted toward me in the driver's seat. He had shiny brown skin and jet black hair trimmed short in a military cut, and flashed me a toothy smile as he checked his big wing mirror. Without taking his eyes off it, he stuck out his left hand and made a rolling gesture. The Japanese obediently formed a neat line and began slowly climbing the steps into the bus.

Thavee pointed to the mirror, and I moved closer to him, looking over his shoulder.

A large black vehicle slowed as it came abreast of us. It was one of those big Ford Expeditions, the kind that was frequently seen around Washington bristling with Secret Service agents and following just behind the President's limousine. The diplomatic plates marked it as belonging to the American Embassy.

I could see that the driver and the passenger were both Westerners, and I closely examined the men's fresh faces, short hair, white short-sleeved shirts, and gold-framed, mirrored sunglasses. I didn't recognize either of them, but I had no doubt they were government types. Unless of course they were just a couple of Mormons out sightseeing.

As both men glanced toward the bus, I involuntarily pulled back from the window.

"Mai pen rai, Ajarn," Thavee said. "Cannot see you. Window very dark."

The van slowed almost to a stop while the two men looked us over. The one in the passenger seat shifted slightly, studying the Japanese shuffling slowly into the bus. He lifted a walkie-talkie to his lips and I could see his mouth moving, but the Ford resumed speed while he was still talking and quickly disappeared down the road behind Manny. I gathered we had passed inspection.

"You sit now, please."

Thavee pulled a big handle and the bus door swung shut with a hydraulic wheeze that was downright liberating.

"Bag on back seat for you, *Ajarn.*"

I made my way down the aisle past the smiling Japanese who were now scattered throughout the mostly empty bus. In the middle of the bench seat that ran all the way across the back, I found a dark blue canvas duffle bag with a heavy zipper. I picked it up when I sat, but as Thavee pulled away from the curb and edged into traffic, I just held it on my lap for a while without looking inside. Up the aisle of the bus, I watched the backs of a dozen or so Japanese heads, and beyond them, the blindingly whitewashed walls of the Grand Palace sliding out of sight.

What the hell am I doing here? I asked myself. *Why am I playing hide-and-seek with a bunch of spooks in mirrored sunglasses? They were representatives of the government of the United States, weren't they? Aren't we all supposed to be on the same side?*

My sweaty jogging clothes were starting to stiffen up since Thavee, like all Thai drivers, kept the air conditioning set on quick-freeze whenever foreigners were around. I gave up trying to understand what was going on and decided just to settle for keeping warm.

I unzipped the black bag and found inside a change of underwear, a pair of jeans, a long-sleeved polo shirt, a dark, lightweight windbreaker, and a pair of Topsiders. Then my groping hand found something else. Down at the bottom of the bag, underneath the neatly folded clothes, was a handgun in a holster and a couple of spare clips. I removed the gun gingerly and my eyes reflexively darted around the bus to check out whether anyone was watching, but no one appeared to be paying the slightest attention.

I had fired handguns at ranges before, but I'd never lifted one in anger or fear and I hardly qualified as an expert. Nevertheless I had no difficulty in recognizing the chrome-plated .45 nestling in the black leather holster, one of the kind that clipped over your belt and could be easily concealed under almost any kind of jacket. One like the blue windbreaker that was also in the bag would do the trick nicely.

Didn't Manny believe me? Did he still think that I really did *intend to shoot Barry after I found him?*

Then another possibility occurred to me, and it was hugely unhappy.

Maybe Manny already knew that Barry had something to do with Dollar's murder and perhaps Howard's, too. Maybe he knew I was the next name on Barry's list. Maybe the ·45 was there for me to protect myself from Barry.

I filed the thought away and shoved the gun back into the duffle. If Barry did have some kind of plan to get me dead — and I still couldn't imagine why he would or, even if he did, why he would be going about it in such an obscure way — I could probably talk him out of it somehow. I had made it successfully through four decades so far, mostly by talking people into and out of things, and so far I had done it without even once getting into a gunfight. I didn't have any intention of changing that now.

Sliding across the bench so that I would be partially hidden behind the empty seats in front of me, I pulled my T-shirt over my head and stripped off my still-damp jogging shorts. When they hit the metal floor of the bus there was a little thud and then I remembered that I had shoved my cell phone into my pocket before I had left the apartment that morning, just in case Anita woke up before I got back and wondered where I was.

So why hadn't she called?

I pulled on the polo shirt and the jeans, then I bent down and retrieved the phone. That was when I realized that I had forgotten to turn it on, which might explain why I hadn't heard from Anita. I sat there holding the phone for a moment and thought about calling her, but what was I going to say to her?

Darling, I'm riding in a bus with a bunch of phony Japanese tourists, wearing some borrowed clothes with a ·45 automatic in a bag on the seat next to me. Why? Well, it's this way. I'm being slipped into Phuket by a semi-retired British gangster so I can find a guy who's been dead for a few years and who may be planning to shoot me. But don't worry. I'll be fine. And I'll try to be home in time for dinner.

Nah, I decided. Maybe it'd be better if I just wait until things clear up a little.

I snapped the cover of the phone shut without turning it on and tossed it into the duffle bag. Then I shoved my sweaty clothes and my running shoes in after it and zipped it up. I pulled on the Topsiders and unfolded the dark blue windbreaker to ward off the chill from the air conditioning. When I did, I saw the big yellow lettering across the back for the first time.

FBI, it read.

Funny, Manny, I thought to myself. *Very fucking funny.*

Looking out the window I recognized the forest of container cranes lining the Chao Praya. We were just passing the main port facilities on the river and that meant we had to be heading southeast. On beyond the docks and the warehouses the expressway would turn into Bangna-Trat Road which was the primary highway to the eastern seaboard. Since that was exactly the opposite direction we would be traveling if the bus were headed to Phuket, I gathered I wasn't going there overland. Manny must have an airplane or helicopter waiting somewhere for me.

A little less than an hour later we passed through the old fishing town of Chonburi and the Gulf of Thailand came into view. Although it was flat and brown, hardly the stuff of great seascapes, the Japanese unlimbered their cameras, rushed to the right side of the bus, and started clicking frantically away. I had assumed of course that these were all Manny's people and just part of the charade he had set up to get me out of Bangkok, but now I wasn't so sure. They certainly looked authentic enough, pressing up against the windows and firing off their Canons and Nikons with little whoops of joy. They were either real tourists after all or this bunch was deeply into method acting.

At Bang Phra, a little town just north of Chonburi, I knew there was a private airfield from which a flying club operated. I'd been there a couple of times with friends who were members and it occurred to me that that might well be where we were headed now.

Sure enough, as Bang Phra went by on our left Thavee began to slow down. He raised his right hand above his shoulder, and without looking back, beckoned me forward. I slipped the strap of the duffle over my shoulder and walked up the aisle until I was standing just behind him, balancing myself against the swaying of the bus.

"You know flying club?" he asked without looking back.

"I've been there."

Thavee nodded a couple of times and bent forward to check both of his wing mirrors.

"I park by hangar. Glider outside. Everybody get out to take picture with glider."

He shot a look back over his shoulder to see if I was listening, although I couldn't imagine what else he thought I might be doing.

"Wait for everybody to get away from bus, *Ajarn,* then go inside hangar. Ike be there."

"Are you telling me that this guy is going to fly me to Phuket in a glider?"

Thavee glanced back again, and after a moment grinned.

"No problem, *Ajarn.* You never fly in glider before?"

I shook my head.

"Then you want good tip?"

"Sure."

As Thavee downshifted and braked, I could see off in the distance a tattered windsock and a large blue-painted hangar with a metal roof. He started a turn off the highway in their direction and then twisted around in the driver's seat and gave me a long, serious look.

"Flap you arm, *Ajarn.* Flap you arm."

THIRTY-ONE

THE HANGAR DOORS WERE WIDE OPEN, but except for two white gliders pushed against the rear wall, their wings overlapping like the carcasses of giant birds awaiting the arrival of a taxidermist, the place was empty.

Could you actually fly to Phuket in one of these things? I had heard that gliders could stay up for hours when the conditions were right, but the only time I had seen one airborne it had been accumulating its hours going around in circles. That was something I was already having no problem doing on my own.

I took a few steps toward the back of the hanger and examined the two gliders more closely. They were odd aircraft, awkward and beautiful at the same time. Their fuselages were thin cylinders, just wide enough to hold two people sitting in single file under an elongated, plexiglas bubble, and their wings were long and spindly, impossibly fragile looking. From the nose of each plane a huge steel ring extended up and forward, and I assumed that was where the tow rope was hooked up to the powered aircraft that hauled them several thousand feet into the air where they were then cut loose to make their own silent way back to earth.

Just as I was unhappily contemplating the place on each plane where the engine should have been, but wasn't, a miniature door in the right-hand wall of the hangar squeaked open. A woman leaned in and beckoned to me.

She was tiny, probably weighing not more than a hundred pounds, and her gray hair was neatly bobbed into a short pageboy. Under any other circumstances, I might have taken the woman to be somewhere in her sixties, but the brown coveralls and black work boots she wore and the red bandana on which she was wiping her grease-stained hands made the issue a little hazy.

I walked toward her and when I got closer I saw the red stitching over the right breast pocket of her coveralls. IKE, it said. Wonderful. Grandma Moses here was about to take me flying in an airplane with no engine.

"Okay, hotshot, let's kick the tires and light the fires," she growled at me with a noise like loose gravel rattling in a sieve.

I thought immediately how American she sounded.

"You're Ike?"

"No, son, I'm the fuckin' Easter Bunny."

I was right. American, without the slightest doubt.

I took a deep breath and glanced back and forth between Ike and the two gliders. "You want me to help you pull one of these out?"

Ike grunted in disgust and stalked away, leaving the little door standing open for me.

"Not those, hotshot. We're taking the tow plane. It's back here."

The tow plane was a yellow Piper Cherokee with a white stripe down its side. It looked old and a little tired, and there was a big dent right in the middle of the vertical stabilizer. On the other hand, there was something about it that I liked a lot. It had an engine.

Ike did a quick walk around, wiggling the wing flaps and poking at some other parts I couldn't identify. When she actually did kick the tires, I almost laughed out loud. Eventually Ike pulled herself up on the wing, climbed from there into the cockpit, and strapped herself into the left seat. I followed, the duffle bag slung over my shoulder.

I strapped myself into the right-hand seat and stowed the bag under my feet, then I slammed the cabin door and snapped the bolt into what I hoped was the locked position. Ike fired the starter and a couple of minutes later she was gunning the engine and dancing down the bumpy asphalt strip. We were airborne.

The little plane climbed out quickly, its engine pulling more powerfully than I would have thought possible from its size. Below us was a monotonous configuration of brown and green sheets streaked with shards of muddy water — long, narrow fields that ran between widely spaced roads like the lanes in a giant's bowling alley. The repeating pattern of oblongs stretched without interruption all the way to the dull, colorless coastline of the Gulf of Thailand and made the world go abruptly horizontal and infinite.

They were rice fields mostly. The flat, marshy land surrounding the delta of the Chao Praya River was an ideal place for growing rice. Building a city there, on the other hand, was a different matter entirely.

After a few minutes we popped like a champagne cork out of a marmalade-colored layer of crud and Ike leveled off in deep blue skies that seemed to go on forever. She nudged our course to the west, pointing us directly across the narrowest part of the Gulf of Thailand and toward the neck of land about fifty miles on the other side that connected Thailand with Malaysia.

Off on our right Bangkok spread all the way to the horizon. The place was a colossus, a thick forest of towering, mostly egg-white buildings that choked the marshy plains as far as the eye could see. When you were on the ground, the city enveloped you, taking away your sense of perspective. Only from the air could you grasp the magnitude of it, and it never failed to overwhelm me.

Ike twisted some dials on the instrument panel, flipped a switch, and pulled a microphone from a bracket over her head.

"Bangkok Control, this is Cherokee Hotel Sierra Golf Zulu X-ray with you south of the field, crossing westbound at five thousand."

After a moment a man's voice crackled out of the radio.

"Golf Zulu X-ray, this is Bangkok Control. Good morning, Ike. You got another load of tourists today?"

The voice's American accent caused me to perk up my ears. Could that really be a Thai flight controller she was talking to?

"No such luck, Prab. Just driving around a little by myself. Don't get many days this nice."

"That's a big roger, Zulu X-ray. Squawk five, niner, niner, seven and report clear of control zone. Bangkok Control out."

"Thanks, Prab. Zulu X-ray clear."

I waited for Ike to explain the conversation to me, but she didn't.

"What was that all about?" I finally asked.

"Just standard stuff. We're on the southern edge of the Don Muang control zone and I always report. You don't have to do it, but I don't want some Chinaman driving a fucking 747 up my butt."

"That didn't sound to me like a Thai on the radio."

Ike's eyes flicked over at me.

"You're not nervous, are you, hotshot?"

"No, I'm . . . of course I am."

Ike nodded as if that satisfied her, then she reached across and patted me on the knee.

"Relax, son. Aviation talk's always in American. Prab went to the University of Oklahoma. Take it from me, he's as Thai as *t'ai chi.*"

"*T'ai chi* is Chinese."

"You know what I mean."

As the mountains behind the western coast of the Gulf appeared over the nose, Ike banked the Cherokee to the south. The Tenasserim Mountains were the spine of the long, narrow umbilical cord of land that separated the Gulf of Thailand from Burma and the Andaman Sea and connected the Buddhist heartland of Thailand with the more Muslim south. Sometimes the slender neck of land was called the elephant's truck for the way it looked on a map dangling from Thailand down toward Malaysia.

Ike didn't seem to have much to say, so I kept quiet as well. We had flown in silence southward along the western edge of the Gulf of Thailand for almost an hour when I spotted the virtually uninhabited necklace of limestone islands that made up the Angthong National Park, and just south of that the resort islands of Ko Samui and Ko Tao. Even from our altitude I could make out the mica-white sands of the islands' beaches, the fringes of spindly coconut palms, and a scattering of tourists basting in the sun. The aquamarine and turquoise layers of the Gulf of Thailand twirled among the islands and coral reefs, knotting together into a spectrum of blues so deep and dense that it looked as if the sea might have turned to black if it had not lost courage.

As we came abeam of the islands Ike pushed the Cherokee's nose to the west and we headed inland over what I was pretty sure was the town of Surat Thani. Tracking to the southwest, we crossed over the isthmus toward the Andaman Sea where Phuket lay just off the coast.

Ike reached out and twisted some dials on the instrument panel, then she pulled down the microphone again.

"Phuket Control, Cherokee Hotel Sierra Golf Zulu X-ray is with you inbound thirty miles north of the airport at five thousand with negative traffic."

"Hey, Ike. How're you this morning?" another American-accented voice responded. "Ah . . . nothing in our pattern at this time, but we're painting a north-bound Thai heavy climbing through flight level one two zero at four miles ten o'clock of your position. There's also a Bangkok Airways Otter about one four miles to your six o'clock at eleven thousand."

Ike bent down and twisted her head to look up through the Cherokee's left window. Then she keyed the mike again.

"Got the heavy. No factor. Zulu X-ray out."

"Roger, Ike. Contact Phuket tower on one twenty three point seven. Have a nice day. Phuket Control out."

I could see the fragile limestone stacks and placid surface of Phangnga Bay coming up just left of our nose, and beneath us was what seemed to be an unbroken carpet of mangrove trees.

"The Phuket airport doesn't seem to be a great place for me to slip onto the island without being seen," I pointed out with what I hoped was an appropriately diplomatic note in my voice.

"It's not." Ike craned her neck up over the instrument panel and scanned the ground below us. "That's why you're not going there."

"But weren't you just talking to somebody about landing there?"

"Yep. Because *I'm* going there."

I figured Ike would explain what that was supposed to mean when she was good and ready.

Below us I watched the Phuket highway twisting south toward the Sarasin Bridges, the twin roadways that were the island's only connection to the mainland. Off to the left Krabi's famous beaches were strung out like pearls tucked into pockets of green satin. Waterfalls gushed down from the low mountains and in some places I could track the course of the rushing streams through the thick jungle canopy until they reached its edge and fell into the sea.

"Just trust me, son. You're in good hands."

Ike changed some numbers on her dials again and took down the microphone.

"Ah . . . Phuket Tower, this is Cherokee Hotel Sierra Golf Zulu X-ray with you. I may have a little problem here."

I stopped admiring the beaches and waterfalls and started listening very carefully.

"Go ahead, Zulu X-ray."

"I've got a rough engine and . . . ah, I'm losing power pretty fast."

I looked at Ike sitting placidly to my left. The engine sounded okay to me.

"Are you declaring an emergency, Zulu X-ray?"

"Negative, Phuket Tower."

Ike absentmindedly keyed the mike three or four times.

"Let me stay with it and see what happens. Be advised that I'm losing altitude and may be off your radar shortly."

Ike pushed the nose of the Cherokee over gently, nudged our course back toward the east, and settled into a gradual descent in the general direction of Phangnga Bay.

"Can you make the field, Zulu X-ray?"

It was a different voice on the radio this time.

"Ah . . . say again, Phuket Tower. You're breaking up. Missed that transmission."

I'd heard every word. The radio sounded fine to me.

"I asked if you can make the field, Ike."

"Cannot copy, Phuket Tower. Repeat. Zulu X-ray cannot copy."

Ike reached for a toggle switch on the instrument panel to the right of the radio. When she flipped it, the dials went dark. Then she turned to me and winked.

With a snap of her wrists on the control wheel, Ike rolled the Cherokee up onto its left wing until we were ninety degrees to the horizon, and then she peeled off like a World War Two dive-bomber making an attack run on a battleship. Another snap of Ike's wrists and the little plane leveled off about fifty feet above the water. Before I could say anything, she banked through a hundred and eighty degrees and crossed inland over a beach. Then she banked steeply again just above the tree line and a short, empty stretch of asphalt road abruptly appeared in the rainforest right in front of us.

As we roared over the end of the road, Ike hauled the plane's nose up to a forty-five degree angle and jerked on a lever between our seats that looked a great deal like a parking brake but which I devoutly hoped wasn't anything of the sort. Her right hand shot straight out, chopping off the throttle, and as the engine dropped to a purr, I heard first the left and then the right landing gear squeal onto the road.

Ike pumped her toe brakes a few times and the little plane stopped rolling almost immediately. Gunning the throttle while she held one brake, Ike spun the Cherokee smartly on its left gear until it was lined up on the roadway pointing back in the direction from which we had just landed.

She reached over, popped my harness release, and shoved open the passenger door. The pulsing of the plane's engine filled the cabin as she leveled her index finger toward the wing. I got the idea quickly enough and scrambled out, dragging my duffle bag.

"Don't fall in the prop, son!"

Ike slammed the door shut behind me and I slid off the wing to the ground just as the engine gave another roar and the Cherokee began its take-off roll away from me. The whine of its engine made it sound like a very large and angry lawnmower, and I clapped both hands over my ears to avoid the worst of the racket.

That was why I didn't hear the jeep as it drove up behind me.

"She's a hell of a pilot, yes?"

The accent was thick and French and smelled of stale cigarettes, like somebody doing a lame Jean-Paul Belmondo. I turned around and saw a man wearing sunglasses slumped over the steering wheel of an open jeep that was dented and covered with dried mud. There was a half-smoked cigarette dangling from his lips, and he was watching the Cherokee disappear off into the distance.

"Now she'll call the little fuckers in the tower with some stupid story about dirt in her fuel or some shit like that and then fly right on into Phuket just like nothing ever happened. Nobody will ever know she was here."

The man shook his head in admiration.

"Big balls for an old lady. Big balls."

I walked around the jeep and pulled myself up into the passenger seat. Pushing my bag onto the floor, I looked the man over. At a glance I took him for forty-five, maybe fifty. Fit looking and wiry with a bit of a burn on his face and forearms, his hair was very long and gray and it hung in a thick mop down to his shoulders. He was wearing a crisp khaki shirt with epaulets, matching shorts, and ankle boots with floppy green socks.

"Welcome to Phuket, *Professeur.* Casablanca with no fucking heroes."

The man straightened up, flicked away his cigarette, and threw me a professional-looking salute.

"I'm Captain Tom, a genuine civilian no longer affiliated with any military unit, government agency, or other form of socially oppressive organization."

"Captain of what?" I asked.

"Ah well, *merde. . . .*"

The man pulled an embarrassed face and shrugged in that elaborate sort of way that only looks right on a Frenchman.

"They used to call me Major Tom, but that sounded so *bourgeois* I busted myself down to captain."

Christ, another one, I thought to myself.

The man checked his watch, either a steel Rolex Oyster or an awfully good fake.

"Enough of the small talk, *Professeur.* We shall go, no?"

THIRTY-TWO

CAPTAIN TOM DROPPED THE JEEP into gear and it gave a little hip-hop as he accelerated up the road.

There was no sign of life around us, but the foliage was so thick that the Taj Mahal could have been a hundred yards in either direction and I would never have spotted it. From somewhere not very far away I could hear muted sounds of surf, and with the heavy smell of salt in the air I gathered we were sticking close to the coast.

As we came to the end of the asphalt surface a track continued straight into the dense rainforest. I braced myself when we left the roadway, but the dirt was unexpectedly smooth and Captain Tom never even slowed down when we hit it.

We drove for a few minutes in silence, then Tom glanced over and pointed to the storage space in front of my seat.

"*Monsieur* Emmanuel said to get that shit for you."

There was a dark blue nylon pouch in the open compartment. I pulled it out and unzipped it and found inside a folded map of Phuket, a gold American Express card, and a California driver's license with a picture that looked as much like me as any driver's license photograph ever had, even though it wasn't me. The credit card and the license were both in the name of Benny Glup, and the driver's license had an address in Redondo Beach, a place just south of the Los Angeles airport where I had actually been once.

I held up the license and gave Captain Tom a questioning look.

"Benny *Glup?"*

Tom shrugged again, this time a little less elaborately since he was driving.

"It's a name, and we had it available. You got some problem with it?"

"Probably no more than the real Benny Glup had, whoever the poor bastard is. Or was."

"He probably never existed. The license is from of a batch of old DEA covers a pal of *Monsieur* Emmanuel's gave us."

The shifting alliances among the players in Southeast Asia were a slippery thing, particularly when you were mostly on the outside looking in. I didn't even want to try and guess what Manny might be doing for the DEA in return.

"Those glasses are for you, too."

Captain Tom pointed at a pair of dark gray night-vision field glasses tucked under the front edge of the seat. I reached down between my legs and pulled the glasses out. Unzipping the duffle, I slipped them inside.

When I got the bag open something made me lift out the .45. Maybe I just wanted to see what Tom would say when he saw it.

His glanced over, but only briefly.

"Piece of faggot shit," he said, hardly batting an eye.

Without slowing down, Tom bent forward and reached around to the small of his back. Lifting his shirt, he produced a black automatic with a nasty profile.

"Now take this sweet *babé* here. Glock 30. All polymer. Even with a fifteen-round magazine it weighs less than thirty ounces and it's got a trigger pull that's silky as pussy hair. Loaded with 230-gram hollow points, you can stop a truck if you can handle the kick."

Tom shot me a quick look to check out my reaction.

"I could loan it to you. Better than that fucking piece-of-shit .45."

"Couldn't you just get me a bazooka instead?" I asked.

Tom tapped his fingers on the steering wheel and thought for a moment.

"Nobody told me you wanted one, but it's no problem if you can give me a couple of hours."

"That was just a joke, Tom."

"Oh, *oui,*" he said, but he didn't laugh.

Captain Tom drove on along the dirt track in silence for a while. Eventually he got around to asking me what I knew he'd wanted to ask as soon as I had produced the ·45, but wasn't sure he ought to.

"You know how to handle a gun, *Professeur?*"

"I'm not going to shoot anybody," I said. "It's mostly just for show."

Tom turned his head and stared.

"Never carry a gun unless you're willing to use it. And never use it unless you're willing to kill somebody. That is what your own famous American outlaw Billy the Kid said, and it is good advice."

I thought that over while I stuffed the ·45 back into the duffle and zipped it up. Then I tucked the bag away under my feet.

"If I recall my western history correctly, Tom, Billy the Kid eventually got shot in the back. Isn't that right?"

Captain Tom flicked his eyes at me briefly and then lapsed into silence again.

After another twenty minutes the track we were following suddenly emerged from the folds of moist greenery and intersected a well-maintained asphalt highway with very little traffic. We turned south, and before long I saw a pair of bridges up in the distance.

"Those are the Sarasin Bridges," Captain Tom said when he noticed me looking that way. "Just across is Phuket Island proper, but Nai Harn Beach is all the way down at the south end. We've still got at least another hour of driving."

"Is that where Barry Gale is?"

"That's where the Phuket Yacht Club is. Benny Glup has a room booked there."

"I wondered what the credit card was for."

"The room's already taken care of — *Monsieur* Emmanuel's got a friend at the hotel — but use the credit card for anything else you want. Order some champagne. The bills don't go to us anyway."

"Forget the champagne, Tom. What about Barry Gale? When are you taking me to him?"

Captain Tom didn't answer my question immediately, but I waited him out. He kept his eyes fixed on the road and didn't speak again until we had crossed the bridge and were rolling steadily down the smooth double highway on the other side.

"*Monsieur* Emmanuel told me to take you to the Phuket Yacht Club, *Professeur.* My instructions are that you're on your own from there."

"But you're going to tell me where Barry Gale *is,* aren't you?"

We slammed through a pothole and Tom fought to keep the jeep moving in a straight line. Slowing down didn't seem to cross his mind as an option.

"The man you're looking for is in a villa on the southwestern tip of the island. It's a few miles east of the Yacht Club."

Tom glanced over to check out my reaction. I tried not to give him one.

"The usual approach to the villa is down past the condominiums at Karon Beach," he went on. "Normally there's no access from the south end of the island where the Yacht Club is unless you go all the way into Patong and then circle back south along the coast again, but you'll be able to get around that since I'm leaving *babé* here with you."

Tom patted the jeep's steering wheel lovingly. Then he pointed toward the things I had taken out of the blue pouch.

"On the map you'll find a route marked out from the Yacht Club up through the ruins of an old tin mine and then onto a four-wheel track that circles above the main road and intercepts it just north of the villa."

"Can't I just use the regular highway?"

Captain Tom looked at me like I had just ridden in with a bunch of tourists, which in a manner of speaking I guess I had.

"That's what they'd expect. Nobody would think you might be coming in from the east, and that could be worth something to you. Besides, the track takes you down on the compound from a little above it so you can see what you're getting into before you get there."

"Are you sure Barry Gale is there?" I asked.

"Not absolutely," Tom admitted with what I thought was undue good cheer, "but we figure he must be. Everything checks out. The description seems right. And we know there's a tall Chinese woman with the guy."

"What would it take to be sure?"

Captain Tom took both hands off the wheel and rubbed the back of his neck without slowing down, leaving the muddy jeep to wobble along on its own for a moment.

"Well, somebody could go up there and ring the doorbell, I guess."

I hoped the rest of the ideas Tom had were better than that.

"Do you know how this guy got here from Bangkok?" I asked, changing the subject.

Captain Tom looked at me strangely.

"Is that a joke, too?"

"No. Why should it be?"

"That was how we found him so fast. I thought you knew."

"Knew what?"

"That he flew down from Bangkok on a Thai Airways flight three days ago."

"Why would I know that?"

"He had a ticket under the name Shepherd with the initial J, so I figured somebody had probably told you."

I smiled and nodded as if I was appropriately amused.

What in God's name was that crazy bastard up to? He was just daring me — or somebody — to come and get him.

The highway was good and largely deserted except for swarms of motorcycles and an occasional pickup truck. Off to our right I caught glimpses of the ocean through thick stands of rubber trees and even over the noise of the jeep I could hear the surf slapping against the rocky cliffs. The road suddenly dipped and then emerged from the trees, and we were barreling along next to a crescent-shaped beach that was deserted except for a small frame building near the surf line that I took to be a restaurant. Just past the building, whatever it was, Captain Tom swung the jeep off the road and headed inland, bumping straight across a rocky, gently rising field as if he had driven it many times before.

We bounced in and out of rolls of black rock terraced like layers of icing on a birthday cake, and avoiding the worst of the gaps between them, Tom guided the jeep at an angle across the rising ground until we had climbed a few hundred yards from where we had left the highway. When we reached a gap between two hillocks, he swung the jeep around until it was headed right through them, facing south and giving us an unobstructed view down the coast, and then he stopped.

Pushing his seat back, Captain Tom stood up and rested his forearms on the top of the jeep's windshield. He pointed with his forefinger off in the distance and I stood up next to him and shaded my eyes with the palm of my right hand. I followed the line of ocean, surf, and rock south until it turned east, twisting back on itself and disappearing from view, but I saw nothing out of the ordinary.

"What am I supposed to be looking for?"

"See that house?" Captain Tom pointed again. "Right there on the end of the point?"

All I saw was a lot of rock.

"Not really."

"Try using the glasses."

I sat down and pulled them out of my bag, then stood up again.

"Look just where the coast seems to end right in the middle of that last gap," he said.

I lifted the binoculars and scanned them slowly over the area Captain Tom was pointing to, but I couldn't find a house.

"I see something that looks like a big wall."

"That's it. That's all you can see from here. The wall goes all the way around the compound. There are several buildings in there, a main house and a couple of smaller ones. You've got to get above it to see down inside. Some people around here call it *Berchtesgaden.*"

I lowered the field glasses and slowly tilted my heard toward Tom.

"What did you say?" I asked.

"Berchtesgaden," Tom repeated. "It's the name of a place in Germany where Hitler. . . ."

"I know what it is," I interrupted.

It was also the password Dollar had used to encrypt his files. What in the world did *that* mean?

I lifted the glasses again and swept them back and forth over the area, but there really wasn't all that much to see. The wall was built of black rock that had been smoothly mortared together into a grim-looking barrier at least fifteen feet high. It appeared strong enough to stop tanks.

"Do you know who owns the place?" I asked Tom.

He shook his head.

"There's been a lot of talk ever since it was built. The story about it being a spa for Saddam Hussein was my personal favorite."

Tom thought for a moment longer.

"Somebody once told me it was owned through some chain of paper companies in funny little countries. That kind of thing."

"Could you find out what the companies are?"

"Probably. Why does it matter?"

"Maybe it doesn't, but I'd like to know."

I'd noticed a pad and a pencil in the jeep's storage box, so I sat down, pulled it out, and wrote down the number of my cell phone. I ripped the sheet off and handed it to Tom.

"Call me when you find out."

"Certainement. So . . . ready to go?"

When I nodded Tom slid back into his seat and turned the jeep downhill. Within in a few minutes we were back on the hard surface, traveling south at a good clip. Several miles passed before either of us spoke again.

"How did you end up here, *Professeur?"* Captain Tom eventually asked. "If I'm not being too personal."

"You mean in Phuket? Today?"

"No, I mean in Thailand. It's none of my business why you're here, but you don't seem the usual type."

Captain Tom glanced over at me, then he tossed out a real classic of a shrug, contorting his whole body into a dismissive gesture.

"Tant pis. I was just making conversation."

I normally did the tale of my dinner with Stanley Ratikun as my party piece whenever somebody asked me why I was in Thailand, but now it felt like a weak and embarrassing imitation of an honest answer. Tom was trying to help me do something that he didn't understand, that *I* didn't even really understand, and I figured the very least that entitled him to was a straightforward answer to his question. I just didn't know how to give him one anymore.

I always told people that I had taken the job at Sasin so that I could live the quiet life, but if that was true, what was I doing in Phuket riding in a drug syndicate's jeep with a loaded .45 at my feet chasing after a guy who had bought a Philippine bank for the Russian mob? Nobody had asked me to do it. As a matter of fact, the closer I got to Barry, the more a very significant selection of people demanded that I *not* do it. So how did I answer Tom's question? What in the world was I doing here?

"I don't know, Tom," I finally said. "I really don't know anymore."

Captain Tom nodded slowly, as if he'd been expecting me to say exactly that.

"Well, anyway," I added for no particular reason, "I *am* here."

"No, you're not." Captain Tom waggled his forefinger at me and grinned. "Ike wasn't here. You're not here. Shit, I'm probably not here either, *Professeur.*"

The jeep suddenly hit another hole in the road and Tom fought the steering to keep control as one front tire skidded down into the hole and back out again.

"But sure as Christ that motherfucking hole is here all right."

THIRTY-THREE

TOM STOPPED THE JEEP at the bottom of a long narrow driveway. It sloped steeply upward for several hundred yards, all the way from a silky crescent of yellow sand to the lip of a towering limestone cliff where the Phuket Yacht Club commanded a flamboyant view over the deep cove that sheltered Nai Harn Beach.

In spite of its name, the Phuket Yacht Club wasn't a yacht club, nor for that matter was it any other kind of club. It was a lavish, extravagant hotel whose doors opened readily to anyone with sufficient cash or the right kind of plastic. Its white, futuristic-looking rooms were cantilevered into stacks across the cliff face and they glistened dazzlingly in the mid-day sun.

"It might make you a little conspicuous if I drove you all the way up to the front door," Tom said as he got out of the jeep.

Oh, right. And naturally strolling into a world-famous resort, the kind of place where you might stumble over Madonna shacked up with Prince Charles, won't make me conspicuous at all.

Tom flipped me the keys and I caught them in the air. Then he held out his hand and we shook.

"Good luck, *Professeur.*"

"Thanks, Tom. Don't forget the rundown on the company that owns that house."

"*Oui.* I'll call you."

Captain Tom snapped me a little salute and strolled away in the direction of an open-air beer bar at the edge of the beach. On my own now, I slid into the driver's seat and started the jeep. By the time I had reached the top of the driveway, parked in the lot, and walked into the hotel's lobby, I was already in trouble. I had forgotten who I was supposed to be.

Then it came back to me in a rush and I went over the desk and gave the smiling girl in a yellow silk sarong the name Benny Glup, stumbling over it a little when I did. She seemed very young to me, but then most Thai women seemed very young to me. Either they really were, or I wasn't, and I didn't like to dwell too much on which one it might be.

The girl's smile briefly changed to puzzlement, as I suppose any sensible person's would when confronted by a man stumbling over his own name. She tapped a few keys on her computer terminal, puckered her lips into a little frown, tapped again, and then her smile quickly returned.

"Oh, Mr. *Glup,"* she sang out happily, as if she had personally been waiting for me most of her life.

"Yes, indeed I am."

I made the claim decisively and noted with some satisfaction how convincing I sounded. Maybe I was getting the hang of this stuff.

"You already registered in room 324, Mr. Glup. It very nice suite. Very good ocean view."

The girl tapped a few more keys. There was a gentle whirring sound and a card key popped out of a flat box next to the computer. She passed it over with another bright smile.

In spite of what Tom had told me, I held out Benny Glup's gold American Express card. The girl shook her head.

"Your suite complementary, Mr. Glup. Like always. Welcome back to the Phuket Yacht Club."

Like always? Welcome back?

"I call boy for luggage?"

I held up my duffle bag and shook my head.

The young girl gave me another dazzling smile.

"Have nice day, Mr. Glup."

Gee, thanks for arranging everything so discreetly, Manny. Maybe next time a couple of high school bands marching around the lobby would be a nice touch.

The suite was pleasant of course, decorated in muted colors and with irritatingly perfect taste. This was a five-star resort after all, and it looked it. I wondered what it cost people who paid actual money to stay there.

I pushed open the glass doors, walked out onto the huge, white-tiled terrace, and stood gazing at the spectacular view. The cove below was horseshoe shaped, and just at its apex clumps of coconut palms stood like sentries guarding the sandy beach. Both sides of the cove were lined with heavily forested hills, the steep cliffs cutting glistening limestone slashes here and there into the thick, emerald canopy. On the right was the Andaman Sea and beyond that lay the Bay of Bengal, and further out, the emptiness of the Indian Ocean.

I went back inside the suite, kicked off my shoes, and lay back across the king-sized bed. Now that I apparently knew where Barry Gale was, I had to admit to myself that I wasn't all that sure what to do next. Did I just go over there and demand to know what the hell he had gotten me into, or was there a better strategy?

I had been assuming I would have plenty of time to decide about that while I was searching for Barry, but it hadn't worked out that way. Manny's people seemed to have fingered him without breaking a sweat, although it looked like Barry had hung out enough signs to get himself tracked down by Helen Keller. Did that mean he wanted to be found — *intended* to be found — or had he just gotten careless?

Either way, I supposed, the problem for me was essentially still the same.

What do I do now?

I stood up, lifted the duffle bag, and dropped it on the bed. Unzipping it, I dumped everything out. There wasn't much. If I was going to hang around Phuket very long, I was going to have to do some shopping. Maybe Benny Glup's American Express card would come in handy after all.

My dirty jogging clothes went into a drawer, my running shoes into the closet, and turning on my cell phone in case Tom called, it and the field glasses went back in the bag along with the map of Phuket, the driver's license and the Amex card. The .45 I held in one hand for a moment, bouncing the extra clips around in the other hand. Finally I shoved them into the duffle too, rolled up the blue FBI windbreaker, pushed it in on top, and zipped the bag.

A slight rumbling in my stomach reminded me that I'd had nothing to eat all day, so I slipped back into the Topsiders, slung the bag over my shoulder, and went downstairs, wandering around the hotel until I found a round pavilion open to the ocean that I took to be a café. Since it was the middle of the afternoon the place was empty. That was just fine with me. I took a table near the rail where there was a spectacular view of the beach, ordered a club sandwich and iced tea from a smiling teenaged boy in a starched white jacket, then pulled the map Tom had left me out of my bag.

The red line drawn on it appeared to leave the paved roadway less than half a mile inland from Nai Harn Beach. Then it snaked back and forth across what looked like mostly open country and headed generally westward until it ended at a point near the sea marked with a circle.

I contemplated the route while I ate my sandwich. There weren't very many landmarks and it occurred to me that some basic reconnaissance might help me to make up my mind exactly what to do. If I drove the route that Tom had marked and took a closer look at the house, maybe something brilliant would occur to me. Bolting the last crusts of my sandwich, I signed the bill — ripping off Benny Glup's signature with a flourish — refolded the map, and walked out to the jeep.

The hotel's driveway was narrow, barely wide enough for a single vehicle where it descended at a sharp angle to the beach. On both sides of the road there were tiny stands selling tacky souvenirs and a few shacks where foreigners in funny clothes perched on rickety stools, drinking beer. Tiny, dark children in shorts and T-shirts circulated among the tourists, tugging at sleeves and nudging thighs, trying to sell packs of cigarettes and handsome garlands made of red roses and white jasmine.

A blond woman in a very short skirt, her skin seared by the sun to the texture of imitation lizard, lounged in one of the shacks close to the road pretending to listen to a man sitting near her. He was old and a little plump with a great shock of gray hair that flopped back and forth as he emphasized whatever he was telling the woman with energetic chopping motions from his hands. Every now and then the man reached down and tugged absentmindedly at the waistband of his yellow and green checked shorts as if he feared they might be about to fall off.

The blond seemed to have her eyes fixed somewhere over the man's head and I got the impression that she might be searching the horizon for someone who was more interesting. It wasn't until I got closer that I realized that she was probably in her sixties. Regardless, she gave me a half-nod as I drove by and shifted just enough on her stool to flash me with her legs. I glanced at her companion, but the old man was still waving his hands, talking to the air, and he hadn't noticed.

Right after that I found the place where the red line on Tom's map began. It was a narrow road that intersected the asphalt from the left and disappeared inland between two dilapidated wooden buildings. There was little more to it than a bumpy track, but at least it was headed in a direction well away from any more old men in checked shorts or women in skirts forty years too short for them, so I turned in without hesitation.

I drove for a long while through pineapple fields while the terrain rose steadily toward some rugged-looking hills to the west. When Captain Tom had stopped the jeep and pointed out *Berchtesgaden,* it seemed to me that we must have been on the ocean side of those hills, the opposite side to the one I was now approaching.

Beyond the pineapple field was a dense forest of rubber trees, all of them apparently planted about the same time, and the utter uniformity of their size and the geometrical perfection of the long rows gave the entire grove the unreal feeling of a cartoon. The track entered the rubber forest slipping between parallel ranks of spindly, white-streaked trees that were set barely ten feet apart and the afternoon light slowly went gray and spongy. Then abruptly I was out of the grove again and climbing once more in the harsh glare of the afternoon sun.

About ten minutes later I came upon a ramshackle one-story wooden building with the roof caved in and I wondered if it was the abandoned tin mine Tom had mentioned. I saw no other obvious evidence of a mine, but then again I really had no idea at all what a tin mine might look like, abandoned or otherwise, so I couldn't be sure. Just beyond the mine, if that's what it was, the road twisted sharply and I saw how far I had climbed.

Out along the horizon was the Andaman Sea. It was slate gray now rather than blue, and it looked to be turning rough in a rising wind. From somewhere, perhaps one of the craggy, shrub-clad islands just offshore where I had heard sea gypsies still lived, the steady breeze carried the pungent smell of salted fish drying in the open air.

Up here the rainforest was thick and luxuriant. Fed relentlessly by the southwestern monsoons, groves of frangipani trees with their cloying fragrance were intermingled with deep stands of coconut palms, figs, and mangos. The jungle was damp and lush. You could hear the solitude.

Down and to the right however, behind the beaches fringed with palms, the forest had been cut away. Where there had not long ago been little more than bananas, coconuts, and empty beaches, the concrete and steel spires of resort hotels were now lined up along Karon Beach like soldiers at attention. In the distance I could make out the sprawling bulk of the Meridien Hotel where it squatted on the spectacular promontory that separated Karon from the next beach to the north. Up there, in the town of Patong, right after nightfall a tangle of neon would be ignited in the narrow streets and the fast food joints, beer bars, and transvestite shows would be thronged with marauding packs of sunburned tourists on the prowl.

The jeep pitched and bounced over the ground as the track became steeper. When I topped a little ridgeline, the ruts swung sharply right and paralleled it for a short run before cutting left again then surging over the top.

On the opposite side of the ridge the deep lushness of the rainforest vanished, metamorphosing abruptly into a vast and ominous pan of bare limestone interrupted only intermittently by lonely clumps of scrubby trees bent and twisted into angry shapes by the winds that swirled up from the Andaman. The twin ruts became an almost invisible track over the rock and the jeep struggled for traction. About a half-mile further on the track swung around a sharp outcropping of limestone and I saw just below me the compound that Captain Tom had called *Berchtesgaden.*

I stopped and backed up until the jeep was out of sight, then I got the binoculars out of the duffle and walked up the road. When I found a point from where I could see the compound clearly, I settled myself in and braced my arms against the rock to steady the glasses.

The track gradually descended for four or five hundred yards on the other side of the outcropping toward the compound. I could see an asphalt road that came from behind a rise to my right and I gathered that was what Tom had described as the normal approach to the house.

The compound had two massive gates that gleamed in the afternoon sun like teak polished to a high gloss. They were flanked with two equally massive brass torches, each of them sticking a good six feet over the top of the wall.

From my elevated vantage point I could easily see over the wall and down into the compound. Inside was what appeared to be a main house with three smaller buildings grouped around it. I studied each of the structures through the glasses, being careful to angle the lenses so that the afternoon sun wouldn't flash off them and give me away. There was no obvious security paraphernalia visible, but of course there wouldn't be, would there?

One of the smaller buildings looked like a large garage with room for several vehicles. It had a huge tank next to it that might have been a gasoline supply. The other two small buildings looked like guesthouses, except that one had four satellite dishes on its roof — three small ones and one very large one. Either there was a sophisticated communications facility in there or somebody watched a whole lot of television. The main house, built out of black rock with shiny brass trim and oversized windows and doors, sprawled across most of the rest of the compound. Overall the effect was something like Wayne Newton does Phuket.

As I studied one of the smaller houses more carefully, the one without the electronic apparatus on the roof, a man came out. I was too far away and the glasses were not strong enough to pick out his features with any clarity, but I followed him anyway as he walked toward the inside of the front gate.

I lost sight of him when my angle of vision was blocked by the compound's wall, but I kept scanning with the glasses and in a moment he reappeared. It struck me that he was walking the perimeter, like a watchman making rounds, and now that he had turned and I saw him from the opposite side, I made out something I had completely missed when I first saw him. In the crook of his left arm he was carrying something that looked an awful lot like an automatic rifle.

I continued to follow the man as he paced the inside of the wall. Then something behind him attracted his attention and I saw him half turn, apparently talking to someone. I swung the glasses in the direction the man was looking and braced my arms to keep them steady.

A woman with her hands on her hips was visible in the half-open front door to the main house and she looked as if she was giving instructions to the man with the rifle. I didn't need to see her face clearly to know who she was.

Beth Staley was a hard woman to miss.

THIRTY-FOUR

ALL OF A SUDDEN A LOUD NOISE that was half tweet and half wail started up just behind me, reverberating like a siren in the silence. I dived for cover and hugged the ground behind the rocks until I realized that it was only my cell phone.

Feeling appropriately foolish, I trotted back to the jeep, dug the phone out of the duffle bag, and flipped it open. Since I was out there on what looked like the dark side of the moon, I was just wondering whether a cell phone would actually work when a man's voice spoke so clearly in my ear that it startled me.

"Professeur?"

"Tom?"

"Oui, Professeur. It is me."

Captain Tom sounded happier after we had identified each other with certainty, but I thought there was still some kind of an odd note in his voice.

"Find out who owns the house?" I asked.

"That was another joke, right, *Professeur?* Like the shit about the bazooka?"

"Look, Tom. Just tell me what you found out. All right?"

"Yes, all right."

Tom paused a beat before he went on and I could hear something hanging in the silence.

"The land title is held in the name of a Thai company, but that company is controlled by another one registered in Hong Kong, and the Hong Kong company is jointly owned by two companies, both of them registered in the British Virgin Islands as non-resident trusts."

"Figures," I said. "Let me guess. The trustees for the companies are both lawyers who are somewhere else."

"Both companies have the same trustee, but that is right. You could say he's a lawyer who's somewhere else."

There was that odd note in Tom's voice again.

"Who is it?" I asked.

"Why are you fucking me around like this, *Professeur?"*

"I'm not fucking you around, Tom. I just want to know who the trustee is."

"You really don't know?"

"No, I really don't know."

"That's strange, *Professeur.* I believe you. But that's pretty fucking strange."

"Why, Tom?"

"Because the fellow we use to run down this kind of stuff never gets it wrong. He says the name of the trustee for both companies is Jonathan William Shepherd. That's you, *n'est-ce pas?"*

There was a long silence and I knew Tom was waiting for me to tell him exactly what was going on, but since I didn't have any better idea than he did, I said nothing.

"You still there, *Professeur?"*

"Yeah, Tom, I'm here. Look, let that go. I don't want to talk about it right now."

And even if I did, I had no earthly idea what I would say.

Captain Tom must have been accustomed to people who didn't want to talk about things because he changed the subject smoothly.

"Where are you now, *Professeur?"*

"I followed the route you marked on the map. I'm in a spot just above the compound and I can see it pretty well. Do you know how many people are in there?"

"Why? What are you going to do? Rush the place with that little faggot ·45 of yours?"

"Maybe."

"Well, shit, *Professeur.*"

There was a short silence before Captain Tom went on.

"I don't know who's in there. The place isn't that big, is it?"

"Looks pretty big from here. You don't know for sure?"

"Jesus Christ, *Professeur,* I know fuck all for sure."

I didn't say anything else. Captain Tom obviously hoped I would tell him what I was going to do, but he wasn't sure he should press the point.

"Hey, I was only making a joke about rushing the house," he eventually said.

"Uh-huh."

"I mean . . . you wouldn't really do that, would you, *Professeur?*"

"Nope."

"Hey, okay. You had me worried there for a minute."

Then Captain Tom played back the last bit of our conversation and noticed that I had left his original question conspicuously unanswered.

"So what *are* you going to do?"

"You got a phone number for the compound, Tom?"

"Ah . . . no."

"Didn't think you would. Then I guess I'll have to go down and ring the doorbell like you suggested."

"Hey, *Professeur,* now wait a minute. If I were you, I'd think about it for a long time before. . . ."

"I have."

I cut Tom off before he could get wound up.

"Ground control to Captain Tom. Over and out."

When I hit the red power button, the cell phone went dead. I shoved it into the duffle and walked back to the rock outcropping that had become my observation post, then raised the field glasses again. The compound looked quiet and sleepy in the late afternoon sun and the guard was no longer anywhere to be seen.

So I was the trustee for the property, huh?

Of course Barry Gale was down there. He had flown to Phuket under my name, and now here he was, surrounded by armed guards and holed up in an elaborate compound I appeared to own. He couldn't have made it any clearer if he had installed a red neon sign on the roof.

Barry Gale *wanted* me to find him, and now I had.

So why wait any longer to ask him what the hell this was all about? I certainly wasn't just going to drive back down to the Phuket Yacht Club now and think about it some more over a Heineken.

In my experience life generally worked best if you just kept moving in a reasonably straight line most of the time, even if a lot of people tried to make it seem more complicated than that. For example, if you wanted to ask someone a question, usually the best approach was to walk right up and ask it. That way, you got your answer without a lot of unnecessary screwing around. Of course, the answer was frequently a lie — but hey, it was a start, wasn't it?

I lowered the glasses and looked around. Barry had picked a hell of a good bolt-hole. Other than using the main road or coming cross-country like I had, the compound was unapproachable. Nobody could get within five hundred yards of the place without being spotted, and even if you *could* get up to it, the walls made it a fortress that would have given General Patton pause. With the gasoline storage and the communications equipment, Barry could probably hold out in there long enough to make anyone stalking him throw up their hands in exasperation and just go away.

Waiting until dark to approach the compound probably wouldn't make any difference, but then again, it might. The element of surprise was always supposed to be a good thing, wasn't it?

Okay, let's just say that I managed to get down there without being seen. Then what?

I could check the place out, of course, see if there might be a way to get past the wall and slip by the guards. Maybe I could give Barry Gale a bit of a shock that way and that would help me get the truth out of him.

Okay, so it wasn't much — in fact, it probably wasn't anything — but it was the most optimistic plan I could come up with on short notice.

On the other hand, it occurred to me that armed guards aren't particularly relevant unless whoever is being guarded expects someone to show up, so it was possible that the primary effect of me suddenly appearing out of the darkness might be to get my ass shot off. That insight caused me to calculate and recalculate the element of surprise a few times, but I couldn't make up my mind which way the balance fell, so I decided not to worry about it.

It was just after five. I walked back to the jeep and settled into the passenger seat, waiting either for darkness to fall or my common sense to return, whichever occurred first.

It seemed unlikely there would be any other traffic the way I had just come — I hadn't seen another vehicle the entire time I'd been driving up — but just in case, I reversed the jeep along the track until I found a good spot to swing it around. I parked it facing out toward the ocean like I was up there to watch the sunset. If anyone did come up the road, I would probably look like just another loony tourist in a tropical daze.

I unzipped the duffle and pushed the glasses inside. When I did, I saw the .45 and lifted it out. I used to shoot some at a range in the Maryland suburbs just outside of Washington, but I hadn't touched a handgun since I'd been in Thailand and I'd certainly never pointed one at a human being. What the hell did I think I was going to do with this one? Use it to threaten Barry?

In my own experience with the somewhat less violent forms of coercion routinely practiced by lawyers, threats only worked when people knew you might actually carry them out. Did I look like a guy who would coolly pull the trigger on someone? And if I didn't, or if I wasn't, then what good was waving a prop around going to do?

Never carry a gun unless you're willing to use it, and never use it unless you're willing to kill somebody.

If I applied the Billy the Kid rule, I'd stick the gun back in the bag right now and forget about it. Still, there were other guys with guns skulking around down somewhere just below me and I would have given a lot right then to know what rules *they* were following.

I stepped out of the jeep and slid the .45 from of its holster. I dropped the clip, hefted it in the approved two-handed grip, and bent my knees into a Weaver stance just like I'd been taught. It all felt familiar enough, I guessed. I looked down the barrel, focusing on the front sight with my left eye open just as my instructor had repeatedly reminded me. Then I racked the slide and dry-fired, feeling the solid clunk of the hammer slamming down where the cartridge ought to be.

Okay, so maybe I *could* use it if I actually had to.

Lowering the .45, I popped the clip back in and worked the slide to chamber a round. Then I set the safety, pushed it back into its holster, and stuck the whole rig back in the duffle bag. I could always decide later what I was going to do with it.

I fiddled with the jeep's passenger seat until I got it as far back as it would go. Then I climbed up and settled into it, propping my feet across the driver's seat and leaning back against the door. The sun was a huge, shimmering disk of red, the lower rim nudging the Andaman Sea. It would soon be dark.

I suddenly remembered a Chinese folk tale about a green flash that supposedly occurs occasionally when the sun sets into the ocean, a brilliant halo of emerald light that flares outward just as the upper rim of the sun sinks beneath the sea. Good fortune and eternal happiness were supposed to be the reward for everyone who saw the green flash, the tale went, but that sounded like far too romantic a notion for the Chinese so I doubted that part of the story. Still, it was a lovely thought, and since I figured I could use some of that good fortune and eternal happiness stuff right about then, I started hoping that this might be my day to see the flash anyway.

I could have been in one of Phuket's many sea-front bars about then, settled comfortably among the crowd of shorts, tank tops, and brown-skinned girls who were always around at the end of the day, wondering if tonight would be the night I'd see the green flash at last; but instead I was slumped against the passenger door of a muddy jeep, all alone, parked on the side of a deserted hill, waiting for it to get dark enough to creep up on a guy who was holed up in a walled estate that looked like it had been built by the Seven Dwarfs on their weekends off from the mine. Not by far my first choice of venues for flash spotting.

In the last light of the setting sun I glanced up the road toward the big outcropping where I'd been watching the compound. A little further along that road, no more than a half-mile away, the answers to all my questions were somewhere inside a lonely compound, perched on the rocky tip of a remote tropical island and guarded by some rented guns.

And how, drawing on the sum total of my entire lifetime's accumulated wisdom and experience, was I going to deal with that?

I was going to wait until it got dark, try to sneak inside, and ask Barry Gale if he would mind very much telling me what in Christ's name was going on here.

That's your big plan?

Well . . . yeah.

It sucks.

By the time I glanced back toward the sun, it was gone. The night had arrived with heart-stopping suddenness and the Andaman Sea looked as if it had turned to molten pewter. The tiny atolls just west of Phuket were a scattering of pebbles flung across its surface, quick frozen into the hardening metal.

I hadn't noticed if there had been a green flash or not.

Rats.

I'd really been counting on that.

THIRTY-FIVE

THE MOON ROSE ROUND AND FULL over my shoulder. It looked like a yellow flying saucer levitating out of the rainforest.

When I figured I had stalled long enough I started the jeep, turned it around, and drove slowly up the track. Just before I swung around the rocks that had been sheltering me I cut my lights, and after I had passed them, I stopped and stood up in the jeep, studying the compound one more time through the field glasses.

The brass torches flanking the wooden gates had been lit. They were blazing with gas flares that shot three or four feet into the air and cast an eerie, yellowish illumination in front of the huge gates. There was a scattering of lights in a few windows, and although I saw no sign of anyone I had absolutely no doubt that Barry and his guards were down there somewhere.

The moonlight was bright enough on the slope for me to pick my way down through the darkness without serious risk, yet still not bright enough to make me unduly conspicuous. That was about as much good luck as I could have hoped for.

I unzipped the bag and took out the .45 and the spare clips. Positioning the holster in front of my right hip, I snapped it over my belt, then stuffed the clips into my trouser pockets. Hauling the windbreaker out of the duffle, I turned it inside out to make the yellow FBI identification on the back a little less conspicuous — somehow I didn't think that would strike exactly the right introductory note with Barry's armed guards — then pulled it on over my polo shirt and jeans.

Taking a deep breath I shifted back into gear and eased the jeep on down the rough track, keeping the headlights doused. The tires made a swishing sound in the dirt and limestone dust as I rolled through the darkness toward the black rock wall.

After about three hundred yards the track dipped sharply and then rose again, and when I reached the top of the rise I stopped and re-examined the view ahead. From that point onward the track faded away, so I backed carefully down from the rise and pulled the jeep off where it couldn't be seen from the compound, then cut the engine.

I got out, closing the door quietly behind me, took the field glasses and walked back up the rise. Stretching out flat so I wouldn't be silhouetted against the sky, I raised the glasses.

The ground sloped down evenly from where I was to the compound and then dropped abruptly right behind it over a cliff and into the sea. The main road was a narrow line of gray asphalt that came in from the north, made a sharp dog-leg west, and ended in a small pad in front of the gates. It was rough and unlighted, really not much of a road, and it appeared to be deserted.

Now that I was closer to the compound I could see that in front of the gates there was a box set all by itself waist high on a shiny post that had to be an intercom of some sort. Above the gates there was another box mounted on the wall. That one looked like a camera.

I swung the glasses back and forth, but I didn't see any other surveillance cameras along the wall. That was the good news. The bad news was that I couldn't find any cover between the rise and the wall either, but with no surveillance and no sign of any guards outside the walls, maybe I wouldn't need it.

While the area around the gate was illuminated by the light from the burning torches, the shadows around the rest of the wall were deep in spite of the moonlight. Unless Barry had himself some spiffy infrared sensors out there, it looked like I could make it unseen at least as far as the wall if I approached the compound from one side rather than head-on toward the gates.

I eased back down the rise and dumped the field glasses in the jeep. Moving perpendicular to the track, I jogged in a half crouch until I was far enough around to the north side of the compound that I couldn't see the gates any longer. Taking one more careful look around and seeing nothing, I drew a deep breath and ran as quietly as I could for the wall. Sure enough I reached the base without any indication that I had been seen and ended up at a spot that was dim enough to make me feel about as secure as I could hope to be under the circumstances.

Up close the wall was just as it had looked through the field glasses. Solid rock, about fifteen feet high, utterly impregnable, and mortared so smoothly that climbing it wasn't even worth thinking about. Staying in the shadows, I worked my way around the compound. I hugged the base of the wall and kept away from the gate, looking carefully for a weak point. I found none.

There were no other entrances at all, and if there was even the slightest variation in the construction of the wall, it eluded me. I soon reached the corner of the compound opposite to the one where I had started. Leaning cautiously out of the shadows, I studied the remaining section of the wall where the gates were. They looked thickly varnished and seemed to fit together in the center with perfect precision. There was no hardware on their exterior, not even a handle or a plate suggesting a lock, and I couldn't see anything like a crack or a knothole through which I could try and sneak a peek inside.

It was an entrance designed to make anyone who approached it feel insignificant, a supplicant begging audience with the Black Prince, and that made me mad as hell. Barry Gale was a slug who had crawled into bed with the Russian Mafia. I knew for certain he'd been involved in one murder back in Dallas and I had no doubt that he was somehow connected to the killings of Howard and Dollar as well. Yet here I was, skulking around in the darkness just to talk to the bastard. My right hand slipped inside my windbreaker and closed on the grip of the ·45.

Let me get this straight, a little voice said. *You're going to pull that peashooter and blast your way in like Rambo, right through a pair of solid teak gates that would probably stop King Kong cold. Then you're going to back down a bunch of goons armed with automatic rifles. That's what you're going to do here?*

With a sigh, I took my hand out of my jacket and looked around again. No, of course I wasn't going to do that, but there was only one other alternative.

I can't believe I'm going to do this either, I thought.

Manny's underground network had successfully smuggled me onto Phuket undetected. I had found Barry Gale's secret bolt-hole, waited until I had the cover of darkness, and then crept all the way to his very gate without anybody spotting me.

And now I'm just going to walk up and ring the goddamned doorbell?

Wonderful, Jack. Really wonderful.

I stepped quickly out of the shadows and rounded the corner into the wavering circle of light cast by the gas torches before I had any more time to think about how stupid I felt doing it. There was a single, red button next to a white number pad on the intercom box and I gave it a solid push.

"Yes?"

The voice that rattled out of the box's loudspeaker was cold and metallic. Worse, it sounded entirely unperturbed. So much for the element of surprise.

"I'm here to see Barry Gale."

It was a wimpy thing to say, and I had to bend down slightly to speak into the intercom, so I felt even wimpier. After all the maneuvering and calculating of advantages and possibilities, now I was just some asshole standing in the dark outside the castle and begging this faceless retainer for an audience with his master.

"Who is this?" the voice asked.

Banks of floodlights set back in recesses at the top of the wall suddenly snapped on and bathed the entrance to the compound so brightly that the flames from the brass torches seemed to have been snuffed out.

I hit the button again. But this time I didn't bend down.

"This is Jack Shepherd."

Squinting against the glare, I let the button go, but then I banged it again with my fist and yelled at the little box.

"I'm sick of this goddamned bullshit. You can tell Barry he's got ten seconds to open this gate or I'm coming back here with every cop I can find and maybe the fucking United States Marines, too."

There was a silence and in it I heard a scraping sound behind me. I turned around quickly, but all I could see were the brown spots still dancing in front of my eyes from the sudden burst of floodlights.

Then there was a metallic click and a bright flashlight came on. The beam played over me and I lifted my hands to shield my eyes. In spite of the care I'd taken in approaching the compound, there was at least one guard patrolling outside and I'd completely missed him. I started wondering what else I might have missed.

Whoever was holding the flashlight stood very still about twenty feet behind me. He said nothing and I could see nothing in the darkness with his light in my eyes. Then I heard a familiar voice.

"Come on in, Jack. I knew you'd turn up eventually."

Barry Gale's voice startled me and I swiveled toward where it seemed to have come from, but of course there was nothing to see except the black intercom box.

"Don't you know it's rude to drop in on friends unannounced, Jack?" Barry's voice continued from the loudspeaker. "You could at least have called so the cook would have had time to put out an extra plate for dinner."

"We're not friends, Barry!"

I was shouting back at the intercom box, but of course I wasn't pressing the button so Barry couldn't hear me.

"And you can stick your goddamned dinner up your goddamned ass!"

The flashlight behind me moved away to one side, but the beam kept me pinned. Whoever was holding the light was maintaining a suitably professional distance between us and I had absolutely no doubt that he was also pointing something at me other than the flashlight.

I saw a movement of the gates out of the corner of my eye and glanced back. The shiny teak panels opened a crack. A man slipped out of the compound and looked me over without expression. He was a local, not particularly big or formidable, but the black assault rifle in his hands more than made up for any other deficiencies.

The man took a few steps in my direction, then stopped, moved off to one side, and gestured me forward with the muzzle of the rifle. His round, slightly shiny face remained expressionless and my eyes kept shifting back and forth between it and the rifle. The man gestured again in an impatient way, this time clearly pointing with his free hand toward the opening in the gates. I walked forward keeping a wary eye on the rifle.

As I stepped between the thick teak panels, someone on the outer edge of my peripheral vision swung a foot and swept my legs cleanly out from under me. I went to the ground and knees pressed into my back as I tried to catch my breath. Practiced hands patted me down. When the hands came to the .45, they snapped the holster off my belt and paused. Then they started over me again. They took the spare clips from the pockets of my jeans, my wallet, and my keys.

"Stand."

It was a man's voice, and I felt the knees move and the weight lift off my back.

I pushed myself up slowly and dusted off with a show of casual deliberation. It was a childish gesture of defiance, but I did it anyway.

When I eventually lifted my eyes, I saw two Thai men a few paces in front of me watching with blank faces. One was the man who had opened the gate and the other might have been the guard I had watched through my glasses patrolling the compound, although I wasn't sure. Both of them were armed, but their weapons dangled casually at their sides. That seemed to me to be a good sign.

"Nice jacket, Mr. Shepherd."

It was a woman's voice from behind me.

"I like the inside-out touch," she added. "Very subtle."

When I turned around, Beth was holding my .45. She had taken it from the holster, but unlike the men's rifles, it wasn't pointed at the ground. It was pointed right at my belly. So much for good signs.

Next to her was one of the men I had seen that day in Lumpini Park, the big one. He was holding my wallet, keys, and the extra clips, so I gathered it was probably his knees that had just been in my back.

"What were you going to do with this thing, Mr. Shepherd?" Beth wiggled the .45. "Shoot Barry?"

"I doubt it, Beth. But you never know."

Beth laughed just like she had laughed that morning we'd been running around the lake, and even in this bizarre and secret place it still had the sound of a happy child in the park on a sunny morning.

"Jeez, that would have come as a real surprise to all of us. Particularly Barry."

I tried to read the expression in Beth's eyes, but now they were cop's eyes and I couldn't.

"Did you come here alone tonight, Mr. Shepherd?"

"What does it look like to you, Beth? You see an army somewhere out there behind me?"

She smiled with her mouth, but I could see her eyes doing calculations as she did. I wondered if she believed me, and what difference it might make if she didn't.

One of the guards walked past me and slipped outside through the opening in the gates. I could hear him talking, probably to whoever had been behind me with the flashlight, but I couldn't make out what they were saying. Whatever it was it must have been the right thing, because a few seconds later he returned, turned his back to me, and murmured something to Beth, after which Beth's body relaxed and she dropped the muzzle of the .45 toward the ground.

"Barry's in the main house. He's anxious to see you."

"I'll bet he is."

"I'll keep your sidearm and extra clips, Mr. Shepherd. You can get them back when you leave."

That sounded encouraging. Beth seemed to think I would be leaving later.

The big man standing with her gave Beth the clips then tossed my wallet and keys across the gap between us. I caught both in the air, which pleased me unreasonably under the circumstances, and shoved them back into my pockets.

When I thought back on it later, I realized that I didn't have the slightest idea what I might find inside that house. Maybe Barry would be lounging around in tennis clothes, chugging Miller Lite and watching the Lakers on a big-screen television. Maybe Barry would be wearing a black suit with dark glasses and hunched over a bank of computer terminals cackling maniacally. Maybe Barry would be buck naked and rolling around in bed with Hillary Clinton.

Well, probably not that.

The big man walked to the gate and closed it again, securing it with quick, economical movements. Beth gestured me toward the entrance to the main house and fell into step behind me still carrying my .45.

"Just don't shoot me in the ass," I muttered.

THIRTY-SIX

THE FRONT DOOR OPENED into a foyer that was well lit but bare. It looked like the decorator had been fired or the owner had run out of money before the job was finished.

The green marble floor was polished to the sheen of a frozen lake and the walls were painted with large murals which appeared to be kitschy scenes of what life was presumably like a few hundred years ago in Phuket, at least for the white guys. A band of dark-skinned, laughing local girls, naked except for a few strategically draped palm fronds here and there, enthusiastically serviced visiting sailors who were sprawled on the beach in varying stages of intoxication. It was just the sort of stuff to go with the brass torches.

"Straight through," Beth said from behind me.

I crossed the foyer and we walked at a stately pace single file along a wide, gallery-like corridor. Through a pair of open doors at the far end I could see part of a large room furnished with comfortable-looking couches and chairs arranged in front of a stone fireplace surrounded by an elaborately-carved marble mantelpiece. Improbably enough for Thailand, there was a wood fire blazing away in the fireplace. It was a scene that suggested Barry Gale had to be standing somewhere just out of sight, probably wearing a burgundy silk smoking jacket with a wide black sash and stroking the head of an Irish Setter.

The gallery itself was lined with oil paintings in heavy, old-fashioned gilt frames and at a quick glance they seemed to be a spectacular collection. I was no art expert, but a couple of the paintings looked a lot like Gauguins, another appeared to be a Monet, and a large canvas that had been carefully lit by concealed pencil-spots might have been a Rembrandt.

"These aren't real, are they?" I asked Beth.

I couldn't see her eyes and she didn't say anything, but I heard her grunt softly. I wondered if that meant that the paintings *were* real, or that she assumed any idiot would know they weren't.

After we reached the big room at the end of the gallery Beth nodded in the direction of one of the couches by the fireplace, then she turned away and walked back to the front door and left me there. Neither Barry Gale nor the Irish setter were anywhere in sight, so not having much else to do I settled back on the couch and looked around.

The room could have been a Ralph Lauren store, crackling fire and all, an American fantasy of what British manor houses ought to look like but never actually did. I'd bet some decorator from New Jersey had ripped a few pages out of an old *Harpers & Queen,* copied as many of them as he could, and then just made the rest of it up from there. In California the result might have been funny. In Phuket, it was scary.

"How do you like my place, Jack?"

Barry came into the room from somewhere behind me, but I didn't turn around.

"Pretty terrific, huh? You see the *names* on those pictures out there?"

He walked past the couch and settled into a red leather wingback chair that was just in front of the fire, crossing his legs at the knee and stretching his arms out along the rolled arms of the chair. He was wearing slacks that looked like black linen, a matching long-sleeved shirt, and black loafers without socks. He looked tanned and rested, not at all like a man on the run.

"So who'd you buy the place from?" I asked him. "Donald Trump?"

"That's a pretty good one," he chuckled.

I chuckled, too. So far we were having a hell of a time.

"Nah," he said after he was done chuckling. "The bank took it off a couple of locals. Two old queens who were part-time politicians, part-time real estate developers, and full-time fuckups. They only *thought* they were Donald Trump."

Barry chuckled one more time for good measure.

"They ran out of money when the Thai economy went into the toilet a few years ago. Left the bastards flat. You might say the bank made them an offer they couldn't refuse."

"And how about your little army outside? Another foreclosure?"

"Beth's worked for the bank . . ." Barry paused to think about it, ". . . oh, almost two years now. I brought her in myself. She doesn't know anything about the heavy lifting, of course. Just the routine stuff."

I nodded.

"Yeah, I can understand how that works. Heck, I'm the trustee for this whole setup and up until a few hours ago I didn't even know it existed."

"Well, I'll tell you, Jack. That doesn't really matter very much."

"It does to me."

"It shouldn't, since you don't really control anything. The whole deal's a double blind. You're only the cut-out. If anyone gets curious and starts poking around trying to find out who owns this place, they'll find that trail leading to you. That's why it's there."

Barry smiled benignly at me. He was apparently enjoying this a lot.

"Okay, Barry, you got me." I tossed out my best shrug. "I'll just sit here until you feel like telling me what the hell's going on. I really don't know what else to do."

"Good decision, Jack. Good decision."

I noticed that Barry was looking over my shoulder, and when he stood up and walked past me I twisted around and saw Beth waiting just inside the gallery. She and Barry exchanged a few words that I couldn't hear and then he walked back and resumed his seat by the fire.

"Came here by yourself tonight, did you, Jack?"

"That's what they say."

"I had it all worked out for you to show up eventually of course, but . . ." he shook his head in mock admiration ". . . I never thought you'd manage it this fast."

"I have friends."

"So do I, Jack, and if you don't give me a straight answer, maybe you'll find out who they are."

So much for chitchat.

"I found some stuff at Dollar's that pointed me to Phuket. Then I got a guy I know to ask around and he located this place. I couldn't tell you how he actually did that even if I wanted to, which I don't."

Putting Mango Manny's name on the table didn't seem fair or necessary, so I didn't.

"You don't need to know any more than that," I added.

Barry's eyes started to dance.

"You've got a pair there big enough to bowl with, don't you, Jack? Not many people tell me what I need to know."

Then he laughed.

"Okay, smart guy, so after your secret pal located me, he smuggled you into Phuket on a private plane or some shit like that. Is that about it?"

I nodded.

"Don't you think someone might have seen you take off from Bangkok?"

"I didn't say we left from Bangkok."

"Then where did you leave from?"

"It doesn't matter, but no one saw me leave."

"And you're just as sure that no one saw you arrive on Phuket?"

"Just as sure."

"So you weren't followed here."

"My friend made sure of that."

"Your friend made sure of that," Barry repeated slowly.

I nodded again.

"So I guess if I shoot you through the head and bury you somewhere out there, no one will ever figure out what happened to you, huh? Except maybe this secret pal of yours."

That thought introduced an unwelcome twist into the conversation, but I pushed on.

"You're not going to do that."

"Really?"

"No."

"And you'd bet your life on that, so to speak."

"I guess I already have."

Barry nodded slowly as if he was weighing the wisdom of my wager. I certainly was.

"How come you're so confident here, Jack? I don't see it myself."

"Because you want something from me."

I looked Barry in the eye and kept on talking.

"You showed up in Bangkok and gave me that cock-and-bull story about being on the run because the ABC had been scammed and you were afraid the Russians would think it was you. But let me tell you what I think happened here."

Barry watched me with obvious interest, but he said nothing.

"I think all that garbage was just to fatten me up. My guess is that you've run your own little con on the bank, skimmed off a bunch of money for yourself, and then led me here because you need me to cover your ass."

"Very interesting theory, Jack. Very imaginative."

"So if you'll just tell me what the hell it is you want me to do, then I can either do it or tell you to shove it. Whichever way it goes, we can put an end to all this diddlyshit and get on with our lives."

Barry was smiling again now.

"I always said you were a smart guy, Jack, and I was right. You really *are* a smart guy."

"I can't tell you how much I appreciate your confidence in me."

"What's more, you've almost got it all right. Still, I'm afraid you're a bit off about one thing, and I have to say that it's something pretty important."

"And that would be. . . ."

"Now that you've shown up here, Jack, you've finished your job for me. I'm all done. I've got no more use for you."

Oops.

Barry smiled. Not knowing what else to do, I smiled back.

"You think I'm crazy, don't you, Jack?"

The thought had crossed my mind.

"When we were working together, you were always the guy everyone looked up to," he said. "You were the man, weren't you?"

"I never looked at it that way, Barry."

"Everyone else did. They never trusted me to do anything if they could get you instead, Jack."

"I'm sorry you feel that way. I think you're selling yourself short."

Barry just shook his head and mimed a theatrical little laugh.

"No, Jack. I just sold *you* short, my friend. And I got a great fucking price for you, too."

I just waited. I knew the rest was coming. Barry was just warming up.

"I bought the Asia Bank of Commerce for Jimmy Kicks just like I told you, a safe little money laundry in a nice out-of-the-way place."

Barry's eyes sparkled with excitement and he was off and running.

"But it wasn't long before I realized I was on to something really big here. Everybody needs a bank they can trust, Jack. Even crooks and criminals."

Barry leaped out of his chair and began to pace the room while he talked, his arms wheeling wildly.

"There's a *river* of dirty money out there, my friend! Drugs, guns, bribes, rackets, scams, outright theft. Shit, it's a fucking *ocean!* I once saw a bunch of garbage bags in a Houston warehouse with fifty million dollars in hundreds in them, just stuffed in there like trash. Have you ever *seen* fifty million dollars in hundred-dollar bills, Jack?"

I shook my head, but Barry hardly seemed to notice.

"Before I got this deal working, all anybody could do with all that money was buy some more dope or maybe a shitty strip mall in Tampa. That's not power, Jack. Cash is power! But not if it's in a bunch of bags in some fucking warehouse. If you can't get your cash into the banking system, you might as well start using it to wipe your ass because that's all it's good for. It's nothing but waste paper."

"A lot of people have tried large scale money laundering, Barry. They always get caught."

"All a bunch of fucking amateurs, Jack!" he sneered. "Just yokels with no vision!"

I nodded in encouragement and Barry took flight again.

"We put the word out discreetly that the ABC was a reliable bank owned by reliable people and that it didn't ask a lot of questions about its depositors. After that the damnedest stuff started turning up on our doorstep. You know why? Because we were part of the international banking system and when folks put their money with us *it* became part of the international banking system! After that I could send it any place in the world without anyone knowing anything at all about it. You know how I did that, Jack?"

He didn't wait for me to answer.

"I am the alchemist!" Barry roared. "I take paper, turn it into energy, zap it around the world, and then turn it back into paper again. In a flash, I can switch a mountain of dirty money into a stream of clean little electrons."

He snapped his fingers.

"Beam me up, Mr. Scott!"

Barry was scaring me. I glanced around the room, checking for exits.

"I wouldn't want you to think I wasn't enjoying our little chat here, Barry, but what has any of this got to do with me?"

"Just be patient, Jack. Hear me out. It was like this. First of course it was mostly just dipshit local scumbags who put money with us, but after the word got around, we had the Russians, the Burmese, the Colombians, the Mexicans, the South Africans, everybody! We started getting into bigger and bigger money, but most of it was just going right through us. I started thinking about ways we could hang on to a bigger piece."

Why doesn't that surprise me?

"Some Burmese jerkoffs had a deal going with the Chinese and suddenly I saw my chance! You know the army really runs the drug trade in China, don't you, Jack? Well, these Burmese yahoos had done a deal with the Chinese army because they were swimming in raw morphine base and wanted to diversify into finished products. They agreed to finance the construction of four heroin refineries just across the border into China from where the opium production was. The PLA would move the raw materials, look after the refineries, and transport the processed heroin to the coast of China for shipment to North America and Europe. The deal was for everybody to split the proceeds from the operation right down the middle."

I shook my head impatiently. It seemed to irritate Barry that I wasn't hanging on his every word, but he went on anyway.

"The problem was how to get the money to finance the refineries and pay off the generals in China without anyone knowing where it came from."

Barry was still watching me, reveling in relating his great adventure to someone he thought would truly appreciate its nuances. He wanted me to be interested in what he was saying. I was, of course, but I tried not to show it.

"The Burmese had a shitload of cash split up among a bunch of shell companies with accounts in American banks, of all places, which the stupid cocksuckers thought was so damned clever of them. The problem was, naturally, that they couldn't figure out how to move any of it from the U.S. to China without being pretty damned conspicuous about it. But I saw the way to do it right away."

Barry tapped the side of his head with one finger and hoisted his eyebrows.

"All the ABC had to do was arrange routine trade financing for a bunch of ordinary businesses the Chinese army controlled: coal mines and toy companies, shit like that. To secure that financing we agreed to accept the cash being held in the American banks by the Burmese. After that we could shift the deposits around through our own system without anybody noticing."

Barry looked terribly pleased with himself.

"The financing was dressed up as if it came from ABC funds, of course, but it was really going to be the Burmese money we'd brought in from the American banks, less our cut, of course. You following me here, Jack?"

"I think I can still grasp the mechanics of a simple back-to-back loan scheme, Barry."

"It was even simpler than you might think, Jack. We took the Burmese funds out of the American shell companies as security for the Chinese loans, but we never made any loans."

It took me a moment, but then I saw the brutal simplicity in what Barry was saying.

"You're telling me that instead of laundering the money that came from the Burmese and passing it through to the Chinese, the Asian Bank of Commerce *stole* it?"

"Not exactly. *I* stole it, not the bank. I personally cleaned the motherfuckers out."

"Why would you think you could get away with that?"

Barry grinned so broadly I thought for a moment he might hurt himself.

"Two reasons, Jack."

He held up two fingers as if I might not be familiar with the number.

"First, what we had with the ABC was a sort of No Tell Motel for money. I mean, it's like this. You're at a nice little motel way out somewhere on the highway with a lady friend and you see your worst enemy with some big-tittied hooker. What are you going to do? Call his wife and say you saw him there? And then when your wife finds out *you* were out there and she asks, 'What were you doing at the No Tell Motel?' what are you going to say?"

Barry laughed some more.

"Hey, it was foolproof, Jack. The money was never supposed to be there in the first place. So who the hell was going to complain that it was gone?"

"What's the second reason?" I asked.

"Well, the second reason — and I'm sorry to have to say this — is you."

"Me?"

"Yeah, you, Jack."

Barry paused and searched briefly for the best way to explain.

"In every business deal I've ever been in, Jack, somebody gets fucked. You know what I mean?"

"Son of a bitch."

"Yeah, you've got it. That's how I'm getting away with it."

Barry wiggled his eyebrows up and down.

"You're the one who's getting fucked."

THIRTY-SEVEN

"It's this way, Jack. Even when you're messing around with money that's not supposed to exist, it still belongs to somebody, and they'll still be plenty pissed when they find out it's gone."

"I can imagine."

"Yeah, that was the problem I had. If the Burmese thought I had their money, they might not come after me publicly, but you can bet your ass that they'd do it privately. Sometimes it's those private complaints that really end up fucking you in the ass. You know what I mean?"

"Not really. It's not a problem I've ever had."

"Well, Jack, that's what I'm trying to tell you here. You have it now."

Barry tapped the side of his head with his index finger for the second time. He apparently liked that gesture a lot.

"Taking the money was easy, but I knew that keeping it would be a lot harder. I needed a patsy. Someone who was such a respected expert in international finance that it would be entirely believable that he was the scam artist here, not me. Someone exactly like you, Jack."

"That's nuts, Barry. Why would anyone in his right mind think that I had anything to do with this?"

"Because your fingerprints are all over everything. The legal work, the fund transfers, even the corporate structures we used. It was all your work, Jack. You put it together."

That didn't make any sense. I'd never had any thing to do with the Asian Bank of Commerce. The closest I'd come to it was ten minutes in a corporate services office in Hong Kong trying to strike up a conversation with a human doorstop.

"You don't know what I'm talking about, do you?"

He had me there. I shook my head.

"I own Southeast Asian Investments, Jack."

"You can't be serious."

"Serious as a fart in a submarine, my friend. Why do you think you got that invitation out of the blue to join their board of directors?"

Barry grinned and spread his palms.

"Hey, I always remember my buddies, don't I?"

The pieces of the puzzle were beginning to slide around in my mind, and they were starting to lock together into a picture that actually made some sort of weird sense.

"The Cambodian shrimp farm I organized was really just a conduit for the money that was supposed to go to China?" I asked carefully.

"Yep." Barry's head bounced up and down. "You're strapped so tightly to ABC and Southeast Asian Investments that it won't take even those Burmese idiots very long to work out that you're the guy in the barrel here."

"And what did I do with all this money I'm supposed to have taken?"

"Ah, Jack..."

Barry spread his hands in front of him in the classic gesture of helplessness.

"I only wish I knew. If I did, honest banker that I am, of course I'd send the information right along to the Chinese who were supposed to get the funds in the first place, but . . . jeez, I guess you were just too smart for me."

The human eye, so they say, can focus on only one thing at a time, and that has always caused me to wonder exactly where that leaves the human mind. There is a technique used in movie making called a rack-focus that tries to duplicate the singularity of the eye's attention.

A rack-focus occurs when there are two things in the picture at the same time, but the one in the foreground is the more important, at least at first, and therefore meant to hold the eye's attention. To achieve that, the camera keeps the foreground in sharp focus and the background is left blurry and indistinct. Then unexpectedly everything is reversed as the camera's focus shifts from foreground to background. The audience's attention is abruptly slammed from whatever it has been watching to what was previously lost in the background, and the whole scene takes on an entirely new perspective.

When Barry finished his story, it happened just like that for me. My mind suddenly rack-focused from the foreground to the background, and everything that had been so blurry and indistinct only a few moments before suddenly snapped into sharp relief.

That was when I started to laugh.

Barry looked puzzled. He figured I was someone who ought to have been pissing himself right about then, certainly beginning to ooze some heavy sweat at the very least, but I wasn't. I was just sitting there laughing at him.

"Laugh if you want, Jack, but I hear someone's looking all over for their money. And they're looking for *you.*"

I sat and shook my head. This was too good to be true.

"How much did you get?" I asked him.

"About fifty million."

I knew I might never get another moment like this again if I lived forever.

"Actually, it wasn't quite that much, was it, Barry? It was more like forty-three million, six hundred thousand. Plus change."

I relished every second of the silence that followed while I stared Barry right in the eye. He tried briefly to look unperturbed, but the effort was a dead loss.

"How the hell did you know that?' he snapped.

I could see the fear. Barry had lost control somehow. He didn't know why or how, and that had scared the hell out of him. Slamming him right then was like slugging a drunk, but I did it anyway. I continued to stare right into his wide, black eyes, and I swung from my heels as hard as I could.

"The money you stole was going to China all right, Barry, but it didn't belong to any Burmese drug producers and it wasn't meant for building heroin refineries in China. It was a CIA slush fund. It was bribe money the CIA was laundering to keep their Chinese networks going."

Barry went completely white. I had never seen anyone go white before. I had always thought the expression to be mostly poetic license, but it wasn't, and he did.

"Bullshit!" he sputtered.

For a moment Barry appeared to be fumbling for some even more forceful way to put his thoughts, but if that's what he was doing, he was spectacularly unsuccessful.

"Bullshit!" he sputtered again, spittle accumulating at the corners of his mouth.

This time he pointed a finger at me, although I wasn't quite sure what he thought that added to his point of view.

"Makes no difference to me if you believe it," I said and tossed out my most ingratiating smile. "My ass isn't on the line here."

"The hell it isn't!"

Barry jutted out his chin and I could hear his breathing accelerate.

"It doesn't matter *whose* money it really was. They still think *you've* got it! You're still the patty in this burger, old buddy."

I shook my head.

"The feds have been all over me for weeks now, Barry. How do you think I knew the exact amount of money you'd got?"

And then I leaned in and added my coldest smile.

"You know why they told me that? Can't you guess why they didn't try to squeeze *me* for it?"

Barry made a disdainful noise, but I could almost hear him thinking.

"It was because they already *knew* that I didn't have their money."

"Oh yeah?" Barry made his noise again. "Then why are they still on your ass, shithead?"

"Because they want something else from me, Barry."

"What the fuck could they want that's worth more to them than fifty million dollars?"

"You, Barry. They want you."

Right in front of me, I watched as Barry Gale began to deflate. Like an old balloon man slowly losing air, his arms contracted, followed by his legs, then his shoulders pulled back somewhere into his neck and he crumpled slowly into his red leather wingback chair.

"That's why I went through all that nonsense to get here without being followed. I wanted to hear your side of the story before I made up my mind what to do about the feds."

I started to laugh again in spite of myself.

"Man, oh man. I can't believe it. You're even dumber than the spooks."

Barry watched me as if I was far away and needed magnification. His eyes shifted back and forth and his jaw worked. He leaned forward in his chair like he was about to rise, but then he shifted his weight and sat back again. He crossed and uncrossed his legs.

Then abruptly an expression like release settled over Barry's face and I felt a shift in the air. He suddenly looked like a man who had just made the altogether pleasing discovery that the law of gravity was still working.

"Was that fifty million really the CIA's money?" he asked in a voice so soft and controlled that it startled me after his screaming fit.

"How else could I have known what the exact amount was?"

Barry didn't answer. Instead he just sat there smiling vaguely at me. I vamped a little, playing for time while I tried to work out why Barry didn't seem worried anymore.

"So what do you think the truth is?" I asked him.

"Me? Oh, I don't know, Jack. The truth is a slippery business."

That was way too elliptical a remark for me. We sat and looked at each other some more.

"What's it going to cost me to fix all this, Jack?"

It still irritated the hell out of me that Barry didn't look concerned anymore, so I tossed out a little jab just to whack him back off his perch again.

"I don't know, Barry. I'll bet the spooks can be real hard asses when they find out that some tin-pot pimp for a bunch of Russian mobsters has tried to scam them."

Barry looked no more concerned than if we were negotiating the purchase of his car and I had suggested a price in which he was just slightly disappointed.

"So what do you do now, Jack?"

Barry crossed his legs and leaned back, like a man making social chitchat without a care in the world.

"You go back to Bangkok now and you meet the spooks, I suppose, and you tell them. . . ." Barry seemed to search hard for a sensible answer. When nothing came to him after a moment he stopped and looked at me with an unexpectedly gentle smile.

"What do you tell them, Jack?"

Is that a trick question?

"I'll probably tell them what happened to their money and where they can find you."

"And then you think they'll just let you walk away? You think after that you can just go back to your life and they'll forget all about you?"

Barry shaped his face into an expression of incredulity.

"Who do you think killed Howard and Dollar, Jack?"

He shook his head sadly, like I had just missed the last question in the lightning round of Double Jeopardy and he could hardly believe my lousy luck.

"You think they had something to do with setting up this deal and I whacked them so they wouldn't tell anyone about it. Is that what you think, Jack?"

"Something like that."

Barry shook his head some more in mock amazement at my naïveté.

"The CIA killed them both, Jack."

"Give me a break, Barry. If you really think you can sell me that, you've been watching way too much TV."

"Think about it. Why did Howard's client files disappear from Dollar's office? Why did somebody take Dollar's house apart? They must have been looking for *something.* Don't you think they were looking for something to tell them what Dollar and Howard had done with the money? I already *knew* where the money was, Jack, so it had to be the CIA who was after Dollar and Howard. Not me."

"I can't see that, Barry," I said.

But I could.

Barry was right. He didn't have to look for the money. He already knew where it was.

"So, the way I'm looking at this thing, Jack, is that the spooks followed the money from Howard to Dollar, and now to...."

Barry stopped talking and pointed his right hand at me, using his thumb and forefinger to make it into a little gun.

"You see my point."

I did. Ray Charles could have seen his point.

"It looks to me like you're standing in a tricky load of goose shit here, Jack. So, just out of interest, tell me . . . what do you plan to do now?"

It was a good question, and right off the top of my head, I didn't have a great answer.

Everything was going too fast. I was usually pretty good at thinking on my feet, but this was ridiculous. A half hour of talking to Barry and I'd already accumulated an array of faceless adversaries big enough to throw a respectable masked ball. It was all getting so complicated that I probably should have been taking notes.

Hurriedly Barry pushed himself out of the leather wingback and strode past me. I shifted my weight on the sofa and followed him with my eyes. Beth had come in again and was waiting quietly at the end of the gallery.

As he had before, Barry crossed the room and stopped too close to her for me to hear what they were saying, but I could see Beth's face and something that looked like disquiet in her expression as her lips moved. Barry folded his arms and glanced quickly back at me, then he said something and Beth frowned. After that she said something else and Barry shook his head.

"I got to take care of something, Jack," he called back to me without turning around.

"That's okay. It's past my bedtime anyway. I'll probably just shove off."

That caused Barry to turn around. It also caused him to jam his hands in his pockets and go back to chuckling.

"Nah, Jack. That's not a choice for you right now. Make yourself at home. I'll be back in a few minutes and we'll get us some drinks, maybe have some sandwiches, and we'll cut a deal here. We're both businessmen. We've done tough deals before. I'm sure we can work something out."

Barry fixed me with a steady eye.

"That's the truth, don't you think, Jack?"

I shrugged and swung my feet up on the coffee table, settling back into the sofa's deep cushions and clasping my hands together behind my head.

"The truth is a slippery business, Barry."

He laughed loudly, too loudly for it to sound particularly convincing, then he turned away and walked quickly away up the gallery. Beth stayed close behind him.

THIRTY-EIGHT

I SAT THERE QUIETLY FOR A WHILE watching and listening to the fire burning, which felt awfully odd. Here I was on a tropical island on the edge of the Indian Ocean. What in the world was I doing staring into a fireplace, for God's sake?

Come to think of it, what was I doing here at all?

When I had set out to storm the Black Prince's castle I figured I was right on the verge of getting everything under control. Of course I *always* figured I was right on the verge of getting everything under control, but this time it wasn't quite working out that way.

Maybe Barry was right. Maybe some kind of feds really *were* responsible for killing Howard and Dollar, either because they were trying to get the Chinese slush fund back or because they were trying to cover up the embarrassing fact that it had existed in the first place. Regardless, why did that necessarily make me the next guy on their list? Even if I could bring myself to believe that agents of the United States government really went around murdering other Americans to keep them quiet, what in God's name would these guys accomplish by killing me?

I didn't know *shit* about whatever they were up to. That, in a nutshell, was exactly the nub of my problem.

I sat there for a while on the sofa with my hands laced behind my head trying to decide what I ought to do now. Surely after Barry came back I could finesse my way past him somehow and work out something. After all, finesse had always been my best punch, hadn't it? A sharply focused argument here, a glib phrase there. Baffle them with bullshit then run for the door. It had always worked before. Why not one more time?

Eventually I got bored wrestling with my predicament and started examining my surroundings. Although right at that moment it wasn't the décor that was getting my attention, it was more a question of where the exits were.

There were two sets of double doors at the opposite end of the room plus the gallery behind me that led to the front door. Along the right-hand wall flanking the fireplace there were a half-dozen windows covered with shades of red and green tartan fabric.

I walked over and pulled one of the window shades aside. Outside I could see only a small section of the compound, but it looked like I was somewhere at the back. The part that I could see was deserted and the moon was just strong enough to light everything with a soft, sourceless glow that under different circumstances might have been romantic. Floodlights, maybe even a pack of snarling German Shepherds, would have seemed more fitting to me, but I didn't see any sign of either.

Out of the corner of my eye I caught a sudden flash of movement behind me and I jerked my head away and let the shade slip closed. A man I didn't recognize had come out of the gallery and was walking quickly across the other side of the room. He appeared to be one of Barry's security guards and carried a weapon that looked like those the guards outside had carried.

Now that I could see the gun in the light, I had no trouble at all recognizing it. It was an AK-47 with a folding stock, a nasty-looking piece of hardware that also amounted to serious firepower. I had played tennis with a couple of SWAT guys back in Washington for a while and one day they'd taken me out to their training range and let me mess around with some stuff they'd taken off a street gang which included a Chinese-made version of the AK. Barry must have been scared shitless if he had the hired help carrying heavy-duty weapons like that.

The man glanced at me without any apparent interest as he pulled out a ring of keys and opened the double doors furthest away from me. He disappeared through them, was out of sight for only a few moments, then reappeared without his weapon and trailed by another man who was also unarmed. They both went out in the direction of the front door without giving me a second look.

I was still trying to figure out what that had all been about when I heard the unmistakable crackle of a radio from somewhere. The noise came and went in sharp little bursts, and having no better idea, I followed the sound until it led me to the double doors that the two men had just passed through. I saw that they'd left them slightly ajar.

I placed my right palm against the upper panel of one of the doors and pressed. It swung open without a sound. I stepped through half expecting to trip some kind of alarm, but nothing happened.

In front of me was a windowless corridor that ran straight for about twenty feet and then ended at an ordinary single door that was standing half-open. The radio was much louder now and I could hear muffled voices in the static. Although I couldn't make out what any of them were saying, the sound was obviously coming from the room at the end of the corridor. I walked quickly down the corridor and through the door.

I wasn't really surprised to find that there was no one in the room. When the two guards had headed for the front door I got a strong feeling that I had been left alone in the house.

My eyes swept over the small space. On the left-hand wall there was a rack holding a dozen or more AKs and piled on the floor underneath them were eight or ten small wooden crates that looked like they contained enough ammunition for a small war. What the hell was Barry preparing for? An attack by the Republican Guard?

In front of me there was a sagging leather couch and some newspapers dumped on the floor, and on the opposite side of the room there was a desk pushed up against the wall with a line of five television monitors mounted above it. The first, second, and third monitors showed gray-toned pictures that were apparently coming from various parts of the compound. The fourth monitor showed the area just inside the main gates. They stood open a few feet and I could see several of the guards hovering together in a little knot and watching something outside. Oddly none of the guards seemed to be carrying weapons anymore.

But it was the fifth monitor that drew my full attention.

That one was displaying what had to be the picture from the camera I had seen outside above the gate. In the glare of the lights shining down from near the top of the wall, I could make out clearly the main road approaching the compound out of the darkness, the intercom box, and the parking pad.

Two white Toyotas and a jeep were parked right outside the gate, and I examined the men who had apparently just arrived in them. There were seven or eight in all, each wearing the chocolate-brown uniform of a Thai policeman. All but one were also wearing dark green combat helmets with red stripes running around them. The only man without a helmet appeared to be the officer in charge. The left side of his chest was emblazoned with a clipboard-sized pad of ribbons and he stood apart and just in front of the others.

I slid into the black swivel chair that was in front of the desk.

Barry Gale had gone outside to meet the police and the scene on the monitor looked like a tableau that had been arranged around him. Beth was standing to his left, and to his right, one of the guards appeared to be talking to the senior officer and translating for Barry and Beth.

The half-dozen or more uniforms behind the officer looked ready to move into action at a moment's notice. In the foreground I could see three of Barry's guards backing him up, but like the guards still inside, they appeared to have discarded their weapons.

No doubt the man I'd seen had been coming in here to put his weapon away when the cops showed up and then had gone out front with the guard who had been watching the security monitor. Well, that would make sense, wouldn't it? It would have hardly been smart to carry AK-47s out to meet the cops.

When I looked back at the monitor Barry was shaking his head firmly, although his body language made him appear more exasperated than concerned.

Still, there was something about the whole scene that didn't look quite right to me. I just couldn't put my finger on what it was.

As I watched, Beth turned her head away from the conversation and lifted a hand-held radio to her lips. When she spoke I could hear her voice coming through a loudspeaker that was mounted on the monitor rack.

"Activity in any other sector?"

"Negative," a male voice with a Thai accent replied immediately, and I gathered it was a guard posted somewhere else around the compound.

"Negative."

"No."

Two more voices. Okay, so there were a *lot* of guards around the compound.

What *was* it about the scene on the security monitor that looked so strange to me? Something was wrong, but whatever it was dangled just out of reach.

The officer was talking to the translator again and pointing his finger at Barry. After whatever he had said was repeated in English, I saw Beth step forward and hold up both her hands, palms out, shaking her head vigorously. The man immediately raised a radio of his own, turned and spoke a few quick words into it.

As soon as he did, Barry turned around and started toward the gates, but several of the cops drew handguns and moved quickly to outflank him, and he stopped. I was still trying to work out what that was all about when two of the other uniforms produced folding submachine guns from somewhere and spread out expertly, covering Beth and her people through widely separated angles of fire.

Now I saw exactly what was wrong with the picture I was seeing.

Thai street cops didn't move like combat soldiers. Thai police generally looked more like the last customers in a pub emptying out at closing time than they did like effective fighting men. These guys obviously weren't police, regardless of their uniforms. They were military.

Somebody was coming for Barry. I had no doubt of it now. He'd stockpiled all this firepower and secured himself behind these walls, then some guys show up and he tells his the guards to open the gates and put away their AKs just because the men are wearing police uniforms.

In Thailand everyone knew that all the really high-class hits were done by the army. Cops were a lot cheaper to rent, of course, but not nearly as good.

What a schmuck Barry is, I thought. *Stupid to the end.*

"Wait a minute."

It was one of the other guard's voices coming through the speaker and Beth raised her radio again.

"What have you got?" she asked.

There was a silence and I saw Beth glance up and look directly into the security camera as if she could encourage the man to answer her more quickly by staring into it.

"More vehicles." The same voice eventually spoke again. "Three. On road."

"What are they?"

"Four-wheel drives. Black ones. Shit. Not see before."

"How close?'

Beth's voice had an undertone of dread that was impossible to miss.

"Two minutes," the man replied.

On the monitor I saw Beth lower the radio and put her lips close to Barry's ear. He still had his back to the guy in charge and was eyeing the uniforms that had drawn down to block his return to the compound.

Everyone else stood motionless and watched.

Beth spoke for a moment, hunching her shoulders slightly and twisting her body to block the Thai cops' line of sight as effectively as she could. Barry appeared to ask her a question, and when she nodded her head, he suddenly broke into a run toward the half-open gates.

The officer started after him, drawing his sidearm as he came, and the other uniforms broke into a trot behind him sweeping the area with their gun barrels. It didn't look to me like anybody was actually firing yet, but I figured that was just a matter of minutes away.

Beth moved to cut the officer off, which looked like it might give Barry time to make the gates if his guards acted fast enough to shield him from the other uniforms. She reached for the man's arm to deflect his aim, but the officer hardly glanced at her. As he cleared the heavy-looking black automatic from his belt holster he kept coming toward the gates and his gun swung up and out in a smooth arc.

I saw the barrel slam Beth on the side of the head, and I saw her go down.

Automatically I started to push myself out of my chair.

So what are you going to do about it? I was already asking myself before I even got my feet under me. *You're a college professor, not a tin-pot action hero with a stunt double.*

I glanced over my shoulder at the rack of automatic rifles, but I could feel a heavy blanket of helplessness settling over me. There were six or eight heavily-armed and obviously well-trained men rushing the gates of Barry's compound and my sole experience with combat weapons had been a half hour at a SWAT range in Washington DC.

I glanced back at the monitor and saw the officer in charge leveling the muzzle of his handgun directly at me, pointing it straight into the lens of the camera. Reflexively I ducked, and when I looked back up again the monitor's picture had turned to static.

If they were knocking out the surveillance systems, I knew what that meant. Barry was going down and there was nothing I could do about it but go down with him. That was something I had absolutely no intention of doing.

I looked around the little room and for the first time noticed another door. Leaping up and grabbing the handle I twisted it.

Locked.

Then I saw the throw bolt just above the handle. It had been secured into a receiver on the door jam and I jerked it open and tried again.

This time the door swung open. A wave of heavy night air flooded in and the room's lights jumped into the darkness.

I banged the switch off with the heel of my hand before the lights attracted any unwanted attention and started to step outside, but then I jumped back into the room and grabbed one of the AKs out of the rack. I fumbled with the magazine in the glow of the security monitors until I remembered how to get it out. From the weight, I knew it was full before I even looked.

I slapped the magazine back in and racked the cocking handle. Fuck the uniforms, and for good measure, fuck the Billy the Kid rule, too. If any of those bastards came at me I wanted something in my hands. I'd decide later what to do with it.

I eased the door closed behind me and stood quietly, letting my eyes adjust to the faint blush of the moonlight and straining my ears for any sound. The compound's wall was at least twenty yards away across open and exposed ground. From where I crouched there appeared no more hope of climbing it from this side than there had been from the other.

Okay, they came up the main road and I had left my jeep behind a rise well away from it, so they almost certainly hadn't seen anything and didn't know Barry had a visitor. Maybe they wouldn't search the compound very hard looking for anyone else after they rounded up Barry and his guards.

If they didn't, I had one idea that might actually work.

One of the guest houses was near a corner of the main house, and if I remembered right, it would largely block the sight-line from the main gate. *If* they didn't know I was there, and *if* they'd already searched the guest house, and *if* I could get there without being seen, *maybe* I could hide out until this was all over.

A load of ifs and maybes, but it was all I had going for me.

Keeping low and pressing myself against the house I began to work my way toward the corner that I guessed was closest to the guest house. None of the windows I passed were lighted, but I stayed in a half crouch anyway and kept my body tight against the wall. When I reached the corner I stopped and dropped flat to the ground. Wedging myself as close to the wall as I could and holding the AK against my chest, I turned my head to one side and inched forward in slow motion. I could feel grit against my cheek and my ear dredged up loose soil like a little backhoe.

When my left eye cleared the corner of the house, my heart sank. There were four men I could see standing twenty or thirty yards away, exactly halfway between the guest house and the gates. Their backs were toward me, but it seemed awfully unlikely I could cross the open space without attracting their attention.

Then I noticed that just beyond these men a dozen or so people were lying face-down on the ground in a straight line, their hands cuffed behind them.

I was still trying to make sense of that when something else finally registered. None of the four men were wearing police uniforms. Instead they all wore loose-fitting blue windbreakers with big yellow letters across the back. The big yellow letters said FBI.

I was just wondering if these guys had gotten their jackets the same place I'd gotten mine when a powerful beam of light hit me directly in the face. Momentarily blinded, I felt rather than saw a boot dig under my stomach. Before I could react, the boot flipped me over and came down in the center of my chest, pinning me to the ground.

"Fuck a duck, Jack, why do you always have to do everything the hard way?"

I recognized the voice immediately.

"Get that damned light out of my face, John."

A big hand wrapped around my upper arm and jerked me to my feet, then relieved me of the AK.

"What the fuck is *this,* Jack?"

Just John had himself a good chuckle while I spit the grit out of my mouth.

"You know how to use one of these puppies?"

"Want to give it back and find out?"

Just John stopped laughing and I looked him over. He was wearing black pants and a black T-shirt and a heavy, six-cell flashlight dangled at his side. Over his shoulder some kind of small submachine gun hung from a sling.

Standing quietly next to John was Jello. He was wearing a khaki uniform that had been stripped of insignia and carried only a service revolver, but it was out of the holster and pointed in my direction. Both men wore dark gray Kevlar vests and over them the same loose blue jackets the four guys around the corner had on.

"We've got him!" Just John called out to someone.

"What the hell are you doing here?" I snapped.

"We're real interested in you, Jack," Just John said. "We like to try and keep in touch with you whatever you're doing. You're a million laughs."

"How did you find me?"

"I can't tell you exactly. A bunch of top-secret shit's involved. I'm sure you understand."

John's voice made it clear that he didn't give a damn whether I did or not.

"Let's just say that turning on your cell phone wasn't real clever, Jacko."

I heard the boots crunching in the dirt behind me before I could say anything else and I saw Just John's eyes flick over my shoulder. It was same the man I'd found sitting in Dollar's office the morning after Howard's body had turned up swinging under the Taksin Bridge, the man who had claimed to be an FBI agent named Frank Morrissey.

"Where'd you find him?" Phony Frank asked Just John, hardly glancing at me.

"Sneaking around back here. The stupid shit...."

Phony Frank waved Just John into silence. "It doesn't matter. Just bring him around front with the rest of them."

Then the man turned on his heel and disappeared back around the corner the way he had come.

"Is one of you heroes going to tell me what the hell's going on here?" I asked after he was gone.

"We've got ourselves a sort of situation, Jack," Just John said.

"No shit."

Then I looked at Jello who had yet to say a word.

"Do you talk, or what, pal?"

"This isn't my show, Jack. I'm just along for the ride."

Jello looked mildly embarrassed and nodded toward Just John.

"If you want to know anything, ask these guys."

"And exactly who *are* these guys?" I asked without taking my eyes off him.

Jello looked away. "Ask them whatever you want to, Jack. Just leave me out of it."

"Leave you out of it? You're wearing the jacket and you're pointing a gun at me, and you say, 'Leave me out of it'? From where I'm standing, old buddy, it looks to me like you're just as much a part of whatever's going on here as any of these other assholes are."

"Come on, Jack. Don't give Jello such a hard time. He's just doing his job," Just John said.

He shifted the submachine gun strap slightly on his shoulder and tucked his flashlight under his left arm.

"Let's take it all one step at a time. Can you just do that for once in your whole goddamned life?"

"One small step for Jack Shepherd, one giant leap for mankind? Something like that, John?"

"You're such a fucking wise-ass, Jack. You break me up. You really do."

Just John cupped my right elbow with his free hand and steered me around the corner of the house. Jello trailed behind as we walked toward the front gate where Phony Frank and the other men in the FBI jackets and the line of people on the ground waited.

John didn't really look all that broken up to me.

THIRTY-NINE

SOMEBODY HAD SET UP PORTABLE LIGHTS at the front of the compound and was switching them on as we rounded the corner. When we walked into the illumination the men wearing the FBI windbreakers turned to watch.

The compound's gates were standing wide open. Just outside, scattered as if they had been hastily abandoned, were three black Cherokees in addition to the old jeep and the two white Toyotas I had seen on the security monitor. The men in police uniforms were lounging against the Toyotas now, just watching the proceedings without any apparent interest, so I shifted my attention back to the FBI jackets and their prisoners.

I recognized Beth and several of Barry's guards in the line of prisoners, but there were also others I didn't recognize. Beth lifted her head slightly. I didn't see any blood and she gave me a half-smile as we approached, so I gathered she was okay.

The Thais in uniform may not have been police, but these guys were all Westerners. Maybe they really *were* FBI and they had just used the Thais to get them through the gate. The whole thing certainly smacked of a textbook FBI operation: come in with such overwhelming force and firepower that resistance was futile and the target collapsed without a struggle.

"Bring him over here!"

Phony Frank was beckoning impatiently at Just John from the other end of the line and I saw Barry handcuffed on the ground in front of him.

"Is that you, Jack?" he called out when he heard our footsteps approaching.

Barry was lying on his stomach and tried to twist his head around so that he could see, but Just John put the toe of his boot on Barry's neck and shoved his face back into the dirt.

Phony Frank looked at me and pointed back down the line at the other people with their hands cuffed behind them.

"You know any of these?" he asked.

I wondered for a moment what the right answer to that was, and what might happen if I got the wrong answer.

"I recognize some of them," I said carefully after a moment.

"From where?"

"From here. A few from before."

I didn't see where this was going.

"Look, partner, these are just some people Barry Gale hired to do routine security work," I said. "If you think you've nabbed a drug lord and his secret army, you've got a real disappointment coming."

Phony Frank walked down the line and pointed at Beth.

"What about her?"

"I think she was in charge of Barry's security."

"Well, she did a piss-poor job of it, I'd say."

Phony Frank laughed and most of the other men who were standing around started laughing, too, but when he walked back up the line again and stopped directly behind Barry, everyone stopped.

"Can you identify this man as Barry Gale?"

Phony Frank pointed to where Barry lay, stomach to the ground and face held in the dirt under Just John's boot.

"Not from this angle. We weren't that close."

Phony Frank nodded a couple of times as if that was a perfectly reasonable thing for me to say. Then he reached down with both hands and in one smooth motion jerked Barry up by an arm and a leg and flipped him onto his back. Poor Barry writhed about uncomfortably, his cuffed hands pressing up into his spine. He looked like a fish that had been gaffed, hauled into a boat, and then left to flap around helplessly on the deck. He also looked terrified.

"For Christ's sake help me, Jack," he whined. "Don't let them kill me!"

"Relax, Barry. It's the feds. They're not going to kill you."

"Oh man, Jack. You don't understand."

Barry breathed in heavy jerks, sputtering slightly from the dirt sticking to his lips.

"You still don't get any of this, do you, you stupid fucking shit?"

"So you're positively identifying this man as Barry Gale," Phony Frank interrupted, enunciating as carefully as if he were making a recording.

"I didn't say that."

"Well is he or isn't he?"

"I'm begging you here, Jack. Don't let them kill me!"

Barry was trying to struggle to his knees, but Just John kept him down effortlessly with one foot. The fear was right there in Barry's eyes. I could see it easily enough, but I still didn't really understand it.

"Just who the hell wants to know, partner?" I snapped at Phony Frank.

I was starting to get very pissed with all the cloak and dagger stuff and I gave him a two-fisted stare.

"Answer the man, Jack. Just answer him," Just John muttered.

He sounded like he was getting pissed, too, but whether at Phony Frank or at me, I couldn't tell.

I folded my arms.

"Not until someone tells me exactly what the hell is going on here."

Just John sighed heavily and bent over. Dropping his flashlight he reached out with one hand and flipped Barry back onto his stomach. When Just John straightened up again, he looked at me and wiped an open hand across his face.

"The ABC was an intelligence operation from the beginning, Jack," he said.

"What did Jimmy Kicks have to do with it?"

"He never existed." Phony Frank smiled humorlessly. "We made Jimmy Kicks up."

I didn't say anything. I didn't breathe. I felt stunned, and suddenly very stupid.

"We needed a bank to get some things done." Phony Frank watched me warily for a moment before he went on. "But then you know all about those things already, don't you, Jack? That story about the Russian mob was just a cover for taking over the ABC. We had to have a reliable Asian conduit to fund a very sensitive operation. It's as simple as that really."

The wind was rising off the Andaman Sea, kicking up little puffs of limestone dust around the compound. It was so quiet I could hear the waves lapping against the rocks somewhere below.

"Who's this 'we' you keep talking about?" I asked after a moment.

"This was a coordinated operation between the CIA and a special White House security unit," John answered.

"Special White House security unit? What's that supposed to mean?" I asked. "Is Oliver North back in charge?"

"That's none of your goddamned business, Jack. You already know a damn sight more than you should and that's another problem we're going to have to solve eventually."

Just John's voice was soft, but something in it made the back of my neck feel cold.

"Barry Gale scammed our operation for a great deal of money and we want it back. On the other hand, we don't want some fucking

Congressman going on CNN someday and claiming we got the wrong guy, so we're doing this by the book. Look over there, Jack."

John point off to my left and for the first time I saw that one of the guys in an FBI jacket was holding a video camera on us.

"If you'll just look into the camera, smile real nice for the folks, and formally identify Gale, we can grab this bunch and it will all be a wrap. Now why can't you just be a good boy, stop fucking around with something you don't understand, and do that for us?"

"You a spy, John?"

"Nah, Jack. I'm just a guy who has to account for the money."

I looked at Barry lying there helplessly on his stomach. I hated to be the one to finger him, but I knew it didn't really make any difference. They had Barry, and although I felt sorry for him, they *should* have had him.

I looked at Phony Frank and pointed to Beth and her people.

"They're just hired hands. Let them go and I'll give you your ID."

I expected him to laugh at me making demands, but he didn't.

"No problem," he said.

He raised his right index finger and rolled it in a tight little circle. The men in FBI jackets started pulling the security guards to their feet and the rest of us watched in silence as they loaded most of them into the jeep and the two Toyotas. Then the guys in the police uniforms got in with the guards and closed the doors.

Two of the men in FBI jackets got into one of the Cherokees with the last three guards, then the one holding the video camera handed it to Jello and got in another Cherokee with the remaining FBI jackets and Beth. She nodded her thanks to me, but didn't say anything. One by one all five cars started and moved out in a convoy with the Cherokees bringing up the rear.

The compound was now empty except for the last of the black Cherokees and our own little tableau. Just John, Phony Frank, Jello, and I remained standing silently around Barry, who was still face-down in the dirt with his hands cuffed behind him. The wind off the ocean rose a little and more dust spiraled into the air.

"Are you positively identifying this man as Barry Gale?" Phony Frank asked again, pointing to Barry.

I didn't say anything right away.

"*Please* just answer the man, Jack."

Just John's voice had a pleading tone in it that didn't really sound like him.

"Okay." I took a breath. "Yeah, this is him. It's Barry Gale."

Phony Frank turned slightly and nodded, holding out his hand to Jello. Jello clicked off the video camera and passed it to him.

Then John took a slow step toward Barry.

Before I realized what he was going to do, he swung his right leg in an extended arc like a football kicker going for a long field goal. He caught Barry squarely in the left ear with the steel-capped toe of his heavy leather boot and Barry's head lifted off the ground. It reached the limit of the length of his spine, then it rebounded into the dirt. After that, Barry screamed.

"*Whoa, whoa!*" I yelled at Just John. "What the *fuck* are you doing?"

"I'm giving this piece of shit a taste of what's coming unless he tells me what he did with our money."

"They're going to kill me, Jack!" Barry screamed again. "They're going to kill me!"

"Shut up, Barry!" I snapped. "They're not going to kill you. The government doesn't kill people. They just arrest you, put you in prison, and somebody *there* kills you."

Then I turned on John.

"You don't have to rough-up the poor bastard. I can tell you how to find the money."

Phony Frank perked up his ears.

"You can?"

"Say 'pretty please.' "

"Fuck you, asshole."

"Okay. Close enough."

I was starting to get to this guy, whoever he really was, and I liked that a lot.

"Everything's on the ABC computer system," I told him. "I can get to it when I've got a computer and a phone line."

Phony Frank looked skeptical.

"You'd need to have the dial-in number for the right part of the bank's network."

"I've got it."

"Then you've got to have the current access codes."

"I've got them, too."

"Gale gave them to you?"

"Nope. I found them on Dollar's computer."

"Weren't they encrypted?"

"Yes, but I got someone to take care of that for me."

"Who?"

"I can't tell you that."

I cut Just John the biggest wink I could manage without hurting my face.

"There's a lot of top-secret shit involved. But I'm sure you understand, don't you, John?"

Phony Frank didn't seem amused.

"Are you just jerking me off here, you little shit? If you are, I'm going to be one unhappy son of a bitch."

"If I had a laptop and a data line, I could show you what I mean. But I don't."

"As luck would have it," Phony Frank said with a nasty smile, "you do."

He pointed at the Cherokee that was still standing in the compound and gave me a little push its direction. Frank, John, and I walked toward it, but Jello stayed where he was.

"Do you roll over and play dead, too?" I called back over my shoulder.

"Look, Jack, stop being an asshole," Jello shouted at me. "I'm just a local cop and these guys are making the rules. Everybody takes orders from somebody."

When we got to the Cherokee Phony Frank opened the passenger door and gestured for me to slide in. He pointed to an IBM ThinkPad clamped into a bracket mounted over the console between the front seats.

"You know how to use that?"

"I think I can manage."

"It's got a wireless modem running a standard Windows communication package. Go into Dial-Up Networking, put in the right telephone number, click on the Dial button, and you'll be in business. Unless you're completely full of shit, of course."

I booted up the ThinkPad and began silently working through the communications screens. When the chirping of two modems connecting wheezed out of the laptop's tiny speakers, Phony Frank and John bent into the Cherokee, watching closely over my shoulder.

The host computer's identifiers started rolling across the screen and I hit the Return key to bring up the log-in box. I shifted my head just enough to block their view as I typed in the access code and quickly hit Return again. When the main screen opened, I began clicking through menus.

"What the fuck is all that shit?"

Phony Frank's mouth was so close to my ear that I felt his breath when he spoke.

I stopped typing and twisted my head toward him.

"Do you want me to stop and give you a lesson on the structure of commercial banking databases, or do you want me to get you the information you're looking for?"

He didn't bother to answer, so I turned back and resumed typing. After a few more moments a large spreadsheet opened and I pointed to the first column of numbers.

"There it is. Those are the dates of every transfer out of the ABC that Barry Gale personally ordered and the Fed wire number for each of them."

Then I opened another file, this one a plain text document with three long columns.

"This is a list of the same Fed wire numbers, but viewed from the opposite side of each transaction."

I moved the cursor around the screen like a pointer.

"Here's each wire number, and when you follow across, it matches up with an amount, a receiving bank, and the account name and number in that bank where the transfer went."

"What's this stuff at the bottom?" Just John asked.

He pointed to another list of names and numbers that appeared as I scrolled down to the bottom of the file.

"Just some notes I made when I was working out all the transactions. They don't mean anything."

"So this is all we need to find our money?" John asked.

"Look, I'm giving you a list of all the banks and account numbers where Barry stashed everything he transferred out of the ABC. What you do with it's up to you."

John still looked as if he thought something wasn't quite right, but Phony Frank was grinning as he stepped away from the Cherokee and straightened up. He spoke in a tone that I thought tried hard to hit a note of respectful admiration, but it came out sounding mostly smug.

"Well, I've got to hand it to you, Jack. You really did our job for us."

"Then I'll start checking my mail for a letter of gratitude from the President." Before he could say anything else I added hurriedly, "You'll need these files. I'll save them to the hard disk."

When I had finished I shut the laptop down and closed it.

"Done," I said, and got out of the Cherokee.

Back across the compound, Jello was still faithfully standing guard over Barry Gale.

"Good dog," I said when we all trooped back, but Jello ignored me.

"Can I load this one up now so we can get out of here?" he asked Phony Frank instead.

"I'll take care of him," Phony Frank replied, bending down over Barry.

When I thought back on it later, I was certain I hadn't seen the gun until he fired.

FORTY

COPS CALL THE ·22 CALIBER COLT WOODSMAN the "hitman special."

The gun is too small to have any real stopping power and it's useless for self-defense; but load it with hollow points, screw on a silencer, and fire it pointblank into a man's head, and it's a foolproof killing machine.

Phony Frank had produced the little gun from somewhere and pressed it against Barry's temple when he bent down, but the two spitting noises it made when he pulled the trigger were the first sign I had that something had gone badly wrong.

"You goddamned bastard!" I screamed uselessly at him.

Just John was ready when I lunged at Phony Frank, wrapping me in a bear hug while I struggled ineffectually.

Jello half pulled his service revolver, but Frank quickly straightened up and laid the muzzle of the Woodsman under his chin. Jello just stood there with a puzzled expression on his face waiting for his brain to catch up with his eyes.

"Put it on the ground, Jello."

Just John spoke in a soft, soothing voice.

"Then we're all going to have a nice little talk."

"I'm not having any talk with you bastards!" I yelled. "You murdered that man in cold blood!"

I kicked back hard with my right heel and caught Just John squarely on his shin, but he never even flinched.

Jello lowered his arm and slowly bent his knees, laying his service revolver flat on the ground. Phony Frank scooped it up and slid it into a pocket of his jacket.

"I'm just doing what they told me to do, Jello."

Phony Frank was watching Jello cautiously, but Jello still seemed more puzzled than alarmed by what was happening.

"My instructions were to locate the missing funds and then eliminate the cause. I guess it's obvious why I couldn't tell you that up front. I'm sorry, Jello. Really."

"You're *sorry?"* I barked at Frank.

"Not for him." Phony Frank nodded toward the handcuffed corpse on the ground. "I'm sorry I had to string Jello along without telling him the whole story."

"But why kill Barry?" I asked. "I got your goddamned money for you."

"Barry Gale compromised a top-secret national security operation. Any way you slice it, we're not going to leave him running around loose now. You can't imagine how much he knows."

"Is that why you killed Howard and Dollar, too? Because of what they knew?"

"Every operation has losses, Jack."

I stared right back at Phony Frank and tried not to flinch.

"Now I know as much as they all did, maybe more. And so does Jello. You going to kill us, too?"

Phony Frank swung the Woodsman away from Jello and took a lazy step toward me.

"Well, you raise an interesting point there, Jack. A real interesting point," he said. "If it was up to me. . . ."

Phony Frank slowly spread his hands in a gesture that left little doubt as to what his preferred choice was.

"But it's not up to me. The guys who tell me what to do say you both walk away. Too many bodies in an operation, they figure, and people start snooping around. Besides, we're sure that when you calm down and think everything through, you'll both be safe bets."

"I'll tell you, partner what, your lapdog over there may be okay, but I'm *anything* but a safe bet!"

Phony Frank was smirking now and I would have liked nothing better than to smash that look right down his throat.

"I don't think you'll be any problem, Jack. You're a player now."

"I'm a *what?"*

"You're a player. You're part of one of the great secrets of history. Look at it this way. If the guys we're backing succeed in overthrowing the Chinese government and end up taking over the whole country like we think they will, you'll probably get a goddamned medal of some kind. A secret one, of course."

Phony Frank looked down and kicked the toe of his boot through the loose dirt. The sound of it in the silence was like a wave breaking over stones.

"Hell, man. Even if the little Chink bastards fuck up and the whole plan turns to shit, you'll be one of the few guys there is who knows how close we really came to changing the world. That's what a player is, Jack. That's you now."

Just John had loosened his grip on me while Phony Frank was talking. I shook him off and took several steps away.

"I'll go to the press and burn you."

"You really believe all that the-truth-shall-make-you-free crap, don't you, Jack?" Phony Frank snorted. "You poor jerk."

"You might get a few reporters going for a while, Jack," Just John said. "But no respectable publication will ever print a word you tell them. We've got that covered. Maybe you'd get your own web page with the other conspiracy nuts, but that's about the best you can hope for."

"It's all wrapped up, Jack," Phony Frank said. "Tighter than a gnat's asshole."

He smiled serenely at me.

"You got no place to go. Nobody to listen to you."

"I've got a top-ranking officer in the Thai police as a witness. That's got to count for something."

We all looked at Jello.

"That true, Jello?" Just John asked. "You see anything here tonight that you might want to talk to somebody about?"

Jello looked at the ground and said nothing. He wouldn't meet my eyes.

"There you go, Jack."

Phony Frank shook his head in mock sympathy.

"A good witness is so hard to find these days."

I stood quietly and looked off across the compound. The wall was too high for me to see the ocean from where we were, but I could smell the salt in the heavy night air.

Somewhere not very far away there were lovers cuddling on palm-lined beaches, fishing boats dragging home nets filled with lobsters, children playing tag on scruffy jetties, and seaside shacks filled with tourists drinking at wobbly tables. Somewhere out there, I reminded myself, life went on as it always had.

But that was beyond the wall, out in the world I had left, or that had left me.

"You really got to face it, Jack."

Just John's voice was gentle now. He sounded like a priest trying to talk somebody out off jumping from a bridge.

"You're on the inside now. You're one of us."

All I could do was stand and shake my head and look at the body face-down in the dirt, arms still handcuffed behind it.

The little Colt had left two small, tidy holes in Barry's left temple. Thin streams of drying blood ran down from each wound and joined together just above his ear into a single, thicker stream. It was a neat, professional job of extinguishing a man's life.

"I'm not one of you," I said after a while. "I'm nothing like you."

I lifted my head and looked at Just John for a long time, then I turned to Phony Frank who met my eyes with a steady gaze.

FORTY-ONE

I HAD TO STAY AT THE PHUKET YACHT CLUB for a couple of days before the man I was waiting for could make the long trip to Thailand.

The morning after they'd shot Barry, I had woken well before daybreak and I sat out on the balcony watching the ocean turn from black to blue steel as the sky slowly lightened. I had ordered a pot of coffee from room service and made a promise to myself that when it was all gone I would decide.

A hard little seed of anger had formed inside me overnight. I cherished it. I nursed it. I willed it to grow.

It did.

And after I finished the last of the coffee, I knew exactly what I had to do.

I lifted the telephone and made the call I had been mentally rehearsing on and off while I had tossed restlessly through the night, struggling with dark dreams that either made no sense, or worse, did.

It took me quite a while to reach the man I wanted, but after I did and I'd told him enough to get his attention, he said he would leave immediately. Still, it would take him at least a full day to get to Phuket, possibly longer.

After that I walked the beach for an hour wondering if I had done the right thing and I fought the part of me that wasn't absolutely sure.

When I got back to the hotel I wandered around until I found a shop and bought some T-shirts and a bathing suit. Around noon I called Anita, but I didn't tell her much. I said that I'd had to go out of town for a couple of days and that I would explain when I got back. Surely the whole story sounded unbelievably strange to her, but I guess she must have heard something in my voice because she didn't question it too closely. She only told me to keep safe and left it at that.

Later in the afternoon I put on my running shoes and jogged listlessly on Nai Harn Beach for a half hour. I was pleased and a little surprised to find that the footing was firm and I began stretching myself, pushing harder and harder until I was up to my usual pace. Almost before I realized it, I had covered several miles and with each crunch of my shoes on the hard-packed sand I became still more certain.

Yes, you've done the right thing. You've got to try at least.

The longer I ran, the more my conviction hardened, and I ran the beach that afternoon until the blood pounding in my ears was all I could hear and the ache of my legs was all I could feel. Then I did it all over again the next morning and once more the next afternoon.

It was after I had run the beach yet again on my third morning in Phuket that I came back and found the man sitting on the floor outside my door. His back was against the wall and his knees were pulled up as he quietly waited for me.

We talked until early afternoon and I told him everything I knew. Then we ordered some sandwiches and coffee from room service and I went over it all again. This time he took notes.

When I was done he started asking long and detailed questions and I answered them all as well as I could. It was almost six that evening before we both finally fell silent.

Tired of talking, we walked out onto the terrace and watched in silence as the sun slid toward the surface of the sea, aiming itself exactly at a gap between two tiny islands that were several miles offshore. Five or ten minutes must have passed without either of us saying another word.

Eventually it was my visitor who broke the silence.

"What made you so sure I didn't know about all this already, Jack?"

"I wasn't sure."

I thought about it some more.

"You just don't seem to me to be a guy who would be part of this kind of thing."

"Too honorable?"

"Not really. Just too smart."

We let the half-smiles hang there for a moment.

"How long have we known each other, Jack?" the man finally asked.

"Oh God, I don't know. We were roommates our last year at Georgetown, so I guess that makes it . . . what? Twenty-odd years now?"

The man nodded.

"Yeah, about that."

The sun hid behind a cloud for a moment and the terrace slipped into a gray half-light.

"I heard from everybody I'd ever met when I was appointed White House Counsel and every single one of them wanted something. I had a million new best friends. You were probably the only guy I'd ever known who didn't call me."

"I was probably the only guy you'd ever known who didn't want anything from you then."

"But you do now."

"Yeah."

"Then lay it out for me, Jack. Tell me exactly what it is that you *do* want."

I put it as plainly as I could.

"I want to be absolutely certain the President knows about this. If he does, and it's what he wants, then there's not a damned thing I can do about it no matter what I believe. But if he doesn't know, he ought to, then he can do whatever he thinks he should."

"That's it?"

"That's it."

The bottom rim of the sun touched the ocean at last and we watched silently as the huge red ball slid through the horizon.

"I can tell you right now, Jack, nothing like this came out of the White House. I don't know who these guys are, but they're not ours. It sounds to me like somebody at the Pentagon or CIA has gone way over the edge."

The man shook his head in disgust.

"I really hate goddamned fucking cowboys like that. There are so many good people who care so much, but sometimes. . . ."

He trailed off with a rueful smile.

Just as the sun's topmost edge plopped out of sight, there was a sudden flare of iridescent green. It exploded out of the ocean, an arc of brilliant emerald expanding like a shockwave until it was swallowed up by the darkening sky.

Damn. So there really was *a green flash. How about that?*

I turned to say something about it and saw that my visitor was holding out his hand.

"I've got to leave, Jack, but I can promise you one thing. I will tell the President the whole story tomorrow. You have my word on that."

We shook and I walked him back inside. We crossed the room through the gathering gloom.

"Oh, hey, I almost forgot," my visitor suddenly said.

The man picked up his briefcase from where he had left it by the door. He swung it onto the desk and snapped open the catches. Reaching inside he produced a box of cigars and handed it to me.

"Montecristos . . . Cubans, no less," I said turning the box over in my hands. "Isn't this a breach of national security or something?"

"Working in the White House has got to have some perks, doesn't it?"

We both smiled, but I suspected at different things.

"It's a real shame you had to give them those bank records," the man said as he closed his briefcase. "Now that they've got their hands on the slush fund again, shutting down these guys will be a bitch."

I scratched at the back of my neck with one hand and made a show of thoughtful deliberation.

"You have to understand that I needed to see your reaction before I gave you the last little bit of it," I said after a pause. "I had to see if you already knew."

My visitor eyed me a moment, a half-smile creeping over his face, and then he leaned against the wall, waiting.

"They have no idea at all where the money is," I said. "No idea."

I paused to let that sink in.

"And now that they've killed Barry Gale, they'll probably never find it."

There was a hint of puzzlement in my visitor's nod.

"But what about the bank records you gave them?" he asked.

"The network I got them into was the university network at Chula, not the Asian Bank of Commerce. What Phony Frank got was a list of transactions I'd made up for the final exam in my international banking class. I don't think they'll be of much use to someone who's trying to overthrow the Chinese government."

My visitor stuck his tongue into the corner of his cheek.

"You're shittin' me," he laughed.

"I shit you not, partner."

The man laughed some more and clapped me on the shoulder.

"You sure you don't want a job at the White House, Jack? You're just the kind of sneaky, deceitful bastard who would fit right in."

I glanced over my shoulder at the red and yellow plumes of the setting sun coloring the sky above the Andaman Sea. They were bombarding the heavens like rockets, bursting against the clouds and sprinkling a dusting of pink and gold across the gunmetal surface of the sea.

"No thanks," I said after a moment. "I'm fine right here."

After my visitor left I took one of the Montecristos out of the box and went back out on the terrace. I dragged a chair around until I could slump back into it and prop my feet up on the railing, then I lit the cigar, cupping my hand around its tip to block off the ocean winds until a red coal was burning deep inside. Taking my time, I nursed a tiny cone of ash into life at its tip.

I sat there smoking quietly and it wasn't long before I was enveloped by a night deeper than any I could remember. I stole away into it and thought back over what my visitor had told me.

Did the White House really know nothing about any of this?

Had no one there ever heard of Just John or Phony Frank, or about the murders of Dollar Dunne or Howard the Roach or Barry Gale?

Maybe he'd told me the truth. Maybe nobody there knew anything.

But then again, maybe somebody there knew everything.

What else would he have said if they did?

I was just asking myself what the real end of the whole story would be when something I had read a long time ago popped unbidden into my mind. In *Death in the Afternoon* Hemingway had written that all stories if continued far enough always end exactly the same way — in death.

Well, I wondered . . . *this time, whose?*

Tilting my head back, I looked up at a canopy of stars that was so radiant, so lustrously deep and rich that I felt a sensation of being released, let loose. It was almost as if at any moment I would be gently lifted away from the earth and drawn straight up into the heavens.

I took a deep draw on my cigar and exhaled in an unhurried sigh. The wet ocean air collected the gray wisps of smoke and tugged them away into the night.

*I would like to express my appreciation to Alan Sargent, my editor,
and to Nury Vittachi and Peter Gordon at Chameleon Press
for guiding this book through a journey to publication that
most writers can only dream about.*

*Above all I am grateful to my wife, Aey.
While this book was struggling to find its feet,
in one way or another, she was always there.*

COMING IN AUTUMN 2002

KILLING PLATO

A Jack Shepherd International Thriller
by Jake Needham

Jack Shepherd returns in *Killing Plato* to confront one of the truly great villains in Asian fiction.

Plato Karsarkis has amassed a fortune in international oil trading. He's rich; he's famous; and he's admired — at least he is until he's indicted by a New York grand jury on sixty-seven counts of racketeering, tax fraud, and money laundering. There's also the matter of a woman he may or may not have murdered, all of which has made him into a latter-day combination of Marc Rich and O.J. Simpson. Then just before his trial Plato Karsarkis disappears and becomes the world's most notorious fugitive.

When Jack Shepherd walks into a restaurant on the jet-set resort island of Phuket and improbably enough finds Plato Karsarkis waiting there for him, he is plunged into a violent spiral of friendship and betrayal that pursues him from Asia all the way back to the life he thought he'd left behind in Washington, DC.

Karsarkis wants Jack to use his White House contacts to get him a Presidential pardon so that he can return to American as a free man. The United States Marshals want Jack to help trap Karsarkis so that they can drag him back to New York for trial. Jack just wants everybody to go away and leave him alone.

Then Jack Shepherd discovers something that chills his heart and changes his mind. The Marshals aren't really in Phuket because they want Karsarkis back.

They're there because somebody wants him dead.